PRAISE FOR JANE NICKERSON

Strands of Bronze and Gold and *The Mirk and Midnight Hour*

"The writing is excellent and the setting is very Gothic and dark... Readers will soon find themselves caught up in the intrigue and mystery." — *USA Today*

"Fans of historical thrillers and gothic romance will be captivated by the rich characters, complex relationships and haunting plot in this terrific debut inspired by the 'Bluebeard' fairy tale." — *Justine Magazine*

"A beautifully woven story...A must read for fans of the classic Bluebeard story and those who like a little creepy with their historical novels." — *Examiner.com*

"A spell-binding tapestry of mystery, romance, and suspense...A gripping gothic tale, with a lavishly described and lushly atmospheric setting and likable heroine." — *SLJ Teen*

"Compelling...There's a languid ease to the prose that invites readers to become fully immersed in the sweltering heat of a Mississippi summer, and Nickerson paints a picture of the Southern landscape that is rustic but ethereal and, at times, eerie." — *The Bulletin*

"Fans of Nancy Werlin's *Impossible*, dark faeries, magical realism, historical fantasy, and star-crossed love will find plenty to enjoy here." —*School Library Journal*

"Far from the typical Civil War romance...[w]ith rich imagery and imaginative subplots driving the storyline." —*Kirkus Review*

A
PLACE
OF
STONE
AND
SHADOW

Also by Jane Nickerson

Strands of Bronze and Gold

The Mirk and Midnight Hour

A
PLACE
OF
STONE
AND
SHADOW

JANE NICKERSON

NORTH LOOP BOOKS
MINNEAPOLIS, MN

NORTHLOOP
BOOKS

North Loop Books
322 First Avenue N, 5th floor
Minneapolis, MN 55401
612.455.2294
www.NorthLoopBooks.com

ISBN-13: 978-1-63413-887-1
LCCN: 2016901853

Distributed by Itasca Books

Book Design by B. Cook

Printed in the United States of America

To Ted

Just because.

CONTENTS

Back in the old time of water,
blood on the stones ran red —
a thousand goats to the slaughter,
a thousand babes from the bed.

Now I, who might be called cunning,
and you, with your beauty and grime,
will wash away in the running
of the old, old water of time.
— Fiona O'Malley

CHAPTER 1

PHANTOM SHADES

On the night before I was to leave for Mississippi, as I huddled on the library sofa, woeful from a foretaste of homesickness, The Two appeared.

It had been so long since they had tormented me that I had thought it over and done. That they were gone forever.

Immediately I was pulled into the past, to all the times I had been their victim. Ever since I was four years old. The experience is always the same. The coldness comes — a chill that withers my skin and sucks all warmth from my body. The points of ice touch my flesh — they are pinching — and the breeze stirs my hair — they are snatching. I *smell* them — carbolic soap and beeswax, with an underlying stink of sweat and onions.

Their voices are shrill. "Look at her. Such a long, ugly nose. Hair like a black horse's tail"…"A gangly, clumsy beanpole"…"But strong. Built for hard labor — like a mule." Followed by shrieks of laughter.

I see them hovering close — Sal with her witchy chin and hard, narrow eyes, and Epsy, puffy and pudgy, with features buried like raisins in rising dough. Both of them in their black and white maids' uniforms and both of them with their faces bloody and half-smashed from their plunge.

For years I did not know their names. I had not known the cause of their deaths. I had tried to ask about them in a round-about way, without letting on the reason. Only last winter Mrs. Gander, the cook, had finally related to me what had happened in our home twenty winters earlier. She had started reluctantly, since Grandmama had forbidden everyone to speak of it, but rapidly Mrs. Gander grew eager.

It seemed that in life the two maids, Sal and Epsy, had formed an unhealthy bond with one another based on mutual wretch-edness. "Nasty, unpleasant, homely girls, always bunched to-gether. Whispering 'psh — psh — psh' — like that — behind their hands. Hated everyone else. Positively encouraged each other to be miserable." Mrs. Gander's eyes glittered. She had ended with, "It's true they'd taken a bit of well-deserved teasing from the other staff, but who'd have thought they'd throw themselves from the third floor balcony? And there they lay sprawled on the snowy flagstones right outside the front door, their bodies all broken and bending every which way. Such a mess to clean up."

Now I felt the familiar, terrible temptation urging me from the library, toward the stairs and up to the third floor balcony — Sal and Epsy luring me to follow them to a similar fate. Their words echoed in my head: "You're nothing but a worry to your grand-mother. You have no friends. You do nothing right..."

But this time was different. This time I knew their names and their stories. This time I blocked out the voices. I swallowed back my terror and let understanding surge in my heart, all tumbled topsy-turvy with exasperation. "Sal and Epsy, if you're so unhappy here, why do you stay? You made your escape once. Do it for good this time and leave me alone." My words fell echoing into the great room.

The scorn of their expressions was replaced by staring disbelief that I had spoken to them. Their eyes bulged and their mouths hung open. Then—poof!—they disappeared with a soft popping sound.

It was just as well they came that night. It made me less hesitant to leave my New York home the next day for Wyndriven Female Academy in Mississippi.

I had first heard about Wyndriven at one of Grandmama's soirees.

Most days I spent my time hunched over a book or pen and paper in some isolated, velvet-draped corner of our mansion. Either that or drifting dreamily along the beautifully furnished, perfectly polished expanses, all sounds hushed by thick Brussels carpets. When I was alone, no one smirked if I knocked into the tea tray and made the liquid slosh out. No one exchanged glances, causing me to wonder what I had done wrong this time.

Occasionally, however, Grandmama insisted I make an appearance in society. Possibly to offset rumors that her reclusive granddaughter was disfigured or feeble-minded or some such nonsense. That soiree was one of those times.

Mr. Charles Stone, a guest at the event, had spoken eloquently of the plight of the South in these first years after the War of the Rebellion. He and his wife, Talitha, had escaped slavery twelve years earlier. It moved me that this man, who had suffered from the South's Evil Institution, should plead for that region. He told

of a Southern minister and his wife who had paid for his education, enabling him to become a lawyer and orator. He cared for
them so much that he had taken on their surname. These good
people had a massive home that had long ago been an abbey in
England, and had been brought over, piece by piece, to Mississippi. They turned it into a seminary for young ladies. Before the
war it had attained an excellent reputation. However, it had been
closed for the duration of the conflict and only recently re-opened.
Mr. Stone feared that his benefactors might be unable to continue
the school due to severe financial losses, as well as the difficulty of
acquiring paying pupils in the South during these troubled times.

I had stood frozen, hearing a siren's call to go to Wyndriven,
to help these people.

Grandmama, at first, had been adamant that I should ignore
the siren. "Why do you think you would be happy there when you
plagued me unceasingly to remove you from the other schools
you've attended? And in the backwoods of Mississippi, of all
places! These days no one from the North would send their child
down there." She smartly tapped one finger on the pamphlet Mr.
Stone had given me. "Besides which, it's in a grim, gloomy ancient
manor. Believe me, my girl, I saw plenty of *those* back in the old
country. Assuredly riddled with rot and mildew." She shuddered.
"And they all had nasty ghosts. Or else some dire curse. Of course
those things are a lot of superstitious twaddle, but I'm not having
a granddaughter of mine exposed to them."

"Hmm. Perhaps I'll come upon the apparition of a walled-
in nun, since it used to be a convent. One can hope, anyway." I
couldn't resist. Grandmama had that effect on me.

She rolled her eyes, made the sign of the cross, and began

fanning herself feverishly.

I had never told Grandmama of my own experiences with particularly nasty ghosts right there in her own home. Or of any of the other spooks I saw now and again. I had never made the mistake of blurting *that* out. Although, come to think of it, it was an Irish peasant legacy I had no doubt inherited through her.

Or perhaps I had the gift because I was born at dead of night. Mrs. Gander once told me that babies birthed at that time have power over spirits and can see the dead. Of course as far as I was concerned, I didn't much believe the "power over" bit.

The only person I ever tried to tell about my Sight was a nursemaid when I was small. I had run up to a skipping child ghost in the park and spoken to him. "She is the strangest child!" my nursemaid said to the other lady with whom she was chatting, as she grabbed my arm. They both laughed loudly, but she slapped my mouth and accused me of telling lies when I tried to explain what I had been doing. I learned my lesson.

I could not let the matter of Wyndriven Academy rest. It was uncanny how badly I wanted to go there when I had never before desired to go anywhere other than the occasional shop. For days I went on to plague my grandmother unceasingly—something I truly was very good at—but to no avail.

It had taken the incident with the wagoner to make Grandmama change her mind.

We had just exited the Arnold and Constable department store, followed by a footman staggering beneath parcels containing the most luscious variety of wearable confectionary. I dearly loved the flounces, puffs, and furbelows that were in style now—I had a hope that they would somewhat disguise my lanky form—

and enjoyed pursuing them. I was flushed with the exhilaration of satisfactory shopping. We had purchased ribbons and hatpins and a bonnet and silk hose and kid gloves and velvet slippers and goodness knows what else.

A heavy-laden wagon stood motionless in the road before us, with one scrawny, washboard-ribbed horse hitched to it, straining under a lashing whip to move forward. The horse's back was striped in bright blood.

My grandmother clutched my arm with sharp fingers. "No, Fiona," she said. "You *will* not."

I jerked from her grasp and flew to confront the astonished driver, where I slipped and slid on ice-rimed bricks and flailed my arms like a windmill to right myself.

"Don't you dare raise that whip again!" I cried, once I had regained my balance. "You should be ashamed to treat a poor animal so." Cruelty to the helpless brought out the tigress in me.

A small crowd gathered to watch the spectacle.

The driver climbed down from his seat to loom overhead. He was a hulking ox of a man (he had to be tall to loom over *me*), with breath like last-month's garbage. He tried to justify himself, but I would have none of it.

"You're a blackguard unfit to handle a horse. Don't you see that the wheel is wedged and the poor creature can't possibly pull forward?"

"You tell him, sweetheart!" someone shouted. A larger crowd had gathered.

The driver was furious, and began to bellow, but Grandmama, who had stood frozen with horror, scuttled up to pour coins into the oaf's hands and to stuff me into our waiting carriage. I allowed myself to be stuffed once the wagoner had freed the wheel.

"You rewarded him for being cruel to the horse," I remonstrated with her once we were on our way.

My grandmother sputtered, but proceeded to deliver a lecture on the evils of making a fool of oneself in public. She spoke with such passion that she lapsed into her mostly-suppressed Irishness and all the ribbons on her much-ribboned cap quivered. "Me girl, it's yourself I'm thinking of. Can't you see how eccentric you look when you go about rescuing horses in the street and scullery maids with toothache every time you turn around?"

"He'd have killed that horse, Grandmama, and Bess was homesick and in pain. Surely, as a good Catholic, you wouldn't have had me ignore either of them?"

"That is all very touching, I'm sure," Grandmama said in a failing voice, "and I'm as Christian as most, but how folks deal with their livestock is no concern of ours. Also you must remember that persons of the scullery maid's class lack the sensitive nerves possessed by ladies. They don't feel pain as ladies do."

"Aren't *we* persons of her class?" I challenged. I was torturing my grandmother, but I could not help it. "Just because Grandpapa and Papa had an indecent knack for making money, which was especially easy during wartime, doesn't mean we're made of different stuff."

"I did not intend—there is nothing we can do..." Grandmama's sentence trailed away.

"Didn't you feel the least bit sorry for the horse?" I could not let it rest.

"I—I—of course it is all very unpleasant, but dear child, you're so impulsive. You cannot poke your nose into every unpleasant thing in this world. Many unpleasant things must be left to their own—er—unpleasant devices. It's just grateful I am that no one I knew was in the throng. It would be so dreadful if...Promise me—promise me—you'll never create such a scene again," she begged, now close to tears. "It won't do at all, at all."

I was on the very edge of my seat, still brittle with energy from my encounter, but I melted at the sight of her expression and threw my arms around her. "Oh, darling Grandmama, I'm so sorry, but can't you see that I can promise nothing of the kind? If ever I come upon any animal or person in such distress, in all conscience I must do as I did just now. You're right, though—I did let my temper get the best of me. I should have assured the wagoner that I knew it was only ignorance that made him treat his poor horse so." I wished I could explain to my grandmother that I *had* to jump into helping, because no one else ever seemed to care as I did.

She sank back into the tufted cushions and said feebly, "Fiona, I thank all the saints in Ireland, you'll soon be going away to school. I only wish we'd known of Wyndriven Academy at the beginning of the term. If ever a girl needed to learn how to act around society, it's you."

"Then I can go to Wyndriven?"

"I suppose so."

When I hugged her fiercely once more, over her shoulder my eye was caught by an undulating coil of mist wafting down the road. It evolved into a ragged, vapory child who melted into a brick wall.

Later, when I considered why Grandmama gave in, I supposed it was in the hopes that the Academy could transform the sow's ear that was me into a silk purse. Perhaps my grandmother also was worried about what I would become if I continued in my solitary ways. Little did Grandmama know, *I* sometimes had a similar nagging fear. I was fretted by the frightening picture of the wild-eyed, poetry-scribbling, specter-seeing recluse I might become if my lonely life remained undisturbed. Perhaps the siren's call was simply my excuse to make another foray into the world.

CHAPTER 2

FORAY

My new maid, my grandmother, and I forayed to the train station the morning after I spoke to The Two. Before boarding the train, I clasped my tiny gray-haired grandmother so hard I lifted her off the ground.

"Put me down this instant!" Grandmama snapped.

I released her. "I'm sorry. I…" I couldn't explain how I was feeling. Tears clogged my throat.

She sighed and straightened her coat. "You must take advantage of what Wyndriven Academy has to teach you." She patted my slumped shoulders. "It's a good-hearted girl you are, you are. I *do* understand, my dearie. I *do* know, but we're here to better ourselves, not stay as we are. If only you took after your father rather than—" She ceased speaking, but I knew she had been about to bring up my actress mother.

All in those few seconds, her final words first touched, then hurt, then angered me. I was suddenly more than ready to board the train.

As we steamed along at thirty miles an hour, my maid, Bridey, and I eagerly watched the changing scenery, grayed through the haze that belched from the locomotive's smoke stack. Sometimes we softly crooned Irish melodies together. I loved to sing, even though Grandmama had disliked it. Too like my mother.

Bridey was wonderful. Servants and I always got along comfortably—indeed, my grandmother accused me of having low tastes in companions. But I was more than comfortable with Bridey. I liked her. I already knew this, even though we had only met a few days earlier. She laughed often, and enjoyed my stylish, showy wardrobe nearly as much as I did. At school she would care for my possessions, my person, and my rooms. And there were a great many of those possessions sent ahead on two drays to Mississippi. Grandmama hoped that nice surroundings would help me to settle in well.

It surprised me that Grandmama had chosen my maid so well, until I realized that only a young, inexperienced servant would be willing to give up civilization to travel to the wild and war-torn South. Bridey had a lilting Irish brogue that made me feel cozy, and a mop of curly brown hair that refused to be confined.

We changed to a stagecoach once we reached Virginia, since the Southern railroad was still in shambles. Now the trip involved much swaying, bumping, lurching, and Bridey looking greenish. She could no longer regale me with stories of the shenanigans of her close-knit family.

The grim realities of what had taken place in this region only a few years earlier were on display. Charred rubble and scenes of destruction, untouched two years after the war's end, left us dismayed. The landscape stretched as a broad black gash of ruin. Federal regiments still occupied the cities, but it seemed that this world was like Humpty Dumpty—all the president's horses and all the president's men could never put it together again.

Once, in a blue-gray twilight, the sound of blasting artillery made me peer out the window. I gasped at sight of a battle waging in the field right beside us. Smoke hung heavy, but vaguely I glimpsed pale soldiers in blue and gray making the motions of killing and death. It took a moment to realize they were wraiths.

Sometimes I was fooled because the ghosts I saw looked and sounded every bit as solid as they had in life. The sightings could occur in such different ways—unfortunately I had yet to figure out The Rules. Perhaps there were none, since the spirits seemed to be individuals who had slipped through cracks in God's plan, so that their very presence defied heavenly laws. One would think that, given this gift—or curse—I would also be given guidance to assist the wretched souls. Perhaps I had been, but was too stupid to realize it.

I squeezed my eyes shut. Surely...surely the battle was a mere image, like a stereopticon slide. I could not bear it if the poor dead soldiers were fighting for all eternity, never realizing that the war had ended and they could move on to rest in their bright home.

Why don't I ever see angels? A flash of something glorious instead of ghastly.

I clutched at the rosary beads in my pocket.

From then on, I rarely looked out the window. At first I passed the time scribbling poetry about the horrors of war, until my heart felt so ready to break that I switched to verses about romance.

Although I had rarely had a conversation with a flesh-and-blood young gentleman, I was intimately acquainted with a good many romantic heroes from novels. In the past few years I had written scads of poetry featuring them. In my dreaming verses, boys with bright eyes and lion-colored hair, or else dark, exotic gypsy-types sporting silver-twisted earrings, would whisper delightful words...

Imagine my surprise when a dark, exotic young man actually boarded the stage in Tennessee. He did not even nod our way, but immediately pulled out a volume from his bag and became immersed in it. I squinted at the title. It was printed in a foreign script.

I sneaked peeks at him. He had long, sleek black hair, dark golden-brown skin, and pleasing features, which somehow contrived to be masculine in spite of their beauty. Perhaps because his nose had a touch of the hawk about it. If only he were as interesting as he was handsome. How did one begin chatting with a stranger of the opposite sex on a stagecoach? The answer was simple: In polite society, one did not.

For three days we traveled in relative silence, cooped up with the young gentleman during the day, separating at an inn at night. I became so used to the boy sitting there with his hawk-nose in his book, that he seemed as if he were merely an attractive extension of the cushioned seat. Or maybe one of the unspeaking sort of ghost.

At last we entered northern Mississippi. It wouldn't be long before we rolled into Chicataw, the town nearest my new school. The delicious, warm air set my winter-sluggish blood flowing faster.

"Do you know what the date is?" I asked Bridey.

The young man glanced up through sooty black lashes. Other than noting that, I ignored him. He had disregarded us—I would speak as if Bridey and I were alone.

Bridey shrugged. "I do not. I have lost track of the days."

"February fourteenth," I announced. "And you know what that means."

"Valentine's Day," Bridey breathed.

"And between you and me, how many beaux do we have?"

Bridey held up her fingers in a circle for zero. "'Tis a pity. And the pair of us so desirable." She glanced sideways at our traveling companion and giggled.

"I have never received a valentine's gift in my life," I said, "so I comfort myself with sweets on this day."

Bridey's eyes danced as I drew an elaborate pasteboard box — violet with stamped silver squiggles and silver ribbons — from my reticule. "I need comfort too," she said.

"Of course I'm sharing."

"That is hard to believe," the young man said.

It was as if the seat had spoken.

He looked at me squarely for the first time. "It is hard to believe that young ladies such as yourselves would have no admirers."

"Thank you," I said, after a little pause. "For finding it hard to believe."

His name, it turned out, was Sebastian Thatoor, his father was an Indian maharajah, and he was bound for Albion Academy, a boys' school near Chicataw. I vaguely knew that a maharajah was some sort of far Eastern royalty. I wasn't sure I believed that part of his background.

When I told Mr. Thatoor who we were and what our destination was, he gave a rusty smile that was more of a spasm. "Then we will be neighbors and it is right that we become acquainted. This is a fine thing." He eyed my box of sugarplums.

In spite of his good looks, poor Mr. Thatoor's manner was painfully gawky. This made *me* far less gawky.

"Oh, are you hungry?" I asked. "Please, help yourself."

"I will...help myself." He reached for a sweet. "I am always hungry."

By the time we arrived at Chicataw, the box was empty.

A chimney standing as a rib,
A burnt-out city, like a sore,
A field in ruins from the flames —
The land becomes the ghost of War.
—By Fiona O'Malley

CHAPTER 3

ARRIVAL

I felt slightly abandoned when Mr. Thatoor was swiftly scooped up by a buggy sent from his school. Bridey, I, and my several trunks were left standing in the dust in front of the Chicataw city hall. I looked about helplessly. A message had been sent ahead about our approximate arrival time, but no one was here to meet us. What would we do if no one came?

Just as I was about to despair, a church bell bonged the hour and a wicker goat cart pulled by two billies drew up. A fine young man leapt out and gave a quick bow. "Miss O'Malley?"

I nodded, taking in the fellow's sack coat cut in the latest style, his buff-colored kid gloves, and his boots polished to an impeccable shine. All proclaimed him the quintessential dandy.

"I'm Harry Petheram," the fellow said, with a quick bow. "One of my sisters is the owner of Wyndriven Academy, while the other is the headmistress."

I bobbed an equally hasty curtsy. "And what are *you*, Mr. Petheram? Besides a brother. You're *not* a teacher."

"Perceptive, Miss O'Malley." He raised appreciative eyebrows. "A schoolteacher is indeed the last thing in this world I would be. I'm not sure what I am actually. I try to make myself useful-ish." He tapped the cart with the handle of his whip. "Sorry for picking you up in this, but no other conveyance was readily available."

"Why, in the city I was constantly dashing about behind a pair of strapping goats," I said, hoping to make him feel less awkward. If indeed he felt awkward, which I rather doubted.

He grinned at me boyishly, although he was not so very young — perhaps thirty or so. "Please call me 'Mr. Harry.' All the students do. It's the Southern way."

I found myself smiling back. Everything was going to be fine. It was a lovely spring day, and Chicataw was a bird-singing, church-bell-ringing, pretty little town with few outward signs of the recent conflict. Everything was going to be fine.

And then I wondered if my smile was too big, so I hastily closed my lips.

"I hope they're muscular goats," I said as I climbed in the cart.

"Oh, yes." Mr. Harry indicated the one on the left. "That one's aptly named Atlas and the other is Billy. The casual observer might think Billy's name is not the most original, and the casual observer would be right. Perhaps you can come up with a better one. Atlas is foul-tempered, but he knows who's in charge, don't you, old boy?" Mr. Harry cracked his whip, and away we rolled.

I tried to think of something pert to say — perhaps a clever name for Billy — but my mind was blank. Mr. Harry was so very smooth. My shyness settled in. No one spoke for several minutes. I was startled when Mr. Harry asked, "And what does a Northern girl like you think of Mississippi?"

"I can't say for certain," I said absently. "We've only just met."

He gave a delighted laugh, although I wasn't sure why. "You know, I'm a Yankee myself. My family first came here twelve years ago. You're going to be surprised by Wyndriven when you first meet it. Everyone is."

As we bowled along, Mr. Harry set me at my ease. He had wonderfully mobile, expressive features, and was most amusing as he regaled us with droll stories of his own school life.

"Hercules," I announced suddenly and too loudly.

"I beg your pardon?" And then Mr. Harry nodded in understanding. "Oh—for the goat, you mean."

"Yes."

"Excellent. So shall he be known all his days." He cracked his whip once again. "Onward, Atlas and Hercules."

We entered a road carved through dense forest. Mr. Harry waved up at the lavender wisteria swathing the branches above. "When we knew you were coming, Miss O'Malley, I decorated the woods just for your pleasure. Spent all night festooning."

Both Bridey and I laughed.

"It's like a wedding canopy," I observed. The grayish brown of winter was flushed with delicate, sprouting green, now and then punctuated by a shock of intense new color. Hard to believe that New York was still armored in ice.

At last we reached our destination. The sweeping front lawn of Wyndriven Academy was one mass of daffodils.

"I think I hear angels singing," I murmured, gazing at the glowing golden waves rippling in a capricious breeze.

Mr. Harry reined in the cart. "They were planted the first year my sister Sophie owned Wyndriven. Once they're done blooming, we'll let the goats out."

I gave him an incredulous look. "Ghosts?" My tone was sharp, and in that moment my warm tingles of excited hope froze into icy shards.

He roared with laughter. "*Goats.* Like these fellows. To graze."

I melted once again, and smiled self-consciously.

"During the war," he continued, "some clever person—all right, I humbly admit it was me—had the bright idea to use them for cropping the grass. Old Mr. Willie, the gardener, took a liking to the beasts so we keep them on. As for 'ghosts,' I guess the place does look haunted, doesn't it? When our resident spook appears to you, it can say (in sepulchral tones, naturally), '*You were warned.*'"

"So there *is* a resident spook?"

He eyed me quizzically. "I spoke in jest." His tone was gentle.

Wyndriven Academy thrust up from the lush greenery, replete with gargoyles, towers, spikes, and stark, stony splendor. "I was told about the building," I said, as I took it in. "Still, I find myself unprepared for such a *monstrous* place."

Mr. Harry clicked his tongue and we moved once again down the drive lined with cedars, dark against daffodil yellow, toward steps rising to an oaken door.

As Mr. Harry helped Bridey and me down, lace curtains fluttered in the windows—we were under observation.

I feared that the pork pie hat which was tilted atop my head in a manner defying all laws of gravity, might slip. Bridey and I had chosen it for this moment because it, along with my crinolette bustle, was the very latest style. I held my head high, mainly to safeguard the hat.

And then my gaze was drawn to a casement on the second floor. The brooding face of a bearded man peered out. As he caught my eye, his expression changed. He gave a faint, surprised smile. I was too nervous to smile back.

"Don't feel anxious," Mr. Harry said, flicking his glance upward. "Everything will be fine." He still held my gloved hand, and now he squeezed it slightly. "Remember I'm here with a ready ear and a stout, manly shoulder, if that gaggle of girls gets too much for you. They have been eaten up with curiosity ever since word got out that such an exceptional young lady was on her way. Already I expect the entire household is agog over your elegant ensemble."

Exceptional. In what way?

I gave him a shaky smile, lifted my skirts, and climbed the abnormally steep steps. Long-legged as I was, I had to scramble to reach them. The sizes felt distorted, as if I had stepped into the pages of *Alice's Adventures in Wonderland*.

Once inside the lofty hall, Bridey was led away by a maid, to await me in my suite, while Mr. Harry took me to the office. He indicated the school motto stenciled in gilt above the door: *Attention, Obedience, Industry, Punctuality.* "My sentiments exactly, except for when I feel like being distracted, rebellious, lazy, and late."

I was still laughing when we entered and Miss Petheram stood from behind the desk. She was long-necked and willowy, too pretty to be a headmistress. Tendrils of soft blonde hair, in a style popular a decade earlier, escaped from their confines to curl about her face. Still, her plain gray jacket over a white blouse, crisp as frost, was sufficiently headmistress-like.

"Harry, you're incorrigible," she said. "Now run along. I'll take care of Miss O'Malley." She reached for my hand as the door clicked behind her brother. "Thank goodness you've arrived at last. I'm sorry to have had you met as you were. Normally I would not have permitted such a thing."

"Mr. Harry explained," I said, "and I enjoyed the ride."

"It's not simply for the cart that I apologize. Girls' schools don't conventionally allow bachelors to reside in them." She looked uncomfortable. "You see, Harry was an officer—a *Union* officer—he attended West Point—and he was quite spent by the end of the war. He needed a good, long rest. After we re-opened the Academy, he intended to leave, but I needed him, and he needed us. Truly, he's indispensable for any number of tasks. He's like an older brother to the students."

I hastened to allay her qualms as I seated myself in a chair in front of the desk. "My grandmother would not mind." Especially since I would never tell her.

Miss Petheram inquired politely as to my trip, and then droned on about the school. "Young ladies live here harmonious-ly as they are gently taught the subtle nuances of grace, polish, and charm."

Now that I looked more closely, the headmistress, like her brother, was older than she had first appeared. Crows' feet puck-ered about her eyes and her skin had the dry, faded look I'd no-ticed before in extremely fair women once past their youth.

I was scrutinizing her too obviously. She averted her gaze uncomfortably, and now sounded like an automaton as her soft voice reeled off the rules—"All talking and laughing, note-writ-ing, conversation by signs, eating, and leaving of seats, are entirely forbidden throughout study and recitation times," etc.

My mind wandered. Evidently Miss Petheram realized this, and, although her lips remained tranquil, her blue eyes twinkled. "Oh, very well. I'm finished lecturing now." She stood to show me around the school. "One more thing." She clasped her hands to her breast as if she were about to reveal something dire. "I wrote to your grandmother that I would try to find a way for you to attend your Catholic Mass, and indeed I did make inquiries. However, the best we can do is take you to the Catholic church in Holly Springs once a month or so. I'm very sorry."

I beamed at her reassuringly. I was not particularly fond of Mass. "Whatever you arrange is fine." Another thing not to tell Grandmama.

Miss Petheram, taffeta skirts hissing, led me now around drawing and sitting and music and class rooms, through bewildering passages, and up and down staircases.

The lavishness of the place was exhausting, although the furnishings did show the wear and tear of a building that had served as a school, as well as barracks for two armies, in the past decade. The beauty—and it was indeed beautiful—had a forlorn quality. Stains, snags, and even slashes marred once-luxurious fabrics, while scratches and chips flawed wood.

Occasionally we would hear piping voices and catch glimpses of girls engaged in various activities.

"I will introduce you to the other young ladies at suppertime," Miss Petheram said, and then added pointedly, "When you have had time to freshen up."

Immediately my hat slid askew. After I straightened it and glanced in a convenient mirror, I saw that my height-of-fashion

crinolette had twisted to the side. My appearance had taken on
the wild, rollicking aspect it so often did. I tried to twitch and tuck
myself back in place.

"A good deal of the building is closed off," Miss Petheram
explained as we passed a barred door.

I thought of those expanses of shadowed, locked, lonely
chambers spreading out around us, and for a moment I experienced a touch of vertigo, almost as one feels when standing atop
a precipice. I shivered.

"Are you too cool, Miss O'Malley? Should we fetch a shawl?"

"No, ma'am," I said. "I only felt sorry for the poor unused
rooms." Even as I said these words, I stepped into an icy spot that
seemed to hold onto the hoarded deadly chill of centuries of winters. Again I shivered.

The headmistress seemed not to notice the change in temperature. "Our staff is currently inadequate and we have had to
put entire wings under dustcovers." A distant look came to her
eyes. "The first time I stayed at the abbey, there was a veritable
army of servants."

"They were all slaves, weren't they?" I asked flatly. I still had
a hard time coming to terms with the South's recent past.

"Mostly," Miss Petheram said, "but not all. It was an unusual
household. It employed a British housekeeper, a Chinese butler,
and a French cook. Oh, and Achal, the valet, was an odd, elusive, *tiny* little man from India. I was always curious about him
because he seemed to be nothing—no personality, no thoughts,
no desires—nothing—without his master. I pitied him. I've often
wondered what happened to him. I really have no idea."

She took note when I wrinkled my nose at a disgustingly gory painting of a stag being mauled by a pack of wolves. "My sister, Miss Sophie, whose family lives in town, meant to make a great many modifications in this place, but she was constantly thwarted in her efforts. Canvases were removed and furniture rearranged, only to be found the next morning back in the original place. No one admits to it, but I expect some of the older servants disliked changes." She gave a nervous laugh. "It was a relief when no one interfered in the decoration of your rooms."

The portraits in a long gallery were more pleasing than the stag picture. I studied them with interest. They were likenesses of the previous owners of the place, after it had become a private home, their fashions changing with the decades. I fancied I could detect a mode of inherited noses that spanned centuries.

I paused before the arresting painting of a young gentleman standing beside a black horse. The artist had been skilled — fire and power emanated from the painted steed, while a vivid, dancing Something showed in the eyes of the youth. There was humor and intelligence in his striking features, as well as...Suddenly I was certain this person had died young. I turned from the portrait in haste.

As we moved along, a tight little headache grew at the base of my skull where my heavy knot of hair rested. Absently, I rubbed at it with one hand while I adjusted hair pins with the other. I had never been in such an *old* place, and the weight of antiquity pressed down. This was compounded by the damp, mossy, cave-like smell of cold stone which seeped up through the veneers. Confusion teased at my mind, as if many different impressions battled for notice. All the lives that had been lived here. All the deaths. The past seemed to close around me as water over pebbles.

I found myself dwelling on the mental picture of the perfectly modern house I would own someday, full of bright rooms with cheerful walls of windows.

CHAPTER 4

A WELCOME

"These spaces were a delight to decorate," Miss Petheram said as she opened the door into my chambers. The sweet, stern lines of her face softened. She paused, as if unsure whether she should continue, then gave a low chuckle. "It was touching how anxious the suite was to wake up and cooperate in becoming pretty."

Her whimsy made me suddenly like her.

She smiled when I told her that my rooms looked so light and airy, I expected them to sprout wings and flit off at any moment. The medieval walls were completely disguised—I might have stepped into the elegantly-furnished, pastel-tinted, silkily-draped modern house I had just daydreamed about.

Plaster garlands bedecked the top of the walls, while below, the paper was in a rose so pale as to be nearly white. The mantels were of fluted, pinkish marble, as was the floor, scattered with fluffy, flowery carpets.

The graceful furniture was what Grandmama and I had picked out back in the city and had shipped here. For a moment I felt confused and dizzy, as if my New York past were colliding

with my Mississippi today. I quickly recovered and moved on to
the bedchamber.

A bed that might have been a cloud, with its puffy white
counterpane and gossamer draperies, occupied much of it. The
curtains fluttered tantalizingly. Through a wide arched doorway
flanked by slender columns, lay the dressing room. Bridey was
already there arranging my toiletries.

"Tomorrow, after lessons, you might explore Wyndriven's
grounds," Miss Petheram said. "They're overgrown, but there's
beauty in the wildness. Do watch out for old Atlas, though—the
black goat. He has a nasty temper and it's his pleasure to surprise
one from behind." As she turned to leave, she added, "You are a
special pupil and your suite shows the care we shall take to make
you happy here."

My peasant ancestors would have been scullery maids at the
abbey, and here I was, a "special" pupil.

I hadn't long to wash, change clothes, and prepare for the
gauntlet of suppertime.

When I was about to head downstairs half an hour after Miss
Petheram left, Bridey gave my shoulder a sympathetic pat. "Sure,
it'll be all right, Miss." I must have appeared terrified. How grateful I was for Bridey.

At my former schools, the harder I had tried to play the part
of a well-bred young lady, the odder I had acted. That was why I
had chosen solitude so often. In solitude, there was no chance for
me to stop all conversation when I said the wrong thing.

In the dining room, the two long tables stretching down the
center, lined with seated girls, were dwarfed by the former banquet hall's cavernous proportions.

Miss Petheram's voice echoed as she stood at the head of the tables. She gave a wordy explanation about where I was from and why I was joining the student body late in the term. She went on to say she knew the young ladies would make an effort to be friendly.

Throughout her speech, I tried to appear confident. I tried not to slouch (as per my grandmother's instructions), and to hold my eyes level with all the cool, surveying stares. I couldn't think how to place my hands, and found that I was plucking at my skirt. I lifted my chin and clasped my fingers together. At last the speech ended, I curtsied, and twenty-or-so heads nodded.

I seated myself in the place Miss Petheram indicated, careful to arrange my bustle beside me first. A carved knob in the tall wooden chair back poked into my spine.

A few weeks from now would I know everyone's names? Was it possible I could ever be friendly with any of them, let alone actual friends?

Scattered conversation ebbed and swelled all around. I was engulfed in Southern drawls. Interesting and lyrical, but it certainly brought home the fact that I was *here*.

Not far down the table, a pretty, dark-haired girl, with unusually large, lustrous eyes, said, "Y'all know how everyone's mad for spiritualism these days? Why, even Mrs. Abraham Lincoln dabbles in it."

"Bite your tongue." This speaker resembled a bad pixie, with her maroon-colored hair and clever, pointed, interesting face. "We don't mention that L name around here."

Pretty girl rolled luminous eyes. "Whatever you say, Trix."

(Ah, Bad Pixie Girl was named Trix.)

Pretty girl continued. "Anyway, my mama sent me sheet music for this 'Spirit Rappings' song. Y'all have got to hear it. 'Rap-tap-tap, lost friends are near you, rap-tap-tap, they see and hear you; 'Tis no fable—beings able—rap-tap-tap upon a table." Her singing voice was nasal.

In the hush that followed, a distinct knocking sounded from beneath the table. Everyone gaped, and then burst into laughter. The mischievous look on Trix's face betrayed the identity of the rapping "spirit."

I shook my head and forced down a buttermilk biscuit. These girls were so very silly. I stabbed at a chunk of something batter-dipped and fried, with slimy innards. "What is this?" I asked the girl across the table, who had been watching me.

She started. "Fried okra," she said, and swiftly looked away.

The meal was all right, but I had trouble eating. I stared down at the dessert—a droopy blancmange—and it leered back. The randomly-set almonds made a hideous, trembling face. I gingerly poked it with my spoon. It quivered.

I shuddered, and then explained to the same girl, "I don't like food that eyes you judgmentally."

She appeared confused, and then scornful. The way they always did.

People were leaving the table. Miss Petheram had stated that the hours following supper were set apart for socializing, so naturally I escaped. I abandoned Monsieur Blancmange and fled toward my rooms, praying I could find the way.

From an anteroom doorway came female voices interspersed with shrill laughter. Something made me pause behind a bushy-leafed aspidistra plant to listen, even though I knew full well that eavesdroppers hear no good of themselves.

"What a queer thing the new girl is. And a carpet-bagging *Yankee* to boot."

I recognized the voice. It was the spirit-rapping young lady. With dismay, I realized it was me she was talking about.

"But Sylvie, Mr. Harry is also a Yankee and you've set your cap for him."

(I had no idea who this voice belonged to, but evidently Pretty Girl's name was Sylvie.)

"You hush your mouth about that."

"Just reminding you. In case you'd forgotten."

"Did you know the new girl brought her own furniture? Took five men to lug in her piano. The academy's instruments ain't good enough." By the sharp, snippy tone, I assigned this voice to the malicious pixie, Trix.

"She's disgustingly rich."

"La, child—only vulgar new money." Trix again. The three voices were each distinctive, although their derisive tones were the same. "And it makes no difference. Wealthy or a beggar, she'd still be laughable. Did you see how she walked around with her long bony face lifted all high and mighty? Ladies, Miss *O'Mooly* is a stuck-up *Yankee* puss, and we're not going to let her lord it over us. Or is it *'lady'* it over us? Whatever it is, she shan't do it. So there. She's nothing but a clodhopper dressed up fancy. Fine feathers do *not* make a fine bird."

From what I remembered at the supper table, Trix had jarringly garish "feathers" of her own. Her dress had honestly been hideous.

If only those girls had known that I didn't consider myself superior to anyone. Except perhaps with my wardrobe. In fact, just the opposite. Probably, though, it wouldn't have made any difference. They were prepared to dislike me before they ever saw me.

I slunk to my room.

Bridey stopped her task when I entered. Her wide-eyed, eager expression told me she had been awaiting my arrival. "It's never guessing you'll be at what I have to tell you, Miss."

I tried to make my face not register the fact that I hadn't the least interest in what she was about to relate. Even though I hadn't. "What is it?"

"Sure and the maid who showed me up here told me murders happened in this place. Lots of them. And not all long ago, either. 'Tis why none of the other servants will sleep over. She asked me if I wasn't afraid, staying nights."

Oh, dear. "And are you?"

Bridey cocked her head to one side, considering. Slowly she grinned. "Actually, I think not. You see, I've the Sight. I've beheld spirits in times past and am none the worse for it. In fact, 'tis hoping I am that I'll come upon a bogle or two. Something to write about to me family. We enjoy a fine ghost tale o' nights."

I nodded with approval. "You're a grand girl for being so brave. I told my grandmother I hoped to see the specter of a walled-in nun, so maybe you'll see that. It's supposed to be a popular haunter of old abbeys, and obviously it makes a fine ghost tale, since it's been used so much. Besides, you and I and the nun are all Catholic, so we'd have something in common." I was being flippant. It seemed the best response.

Of course from the moment I set foot in Wyndriven, I had been waiting jumpily for the spectral nun sighting. However, I was not about to mention my own gift of the Sight to Bridey. For one thing, if her ability had not allowed her to meet up with The Two during her few nights spent at my grandmother's house, then I doubted she would have trouble here. "But you know if you're ever nervous about sleeping in your own room, you can always stay on the sofa in here."

Bridey adamantly shook her head. "No, indeed. It's snoozing in me own cot I'll be. Did I tell you I shared a bed with two sisters at home? Yes, I did. And I was in the middle. Always someone breathing on me. I'll be most happy upstairs in the old servants' quarters. I put me things there already. So high up I don't believe any bogles will care to make the trip, more's the pity."

"Did the maid tell you any details about these murders 'most foul?'"

"Nothing more. Took her long enough to figure out how to bring up they'd happened at all, at all. I shall ask her next time I see her." Bridey returned to shaking out and hanging my far-too-many (if there could be such a thing) gowns in the wardrobes.

The words of the school girls echoed in my mind. At thought of them, an aching hollow gaped somewhere in my middle, but my eyes remained hot and dry and tearless. I busied myself arranging the framed silhouettes of my parents on the mantel. Perhaps if my mother had been in my life, I could have confided Things to her. Things about other girls. Things about ghosts. The line from the poem by Whittier came into my head: "For of all sad words of tongue or pen, the saddest are these: 'It might have been!'" Because my mother had not been in my life since I was four years old.

My mother had performed in musical theater when she met

my painfully shy, exceedingly intelligent father. Eventually, she had abandoned us both to tour Europe with her old company. We never saw or heard from her again. That was when we went to live with Grandmama. That was when I first saw spirits.

My faint memories of my mother were of someone filled with laughter and light-heartedness. My memories of her leaving were sheer agony. I could only watch her go, devastated by the choices of powerful grown-ups and helpless to save what I loved. Sometimes I wrote myself letters from my mother describing the things she did and how much she wished I was with her. Often that helped. If I was in a low mood, however, I would imagine her with new replacement daughters, completely forgetting me. That did *not* help.

I went on to arrange my beloved books on their shelves. Each volume must be situated according to its friends. Jane Austen's novels liked to be sandwiched between Ouida's and the Bronte sisters' — that sort of thing. I began to feel better as I handled them, and I softly sang "When the Corn is Waving, Annie Dear." Bridey hummed along.

When I finished, I reached for a dress to hang as well.

"Oh, yourself mustn't be doing that, Miss," she said, shooing me away. "Rest up for your first school day tomorrow. There you go now."

I clutched a cherry-colored silk faille to my chest. "Please let me help. I adore handling my dresses. I love how they feel. I even stroke them — they're my pets."

A giggle escaped from Bridey. "Is that the way of it? Of course I'll *let* you help if you want to so bad."

After we finished putting everything away, and Bridey

was about to leave, she stopped in her tracks. "Ooh! Your light. Mustn't forget that." We gave each other a look of mutual understanding tinged with shame. The fact was, both Bridey and I were afraid of the dark. We had discovered this about each other early in our travels.

After Bridey left, the rosy glow of the fairy lamp she had lit cast such weird shadows that I wasn't sure if it helped or hurt.

I lay against my pillow, trying to become used to those strange shadows and the strange sounds and the strange feel of this place. The things the girls had said slithered again into my mind. I winced, and drew my knees to my chest. It seemed to me, as a person who had experienced a great deal of exquisite social embarrassment in her sixteen years, that humiliation can be worse in some aspects than tragedy. At least there is dignity in tragedy, but in embarrassment there is only gut-wrenching pain and the cringing hope that no one else will learn of it.

I sucked in my breath so that it felt as if I were choking. I had always known I was odd and unattractive—early on The Two had made sure of that—but somehow I had hoped no one here would notice. I reached for my handkerchief on the bedside table and turned my pillow over so the feathers would fluff and the linen would be cooler against my neck, as I prepared for a good cry.

My sniffing drew in a whiff of pipe tobacco, with an underlying scent of something spicy-masculine, as of gentlemen's cologne. My window was open—perhaps Mr. Harry was outside below, smoking. Or the bearded gentleman I had glimpsed earlier, whoever he was.

A sound met my ears. Footsteps pacing the floor above. I didn't like to think of so many strangers so close. But then again I didn't like to think of the empty rooms either.

Or no. Not upstairs. I gave a short gasp. The footfall was right here in this room. Around my bed. I clutched at the covers. Now the quiet tread moved toward the window. I forced myself to look.

The draperies were open. Bars of moonlight sliced through the hazy silhouette of a broad-shouldered person standing with his back to me, gazing out into the darkness.

Of course. My room is haunted.

They come out from the corners
And the inbetweens —
Those shuddering like mourners,
And those seldom-seen.
They crawl out of the mirrors
And hang above the beds--
Those loveless and those dearer,
Those pale and passed, those dead.
— By Fiona O'Malley

CHAPTER 5

MY HERO

My darling dress was reluctantly shrouded in the voluminous black silk apron that all students were required to wear during lessons. Although Bridey had thought it peculiar, I had dressed behind a screen that first morning, in case the ghost who shared my quarters was still drifting about unseen. With any luck he wouldn't be unseen *behind* the screen. My hope was that if he were invisible to me, I was invisible to him as well. The idea of a phantom in my bedchamber was not pleasant, but The Two had somewhat vaccinated me against terror of random spooks, since no other specter could possibly be worse than they. Mostly I felt tired and resigned.

I had classes in aesthetics, elocution, moral philosophy, posture and poise, fancywork, dance, and handwriting. The younger girls had more academic subjects, but we sixteen- and seventeen-year-olds were considered to have moved beyond book learning. They did not want us turning into intellectual bluestockings, after all. I did not mind the lack of schoolbooks—I was perfectly capable of turning myself into a bluestocking without formal instruction.

From the evening before, I recognized Trix and Sylvie. They made up two of the three girls who seemed glued to one another and were in all my classes. Turtle Nose was the third. I hadn't noticed her previously, although she certainly resembled a turtle—something about the nose. While Sylvie was darkly beautiful, Turtle Nose was darkly plain.

Our handwriting class was taught by a swarthy, strong-featured woman named Miss Wright. She strode between the desk rows, scrutinizing our copperplate—an exercise in aphorisms in alphabetical order. *Afflictions are often blessings in disguise, By its fruit the tree is known*...I bent my head over my paper so she couldn't see mine, but the girl who sat across from me was not so lucky. "You'll come back in here after supper, Miss Clegg," Miss Wright rumbled in her deep voice, "and redo every line of this chicken-scratching."

Miss Clegg flushed a shade of purest puce. She was mousey-haired and flabbily overweight, with an unfortunate complexion. Her face was pitted with smallpox scars. My heart went out to her. I had always wondered if I would have had the strength of will not to claw at my skin if ever I had been cursed with the disease. I feared that I would not.

There but for the grace of God go I.

In the dining room, once again, no one spoke to me. When Miss Clegg rose and trudged from the room, I waited just a moment to follow. I wanted to introduce myself to the girl. Being an outcast would not be nearly so disagreeable if there were two of us.

Miss Clegg dropped down at a desk in the classroom, gave a great sigh and, without looking up, reached for a sheet of paper.

She dipped her pen and began apathetically scratching away, hopefully not like any sort of fowl.

I seated myself across from her. "I saw Miss Wright scornfully glance at my penmanship. I bet she'll bring it up tomorrow, so I might as well redo mine now too."

"Suit yourself," was all Miss Clegg said, but the look she gave me showed she thought me a fool for doing so.

The only sounds in the room were the ticking of the clock, the scraping of our pens, and an occasional clicking sound, which I discovered came from Miss Clegg biting the nails on her left hand while her right hand wrote. Once in a while there was also a sigh from the girl, as though the act of lifting her pen was almost more than she could manage.

"Oh, my goodness," I announced abruptly, "the writing teacher is named Miss *Wright*."

"You only just realized that?" My companion set down her pen. "I'm Dorcas Clegg, by the way."

"Fiona O'Malley."

"Of course. I know. Everyone knows. Cassie Humphrey's mother is kin to someone in New York who knows your grandmother, so she told Cassie you were coming and Cassie told everyone else. Even me, and no one ever bothers telling me anything. But Cassie's tongue is hinged in the middle. We know all about you. You're a rich Yankee and all your family's money came from making cannons or something like that."

I was taken aback by the tone of her voice — soft and sultry and lilting. Beautiful. This, along with the outpouring of words from such a limp, listless sort of person surprised me so much that for a moment I could hardly process what she had said. When I did, an ink blot spread from my nib. "I really don't know about our finances. My grandmother gives me clothes and is paying for the rooms and everything. I wish Cassie hadn't spread all that around. About the money and the firearms, I mean. It makes me feel guilty."

Dorcas Clegg eyed me with a dull curiosity. "An inconvenient way to feel. Understandable, though—the war being so fresh in our minds down here. I wonder that you dared come South at all."

I lifted my shoulders. Perhaps she would drop the subject.

She picked up her pen, but did not use it. "So, do you really have your own maid and a whole lavish suite of rooms to yourself?"

"Just a bedroom and sitting room. And a dressing room, I guess."

"'Just.' Most of us are crowded four in one chamber. You know it's not exactly common at Wyndriven to have rooms redecorated just for you."

"Now I'll feel guilty about that as well. Anyway, you're welcome to see them any time you want."

The door to the schoolroom flew open suddenly, and Trix swept in. Over her shoulder, she announced, "Here she is." Sylvie and Turtle Nose sidled in after.

Trix held out a fancy box tied with a satin ribbon. "A gift for you, Miss O'Malley," she purred. "Some welcoming caramels from all of us."

"Why, thank you." I took the box, confused and a little mystified by such an attention.

"Open it," Sylvie said, drawing closer. "You do like caramels, don't you?"

"Love them." I untied the ribbon, and didn't even realize until later, that Dorcas had whispered, "Watch out," and Turtle Nose had flicked a quick, apologetic look my way, just as I lifted the lid.

I trembled first, then gagged, gave a strangled scream, and dropped the box.

Earthworms, writhing pinky-gray and nauseating, spilled onto the parquet floor about my feet. I kicked out as one touched my slipper. Mindless, I jumped over them and tore from the room. Behind me the girls dissolved into laughter. "What? You don't *love* those caramels?" Trix called after.

I couldn't bear it. Any of it. I hated girls.

Some instinct led me to an outside door. I would keep running until I boarded a stagecoach, and then never stop until I reached New York. I would beg Grandmama to hide me away forever in some book-stocked cranny. Preferably entered only by a secret door.

However, the breeze, chill and scented sharply with pine, slapped my senses back into me. I halted on a creeper-filigreed path. This time I would not, could not run away. No matter what, by my own choice, for good or ill, I would remain at Wyndriven for the next four months.

At least it wouldn't hurt to hide out for a while until the sun set and I could slink undetected up to my haunted bedchamber.

After which another day would begin and I would have to attend all those classes and see those detestable girls, laughing behind their hands. And the next day would be the same, and the next...

Just ahead, rising above a brick wall, were the spires of a medieval chapel, oriel windows glittering and gargoyles grimacing.

In the center of the wall was an iron gate. There is something so tempting about a gate, and a church would be comforting. The gate clanged musically when I flung it open to enter a grassy church-yard, suitably somber for my mood, complete with a willow tree bending mournfully over a couple of ivy-shrouded tombstones.

I climbed the stone steps and turned the knob on an elaborate, iron-banded door. Locked.

Being unable to enter made me want to do so all the more. My rosary beads were in my pocket, and I yearned to pray in a house of God. To clear my mind of slimy worms and malicious girls — one being as bad as the other. The chapel had seemed like a well-timed gift. Of course it was not. The day's only present was a box of wriggling nastiness. My stomach lurched again at the image. A bitter smile quirked my lips as I realized the irony that a ghost's smashed-in head no longer fazed me, but here I was, physically ill at the mere thought of earthworms. How did Trix know I would be undone by the creatures? I sank to the top step and buried my head in my arms.

"I beg your pardon, Mademoiselle, but would it help to talk about it? I have a sympathetic ear."

At the first sound of the voice, I flinched and slowly raised my face.

Looming above was the bearded man I had seen watching when I first arrived.

Painful heat rushed to my cheeks. I shook my head and started to rise, to flee again. "N-no, sir," I stammered. "Really, I'm all right. Just tired."

"Ah, the eternal excuse of ladies. Perhaps you also have a headache." His voice was deep and mellow, charmingly accented.

In spite of my misery my lips twitched in the ghost of a smile, as I brushed off the back of my skirt. "Not yet, but it almost certainly is coming on."

"No, no. Sit back down, *s'il vous plait*. I did not mean to disturb you. I will leave immediately if you wish. It is only that you looked so unhappy, and sometimes it helps to talk."

I lowered myself back to the step. "Are you — are you associated with the school in some way, sir?"

"Not with the school, but with the building. For many, many years — indeed, since the abbey was first brought to Mississippi — I have overseen it."

"So you're some sort of manager?"

"That is not my actual title, but it's as good a name for what I do as any. The owner, So — Madam Stone — was once my intimate friend, but we have since had a falling out. It saddens me that I rarely see her these days. You have not met the lady yet, I suppose?"

"Not yet."

"When you do meet her, perhaps afterward you will tell me how she goes on. It is regrettable the distance between us now when once we were so close." His velvety voice was suddenly husky, as though he were laboring under some strong emotion. I sensed a romance — unrequited love — and pitied him. I nodded.

"As for the other Petherams," he continued, "they ignore my existence. I believe they will not mention my name." He lowered the lids of his honey-colored eyes in a kind of pain, and I felt more sympathetic to him than ever, as I always did any victim of injustice. He shook himself a little. "But enough of unpleasantries — I saw you from the window when you arrived. And you saw me, did you not?"

"Oh, yes."

"I was surprised at that. I had thought I was perfectly stealthy, peeking out at the new arrival."

"You and everyone else. There seemed to be someone peeking stealthily from every window."

He laughed. It was a deep, rich sound, and most appealing. Everything about him was appealing. At least for an older man. He had to be quite forty. He was terribly handsome, and richly dressed. I was particularly delighted by the twisted silver hoops in his ears. Intriguing.

"Now," he said, "will you not tell me what has made you forlorn?"

As I studied him more closely, there was a touch of romantic dishevelment about his edges. He was bare-headed, his cravat was loosened, a bit of shirttail peeked from beneath the burgundy brocade waistcoat, and a lock of black hair fell across his forehead. Intriguing-er. He might easily be the mysterious master of the house in one of my Gothic novels. And the master was nearly always a misunderstood, but worthy man.

I suddenly believed that there was enough experience, intelligence, and sympathy conveyed in this stranger's features to risk confiding in him. Besides, he hadn't seemed like a stranger for more than a moment. "It's some horrid girls. They decided to dislike me before they ever met me. Not surprising: I've never had the gift of making friends." The words hung in the air. "Which I don't mind," I lied quickly.

"Oh, ho," he said, "I think now you are telling a story."

"No!" I cried. "No, it's true." I said more softly, "I do prefer my own company, if the others will simply leave me alone. But if they're going to single me out for ridicule…"

He shook his head in disbelief. "To me you seem *tres sympathique*. I cannot think of the last time I had such a stimulating conversation. I detect a slight north-eastern accent. How did you come to Wyndriven Abbey, of all places?"

Poor man. He must be lonely indeed if he thought the conversation of the last few minutes had been stimulating. I took a deep breath as it flashed through my mind how all this had come about, and when I remembered the way I had worn down Grandmama, I laughed at myself. Well, a person can't laugh at nothing and not tell someone why, so I told the man all about it. And I don't quite know how or why, but from there we got onto discussing my home in New York, as well as places in the city which he had visited.

"Have you been to the chocolate shop on the corner of Ninth and Broadway?" I asked.

"*Mais oui*. The one where you may watch the wheel in the window go round as the white stone rollers grind chocolate into paste. Délicieux." He pinched his fingers to his lips, kissed them, and opened his hand. "What I would not give for a taste right now."

"Me too. And their caramels — oh." I pulled a face.

He raised his arched black brows. "*Pauvre petite*. Is there something distressing about the memory of caramels? Out with it — I am dying to know of the so frightful caramels in your past."

"They weren't caramels. They were earthworms filling a candy box that the beastly girls *told* me held caramels. Just today. That's why I was so miserable. And I have the greatest horror of worms. How could those girls possibly have known that earthworms are the creature of which I'm most terrified? That I have nightmares about?"

"Certain spiteful young ladies wield a talent to sniff out weaknesses in others."

I groaned. "I may never recover. Never open another candy box. It was the red-headed one who gave it to me. It was her idea, obviously."

"Red heads can never be trusted. I have the greatest aversion to flaming hair." He paused, and I shot him a quick glance, expecting to see that he was jesting. An odd expression was on his face. He shook himself as if shaking his mind free, before he continued. "I am only present here now and again, but I have seen this girl. Her name, I believe, is Trix."

"Yes. That's her. And then there are her minions, Sylvie and Turtle Nose."

"But…turtles do not have noses. At least not obvious ones." The laugh lines around his eyes deepened.

"Well, this girl does."

"I understand. Or rather, I do not, but that is neither here nor there." He slapped his hand against his thigh. "I tell you what you must do. You must hold your head high because you would never stoop to such Trix-ish tricks. You will be more subtle. I have seen this thing before—the ringleader followed about by toadies. She will pick someone she supposes is helpless, and in your case I expect you make her jealous as well, to prey upon. You must show no fear because you are *not* helpless. And then you will undermine this Trix by stealing away her toadies. Have you anything you can offer, to lure them to your side?"

How amazing to have someone in this place willing to help

a girl like me. "I'm not sure," I said doubtfully. "I have a hamper full of goodies. Grandmama knows of my sweet tooth, and she packed it for me. And of course there's all my jewelry and gowns and such. Should I offer to share them with Sylvie and Turtle Nose? In the privacy of my exquisite new rooms?"

Mischief lit his eyes as he clasped his hands together. "*Parfait!* What a clever girl you are. You will win them over completely. Trix, meanwhile, will be devoured by jealousy."

"Hard to imagine I could ever make anyone jealous." I looked down at my hands awkwardly. "Thank you. You are so kind. It's nice to have someone on my side." As we had talked, the sky had changed from blue to pink to violet with the setting sun. "I better go in, I suppose."

"It has been a pleasure. I hope we shall see much more of each other in the future. You must inform me if our scheme succeeds."

"We haven't properly introduced ourselves. Will you tell me your name, please?"

"You may call me Monsieur. And you are—?"

"Fiona O'Malley."

He gave a slight bow. "*Enchanté*, Mademoiselle O'Malley. An Irish lady once told me that having an O attached to your name means you are of royal Irish descent. Did you know that?"

"No, sir."

"Well, now you do. You are an aristocrat and must never think meanly of yourself. And so I shall say *au revoir*." He turned on his heels and went around the corner of the building before I could even sputter out a goodbye. Or an *au revoir*. Perhaps I would begin charmingly peppering my conversation with French phrases.

Did Monsieur…? Yes, he did. He had a very slight limp.

He was so different from anyone I had ever before met. In real life, that is. He seemed appreciative, wicked, fascinating. And he wanted to help me.

My hero.

CHAPTER 6

INFORMATION

Dorcas, Turtle Nose, Sylvie, and I are frolicking about my sitting room in mad revelry. We are decked out in my most fabulous gowns. We are dowsed with French perfume, consuming chocolates at a shocking rate, and shaking with merriment at jokes that only the four of us understand. Trix peeks wistfully in at the doorway.

Only…

My daydream kept dissolving half-formed.

Monsieur made me think of the sort of uncle I had always wished I had — an interesting, elegant, amiable, cosmopolitan gentleman, with whom all the girls at school would be infatuated, but I would be his favorite. (Although — oh dear — not at all in a *romantic* way. Much too old.) However, now that I considered it, his suggested scheme made me uncomfortable. If it came to contests in cruelty, I preferred not to win.

I had been hunched at my dainty desk, laboring by lamplight over a letter to my grandmother, when my shabby little musing had caused me to put down my pen. I lifted it now, but paused, struck with the sensation that someone was standing behind me.

Slowly I turned…

And there stood Dorcas Clegg, peering over my shoulder to read what I had written.

"I knocked," she said, in her pretty, surprising voice, "but you didn't answer, so I came on in."

I covered my letter with another sheet of paper. "I'm glad you came. Gives me an excuse to stop writing."

"To your grandmother."

Evidently Dorcas had managed to read a bit. "Yes."

"And you wrote how happy you are here. Are you really?"

"No. But it's what one says." This struck me as funny and I began to giggle.

Dorcas stared for a minute, then broke into a shy smile, the first I had seen from her.

She began to wander about, listlessly touching a perfume flask of Venetian glass, limply picking up a paisley shawl to untangle its fringe. "You have pretty things."

"I told you my grandmother had these rooms prepared for me. She hopes the pretty things will make me more confident."

"Do they?"

"Sadly, no. It would take much more than that. I do like everything, of course, but it's a bit overwhelming and it sets me too much apart from everyone else. Thank you, by the way, for trying to warn me about the worm box. I hope you won't get in trouble because you did."

She wrinkled her nose. "Oh, Trix and Sylvie and Mary Dell don't care enough about me to bother punishing me."

Mary Dell. So, that was Turtle Nose's real name. I liked it. It sounded so Southern.

"Ooh!" Dorcas squealed, turning around and holding up a snood with black pearls woven into the mesh. "How beautiful."

Already I knew that Dorcas must really love the thing, since she was not the squealing sort. "Take it," I said. "Please. The pearls don't show up in my black hair. Now tell me more about those girls."

Dorcas, as she stuffed her hair into the snood, informed me that Mary Dell, so plain, and Sylvie, so pretty, were twins, and that neither was nearly as bad as Trix, who had once called Dorcas "Swiss Cheese Face" because of her complexion. I expressed my disgust at such name-calling, and felt ashamed for having thought of Mary Dell as "Turtle Nose."

I picked up a box of pastel-frosted confections, each topped with a delicate candied violet, from my bedside table. (Sometimes, I must admit, I ate sweets in bed.) "Won't you sit down and have a cake?"

"You don't have any peppermint tea, do you?" Dorcas asked.

"Sorry, I don't."

"I'd better not eat much, then. I've a bad stomach left over from when I was ill long ago. My belly is constantly twisting and growling."

"Embarrassing in class."

"Oh, you should see Trix's expression when she hears it."

"I bet she doesn't sneer at you nearly as much as she does at me. I'm sure that to her my very existence is much more distasteful than any measly old digestive difficulties."

Dorcas laughed. Her faded eyes brightened. "Huh. I've never thought my stomach problems were funny before."

My heart brimmed with sympathy. "Well, they aren't of

course, but it helps sometimes to make light of that sort of thing. Does wearing a corset make it worse? I do so hate corsets."

"Oh yes. All our innards squeezed into the wrong places. Anyway, that's why I was asking about peppermint tea. It helps some."

"Was the illness small pox?"

"Obviously."

"Were you the only one in your family who got it?"

"It killed my mother and my sister." She began to gnaw on a fingernail.

"I'm so sorry."

"Actually, it was more tragic for me when my nurse ran off during the war, since I don't remember Mother doing a thing for me—not a sash tied nor a tear wiped. Mammy did all that from the time I was a baby, yet she didn't even say good-bye when she left. And then my father remarried last year and my new step-mother couldn't abide the sight of me. She actually said so, right out. That's when I was sent here."

Poor, lonely, unwanted girl. "My mother abandoned my father and me twelve years ago." My eyes widened in surprise at myself. Had I really just said that? I had never before revealed this to another person.

We moved into the sitting room where Dorcas wilted into the soft armchair beside the hearth and I ensconced myself in the rocker. Dorcas, who was fleshy, barely nibbled part of one cake while I, who was a beanpole, downed four. Unjust.

When I die and go to heaven, I shall demand an explanation of such unfairness from the Lord.

Now Dorcas told me that Trix kept a snake in her room and

when I asked why, she said, "Because she thinks it shows she's unconventional." Because of what I had overheard, I asked if Mr. Harry particularly liked Sylvie. Dorcas said he must, since she had once heard him whisper to Sylvie that she was driving him insane. Although, Dorcas commented, she did not know how he could continue to visit his lady friend, who lived in rooms above the Cotton Bottom Tavern in Chicataw, when it was Sylvie who drove him insane. "Mr. Harry drinks a lot," Dorcas concluded. "Carries a flask in his breast pocket."

Such an interesting and informative conversation. "Goodness. How do you know all this?"

She lifted her hands. "Folks think I'm too boring to notice, so I see and hear things I'm not meant to."

At first I had been as wrong about Dorcas as those other people, but now I knew. Dorcas was *not* dull and dense. In fact, she was astute. She was simply beaten down by her stomach problems and unattractiveness and unwantedness. Well, *I* would care about her.

Later I was to learn that Dorcas indeed knew a great deal, not only for the reason she mentioned, but also because she had a habit of slipping into a room silently and waiting to be noticed before she said anything. She would drift around the place as quietly as a ghost, so no one knew when she was standing behind them, watching and listening.

She drooped now and drew a little closer to the fire. "Here's something else you don't know. I mean, Miss Petheram certainly doesn't advertise it." She glanced around as though she feared someone might be listening, then lowered her voice. "There were murders committed in this house. Women were butchered here."

"*Here* here? As in my rooms?" I asked.

Her face fell. "Well, I don't know *exactly* where he did it. I only know he did it."

This must be the killings that Bridey had spoken of on my first day here. I shrugged in an off-hand sort of way. "Most ancient places must have had murders take place in them. Not to mention all the people who have passed on cozily in these bedchambers. Everybody dies eventually and I guess they have to do it somewhere."

"But this was recently—this was the last owner before Miss Sophie. When Wyndriven was in Mississippi. That's why no locals send their girls here. The murderer slew a bunch of wives. Married them and then slaughtered them, one after another. I think there were twelve he killed."

"No! Really? Shouldn't he have learned after the first half dozen that he didn't enjoy wedded bliss? Why would he keep on getting married?"

"Because he was a raving lunatic, I suppose."

"Would the Petherams have been around here at that time? Did they know the murderer?

"I don't know. I've tried to find out, but I can't ask them, and the students and servants don't know much—at least not the maid who was telling the story." Dorcas's expression brightened as she thought of another tidbit she could impart. "The killer sawed their bodies into little pieces and buried the scraps all over the gardens."

I carefully kept my dismay from showing. Think of the ghastly possibilities of dismembered ghosts in the house. "Uprooting bones and fingers must be nasty for the gardeners," I said. I was being facetious, of course. I had to be.

Dorcas gave a reluctant laugh. "It does sound pretty unlikely, doesn't it?" She pondered for a moment, then, "Well here's something I know for a fact is true—Miss Petheram has been betrothed to Mr. Crow, the headmaster of Albion Academy, for *ten whole years.* You'll see Mr. Crow when the Academy boys come to Wyndriven for a social."

I wondered if Mr. Thatoor would be with them.

Bridey entered just then, and I sent her off for peppermint tea. Once she returned and Dorcas had a cup to sip, Bridey busied herself straightening my dressing table and smiling mysteriously. Either the task was more amusing than I would have thought, or…I looked at her closely. There was a new energy vibrating in her. Her cheeks were flushed.

"Mississippi must agree with you, Bridey," I said.

With a mischievous sparkle in her eyes, she said, "Or at least a certain shopkeeper in town does."

"Ooh, tell us more."

Dorcas sat up straighter to listen.

"Ah, now," Bridey said, "what would there be to tell? I've only met him this morning, when I walked into town to buy black wool to mend the embroidery that's unraveled on your pink dress."

"Yes," I said, "maybe so, but the fellow must have said something interesting to make you so fluttery."

Her pretty color heightened. "His name is Conor Maloney and he's a fine Irish lad. His dad does be owning Maloney's Mercantile. Conor asked me if I would be coming into town often and I told him I didn't know. So he said he would be arranging more deliveries to the school, if I'd be here."

"Hmm," I said, "I'm sure there's some things I'll need from Maloney's in the next few days." I glanced at the clock. "Oh, goodness. I didn't realize how late it was. Dorcas, I'll walk you part way to your room. Bridey, you were very late coming to me."

She started to offer an excuse, but I stopped her. "It doesn't matter. Go on up to bed. You needn't wait around to help me undress."

Twenty minutes later I was returning to my rooms, and thinking about Dorcas's tale of murder and mayhem. I prayed that I would never see severed heads or raggedy limbs floating about my pillow.

I swung open the door into my sitting room and stopped short.

Within the glow of lamplight, a man stood with his back to me, facing the mantel.

CHAPTER 7

TALKING TO THE DEAD

His head was bowed and one hand rested on the mantel. He was tall, with a slim waist and broad shoulder muscles that swelled his loose white linen shirt.

When I had seen my resident ghost the first time, he had been slightly translucent. Now he appeared solid and opaque as the marble beneath his touch. A black ribbon tied back his long hair, which was a sun-streaked brown, and wavy and unruly, so that some strands had escaped from the ribbon. His figure and bearing proclaimed him young, although I could not see his face.

Suddenly I couldn't bear it if this person should turn around and there would be a bullet hole in the center of his forehead, or his throat would be slit, or...I nearly fell over in my hurry to back out into the hall.

I closed the door and leaned my head against it, breath heaving.

"Fiona, child," Miss Petheram said from behind me. "Is something wrong?"

I faced her and stretched my lips into a bright, most likely appalling, smile. "No, ma'am." My mind worked frantically to find an acceptable reason not to go into my rooms. "It's only that I need to get something I left downstairs."

"Well, hurry then. It's nearly midnight. Lights were supposed to be out two hours ago." She sniffed and brought a crumpled handkerchief to her nose. "I should be long asleep myself."

"You needn't wait for me."

"Will you go straight to bed after you fetch whatever you need to fetch?"

I gave a half nod, which I hoped wasn't a binding promise. I lowered my eyes so she wouldn't see my expression. I wished I could tell her what was in my room. But I couldn't. I was forever alone with this unnatural part of my life. And I could not ask Miss Petheram to give me another room when she had worked so hard on this one. Eventually I would have to return to it, but hopefully not until morning light.

"Very well," she said. "It's all dark downstairs so take a lamp."

She must be wrong. Someone else had still to be awake below — the faint, deep notes of a cello wafted up to us.

I took a light from a nearby stand, and could feel the headmistress watching as I headed down the staircase, the mahogany rail smooth beneath my fingers. It was only at the last step that it registered that Miss Petheram had been crying. Her eyes had been red, poor thing. She always seemed so cool and serene, and yet… There was more to the headmistress than met the eye. I started to turn and follow her to ask what was wrong and if I could help, but stopped myself. Most old people didn't like young folks to know they were unhappy.

For a moment I paused at the bottom of the soaring staircase, unsure where to go. The hall was shrouded in darkness save for my island of lamplight and some dim greenish moonbeams that drifted in through an arched window. The cello music wandered and twined down from a corridor opening to the left. It was tantalizing—in a bad way. Normally, music was my escape to a sweeter, brighter world. But these bleak, discordant notes...They did take me to another world, but a disturbing one. They squabbled, wrangled, and snatched— yet wove their way into my blood. I wondered what twisted quirk in the cellist, obviously talented, made her choose such a sound. Who could it be? A sneaky peek couldn't hurt.

I followed the music to a closed door, set my lamp on a nearby surface, and softly cracked open the door.

Inky blackness lay within, yet the sound poured out like an engulfing wave. I fell back. Playing music in the dark? I picked up the lamp and held it inside the opening, not caring now if I was detected.

It was a music room, beautifully paneled and proportioned, with a piano at one end, a harp at the other, and a cello leaning on a stand in one corner. With no one touching it.

The music no longer came from the room; it was everywhere. Especially inside my head. I stumbled to lean against a wall while I clutched at my hair as though to pull the notes out.

A low stern whirr sounded close by, the great clock in the hall began to strike midnight, and the music ceased.

Once the bonging stopped, the house was absolutely silent.

It took me a moment to recover and stand straight. Some troubled, spectral midnight musician. Oh, this Wyndriven Academy was an uncanny and worrisome place. Only two ghosts had haunted my grandmother's house, but here...So much history. So many deaths. How could I live here if phantom men and musicians and murdered wives flitted constantly about? How could I stand it? I felt as if I were chased from place to place by spirits.

A destination was called for. The library — if it was find-able. Once there, I might choose a cheerful novel and curl up in one of the chairs. Or maybe I would lie on the tiger skin rug I had noticed during my tour, and sleep with my own head resting on a tiger's, which might incite interesting, albeit uncomfortable dreams. After the dawn began streaming in, but before anyone else was awake, I would steal back up to my own rooms, where, hopefully, the phantom would be banished with the night.

I headed in the direction where I believed the library lay. Not this massive, paneled entry. Or this one. *This* one. The door groaned as I opened it.

Some frantic shushings sounded and then —

"Oh, it's only the new girl," Trix said. "Who told you we were here?"

She, Sylvie, and Mary Dell sat around a small table. They dropped each other's hands which they had been holding. The feeble, flickering glimmer of a single candle made their faces wraithlike in the gloom. Trix's expression revealed hostility, Sylvie's showed relief, while Mary Dell's reflected guilt.

"N-no one," I stammered. "I left some things down here." Even as I said it, I wished I hadn't.

"So are you going to tell The Petheram on us?"

"Of course not."

"You'll be sorry if you do," Trix snapped. "Get your stuff and get out." Looking about frantically, I snatched up a random wooden box and a book, both of which were huddled on a stand in a nearby niche. While still holding the lamp with one hand, I clutched the box and book to my chest with the other, as though they were very precious.

"You say those are yours?" giggled Sylvie. "We wondered who had been reading *How to Write a Love Letter.*"

"Yes. No. Oh—" I tried to sweep from the room with dignity, but my skirt brushed against a pile of papers and sent them fluttering. I stooped to feebly gather them up.

"Leave it!" Trix ordered.

I obeyed.

Off down the passage I scuttled as fast as I could with my arms full. I didn't care that the ghost might still be in my room. All I cared about was putting a distance between myself and Trix and Company. Who had been having a séance. Couldn't even *they* feel that Wyndriven was a dangerous place to trifle with such things?

The hard marble of the staircase gave way beneath my feet to the thick plush of the hall runners, and I was in my own bedchamber corridor. I confronted my doorway, squared my shoulders, and entered my sitting room.

The young man now sprawled on the sofa. Although the room lay in darkness, a pale glow emanated from him, revealing him clearly. No gaping wounds or signs of death showed, thank goodness. His front was as attractive as his back had hinted it should be. I moved to set down my burdens. The book dropped to the floor with a thud.

The fellow jumped up, startled, then gave a courtly, old-fashioned bow. His clothing seemed to be the style of the past century, sporting knee-length breeches, brown boots, and a shirt with full sleeves gathered to a ruffled wrist. He had a tanned skin, as if he had spent a great deal of time outdoors. Once.

The vibrant young man with the horse. From the portrait.

He gave a friendly smile. "Miss...? You must be one of the guests I haven't yet met. Have you lost your way? I'm Wyndon. I'm afraid this is my room you've stumbled into. Don't be embarrassed. An easy enough mistake. House is like a maze. Now, where did you intend to go? I'll put you on your course." His accent was cultured British, his tone hearty and confident. He seemed a person whose habit was optimism.

He doesn't know. He really doesn't know.

He spoke so naturally, not as if he were dead at all, that I answered him just as naturally, not as if he were dead at all. And I realized now that the scent was there—the fragrance of tobacco smoke and spicy gentleman's cologne from the night before.

"I'm so sorry, Mr. Wyndon, This is very awkward, but—"

"I'm not Mr. Wyndon."

"Excuse me? Wasn't that the name you just told me?"

"Yes, but it will be more proper if you address me as *Lord* Wyndon. Because that's my title, you see. Your accent—are you from the colonies?"

"I am an American. Fiona O'Malley."

"Irish!" he said.

"Well, my grandparents came over from Ireland."

"What a coincidence! My grandmother also came over from Ireland. She was one of the Lightfoots of Glanling." He chuckled. "I always think I should say she's one of the Light*feet* of Glanling. Well, tomorrow we'll have to see what else we have in common. But now let me escort—" He moved toward the door which I had closed behind me.

"No," I interrupted, and raised my hand to stop him. "As I started to say, this is very awkward, but, um, I need to explain something which might come as a great shock."

He rubbed his jaw. There was a little stubble on his chin. "Well then, I shall prepare myself. But really, this won't do—you being in a gentleman's private suite and all." He spoke firmly. Had I not known what I knew, I would have scurried out into the hall.

"Actually, this is *my* room," I said.

His smile fled. First his jewel-blue eyes regarded me blankly, then quizzically. "In these big houses it's easy to get confused. Let me take you—" He broke off when he reached for the doorknob. His arm went through the oaken panel. With a gasp, he pulled it in, and tried again. He staggered backward into the center of the room.

"It's what I was trying to tell you," I said weakly, my throat constricted from compassion. "You're—I hate to tell you this, but you're—well, you're no longer living."

"I'm *what*?"

"You're dead. You're a spirit."

"I'm…?" He shook his head as if to clear it. "This has got to be a dream. Yes, that's it. A nightmare. You're a nightmare." He put both hands about his head. "Oh, my skull aches."

I said nothing, while he absorbed the impossible. How tragic to have a headache even after death. And how painful for me to be called a nightmare.

From behind his hands, in a broken voice, he said, "It's not true. If I'm dead, why am I still at the abbey?"

I couldn't think what else to say, so I said nothing.

He lowered his hands. "This is my sitting room. Although, now that I really look at it, it's much *pinker* than it should be. And this—" he moved into the next room—"is my bedchamber. The furnishings are different, I see now, but this is the fireplace and these are the windows. The view, though..."

"This used to be your room," I said carefully, "a hundred or so years ago. Earlier this century your whole house was moved kit and caboodle to the United States of America and put back together here."

"The *United States*? How extraordinary. You're saying we're in the Americas?"

"Yes. There was a war and we won our independence from Britain. I'm not sure when you lived so I don't know how you left things."

"It is—it was 1745."

"It's now the year 1867. Don't you remember anything at all of these years? Were you just sort of...here, but not here?"

"Last I remember is being out riding Banner, my horse, on my estate—in Berkshire. I was by myself, galloping over the countryside as I like—liked—really, this is all so incredible—to do when we had guests and I needed an escape. And then, I'm not sure. It's hazy. But, what about everyone I know? Marietta? *Where is Marietta?*"

I didn't answer. I didn't have to.

His face contorted, and he sank to an armchair as if his spectral body had turned to jelly, and hunched there with his head buried in his arms.

He was in pain of so many different layers and facets that I couldn't begin to comfort him. I watched helplessly, as gradually he faded away. He was "out" again, possibly back to wherever he had been slumbering for the last hundred years.

"I'm so sorry, Lord Wyndon," I whispered.

Strains of music in the night--
Does no one hear but me?
Sad and haunting, or sweet and mild;
Or fierce and strident, mad and wild;
Does no one hear but me?
  — By Fiona O'Malley

CHAPTER 8

THE ORANGERY

The faint rustle of riffling paper tickled my ears as I lay, fully dressed except for shoes, on top of my bedcovers. My eyelids fluttered open. The filmy bed curtains were waving, washed pinky-gray with dawn. I lifted up the gauze and peeped from beneath, expecting to find Lord Wyndon back in the chair where he had disappeared last night. I wished to see him again, speak to him, to aid in any way I could, which admittedly was not much. I...*liked* him.

He was not there—at least not that I could tell. I was disappointed.

On a table between the bed and window I had left several books, and one of them—a thick one—lay open. I swung my feet over the bedside and slipped out to pad across the cool marble.

It was the Bible. Open to the book of Revelation. "...And the city lieth foursquare...and the building of the wall thereof was of jasper stone..." A description of heaven, pearly gates and all.

He had been reading about what he was missing.

Bridey came in to assist me in dressing, and was shocked to

find me still in my yesterday's gown. I had no excuse, so I merely lifted my arms for her to help me change. She was still shaking her head over it when I left my room.

Up until elocution class, I was distracted by thoughts of Lord Wyndon. And then, in elocution class, I was distracted by Monsieur.

A monotone-voiced young lady was reciting Lord Byron's "Maid of Athens," managing the impossible by making even the most sumptuous passages tedious. It hurt me, so I glanced away. My eye was caught by a movement outside the open door.

Monsieur was passing in the hall. I recognized him first by his marvelous physique. Today he wore a black coat with a waistcoat of golden satin. He glanced in, paused in mid-stride, and looked inquiringly my way. I peeked around. Everyone appeared to have eyes glazed over. I gave Monsieur a friendly-but-surreptitious smile.

He smiled back and I watched with interest as he ran his fingers through his hair to make it stand wildly on end. Next he plunged to one side and clutched his hands to his breast, dramatically illustrating the line from "Maid," "Give, oh give me back my heart!" He went on with greatly exaggerated gestures throughout the poem. When the girl reached the "By that lip I long to taste," he slowly, caressingly, passed his tongue over his lips. I averted my gaze in confusion. Was Monsieur in some wince-able, embarrassing way *flirting* with me? Surely not. He was too old for that sort of thing, and I too young.

When I looked up once more, it was at the line "Though I fly to Istanbul," and Monsieur's elbows were bent and flapping comically. I burst out laughing. Everyone in the room turned to stare. I clapped my hand over my mouth.

The girl who was reciting appeared bewildered, and Mr. Moss, the teacher, glared at Monsieur, marched over to the door, and slammed it shut. "Kindly refrain from distraction, Miss O'Malley."

"I'm so sorry," I said to the girl up front. "Please excuse me." Next time I saw Monsieur, I should take him to task. But even though he had made me act the fool in front of these strangers, I still felt like laughing. Obviously I had been mistaken about the flirting bit.

As Dorcas accompanied me to the banquet hall for luncheon, she kept trying to tell me things. I did want to be her friend, but I was thinking of all I needed to learn about Lord Wyndon. If I were to help him, I must better understand his unnatural condition. He could sit in a chair without sinking through, but his arm had penetrated the door. What if I tried to touch him? I found my cheeks foolishly burning at the notion. I hastened to explain to myself that by "touch him" I meant as in taking his arm. In case myself had mistook my meaning.

I responded to Dorcas vaguely until the headmistress's name leaped out.

"Uh-huh," I had said before my brain focused on what Dorcas had been saying. It focused forthwith. "What's that? Sorry. I said, 'Uh-huh,' when I wasn't actually listening. What was that about Miss Petheram?"

"She broke off her engagement to Mr. Crow."

"How do you know?"

"I needed to ask her about mailing some letters, so I went to the office before breakfast, and Mr. Crow was there. They didn't see me because the door was open to the big cabinet and I was standing behind it. Mr. Crow was saying, 'What is of such importance that I must attend you so early?' Miss Petheram said, really low, so I had to listen hard, 'Roland, I was up all night thinking—are you truly in love with me?' He mumbled so I couldn't hear well. And she made a sort of choking sound, and said, 'If you don't know, then you aren't. If you really wanted to marry me, you'd have done it years ago.' And he said, 'How can you say such a thing? You know it's only that Mother—' And Miss Petheram almost *screamed*—I like to jumped!—'Your *mother*! She manipulates you,' and something else, but she was crying so much it was garbled. And he said, 'I'm surprised that you, Anne, should be so unfeeling toward a frail old woman.' And she cried out, 'Frail!' Then I heard them moving and I hurried into the hall, because maybe they wouldn't like to know I'd been there. Mr. Crow came out a few minutes later, walking fast and with his lips all squashed together, and when I went in right after to ask Miss Petheram about the letters, she had to compose herself and she didn't have her pearl engagement ring on anymore." She finally took a breath. "So that's how I know."

It was amazing how accurately the usually bland Dorcas could mimic the expressions in others' voices. I nodded with appreciation. "Goodness, you certainly are talented at hearing things. And repeating them so nicely."

She gave a shy-but-smug smile. "Thank you."

"Poor Miss Petheram to have wasted her youth on that man." If only I knew a wonderful fellow for her to fall in love with and they would marry and I would be her bridesmaid (crowned with a lily garland)...

I firmly reigned myself back to considering the subject of poor, exiled-from-paradise Lord Wyndon.

Was it possible that the moving of his house separated him from his portal, or whatever entrance one needed in order to flow into heaven? If that were the case, how could he ever leave Wyndriven? There had to be some key, some law. If only I knew how it all worked.

"Fiona! Did you even hear what I just said?" Unfortunately, Dorcas kept jerking me back to the present, expecting me to chat with her. Since leaving Grandmama's house, I had experienced such a lot of unaccustomed company and conversation. It boggled my mind, used as I was to drifting through my days in silent musing. Evidently when you were around people, they expected you to pay attention to them. And so much of this new interaction had been with gentlemen—Mr. Thatoor, Mr. Harry, Lord Wyndon, and Monsieur. Thankfully, only one of them was disembodied.

The sounds of shrill girls' voices reached out to jab at me from inside the banquet hall. For once, I did not feel like eating. Instead, I positively *hungered* to be alone. I made an excuse and deserted Dorcas.

In search of an isolated spot for reflection, I headed toward the outside doors. Mr. Harry was midway down the corridor, apparently juggling carpentry work with polite attention for the two admiring, very young ladies clustered on the window seat beside him. Mr. Harry wore a dark brown sack coat today. Somehow his stylishness reassured me—everyone else in this place was sadly several years out of fashion. Including Monsieur, in spite of his elegance. Understandable, due to the war, but still it made me feel dreary for their sakes.

A smile tugged at me when one of the girls commented, "How well you use your hammer, Mr. Harry."

In reality, he looked rather inept as he attempted to replace some molding. He grunted something around the three nails he held between his lips. I guessed he wished they'd leave him alone so he could curse occasionally and take a swig from the flask that bulged in his breast pocket. At sight of me his eyes lit up. "Miss O'Malley," he mumbled before he spit out the nails. He looked a bit sheepish. "As you see, I am the unhandyman around here. You'd think my brother Junius would hire someone more proficient, but that fellow is remarkably tightfisted."

"*Another* Petheram?"

"Yes. It's unlikely you'll ever meet Junius, though. He's busy with his flibbertigibbet wife and promising brood of young'uns, plus he oversees a good many properties, so he has the devil— excuse me, I mean the Old Scratch—of a time getting around to everything."

No wonder they needed Monsieur to help with the place as well. I nearly asked Mr. Harry about Monsieur, but held my tongue. Monsieur had said they were not on good terms.

Mr. Harry was watching me closely. "I've been wondering how you were adjusting to life at Wyndriven?"

"Well enough, thank you."

"Don't love it yet, eh? I understand. Being surrounded by a sea of overwhelming crinolines takes getting used to."

The girls flicked measuring glances my way.

I nodded. "I can breathe better if I get outside by myself now and then. That's where I'm going now."

"You might want to explore the orangery," Mr. Harry suggested. "It's unlocked."

"Is that the glasshouse? I saw it yesterday. Thank you for the suggestion." I left Mr. Harry to his young ladies in their over-whelming crinolines.

Outside, I scanned the grounds to get my bearings. Over near the edge of the woods, a couple was moving together, arm in arm. By squinting, I could make out that it was Bridey, along with, ev-idently, Conor-the-grocer's-boy. She oughtn't to be with him in the middle of the day when she should be caring for her duties, as she was paid to do, but I didn't blame her. Nor did I blame her for clinging to Conor's arm—it looked to be a nice, strong arm to hold onto.

I nearly stumbled over old Mr. Willie, who was pruning away the poking-out bits on an azalea bush. He was a shaky, withered, gnomish fellow, far too ancient to do the work he did. I was about to make some pleasantry (as mannerly people are supposed to do) about the beauty of the grounds, when his legs suddenly gave way and he came down hard.

"Are you all right?" I hastened to ask the poor, felled gardener.

He drew a yellow-spotted handkerchief from his waistcoat pocket, mopped his forehead, and left the cloth over his face for a moment. Finally he removed it and said, "I am, Miss. Though the sticks stabbing in my hind end don't feel too good. Ain't young as I used to be." Never once did his eyes meet mine as he spoke. He seemed to look carefully at my chin.

"Sticks in the hind end wouldn't be pleasant at any age. Let me help you up." I reached beneath his elbows and assisted him over to a marble bench. He was such a shriveled fellow that a strapping girl like myself could possibly have carried him with no problem. I had been about to suggest it, but stopped myself in the nick of time. From what I had seen, men—even old, fragile ones — were often silly about showing weakness.

He thanked me, and then explained solemnly, "I gets the misery in my legs sometimes and they plumb give out."

"Perhaps you shouldn't work so hard."

A little light sparked in his eyes. "By jingoes, if the day happens when I got to forsake my work, it'll be the day they might as well clonk me on the head and plant me in the ground and be done with it."

I was immediately put in mind of the body parts supposed to be buried in the gardens. Perhaps someday I could ask Mr. Willie about them. But not today.

I made sure he was firmly seated before I left him.

The orangery would be a whimsical retreat, with its glass domes and turrets and twining latticework of curling metal vines. I turned the handle of the ornate grilled door, was met by a smell of warm, damp earth mixed with steamy greenery, and entered the tropics. The place was lush with arching brilliant blossoms and glowing foliage. Orange, lemon, and lime trees, and others whose vivid fruits I did not recognize, were espaliered against the walls, while rainbows danced everywhere from sunshine through misted glass. Pathways paved with a mosaic of gold and brown and black tiles meandered throughout.

Humidity made the air thick. I pushed up the sleeves of my gown as I proceeded inside. I caught myself with a jerk when my feet nearly flew out from beneath me — the lovely tiles were moisture-slimed. I went more slowly, delightedly absorbing the fantastical beauty of the place, until I came to a black iron bench beside a still, stone-walled lily pool. I sank down to the seat, and bent over to dip my fingers in cool water, letting it dribble back down into spreading rings.

A reflection in the shining surface made me look up.

Monsieur stood beside me. "You escaped." His eyes twinkled with understanding. "There is nothing so stifling as a house full of strangers."

"Especially loud schoolgirl strangers," I said. "Southern accents are nice, but sometimes I can't listen to them chatter another minute."

"*Oui*," he said. "Outrageous for the abbey to be so occupied these days—sniggering young females pretending to be well-behaved, while just below the surface....but it was even worse when the armies occupied it with their booming, common voices and rough boots." He sank down next to me.

"You've changed," I said, surveying him.

His eyebrow twitched slightly. "In what way?"

"I mean your clothing. This morning you wore a black coat, and now it's brown."

He relaxed. "I wear clothing appropriate to the setting. This coat is more suitable to the orangery."

"Everyone in class thought I was crazy when you made me laugh during Lord Byron's love poem," I said, shaking my finger at him.

"*Je suis désolé*," he said, lowering his black lashes demurely.

It made me laugh again because he could not have looked more *un*-sorry. "Mr. Moss might have scolded you soundly."

"That would certainly have added to the excitement if that sorry excuse for a man had tried to put me in my place." He stood now and wandered over to the glass wall, gazing out. "My parents once entertained Lord Byron at their chateau in France. I was young, but I could see that he was indeed—what is it Lady Caroline Lamb said of him?—'mad, bad, and dangerous to know.'"

"And so," I looked speculatively at Monsieur, taking in his still-tussled hair and loosened cravat, "did you take lessons from him?"

There was a moment of shocked silence. Monsieur's jaw tightened as he stared at me. What had I said? "I beg your pardon," I apologized hastily. "I thought that would be a funny thing to say, but I guess it was actually obnoxious."

Monsieur's features relaxed, but still his tone was cool when he spoke. "Do you always say whatever pops into your head, Mademoiselle Fiona?"

"Quite often. I'm trying to learn restraint, but it's slow coming."

He laughed then, and I was relieved. "Well, don't learn too much. You might lose your charm."

I had never before been called charming. I beamed.

"I am glad," he said, "that you have discovered the orangery. It is a soothing place." He glanced around, with dark reminiscence in his eyes. "One night, years ago, I lit a great many candles and placed them in the trees. It seemed a fairyland the way they glowed and reflected in the black glass."

"I would like to see it so."

His lips quirked into a grimace. "I am afraid it became a painful memory." He stood abruptly and turned away. "Since that time I have never again allowed candles to burn in here. If someone lights one, poof! I extinguish it immediately."

For a moment we said nothing, and I wondered if the pain had something to do with the failed romance I suspected he once had with Miss Sophie.

His head lifted as if he shook himself from his reveries. He sat back down and looked at me closely. "Confess, now. You are not going to follow my advice about Trix, are you?"

"I don't think I could. It would be too mean."

"Indeed? Sometimes, with some people, harshness is necessary. You may yet avail yourself of my advice. So, has the vixen been up to anymore tricks?"

I paused, and let what I hoped was an impish smile spread across my face. "Well, I surprised her and her cronies having a séance."

"No!" He gave a bark of laughter. "*Not* a séance? It cannot be."

"That has to be what they were doing. They were in the library holding hands around a table. At dead of night, no less."

He flexed his long white fingers, with an air of wicked, delighted mischief. "They share a fondness for spiritualism, do they? Oh, we can have fun with this. Picture it—the table rising and a hollow moan echoing through the murk. The candle guttering out and those young ladies running screaming, mindless with terror, into the shadows. Too delicious, and they would deserve it, making a game of such things."

"Could you really manage that? How? How could you make the table rise without them seeing you?"

"Oh, I have my ways."

I sighed. So tempting. "Please don't. It would be mean."

He rolled his eyes in an exaggerated fashion. "And Mademoiselle Fiona has a heart as sweet as treacle. Oh, very well. I will restrain myself. I wouldn't want to be 'mean.' Although, did I mention I cannot abide redheads and their sly ways? Now, what were you yourself doing wandering downstairs in the spoooooky—" he waggled his fingers at both sides of his face — "midnight hours?"

For a fraction of a second I considered telling him about my genuine ghosts, since something in Monsieur's manner invited confidences, but stopped myself. Monsieur had been sympathetic. I did not want to see his expression change if I confided in him. Disbelief, and worse — a look that showed he doubted my sanity. "I couldn't sleep," I said instead, "so I went down for a book."

"And thus startled the ridiculous spiritualists."

"We startled each other and it made me equally silly. I was shocked into saying I was seeking some possessions of mine that I'd left in there. I grabbed up a wooden box and a book called *How to Write a Love Letter.*" To my own amazement, I began to giggle.

Monsieur gave an appreciative nod. "You had presence of mind. Such a useful volume to study and master at your age. And what treasure lay in the box?"

"I haven't looked," I said. "I dumped the things down in my room and haven't noticed them since, except to step over them. Doubtless my maid is wondering how they got there."

"Perhaps she realizes you are a girl of many surprises." He gave me a considering look. "Do you know, I think you misjudge your capabilities. If you put your mind to it, you could indeed be skilled at mischief. Against people who deserved it, that is. Those shrews have abused you, and certainly other unfortunates, with their malice. You have pluck and spirit, which their lesser targets almost certainly do not. Even if you do not care enough about yourself, those others need you to defend them, to repay the mistreatment."

I remembered Trix's "Swiss cheese face" comment to Dorcas, and felt ire once more kindle down my spine. Still, I hesitated.

"What about loving your enemies?"

He gave a very French-looking gesture, brushing away my words. "Christian sentimentality." His tone was dry. "I have always noted that the meek, with their mealy-mouthed, whiny ways, inherit nothing at all in this world. You must stand up for all victims and teach those abusers a well-deserved lesson."

His words had an allure. Vaguely I knew that I shouldn't agree with him, but...It was hard to think clearly while listening to his beautiful, beguiling voice. "It's true that decent people *should* defend the oppressed," I said slowly. "I've often tried to."

"Of course you have. You are a brave girl. And Trix has caused a great deal of injustice. Isn't it time she is paid back? How good it would feel. It would heal you of so many slights. You have suffered numerous humiliations, have you not?"

I blinked rapidly and looked down at my hands.

He knows. He understands.

I glanced back up to find Monsieur surveying me with a speculative, satisfied expression.

"Why are you pleased with me?" I asked abruptly.

He looked—ever so slightly—taken aback. An unusual sensation for him, I guessed. "Er—simply because you are you, of course, Mademoiselle Fiona."

My stomach felt shaky. "Excuse me. I'm so sorry. I really need—I must go back to class." I sprang up and stumbled awkwardly down the path, slipping once on the tiles and catching myself by clutching at an overhanging branch. Delicate leaves showered down.

CHAPTER 9

THE TWISTING THING

That evening, after a twilit stroll around the grounds with Dorcas, I entered my sitting room to find Bridey kneeling beside the little chest from the library. It was about a foot long and ten inches wide, fashioned of some pale wood, carved with an intricate design of scrollwork. The lid was open, and Bridey's splayed fingers dropped bits of tattered cloth back into the cavity as if they burned.

"What *is* that stuff?" I asked.

She stood abruptly, her face drawn. "Don't you know? It was yourself brought it in here."

"It's something I accidentally picked up in the library. I hadn't looked inside." I knelt and inspected the chest's contents. Scraps of shredded cloth—embroidered canvas—filled the box. It had been some sort of small tapestry. "This was stunning once." I gingerly held up a bit. "See—beautifully stitched. And some of it is hairwork, in reddish shades. Why would someone do this?"

The tapestry had been deliberately, viciously destroyed. The frayed bits hadn't been cut with scissors; they had been stretched, twisted, and savagely ripped. The shreds seemed to writhe. This cloth had aroused powerful emotions. Someone had hated it, yet refused to part with the remnants. I shuddered at such warped emotions, as I let the lid fall shut with a crack. "I'll—I'll take it back."

Bridey was still staring at the box. I noticed that she was wearing her green glass beads and her exuberant hair was bound with ribbon. She wrapped the ribbon ends round and round her finger.

I sank to the floor, letting my skirts poof up around me. "You must be seeing your young man this evening."

"I am. Conor sent a note. I'm to meet him by the lake once I'm done helping you." I expected her to smile as she said this, but she did not.

"Then go ahead and go. I can undress myself. Tonight I really will do it."

She hesitated. "'Tis kind you are, but—"

"But what?"

"Won't you take that nasty box out straight away? It sets me skin crawling."

I made myself laugh. "Don't you worry about the distressing box. I'll get rid of it."

Still, she would not leave. I watched her for a moment as she hovered about, ineffectually picking up this or straightening that.

"What is it, Bridey?" I asked finally. "What's troubling you?"

She bit her lower lip. "This grand house built of stones so old..."

"What about this grand house?"

"'Tis not right. Something feels *off*," she said in a rush. "We made sport of it on the first day—the past and the possible spirits—but we ought not to have. I keep a lamp lit in me room all night—the fairy light isn't enough in this place. Others have felt it too. They've had an impossible time keeping servants."

"I expect that's because of the war and the Negroes' new freedom. Also they can't pay much."

She shook her head. "'Tis not the real problem. Miz Jump's tongue is hinged in the middle—her as is the cook, and they all call her Miz and never Missus as we would say. Anyway, yesterday Miz Jump told of eerie happenings here. There's a bogle, for instance, who moves furniture about."

I burst out laughing.

"'Tis what she said." Bridey gave a reluctant grin, even though she had just told me we shouldn't make fun of such things.

"Do you suppose we should leave out a bowl of milk for it every night, as they do for the wee folk in Ireland?"

"The rest of the staff isn't after finding it funny. If Miz Jump doesn't hold her tongue, she'll soon have no more kitchen maids with handy ears to box. It's true what the maid told me—not a servant but me will sleep in the house. A shadow sometimes watches over them as they work, they say. Some have felt a cold breath on their necks. I told you before, I've the Sight meself—not so much as me gran—but I do have it. I've sensed cold spots here, and then too, I saw…Something…last night."

"Really? What exactly?"

She made circles in the carpet with the toe of her boot before she spoke again. "I was taking a short cut to some backstairs down a hallway that's not much used, when some smoke rose up ahead."

"Smoke? As in something burning?"

"Smoke as in something not burning. 'Twas oily and black

and about the height and width of a big man. It—it had eyes. It coiled and wriggled and squirmed and moved toward me, so that I turned on me heels and ran fast as I could back to the kitchen where some others was yet gathered."

In spite of myself, the hair stood up on my arms. I had never seen such a specter, and prayed that I never would, but if I did…

"Maybe somebody went that way a second earlier with a smoking lamp," I said weakly.

Her jaw tightened. "That wouldn't explain the eyes. Nor why the Thing was growing arms."

"Arms?" My voice squeaked.

"Arms and legs. Sort of nubbins poking out, fighting to take form."

"How frightening." I swallowed. "I've never…"

"'You've never' what, Miss Fiona?"

My hands twisted together. "I have never told anyone this, but I'm like you. Sometimes I see things most people can't. Spirits."

Bridey knelt beside me with eyes as wide as those of the teacup-eyed dog in the Tinderbox story by that Mr. Andersen. "So you've the Sight as well."

"It's happened to me since I was small, starting with a pair of spooks in my grandmother's house." For a moment I considered telling Bridey more about Sal and Epsy, but dismissed the thought. I hoped to ease her mind, and The Two, with their taunts and their goading me toward suicide would not help with that goal. Leo, on the other hand…"And I have seen a young man in this place, but that's how he looks to me—like a young man. And he's harmless. Even—even rather nice, strange to say. Besides, although the dead do walk at times, they have no substance to hurt anyone. And why should we assume they would want to, anyway?"

"Ah, but what about possession?"

"Possession?" I seemed to constantly echo her words in question form.

"Such as the pigs in the Good Book who ran off the cliff because of the devils entered into them. Where the bogle does ooze into the living flesh and drives out the person's own soul, to take over the body. Me old gran had a friend who liked to walk o' nights in the church yard, and one day the friend commenced acting all strange-like. When me gran looked into her eyes, *someone else looked out*. Her folks sent her to the lunatic asylum in Dublin, but me gran knew what it was really ailed her. What nasty, unnatural creature hunkered down inside the poor woman's body."

I shook my head vehemently. "No. Don't even think of such a thing. If you see that smoke again, the only way it can hurt you is if you're frightened, and go running off headlong, which is perhaps what happened to the stupid pigs. Instead, back carefully away. And always, always carry a light as it gets dusky."

"I do." Her face flushed and softened. "And if Conor isn't the sweetest boy-o. He and I had no need to *make* a friendship. We knew each other well the moment we set eyes on one another. So I confessed me fear of the dark, and he gave me his own bright lantern to take about at night. He's heard the stories and doesn't much like me being here. Says he might just have to carry me off someday." As if she couldn't help it, she gave a little wriggle of excitement.

"Not *too* soon, I hope. I would miss you terribly." I reached into my pocket and drew out my onyx and silver rosary beads. "Take these and carry them in your apron. Maybe they'll keep that thing away." My voice shook a little, and I saw that Bridey responded to my tone by looking frightened again. I straightened my shoulders and firmed myself up. "Don't worry. It's true that what you've seen is a type of spook I've never before encountered, but I've seen plenty of them and I'm unscathed. Or at least not very scathed. If you do see it again, come tell me. We'll go to Miss Petheram." I put the beads in her palm and enclosed her hand in both of mine for a moment.

"I thank you," Bridey said, looking down at our hands. "But I'd not be asking the mistress for help. What could she do?"

"I don't know. She just seems, well, *capable*. But if you really are too scared, I could send you back to New York." Even as I made the offer, my heart sank at the sudden loneliness brought on by the thought of Bridey leaving.

Bridey gently withdrew her hand, and lifted her chin. "I'll not be after letting any bogle scare me away. For one thing, there's me lad Conor now."

"Then do you want to sleep in my room? You wouldn't have to use the sofa. We could move a cot in here."

She gave a short laugh, told me no thank you, and sailed out, closing the door behind her. I guessed she desired the privacy of her own room so I wouldn't know how many evenings she spent with her lad.

For a moment I stood staring at the door. I shivered. Either my imagination was too vivid, or Bridey's description of the twisting Thing painted too striking a picture—I kept seeing it in my mind.

What are these phantom shades
That no one else can see?
They come and go like shadows;
They jeer, and torment me.
Yet sometimes they laugh, and speak to me;
Sometimes they smile, and bless,
And comfort me when I am sad,
And ease my loneliness.
  — By Fiona O'Malley

CHAPTER 10

LEO

I could not return the chest to the library just yet. Not only was I squeamish about braving the dusky, echoing halls right after Bridey's ghost story, but if Trix and her cohorts were out and about tonight, and encountered me carrying these things...oh, they would have fun with it, wouldn't they? However, I did not wish Bridey to be disturbed by sight of the box again before I could rid myself of it, so I hauled it into my bedchamber. After I undressed and slipped on my nightgown, unencumbered by hoop and petticoats, I wriggled under the bed on my belly to shove the box deep within the dark recesses.

As I started to scoot back out, I drew in my breath with a grunt and discerned the scent of tobacco and spicy cologne. Oh no. Frantically I shoved down my nightgown over my bare legs as I emerged, and tried to recover some measure of dignity as I sat on my heels.

Although, why should I be embarrassed? I tossed back my disheveled hair with defiance. After all, being a spook was definitely not the most exalted of states in which to find oneself. Lord

Wyndon was in no position to scorn me.

My defiance was wasted. Lord Wyndon had no interest in me or my unseemly apparel and situation. He slumped in the chair by the table where I had last seen him, his back hunched and his head in his arms. Still attached to his shoulders, of course—he wasn't *that* sort of ghost.

He glanced up as if he felt me watching, inclined his head slightly in some remnant of his former courtly manners, and gave a mirthless smile. "So you, Miss O'Malley, are still here and so am I. This is all real. I suppose I must come to terms with it."

He continued to ignore my nightgown, so I supposed it was best for all concerned if I ignored it as well. "It's something that would be hard for anyone to comprehend, my Lord." I wished I dared pat his back in a comforting sort of way. Or at least dared try. "I can't begin to imagine how you're feeling."

"Don't call me 'Lord.'"

I gave him an exasperated look. "But you said—"

"That was before I knew that I'm not Lord Wyndon anymore. I'm nothing. Nobody. Evidently there's not enough left of me to prevent me from oozing through solid doors."

"It must feel interesting to be able to do that." I tilted my head to one side, contemplating the possibilities. "There are so many things you can do now that you couldn't before."

He studied me sharply, eyes narrowed, as if he could hardly believe what I had just said.

"What?" I asked.

"It's simply…Miss O'Malley, you amaze me. Are you saying what I think you're saying so matter-of-factly?"

"It depends on what you think I'm saying."

"Are you telling me to consider the pleasant parts of being dead? Of finding myself a wraith?"

I considered for a moment. "I suppose I am."

He raised his eyebrows, which were darker than his tawny hair. "Interesting, you think."

My cheeks grew warm. It had been a stupid, insensitive thing to say. I opened my mouth to apologize, then closed it when I saw he was grinning. It was as if a sudden light came over his face.

"Most would have called it horrifying," he said. "But perhaps society in your time is more familiar with the supernatural than it was in mine?"

"No," I said. "It's not. Generally ghosts are still confined to chilling stories told by firesides as the coals die down. I'm different from most folks, though."

"That's obvious. But why specifically?"

"I have seen specters since I was a little girl, so I can take you more in stride. I've thought a lot about it. My guess is that spirit bodies are not so very different from earthly ones. They both hold personalities—the spark that makes us *us*—just the same. Perhaps ghosts are simply formed of finer materials. So, I'm not afraid of you. Especially since you show no signs of your death. You know—no stab wounds or small-pox pustules, that sort of thing. I never quite get used to that."

"And you see 'that sort of thing' sometimes?"

"Yes."

He eyed me with pity as if he were picturing the four-year-old I had once been. "Poor little girl. You must have been out of your mind with terror at first."

I nodded, and looked away, remembering those long-ago encounters with The Two. I had screamed and screamed and refused to be comforted by my beside-herself nurse, as The Two sneered over her shoulder.

He rose and drew closer. "You would think I would understand more about this condition than you do, since I am *in* it, but I know nothing. Do you suppose—" he gave a deep shudder—"is it possible that this is all there is? That after death everyone is doomed to wander in this between place? Each alone in his own private hell with no prospect of heaven? I see no other spirits, so we're even cut off from each other."

"No!" I said sharply, stung by the awfulness of the thought. "I don't understand much, but I do know that this thing that has happened to you is rare. I don't know how I know, but I do, with every fiber of my being. By far, most who have passed on have passed on to the heavenly sphere. You are the first spirit I have really spoken to, but perhaps others, who have been aware of their circumstances longer, understand the abilities and limitations better. It's a stimulating question and, from now on, if I see specters, I'll ask them about it. I'll try to learn what I can."

"Well, then, I'll attempt to make myself see it your way. I am still me and that's all to the good. I guess. At least I haven't returned to earth as a mealy worm."

I shuddered. "Thank goodness. I truly couldn't stand here with you calmly if you had."

He grinned, looked down at himself, and flexed his arms. "I shall see what this insubstantial body of mine is capable of. I used to consider myself an athlete. Do you think perhaps I can leap to the ceiling? Above the ceiling? To the moon? Can I fly? I've always wanted to fly."

"Me too. Maybe, my Lor—I *really* have to have some name for you, sir."

"Then call me Leo. My given name."

It fit him. There was something lion-esque about his shock of unruly, goldy-brown hair. He turned on the heels of his tall brown boots and strode toward the outside wall.

"And please call me Fiona." I scrambled after him.

Without flinching he walked into the wall. The front of him melted into it, and I expected the rest of him to follow, but instead his back remained in the room, as if the plaster and wood were gelatinous, and he was stuck in the gooey stuff. He pulled back in, with a sort of sucking sound. Now he made for the sitting room and the door into the corridor. First he thrust his arm through, but when he tried to move his whole body into it, he went part way, then halted. He lurched backward, eyes slightly unfocused. "I can't," he gasped. "I can't leave these rooms."

"Oh dear."

He went into the bedroom, dropped into the chair once again, and rubbed his temples. I found myself staring at his hands—they looked hard and strong, with the bones showing a little under the skin. How remarkable that there should be the outline of bones. He wore a signet ring on one finger.

"I had hoped you could move with unearthly freedom now," I said carefully, "although I've heard that spirits are often limited to certain areas. I'm so sorry."

He visibly struggled to compose himself. His jaw set. "Perhaps this is where I died. In bed no doubt. Maybe that's why I can't leave."

"Don't you remember anything at all of the—of the end?"

He shook his head.

I seated myself on the edge of the chair across from him. "I have been thinking about your situation," I said tentatively.

"And what conclusion," he asked, after a moment, "have you reached?"

"It seems to me that if you can remember how you met your death — if it was murder or something awful like that — "

"'Something awful,'" Leo repeated, muttering under his breath. "Decapitation, strangulation…"

"Yes." I nodded, eager. "Like that. Then maybe we can figure out why you're still here. Perhaps — "

"Perhaps if we understand that, we can send me on to my just reward. In your years of association with the disembodied, have you had much experience in sending poor, lost souls to their just rewards, Miss — Fiona?"

"No. But it doesn't hurt to try, does it?"

He gave a short laugh. "You're right. No more feeling sorry for myself. It is what it is. No one has any patience with those pitiful, wailing, moaning specimens of spooks. So — I'll try to remember what happened. I will be a bit queasy if it was decapitation, though." His mouth tightened. "It all feels as if I'm trying to snatch at a dream. I start to recall and it eludes."

"Why don't you tell me about your life leading up to your death? Maybe then it will come more easily."

"My *death*. So extraordinary. All right, I shall attempt to collect my thoughts, and tomorrow night I will tell you — in a nutshell — the life story of James Leo Lightfoot Stafford — Lord Wyndon — so that perhaps we can advance his death story."

I opened my mouth, but he spoke first.

"No, not now. I don't seem to need any rest, but I can see you are weary unto death. Go to bed, Fiona."

He rose and gazed at the window draperies as though they were open and the view a troubling one. I scrambled to pull back the brocade panels so he wasn't staring at nothing. The moon shone around the hard-seeming lines of his body as I slipped obediently between my sheets.

CHAPTER 11

BURNING BRIGHT

It was difficult, the next day, to wait till nighttime for Leo's account of his life. All through my lessons, there were only teachers and girls to look at, and who wished to look at teachers and girls when they wanted to be with either their intriguing adopted uncle or their intriguing specter friend? I didn't think I could make it through all my classes, and yet, as usually happens, I did.

After supper I evaded Dorcas and slipped outside for a solitary sunset stroll. I was not surprised, or disappointed, however, when Monsieur's long legs stepped into place beside me as I skirted the rose garden. "This light," he said, "reminds me of an evening I spent in India when I hunted the ghost tiger."

I looked upward. The great, rosy sky had a polished look to it, like glazed china, and all the air was flushed pink, as if the glaze had oozed downwards, washing over the world. "I hope you mean to tell me about it. It's interesting that you had a tiger adventure, because you remind me of one. A tiger that is. Something about your eyes. 'In what distant deeps or skies burnt the fire of thine eyes?' That's from that poem by Blake."

He smiled. "I am flattered. I admire tigers. If you wish, I will tell you the tale. Not here, though. Let us go climb onto the ruins of the folly. It was patterned after an Indian temple, so it would be a suitable setting for the telling."

"Oh, I'm so glad Wyndriven has some nice romantic ruins."

He pointed. "They are a distance ahead, at the top of that hill, near the edge of the woods."

We walked for several minutes. The great heap of toppled stones lay in a jumble of crumbled slag, fallen columns, and massive blocks, all leprous with lichen and tangled with creepers. I glanced down at my dress, fashioned of exquisitely embroidered delaine fabric, shrugged, and surged onward. Monsieur ascended the mound ahead of me. I was surprised, and rather discomfited, that he did not reach behind to offer his hand to assist. Most ungentlemanly. I clambered clumsily up and around the stones, hoping that none of the vines were poison ivy. I slipped once and caught myself before I could bark my shins. As I did so, I noted carving in the blocks, delineated with emerald moss.

"This must have been beautiful before it fell," I said, between heaving breaths.

Monsieur seemed unfazed by the exercise, moving easily and adroitly. "It was. And beguiling. Others did not appreciate it, however. They found it an eyesore. Their goal was to wipe it off the face of the earth, to dump the blocks into the river."

I assumed that by "they" he meant the Petherams and Stones.

I pushed escaping tendrils of hair back from my face. "Why is it still here then?"

"It proved unlucky to move the boulders," he said, without looking backward. "Accidents occurred. Scaffolding collapsed.

Stones fell, limbs were crushed. After the second broken worker, Sophia decided the ruins could stay as they were."

Triumphant now at the top of the heap, Monsieur tossed his coattails back and settled himself on a block, waiting for me to find my own seat. The fading light etched lines into his lean cheeks.

I twitched my skirt away from where it was caught on a rough outcrop and ripped it. "Bridey is going to be upset with me."

His hard bright scrutiny took in my skirt. "Bridey is the name of your Irish maid?"

"Yes, sir."

"I have seen her at times about the place." He chuckled. "I believe I make her nervous."

I was too busy managing my feet in the rubble to give a thought as to why Monsieur would have taken notice of my lady's maid. "Well, don't. I like her," I said. "I expect, though, that you make a great many people nervous. Even the ones you bother to fascinate. You're that sort of man—so—so *kingly* and ridiculously handsome, but mocking and severe."

"Do you indeed find me ridiculously handsome?" His eyes glittered.

How annoying he was. "You know perfectly well that you are. Just remember, handsome is as handsome does."

"Spoken exactly as if you were your grandmother. And what about kingly?"

"Oh, hush. I couldn't think of the right word. With your elegant bearing, is what I meant."

He threw back his head and laughed. "Ah, Fiona, that is precisely the sort of comment that makes you so unconventional— very few would have told me such a thing out loud."

I felt particularly ungainly as he watched me finish my climb and drop down onto a level wedge just below him. "You'd better tell it fast," I said.

He gave an enquiring look.

"We'll have to climb down before it's dark," I explained.

He nodded and began. "A certain village in northern India was haunted by a *bhoot*—a spirit able to assume the form of an animal. In this case, it was a great white tiger. The beast had carried off two children to eat and—"

"The ghost could eat?"

"So it seemed."

"And carry off children?"

"So it seemed."

"But—"

"Hush, Mademoiselle Fiona."

I hushed for a while.

"After the second child was carried off, and they found the leftover gnawed-on bits and pieces, the natives began to suspect that it was not, in fact, a *bhoot*. For one thing there was, as you so astutely noted, the fact that it ate, and that it could perform physical acts. And for another—what on earth is it now?"

I had gasped and was pointing into the woods. "Someone was there. A young girl. She looked all wild, blending into the trees. When she realized I saw her, she ran off as if she didn't wish to be noticed."

"Kindly refrain from noticing her then. Now, do you want to hear the story or not?"

"I'm sorry. Please go on." Still, I couldn't help but continue wondering about the elusive, shadow-dappled girl. She had a dusky, pointed face and slightly slanted, wary eyes. With black hair spread around her like a shadow. I could not see anything below her neck, but I imagined her to be feathered and furred and hooved, an elemental spirit of the forest.

"Those who had glimpsed it," Monsieur continued, "now realized that the tiger's feet did not face backward, as is the tradition with *bhoots*. Instead it was a flesh and blood creature, but with fur as white as snow, crossed with dark stripes, and eyes as blue as sapphires. The village hunter determined to track it down, and I determined to kill it.

"The beast evaded us again and again. Just when we would think we had it, it had vanished, as if it were indeed a *bhoot*. I began to admire its cunning. But the day arrived when, at last—*le voilà!*—we had the animal cornered in a ravine. I will never forget how it appeared there, unafraid, blue fire in its eyes. I looked into its gaze and knew its hunger, the smell of blood in its nostrils, the power in its great muscles and claws. It lowered its head and began to slowly move toward us, preparing to spring, intense and elegant. *Le Magnifique!*"

"And so did you choose not to kill it? Instead to carry it off where it could harm no one again?"

"Certainly not. I shot it first, then slit its throat. Its pelt graces the floor of the trophy room here at the abbey. Blue glass was used for its eyes."

I wrinkled my nose. "Tragic."

Something in the rubble caught my eye and I scrambled from my perch. The object was some sort of small statue or gargoyle…I heaved the thing up to study. "You think this is meant to be a monkey? How ugly. Look at its leer. Like a nasty, lecherous old bald man."

"Mademoiselle Fi—"

Even as Monsieur began to say my name sharply, the statue slipped from my hands and crashed to the stones below, where it shattered. I gaped after it, shocked, but I was more shocked by Monsieur's tone of voice when he berated me.

"Clumsy fool!" he bellowed, standing and looming above. "That monkey was ancient—crafted by hands that have been dust for a thousand years! A treasure! You with your bumbling ways, how dare you touch it?"

"I—I'm sorry. Could it be mended?"

He turned his back for a moment, tearing his hair, then whirled around. "Mended! I—will—not—even—respond—to such a stupid question."

I wanted to run off sobbing, but could not move as I stared at Monsieur's changed countenance, his lips thin and cruel, eyes blazing gold. Where was the amiable uncle I wanted him to be?

At sight of my face, he pulled himself visibly back in check. He stretched and flexed his long white fingers a few times before giving a flick of his hand. "Bah! A thousand or so years, a lump of stone— what does it signify? It is no matter." His words sounded strangled.

I could not speak. I shook my head and started down the rocky heap.

"Forgive me for losing my temper, Mademoiselle Fiona!" Monsieur called after me. "I am a beast to have spoken as I did. Please tell me I am forgiven."

I turned and faced him. The temptation of tears was gone now. Instead I was stiff and bleak. "There's nothing to forgive. You're right. I am a gawky oaf. I can't tell you all the things I've broken in my life."

"But ah! All is readily pardoned in a lady so charming. Please—I shall not rest tonight if you leave feeling hurt."

"I'm fine," I said, once more threading around and over the stones with ungainly speed. "I simply need to get off this—this *oaf-trap* before I kill myself."

Monsieur was a stimulating man, a fascinating man, but if he thought I was charming, I pitied those of whom he thought ill.

When Bridey fussed over my unfortunate dress that evening, my chin trembled from wanting to cry. Why must I ruin everything? I was indeed a clumsy fool. Everyone saw it. Everyone noted it.

Still, I could not quite fathom Monsieur's extreme reaction to the broken statue. It wasn't entirely my fault—if it was so ancient and valuable, why had it been left in a pile of debris?

Lord Wyndon flickered into the room, seeming to bring with him both moonlight and warmth. I was immediately distracted from my pitiful shortcomings.

Bridey giggled when I stepped behind the screen for her to help me don my voluminous nightgown. "You are the most modest girl in the world. You don't want the furniture to see you undress."

I managed a laugh as well. "We mustn't make the footstool jealous of my figure." As I sat afterwards at the dressing table while Bridey brushed and braided my hair, she announced, "Conor told me something today. He knew I was worrying about no mass to attend, and he mentioned a fellow who used to be a Catholic priest. He has a mission among the Choctaw Indians on the other side of town. Conor and his dad go to him sometimes, and he'll hold a mass since there's no one else around who can do it. Conor's going to take me to meet him soon. You could go too, if you like. They call the man Father Paul."

"He used to be a priest?"

"He did. He still believes and all, and all. And he still knows the ways. 'Tis only he wanted a family someday."

Suddenly I longed to talk to a priest—or someone who was like unto a priest. I couldn't tell him my secrets, but it would be nice to speak to the man, to feel his reassurance. At least I could ask his advice about participating in the school's morning prayers or attending one of the protestant churches in town. "Thank you. I would like very much to go with you."

Lord Wyndon wandered up behind Bridey's mirrored shoulder. He peered closely at my own reflection, and something about his look stirred me as if it had been a touch. I blinked and swallowed. My expression became a grimace.

Bridey laughed. "Did I tug too hard on your hair?"

"No. I'm just not feeling well."

"I'll make you a warm caudle before I go out to Conor. Me gran used to whip up caudles of cream and ground almonds, honey and ginger. Most calming and 'twill ease whatever's out of sorts. I'll have to find where Miz Jump keeps the ingredients, though, so it might take me a bit. She hides things in odd places because she's so sure everyone steals from the pantry. Though there's not a servant 'twould dare. But I'll bring it to you tonight."

"I'd like that." I hesitated. "You're not frightened of seeing your smoky ghost as you go about the place, are you?"

Before answering, Bridey finished my braids and tied the last ribbon with a flourish. "No. Not really."

"Perhaps this Father Paul could give us some advice about

it." I turned around on the stool so I could face her. "I'm sure everything will be all right. You know, Bridey, as I was trying to say when you told me about it—couldn't spirits be good or bad just like people? They simply can't help scaring us. Maybe the smoke is nice smoke."

She was bundling the gown I had torn at the ruins into the basket where she put all my abused garments awaiting mending. She sniffed. "You haven't seen it. Or felt it. 'Tis not here for any good purpose. If 'twere a good spirit, it would have passed on to heaven where it belonged."

I heard Leo's breath catch.

"That's not always the case," I hastened to say. "Why couldn't it be someone who loved this place, who wants to hold on to the surroundings where he was happy?"

She wouldn't meet my eyes. "That oily, nasty thing is not a sweet, gentle, home-loving bogle. It's a devil out of hell, and what would it be wanting, but the ruination of our souls?" And on that pleasant note, she curtsied a good night.

Leo was restlessly pacing back and forth, his mouth set in a grim line. He halted when the door closed. "Fiona, promise you'll be wary of this smoky apparition."

His abrupt tone was one I'd never heard from him before. And something about it irked me. "Why should I make such a promise? As I said to Bridey, I'm not convinced we must assume it's something bad. And we agreed that I'm going to start questioning spirits if I come across them. For your sake."

"I'm asking you," he said, exasperated, "because, from the sound of the thing, it's not a benevolent 'bogle' like myself. And you must take care of Bridey—I've grown fond of her as I've seen her these few days, bustling about setting your messes to rights."

I winced at his mention of my messes, although that was what they were, and it was my maid's job to deal with them. Eclipsing this was an even more unreasonable twinge of…something…over his fondness for Bridey. I squashed it immediately. Definitely unreasonable. "I'll take care of us both," I said shortly.

"How?" Leo challenged. "Exactly how do you intend to do that?"

"I don't know, but I'll do it."

Leo's lips compressed. There was a long moment.

"Are you all right?" I asked at last. "You look…"

"What? How do I look, Fiona? Annoyed? Frustrated? Angry? Can't you imagine how sick I am of my…my uselessness?" He shouted the last word, and stomped over to the outside wall, where he smashed his fist into the wallpaper. It went right through.

He withdrew his hand and slowly turned around, sheepish. "Well, that was stupid. Sorry. Sorry for acting the brute. It's just that I hate being unable to do anything. I feel rather protective, in my lordly way, of the two girls in my tiny world."

"Hmm. Do you? Well, you can start by not trying to break it down. That was interesting, as well as silly. I have never before in my life wanted to punch a wall."

"Perhaps someday the primal Fiona will come out and you'll try it. Resist, though, because you'll feel a fool afterwards."

"Well, Bridey and I are fine for now, so you may remain calm. I admit I really am concerned about Bridey's smoke, but I don't want to get her scared. Thus far you're the only spirit I've seen in the place, although I have felt and heard things. What about you?

When you were alive did you ever notice anything supernatural at Wyndriven? Or has anyone else drifted in here since you've been haunting my rooms?"

He shook his head. "Back when I was a mortal, the servants used to say that the specter of a walled-in nun lingered in the abbey. I never saw it, though."

I gave a short laugh. "Before I came here I was hoping I'd have such a sighting."

"Do you suppose different spirits are in different levels of existence and that's why we aren't constantly running into each other?"

"Possibly. I hadn't thought of that. Or maybe there simply aren't that many of you wandering about and you're confined to certain areas." I moved into my bedroom to pour a glass of water from the carafe beside my bed. Leo followed. "Did you hear Bridey tell me about the priest? Or rather, ex-priest?"

"Yes."

"I could ask his advice." I gulped down the water. "I wouldn't tell him your exact situation, but I could question him—theoretically—about how to help a spirit go where it needs to go."

"What if his only suggestion is exorcism?"

"Then we would ignore him, because that thrusts a spirit down to hell."

"And I would far rather remain at Wyndriven Abbey." He rubbed his knuckles that had hit the wall, as if they were smarting, even though he couldn't have hurt them. "So, are you ready for my Life Story?"

"As long as it doesn't involve *bhoots*," I muttered.

"I beg your pardon?"

"Nothing. I'll tell you later."

"Are you too tired? It can wait till tomorrow or...whenever."

I smiled and shook my head. "*I* can't wait even if you can. Let's go in the sitting room." I went ahead of him, settled myself cozily in an armchair, and tucked my feet beneath me. "Pray, tell on."

CHAPTER 12

HIS STORY

"I was born here at Wyndriven Abbey—or should I say *there* at Wyndriven Abbey, since this building was then in England and you tell me we're now in America? Baffles the mind." Leo leaned forward, rested his elbows on his knees, and rubbed his chin. "My father wed late in life. He was a scholar, and one day he awoke from his studies and thought with surprise, *I'm middle-aged and have no heir.* He straightaway dusted himself off and wed my mother who efficiently produced two sons and died at my birth."

"So you are motherless like me." I gave a little sigh. "Or rather almost like me. I did have one for a few years. Were you often sad because of it?"

He looked at me thoughtfully for a moment, then shook his head. "No. Not me. I can see how one would feel the loss terribly if one had known a mother, but I never had. Actually, mine was a splendid childhood." I waited for him to continue, but he did not. Instead he said, "I take it yours was not?"

"Splendid? No, it wasn't." Then, lest he think I was whining or begging for sympathy, I added, "Of course I was far more fortunate than many. I wanted for nothing money could buy. Why, you should have seen all my books."

Even though I hadn't begged for it, he gave me a look full of compassion, which embarrassed me, so I asked, "Of what splendors did your splendid childhood consist?"

"Oh, freedom mostly. For all he had desired an heir or two, my father never seemed to notice my older brother, Edwin, and me much. We were given the run of the estate and explored every inch of heath and woodland. We were wild things, I suppose. We had guns for hunting and horses for riding and poles for fishing. We got each other in a great many scrapes, and got each other out of them. We had a tutor, but he never seemed to care much if we learned anything. Luckily I liked learning or I would have grown up a complete dunderhead. Or rather, it wasn't *only* that I liked learning — there was also this girl…"

He paused, gazing intently between the opened draperies, but not as if he was seeing anything. I waited, gazing intently at *him*. He was not a traditionally handsome young man — his features were too irregular, his jaw too square and determined, his mouth too wide and his brow too broad. However, just as his painted face had captivated me, so did his face in person. Or rather, in spirit.

"Was the girl named Marietta?" I asked eventually.

"Yes." He swallowed with obvious difficulty. "Marietta. How on earth did you know?"

"You mentioned her name once. When we first met. Who was she?"

"A sort of cousin. Also my father's ward. She came to live with us when I was twelve. She was the most beautiful creature

I had ever before seen—dainty and delicate with glossy brown curls and small hands and a tiny waist and the prettiest little ways. My father ignored her every bit as much as he ignored us, but Marietta had no desire to run about uncivilized as we did. I wanted to be near her, so I tamed myself and groomed myself and studied my books and hung about, listening to her read, or turning the pages of her music, or walking with her in the garden."

I felt wistful. *No one will ever think of me as dainty and delicate. Or as having pretty little ways. Or small hands, for that matter.*

I flushed then, knowing I was insecure and jealous, and worse yet, jealous of a girl dead nearly a hundred years. Absurd!

"She had a lapdog—Fenris—a small red and white spaniel—and she would hold him up to her cheek and speak sweet words to him, her big brown eyes next to his."

And I can't abide small dogs—always yapping and growling and snapping.

"Marietta was the only person Fenris liked. He would yap and growl and snap at anyone else. She would scold him because she thought he hurt my feelings." Leo's lips stretched in a smile I thought rather silly, as he remembered. "Marietta also worried that my feelings were hurt because of my father's neglect. They weren't, but I didn't let her know, since I enjoyed her attempts to make it up to me."

"So you fell in love with Marietta as you grew older." I didn't ask it as a question; it was a given.

"Of course. Who could help it? I didn't suppose there was any hope, though. Marietta with her beauty and fineness and me, a younger son with no comeliness and few prospects. When I was sixteen my father purchased my commission in the navy and I went to sea. It was—it was not a pleasant time. I had never before been more than a few miles from home, and I did not get on well with the captain. He called me insubordinate, although I did not understand why he found me so. He would tell me to wipe that look off my face, and, in bewilderment, I would try to change the set of my features. Nothing seemed to help. Why are you staring at me like that, Fiona?"

"It's the humorous quirk to your mouth, I bet. That made the captain call you insubordinate, I mean. It causes you to appear as if you're finding everything amusing, even if you don't."

"Oh. Well, you're right—the expression has nothing to do with how I actually feel. I could have assured Captain Hardy that I found very little funny on board the Valiant. All I wanted to do was go home. When I slept I would dream I was at the abbey, and Marietta would be with me as well. I would picture her small white hand tucked in the crook of my arm, or her expression as she looked up at me. At first I worried that while I was gone Edwin would woo and win her, but to my amazement, he had no interest in that direction. And so I let myself begin to hope.

"And then, a week after my twentieth birthday, came the shocking news that both Edwin and my father had succumbed to cholera within a few days of each other. I was Lord Wyndon and had inherited everything along with the title."

"So you went home to Marietta."

"I went home anyway. I raced to Wyndriven, hopeful, in spite of my grief over my family, that I had a chance with her now."

"And did it all play out as you desired?"

He gave a rueful smile. "Does it ever? Instead I found that she was being courted by another man. My cousin Godfrey. He was next in line for the estate and everything that I was not—smooth, handsome, talented in all the cultural arts. He seemed the perfect match to Marietta's perfection. I couldn't compete. When Godfrey was around—and he was always around—I was tongue-tied and awkward. I picture myself with a glum, hang-dog countenance, mutely watching Godfrey and Marietta as I withered inside. Finally I could no longer bear to see them together. I had a good many entertaining friends. I began to pass my evenings with them at the Red Stag—a public house. Most of my daylight hours were spent outdoors. I would ride about the estate, surveying fields and checking on tenants. I purchased a new horse, a fiery beast, and I spent weeks breaking him."

Leo's storytelling was as captivating as Monsieur's. He had the sort of deep, almost-echoing voice that went with his broad chest. It was pleasing in a different way from Monsieur's voice— more substantial and gravelly, less velvety and coaxing.

I had been watching his eyes as he spoke, the luminous blue shining when he mentioned Marietta, darkening when he told of the deaths of his father and brother, clouding when his memory blurred. Now he rose and began pacing, long strides back and forth across the room.

"So you just turned Marietta over to Godfrey?" I asked.

He whirled around. "I told you it was no use. I didn't have a chance."

"But you didn't even let her make a choice," I cried passionately. "And besides—the way you talk about her—you couldn't possibly know who she would like. You don't even know what *she* was like."

"I did tell you," he said coldly, "that she was beautiful and delicate—"

"With infinitesimal hands and waist. Yes, I heard you. Was she any more to you than a lovely face and body? You've made her sound as if she had about as much character as—as that." I pointed toward the figurine on the mantel.

"As that china shepherdess?"

"No. Even less. As the sheep. Had Marietta no personality? What were you in love with? The way she patted her nasty little dog?"

"N-no—no." He sputtered, taken aback. "Of course not. I haven't described her well at all. Marietta was kind, for one thing. She would speak to the poorest yokel as if he were gentlefolk. She laughed at my jokes, and made her own. And until Godfrey showed up, she was the easiest person to talk to that I've ever met." He pressed his fingers into the upholstery of the back of the chair. Or at least he prodded so hard that his fingers disappeared into it. "Are you always like this, Fiona?"

"Like what?"

"Blunt."

"I'm afraid I am quite often," I said mournfully. This was the second time in two days that someone had rightfully accused me of speaking without thinking. "It really is a character defect of mine. But what happened next? Did Marietta end up with Godfrey since you so ridiculously left her to him?"

"I don't know. This is where—oh." He sank back into the chair.

"'Oh,' what?"

"I remember now."

I waited, and when he didn't immediately continue, I waved him on. "Don't stop. What do you remember?"

"I was out riding Banner — the horse. He had finally learned who was master, or so I thought. But this time — how remarkable — to me it seems as if it was only a few hours, or, at most, a couple days ago — he was skittish. Tossing his head and rearing. I had the devil of a time holding on to him. Then, suddenly, I couldn't control him any longer. He tore into the forest, arched his back, and..."

"And?"

"And cracked my skull against a limb."

We were silent for a moment, taking in the enormity of Leo's death. I peeked up at him, to see if I could tell how, exactly, he was taking it. He didn't look upset. Instead he appeared thoughtful. When he spoke at last, he said, "I wonder..."

"What do you wonder?"

"Well, what spooked Banner? It wasn't in his character to buck like that. Run, yes, he could run like the wind. But he acted as if someone had slipped a burr under his saddle or something. I should have checked, although one doesn't automatically assume such a thing."

"Could someone have meddled with him?"

"You're saying it might have been deliberate? But who would have wanted me out of the way?"

"Godfrey, of course. Presumably he had everything to gain from your death — your property, and, well, Marietta. Perhaps you're here for revenge. Do you want to get even?"

His forehead creased.

"Not that I know of at this moment. It's all so fuzzy still, but what would be the point after I've been dead for a hundred years? Anyway, they must have carried me back here to my bed. The agony." He rubbed his head once more. "Something sucked, tugged me upward, and before I knew it, I was looking down at myself from a height around the ceiling. Marietta had wrapped her silk scarf about my head. She was weeping. That's all."

"What do you mean, 'that's all?'"

"I mean, you aggravating girl, that the next I was aware of anything is being in this room shortly before you entered it that first night we spoke. And at that time I had no recollection of the whole business of my death."

"But what about those hundred years' worth of years?"

"No idea. All I know is they flew by without me noticing them."

"What do you think happened to Marietta and Godfrey?"

"I suppose Godfrey inherited Wyndriven and he and his descendants ruined it. How else did it end up here? Doubtless Marietta married him and became Lady Wyndon."

"You say she was tiny and brown-haired?"

He nodded.

"With dimples?"

He nodded yet again.

"And did Godfrey wear a silly wig and have a mole on his cheek and a mouth like a girl's?"

Leo gave a twisted sort of smile. "Yes, he did. How did you know?"

"Because there's a portrait of him in the gallery. Of him and Marietta. With a throng of sweet small children and a particularly fat red and white spaniel sitting between them. I'm so sorry."

Leo's jaw tightened as he turned his face away.

"And now you'll never know if she would actually have preferred you."

"Thank you," he said gruffly. "I hadn't thought of that."

"Of course she may have married Godfrey because second best was better than nothing after you were gone. You wouldn't have wanted her to remain alone and childless forever, would you?"

He shrugged.

"They were remarkably pretty children. If the painting wasn't so enormous, I would try to sneak it in here for you. So you could see Marietta one more time."

Leo said nothing, just looked down at his hands. It had all happened so long ago, but to him it was fresh. And painful.

He stood abruptly and strode to the window, staring off as though he wished he were out there, running as far away from this place—and me—as he could get.

I silently considered his back for several minutes. "You know what we should do?" I said, after giving it some thought. "Since you hate being limited to these few rooms, and will soon grow bored to death—or whatever—here, why don't we work on helping you get into the rest of the house? Maybe even outside." When he didn't answer I went on. "At least it would make a change."

Without turning he said in a muffled voice, "You've seen I can't leave. I'm stuck here forever. And ever. And ever." He drew his sleeve across his eyes.

"We don't know that," I said loudly, and strode up to him so he had no choice but to look at me. "If something is bad, you shouldn't just wring your hands."

"I'm not wringing my hands."

"You're wringing them mentally. What you need to do is take action. You have to at least try, instead of wallowing like a—a wallower."

He snorted. "And just how do you yourself generally face life, Miss O'Malley?"

"Oh," I said, "before I came here, I was a particularly shameful hider and wallower. That's how I know it does no good. Therefore, *I* am planning on exploring the books in the library to see if there's something that will help us figure things out. There's ever so many peculiar books there — some are bound to be on spiritualism. As for *you*, whenever you're in this room and I'm not around, you ought to work on calisthenics. There's got to be ways you can strengthen your puny, weak spiritual body."

"Weak and puny."

"Oh, not in appearance — in appearance you're a strapping fellow — but in feeling. Your spirit body's never done *anything* before, you see. It can't help it. And exercise your mind, too. Concentrate as you try to — " I made a squeaking sound. "You read the Bible the other day."

He stared blankly. "Yes. For solace."

"You turned the pages with your ghost hands. You made something move."

"I did, didn't I?" Leo said slowly, realization dawning on his face. "I wonder how? I did it without thinking."

We pondered this for a moment.

"At least it gives me hope," he said finally.

"And there's other things we can do, so it won't be so dreary for you. I'll catch you up on the last hundred years of books and music. I'll read you Dickens. You'll love Dickens! We'll play cards."

"Cards?"

I grinned. "Yes. I'll figure out some sort of holder or something for you until you can hold them yourself. Let's have some fun, Leo."

He bowed his head and covered his face with his hands. His shoulders began to shake, and I feared he was weeping, until he lowered his hands and I saw he was laughing silently.

"Oh, you think it's impossible to have fun here with me?" I asked. "I'll have you know that I have it in me to be an exceedingly entertaining person." I ended the sentence laughing, until an enormous yawn swallowed the laughter. "Well," I said, "When do you think you're going to poof out?"

He lifted his head. "I have no idea. I don't seem to have any control over poofing—a terrible word, by the way, Fiona—or I would have done it right after you told me about Marietta and Godfrey's family portrait."

"So...I know you don't remember anything about all the years after you died until I walked in on you two days ago, but what happens nowadays when you fade sadly away?"

"It—well, it seems as if I fall asleep, or...not even that—as if I fall into nothing. I have no thoughts, no dreams, when I am not present and visible to you here. It was long after you were asleep last night that I faded out, but I came back into being once during the day, when you were gone. And then back out again until you were here tonight."

"Now, when you're invisible, you really are not present? You have no recollection of me changing clothes or...other private things? It's just—you know..."

For a moment he looked confused, then his eyes focused with understanding, and he turned abruptly offended. "I would never do something so ungentlemanly as to spy upon a lady."

I looked down at the carpet. Couldn't I ever hold my tongue? "I had to mention it," I mumbled miserably. "Can't you understand how horrible it would be for a lady if an unseen gentleman saw *her* when she couldn't see *him*?"

His mouth had a quirk of a smile. "It can't be a situation that has happened often before. But of course I do understand." His tone was gentler. "And since we seem fated to share these rooms for the time being, I promise I'll always let you know when I know that I'm here." He gave a slight bow. "Goodnight, Fiona. And, in case you haven't thought of it, I hope you understand as well, that having no body also puts a fellow into a devilishly vulnerable situation. You know, being absolutely skinless and helpless to affect the world. At least for the time being."

Looking at him, I felt a little tremulous. It had been a very long day. "You're so *nice*, Leo. And such a gentleman, even if you do use the word 'devilishly' around a lady. I don't blame you, though—it's an awfully *striking* word, isn't it? I'm glad it's you who is haunting my rooms."

Houses can have eyes, it seems
And other human parts
Can you hear the creaking-beating
Of its dusty wooden heart?
—*By Fiona O'Malley*

CHAPTER 13

THE TOUR

Morning came, but Bridey did not.

Such a thing had never happened before. Obviously, the slugabed had been out too late with her boy-o. That was it. Come to think of it, Bridey had not returned last night to give me the promised caudle. And it had sounded so delicious. Perhaps she was *still* with Conor. Oh dear.

My hands kept getting in each other's way as I worked at tightening my own stays and buttoning my own buttons and fastening my own jewelry and arranging my own hair. I did all right with the jewelry and buttons. With the stays I failed miserably—I had to wear my gown with the largest waist—and with the hair I failed marginally. I should have to reprimand Bridey. Reprimanding went against my nature, but I could clearly hear my grandmother's voice saying: "The girl mustn't begin forgetting her responsibilities simply because she has a beau and her mistress is young and weak." And Grandmama would have been right.

At breakfast I asked the serving maid if she had seen Bridey. She had not.

"Could she have eloped with Conor?" Dorcas's dull eyes gained a little luster at the titillating possibility.

"I don't *think* so." But now that Dorcas had planted the thought in my head, it wouldn't leave. If Bridey didn't show up after class, I would have to believe she might really have done it. Anger and a sense of abandonment stirred in my breast. It was hard to credit she would leave, without a word, but how much did I actually know about my maid? That she had a large family, was frightened of the dark, had some experiences with the supernatural, and sometimes forgot her responsibilities. I had thought of her as a friend, but really, she had only been a paid servant. If she truly was gone, it would be a muddle. I would have to get into town to Conor's family and find out what they knew. Then I would have to write my grandmother, and she would blame me.

We were dismissed early because the teachers and most of the staff had been promised a partial holiday for some unexplained reason.

I thought of consulting Miss Petheram about my Bridey problem, but I didn't want to get my maid into too much trouble. Also, as I was walking past the office, Mr. Harry emerged with a face like a storm cloud, closely followed by Monsieur. Monsieur caught my eye and winked. I was in no mood for winkage, besides being still rather upset with him for the way he had acted when I broke the monkey, so I sailed on past without acknowledging him. After an interview with those two, Miss Petheram could be in no mood to bother with me. I wandered to my suite, hoping Bridey would be there so I could stop worrying.

Only Leo was present, reclining on the sofa.

"Has Bridey come in today?" I asked him.

He looked up. "No. Haven't seen her."

"I'll have to check her chamber upstairs. I'm ashamed I have no idea where it is." A considerate mistress would have inspected her maid's living conditions, but it hadn't occurred to me.

The hall door flung open, and Trix stood staring at me. "You are so strange," she said.

"I'm just…"

"Ye-e-es?"

How could I explain away what appeared to be a nice little tête-à-tête with myself? "Nothing."

"Thought so. Well, out, out, out, if you want some fun. All the older girls are coming along."

I hesitated. Was this some new hoax at my expense?

However, from the hall, someone called, "Hurry! We don't know how long she'll be gone." Behind Trix, a crowd gathered. Dorcas was there.

Leo waved me on, so I went out the door.

"What are we doing?" I asked. There were thirteen waiting — all the older girls. I recognized faces, but still knew only a few names. Everyone seemed to be bubbling with excitement, like ants when their hill is disturbed.

Trix flashed a wicked grin. "I'm taking y'all on a tour to explore the forbidden reaches of Wyndriven. Penny apiece."

I searched in my pocket. "I haven't any coins with me."

She rolled her eyes. "I don't actually expect you to pay. I was jesting. Although how can a rich girl not have any money? Anyway, I snitched The Petheram's keys while she went on some errand or other. The younger girls are all penned up with Miss Daphne. Miss Daphne's the housekeeper, in case you don't know.

Supposedly she's in charge of us too this afternoon, but she shan't ever know what we're doing, and all the other adults are gone." Trix herded us on down the corridor.

"Why is Trix including me?" I whispered to Dorcas as we trailed along at the end. "I thought she hated me."

Dorcas shook her head. "No. You're not that special. She doesn't sneer at you any more than she sneers at everybody."

We scurried to keep up. Dorcas looked pale and drawn. She clutched her stomach.

"Are you all right?" I asked. "We don't have to go with them if you don't want to."

"I want to. My innards always hurt when anything interesting is happening." She gave a doleful smile which I guessed was intended to be reassuring.

I fretted with the bangle on my wrist. "Bridey still hasn't shown up. While we're roaming the far reaches, let's see if we can find her room. It's somewhere up near the attics—in the long-ago servant's quarters."

Trix led the way as if she knew where she was going, although she didn't. Dorcas had told me that none of the girls had seen more than bits and pieces of this vast, monster of a building.

At first I planned to pay careful attention to everything so I could describe it to Leo later, but that plan soon faded. I felt myself hanging back. Bridey's disappearance left me in a pensive, anxious mood. I hated the thought of what I would have to say to her if she came waltzing into my room in a few hours, pretending nothing was wrong. I would have to act like a real mistress.

We wandered beyond the places Miss Petheram had shown me, through massive, dusky spaces and minute ones, up and down sweeping staircases and crooked, narrow back stairs, into surprising nooks and crannies. We climbed a twisting stone staircase. Carrie-something-or-other stumbled and banged her knee on a step. She gave a yelp.

"Legend has it," Trix said over her shoulder, eyes snapping, "that ghosts of the old family reach out to catch your ankles."

"Naughty ghosts." Sylvie giggled.

"Their name was Wyndon," I said, too loudly.

"Whose name was Wyndon?" another girl asked.

"The family who owned Wyndriven Abbey. Back in England."

"How on earth do you know that?" Trix said.

"Oh...you know. Their portraits are in the gallery. You've all seen them."

The dim, unused chambers were lofty and sumptuously adorned, but they smelled lonely and ancient and eerie. Carpets had been rolled up, and paintings and tapestries covered for their protection. In the gloom we could only make out shapes of things swathed in pallid holland covers. A person could be underneath, silent, hiding, and we would not know.

As we continued on our way, we became oddly quiet for a group of girls, whispering when we spoke and practically tiptoeing. Even our sneezes were subdued, as we stirred up dust on the floors.

We entered a vast hall lined with odd, partially concealed shapes. Trix twitched off one cover, and several of us let out shrieks, because a naked man stood there jauntily, holding a bunch of grapes before his mouth, coldly glowing in marble. This place was a sculpture gallery. We uncovered more figures from many different cultures, created in bronze and stone, marble,

plaster, and wood. One blue-skinned, many-armed female creature poked out a purple tongue. "What *can* she have been eating?"
Trix giggled.

"I wonder if one of the wives was killed in here?" Dorcas
whispered. "It seems like the sort of place where someone would
murder someone."

We covered up the statues and left hastily—too many blind
eyes watching. I could sense what everyone was feeling—that *we*
were the ones exposed.

Actually a lot of the empty rooms seemed like places where
someone could have murdered someone.

We headed upstairs, to the part of the house still used, and
peeked in bedchamber after bedchamber. After we came upon a
room with Miss Petheram's dove gray wrapper spread across the
bed and her books upon the nightstand, the Carrie girl shuffled
her feet and said, "She'll return any minute, and we'll get caught.
I'm going back down."

Trix mocked Carrie for being a chicken, but all the other girls
except for me, Dorcas, Mary Dell, and Sylvie, left with her.

Our diminished group continued our tour. In the portrait gallery I inspected Marietta's family portrait carefully, trying to remember details to relate to Leo.

Mary Dell pushed her hair back from her face. "Trix, hadn't
we better stop here? We really are going to get caught, and I'm
doing poorly enough in my lessons that I don't dare get on Miss
Petheram's bad side."

Trix tapped her foot, looked from side to side, and finally
sighed. "I didn't actually steal the keys, you know."

"Then how'd you get them?" Sylvie asked.

"If you must know, The Petheram let me have them. She said it might be interesting for us to poke about and she knew we wouldn't hurt anything. She even informed Miss Daphne. I just thought it would be more fun if y'all were nervous and I could keep scorning you for it. I managed a little of that, didn't I?" She chuckled unrepentantly.

Sylvie stamped her kid slipper, but she was laughing too. "Why, you provoking creature. Every second, I was quivering with fear of being apprehended. All right then, let's go on."

I paused, examining a steep, dusky flight of rickety stairs, which I guessed led to the old servants' quarters. "I need to go up there."

"Why?" Trix demanded. Every time Trix asked a question, it sounded as if she was issuing a challenge

And every time I was around Trix, I felt as if whatever I was doing or saying was particularly stupid. I could feel a foolish look coming over my face as I explained about Bridey.

Sylvie seemed fascinated. "You really think she might have run off with a boy she's only known a couple days? How incredibly romantic."

"Well, she's missing and she's sweet on him. I've got to at least seek out her room to see if her things are gone."

"So you don't know for sure where she's been sleeping?" Trix exclaimed. "You didn't even make certain your maid was well-situated? You, with your whole suite of fine rooms."

I could feel the guilty color rise in my face. "I meant to," I mumbled.

"Hah!" exclaimed Trix.

"Well," Mary Dell said comfortably, "we'll all go with you,

won't we, ladies?"

Even Trix, after considering for a moment, nodded.

Eventually, down a narrow corridor carpeted in rough drugget, we found Bridey's pitiful chamber, and I felt more ashamed of my thoughtlessness than ever. It held a sagging rope bed and a plain pine bureau. Bridey's toiletry articles were scattered on top of the bureau, and her few extra clothes hung on hooks.

"Why didn't she take her things?" I wailed. "If she eloped with her new beau, she'd have taken her things."

Trix shrugged. "She's a servant. And Irish. Who knows what they'd do?"

The anxiety I'd felt since Bridey hadn't shown up in the morning settled like a lump of ice in my stomach.

"You'll have to talk to the other servants," Dorcas said. "And we'll get Mr. Harry to take us to Maloney's Mercantile. Maybe Conor's family will know everything."

No one else gave another thought to Bridey's disappearance. I was mute now and my steps grew automatic as Trix continued our tour. I was horrified by how alone Bridey had been each evening, how far from every other living soul. As we made our way down a murky little back staircase which led all the way below to the service area, I wondered if this was the place she had seen the evil smoke. Goosebumps rose on my arms.

On the main floor, inside the green baize servants' door, Trix led us through a passage lined with larders and pantries, a washhouse, and storage rooms. Dorcas and I dropped back even farther. When we reached the kitchen, Dorcas and I remained in the center of the space. Something squeezed my heart, as Trix cast open the door to a dark, gaping hole. The cellar stairs.

"Below us are the dungeons," Trix announced, glancing back, "where enemies of the Wyndons — thank you, Fiona, for that tidbit of information — were chained and left to rot. You can smell it still, can't you? Like a dead rat in the walls."

A draft of foul, stagnant, damp-earthy air wafted up from the blackness.

"That's silly," Dorcas dared to say, although her voice wasn't entirely steady. "It's just a cellar dug here. When they picked up the stones to bring them here, they wouldn't have brought the dungeons."

"Good point." Trix actually looked approvingly at Dorcas. "Well, it certainly *smells* as if prisoners are rotting down there. But if it isn't a dungeon, perhaps it's the wine cellar. Wouldn't that be fun? The Stones are teetotalers, so there should be plenty left for us to sample."

"Except," Dorcas said, "for the two armies that stayed here. And Mr. Harry."

"Getting a bit uppity, now, aren't we, Dorcas, my child?" Trix grinned to show she was teasing. "We'll simply have to see what's down there. Here, hand me that candle, Mary Dell. For the climax of our tour, we must descend into Hades, unless y'all are too chicken. I myself find it darkly fascinating."

I wanted to beg her not to do it, not to go down, but I couldn't say a word. I watched as Mary Dell lit a straw in the glowing fireplace coals, touched it to the candle wick, and for a moment the flame flared brighter as she brought it to Trix. Something about the jaunty set of Trix's shoulders as she plunged down the steps seemed a bit too deliberate. I suspected she was not as confident as she pretended. However, she put on a good show. "Have y'all ever had brandy? Tastes disgusting, but such a kick. I love it! Used to steal my papa's all the time."

Dorcas grabbed my hand and briefly held it in her pudgy, clammy one, before we dropped into single file down the teetering stairs.

I was not even surprised when Sylvie, who was just behind Trix, first gasped and then screamed. Something in me must have known what we were going to find.

Bridey just lay there.

I cried out her name in a hoarse voice I didn't recognize as my own.

Of course she didn't move.

Sylvie, sobbing, pushed past me back up to the kitchen. The rest of us slowly made our way down the last steps.

At the bottom, in the little circle of candlelight, my maid's curls were spread out on the stone floor. Her neck was twisted in an unnatural position at odds with her crumpled body. A thin stream of blood trickled from the corner of her mouth. She stared straight up as if in horror at her last sight before the fatal tumble downwards. Nearby lay a puddle of hardened wax which had been a candle. Bridey, who was terrified of the dark, had lain here alone in the blackness all these hours.

Close beside me, I felt Dorcas shaking like a jelly. The sight, the silence, the smell of death closed over us.

"Why ever did she come down here?" For once, Trix's voice was a whisper.

I gulped. "Last night she was going to make a drink for me. She must have been looking for ingredients." Steeling myself, I knelt down beside the body and lifted Bridey's hand. I had read that one should seek a pulse. I had never before touched dead flesh. It was curiously stiff and cold. Something was still clutched in her tightly clenched fist. The rosary beads I had given her.

"Would all of you please go up and tell Miss Daphne and Mr. Willie what has happened, and see if the Petherams are back?" I said, when I could speak. "I'll stay here. I shan't leave Bridey alone."

Dorcas hesitated. "I'll wait with you." Her skin was spongy gray, as if she were going to lose her luncheon at any moment.

"No," I said, shaking my head. "Please don't. She was my maid and my friend. Leave me alone with her for a few minutes."

Dorcas glanced back once, but followed the others upstairs.

My eyes raked the shadows beyond the candlelight, fearing that I would see the pale shade of Bridey keeping vigil over her body, looking back at me.

My teeth began to chatter and I could not still them.

What if She should come —
Bridey, my poor little maid — from that strange place?
What if I should look upon her face, as it was before,
And see her bloody and broken, lying on the floor!
My heart is filled with dread;
Can I forgive my friend for being dead?
— By Fiona O'Malley

CHAPTER 14

WHAT LIGHT...?

Feb. 20, 1867

Dearest Grandmama,

Something tragic has happened. Bridey Flynn, my maid, has met with an accident – she fell down some stairs and passed away two nights ago. I hadn't known her long, but I was very fond of her, and I grieve for her. Bridey will be buried in a Catholic Cemetery and the funeral mass tomorrow will be read by a priest named Father Paul...

Mr. Harry had contacted the priest who was no longer a priest. I wiped away tears as I went on to request that my grandmother notify Bridey's family as well as give them a sum of money. I also asked that she not send me another maid. I knew she would argue that those in the domestic employment sphere needed the work as much as we needed to be served. However, replacing Bridey at this moment was unthinkable. At least for the time being, I should manage as the other girls did at school, tending to our own things and helping one other. I had no clear idea how to go about doing this, but I would figure it out.

I tapped my pen against the inkwell. I had started another

letter to Grandmama on the day I arrived at Wyndriven, but had never finished it. I pictured the old lady now, wandering alone in her echoing house, and was filled with remorse. I couldn't leave the letter as it was. Even though I was tired and sad, I wrote several more paragraphs, naming different girls and pretending that we were friendly with one another, and telling her how accomplished I would soon become due to my lessons here. (I hoped to demonstrate this with my already much-improved penmanship.) It would make her so happy to believe I was on my way to becoming normalized.

Tomorrow afternoon, I would gather up Bridey's possessions, and send them in a parcel with the letter. Grandmama could turn them over to the Flynn family. Two envelopes lay on my desk — one for the Flynns and one for Conor, each containing a curling, brown lock of Bridey's hair which I had snipped earlier today, and bound with bits of crimson thread.

I undressed, bringing on a cramp between my shoulder blades as I twisted to unbutton myself. The night before, Dorcas had helped, but I couldn't expect that every evening. I slipped on my second-best nightgown and climbed into bed, leaving my gown, stockings, and underclothing mounded on the dressing room floor. Eventually I must learn to be tidy, but not tonight. I lay on my side and pillowed my head on my hands.

A lop-sided moon shone through the window, pure white and luminous. It drenched my room with dull silver. I pictured it gently bathing Bridey's coffin (supplied by Maloney's Mercantile) down in the blue salon, softening all the outlines. Women from town had washed her body and dressed her in my very best, laciest nightgown. It wouldn't itch her as it had always itched me.

I prayed that Bridey's spirit was safe and happy in the next world. How was it that, although I had a sure knowledge that personalities continue after death, I still grieved? Because it was such a loss, I supposed. Such a waste of a young life. Because I could not see her or talk to her.

Or could I?

Please, no! I could not bear for Bridey to appear to me now. I had never before seen the specter of anyone I had known in life, and I hoped I would never have to.

How had it all happened so rapidly? One day she was there. The next not. I tried to find some *reason* for it. To make some sense out of Bridey's death.

I forced myself to entertain the question I had been suppressing: did the smoke Bridey had seen have anything to do with her plunge down the stairs? Had it frightened her and caused her to misstep? It was certainly a possibility

The shiver in my bones made me believe it was likely.

What a beautiful day. The world was honeyed by amber sunlight, and a breeze blowing across new grass brought fresh scents of spring. We stood in the Catholic cemetery at the top of a forested hill near Father Paul's mission.

It was a relief to me that prayers had been offered at the funeral mass for the repose of Bridey's immortal soul. Father Paul spoke in English now, rather than Latin, reminding us of our need for salvation and grace, and asking for consolation for those who mourned.

He wore regular clothing, with no vestments. He made me think of an old-testament prophet, except that he had no beard.

He was tall and angular and grave, with roughhewn features, and eyes deeply set beneath heavy brows. He frightened me a little.

Trix, Sylvie, Mary Dell, and Dorcas were present. It had been obvious that they should attend the service because we had been together for the discovery of the accident. Still, the others were not particularly friendly to Dorcas and me, and we had little to say. We all wore black, although at one point Trix had reminded me sharply that this was the only time I should dress in black for Bridey. After all, she said, one simply does *not* wear mourning for a servant.

I was vaguely interested in what Trix deemed appropriate apparel for the funeral of a servant. Her bonnet, clotted with a swarm of huge bruise-colored cabbage roses, was distractingly ugly. Something about her — and it was not the bonnet — made me take a second look. Mary Dell had been fussing over Trix because her weight had been falling off — her dress did indeed hang baggy. Also, there was a pinched look about Trix's face, and dark shadows beneath her eyes. I had only known her for a few days, but even I could tell that something was not right with Trix. Surely it had nothing to do with Bridey. She looked consumptive.

Besides us girls and Father Paul, only Miss Petheram and Conor were present. Poor Conor's face was such a study in confusion and grief that it hurt to look upon him. When I had glimpsed him with Bridey, from a distance, he had seemed a young Irishman so hard and lean he might have been made from a coach whip. Now he appeared bent and beaten.

Dorcas nudged me. "Doesn't Miss Petheram look nice? Do you suppose the priest notices?"

Shocked, I shushed Dorcas, but now I could not resist examining our headmistress. She truly was extra pretty today, in spite of her dark, drab garb. The sunlight meandered beneath her bonnet to make her irises shine extra blue and tint her cheeks with rose, and the breeze sent tendrils of blonde hair across her forehead, softening her features.

"See, you're looking too," Dorcas hissed, when my glance now wandered back toward Father Paul. He, however, appeared to take no notice of Miss Petheram.

It was Conor who threw the first clods of earth onto the casket before the gravedigger commenced filling in the hole. We all watched as shovelful after shovelful showered down. Somehow the repeated motions made death very real. Bridey's body was laid to rest so far from her family. So far from her home. I had brought her down here. She had died serving me.

After the brown dirt was mounded, Conor continued standing there, staring, bewildered, staggered. He had met Bridey such a short time ago, yet I was certain that visions of a happy future had already been dreamed. And then inexplicably snatched away.

Dorcas nudged me. "We'll wait in the wagon."

I nodded. "Shan't be long." I approached Conor and held out the envelope containing Bridey's hair. He started. "I cut this for you. Bridey would want you to have it to remember her by. She — she really cared for you. You were all she thought about from the minute you first met."

He looked into the envelope and his eyes welled. He mopped them with a large handkerchief as he thanked me. I couldn't think what else to say, so I left him and went to Father Paul's side.

"Father," I said, "I appreciate all you've done for Bridey. It would have been very important to her. She told me that a former priest lived near us and we'd hoped to meet you — obviously under other circumstances."

"Actually," he said, "I am not a 'former' priest. Once a man has been ordained to Holy Orders, he is always a priest. However, since I have been reduced to laity, I may only exercise my priestly faculties in time of need." He examined me from beneath craggy brows as if measuring me in some way. "You are Miss O'Malley. Conor told me that Miss Flynn's mistress was a good Catholic girl."

"I am. Or rather, I don't always act as I should, but I do try. There are some things I need to ask you. I have been wondering if it would be wrong of me to attend church in Chicataw with the other girls because — because — "

He gave a grave smile that lessened the somber quality of his face. "I understand. Because there is no official Catholic parish hereabouts. Someday there will be of course. You must do the best you can with those circumstances you are given, and the best you can do for now is to attend the worship services available."

I shuffled my feet, wondering how to word my next inquiry, which concerned dealing with the evil smoke. Finally I simply blurted it out. "I have another question — an unusual one. You say you can do priestly things in time of great need. What about exorcism? Could you perform an exorcism if a spirit somewhere needed to be got rid of?"

His eyes flicked toward the casket.

"No," I said quickly. "Not <u>Bridey</u>."

His mouth went straight and unsmiling. "Miss O'Malley, devils are powerful beings and dangerous to deal with. Spiritualism is not something to be toyed with. I hope you young ladies have not been dabbling in such things? No séances or attempts to communicate with the dead?"

"I have never participated in a séance," I told him truly. "I know that sort of thing is serious. I was only asking in a theoretical sense. If I were ever to ask you in a real sense, it would only be as a last resort. And I would never want you to exorcise a whole house, just one spirit from it."

His sardonic left eyebrow quirked. "You don't understand what exorcism is, do you?"

"Not really, I guess. How could I?"

He smiled faintly. "Correct. How could you? Exorcism is used only on people who are possessed by demons. Performing such a rite thrusts the invading spirit down to hell, separated forever from God. Objects, such as houses, may be *ob*sessed. In that case a priest may bless the building."

I opened my mouth to say more, but closed it, because at that moment, Miss Petheram approached, and Father Paul looked up. The breeze blew her bonnet back, the sun shone bright on her face, and I witnessed something I had only read about in novels. Both their pairs of eyes took on the same misty stare.

"What lady is that which doth enrich the hand of yonder knight? O! She doth teach the torches to burn bright!"

Father Paul didn't actually say this, but he looked as if he felt it.

I shook myself from the spell of wonder I was somehow included in, and introduced my headmistress. Father Paul took her hand and forgot to give it back, as the two of them began discussing the beautiful setting and the splendid weather — anything but the grave and the girl that lay so close. It was as if I were not there. I speedily took my leave.

The week after Bridey's burial was a difficult one. I felt the loss of my maid, companion, and friend, but was ashamed that often I missed her mostly because I had such a hard time performing for myself the tasks that she, and a line of other servants before her, had always performed for me. I felt as if I had entered an alien world — the world of ordinary people who did not have their own private lady's maid. I could have asked Dorcas how to manage, but it embarrassed me that I knew so little, and so I blundered about on my own. Dorcas was, however, kind enough to pull my corset laces for me, because that was truly impossible to do for oneself. I had to dash down to her room each morning, my wrapper flapping, for her assistance.

My underthings needed laundering and I must find out how one went about doing that. I raked myself over the coals because I realized how much trouble I had made for Bridey through my carelessness. One day I clumsily attempted to stitch up the rent in a skirt I took from the heaped sewing basket. I awkwardly poked and pulled at it with a needle and thread, but gave up when I saw the lumpy mess I made. I had only executed decorative fancywork in the past, and I was not proficient at that.

Well, thank goodness I am rich. I shall simply give these things away and buy new ones.

I was pathetic.

In the still-cool evenings I shivered since I did not know how to lay a fire. In the mornings, I swiped at dust on furniture, whacked at carpets and floorboards with a broom, and ineffectually attempted to smooth out my bedcovers. My rooms looked as if a whirlwind had blown through them.

And I looked as if I had stood in the center of that wind.

Leo caught me weeping one afternoon when I was trying to complete my toilette for supper. I wept with frustration because I couldn't find one of my rose-beaded slippers, the bow on my collar was crooked, I couldn't fasten my morocco belt because my stays weren't pulled tight enough, and strands of my coarse black hair poked wildly out of the chignon I had tried to knot it in. I lay my head down on the dressing table and bawled.

"What is it this time, Fiona?" he asked gently. "Still poor Bridey? She wouldn't want you to grieve so."

I lifted my head, aware of my tear-ravaged face, but at the moment I didn't care. "N-no," I hiccupped. "This time it's my d-devilish hair."

He laughed, but immediately choked back the laughter when I glared at him through my tears. "It's not so very...devilish," he said. "You look fine."

"Fine?" I cried. "I look awful. There's bits and pieces of me flying away and poking out in every direction. I look as if a three-year-old tried to paste me together from scraps. I love pretty things, but I don't deserve them. I'm nearly seventeen years old and I'm as bungling as a helpless babe."

"You're a lady," he said quietly. "No lady is expected to perform these tasks for herself."

"Well, what useless, frivolous, ridiculous things we are, then." I raised my chin. "Even though it's awful about Bridey, I'm glad — glad — that I'm being forced to learn to fend for myself."

"You'll get it right eventually."

"I will," I said, and realized I was still glaring, but with determination now. "And until I do, must you stand around in here?"

He looked nonplussed. "Yes. I must. As you well know."

"True," I admitted. "But for now, while I'm trying to learn to take care of myself, will you please not look at me?"

He cocked a humorous eyebrow, but said only, "Very well, my proud beauty," and meekly turned away.

At the end of the week, as we were taking a turn about the flag-stone terrace after supper, Dorcas told me something that stopped me in my tracks.

"They're saying that Bridey haunts the cemetery."

"Who is saying that?" I demanded.

"The maids were talking as they cleaned up the tables. One of them is being courted by a Choctaw fellow who lives near the Catholic mission. He told her a light has been seen hovering about the graveyard hill every evening since Bridey was buried. It stays there all night long."

"That can't be so!" I cried. "I don't believe it."

Dorcas shrugged placidly. "Only telling what I heard."

I moved over to the balustrade and stared out over the gardens, my knuckles pressed against my lips as I thought what to do. Bridey's spirit must not linger, lost and alone in the dark. What a horrifying image. Dorcas stood behind me, her breathing soft and heavy, patiently waiting for me to speak again.

I made a decision. "Dorcas," I turned and said, "do you know how to harness the goats to the cart? I haven't an idea how to do it."

Her forehead wrinkled. "I suppose I could do it. I've seen it done. Why?"

"Because tonight you and I are going to visit Bridey's grave. It's too far to walk, so we'll take the cart."

She shook her head so hard her limp brown hair flew in her

face. "Oh, no we're not."

"Well, then, I am. But will you at least help me harness the goats?"

"Why would you go there? I'm curious to see the light too, but it's much too much trouble to snitch the cart and travel all the way through the forest and across Chicataw in the middle of the night."

"I owe it to Bridey. If she's not at rest, and it really is *her* there, and not some moaning bedsheet, we can't leave her so. She needs help and I have to help her."

"How?"

"I don't know, but maybe she can tell me what's keeping her here."

"All anyone has seen is a light. How could she talk to you?"

I sighed. "Because, well, sometimes I can speak to spirits."

"*What?*" Her face showed bewilderment, before she grunted. "Stop it. I actually thought you were serious for a second."

"I *am* serious. I've seen them since I was little, and lately I've been able to talk to them."

"Really? Real ghosts?"

"Yes. Really real ghosts. Don't you go telling anyone, though, because it's not something I'm proud of, and I don't want it spread about. Do you believe me?"

"I don't know. I'm being honest. I don't know. I do believe that spirits can walk the earth because plenty of folks have seen them. And you ain't a liar. But just…give me a while to think."

"Won't you go with me while you're thinking? Please?"

Dorcas's thumb nail clicked between her teeth. "I guess so. You would never be able to find the way or drive the cart. Because even though I like you, you often haven't much sense."

That night, after the clock in the hall bonged a single note, Dorcas and I met at the bottom of the great stairs, each cloaked in a mantelet and carrying a candle. Dorcas put her finger over her lips when I opened my mouth to greet her. She led the way to a side door, and out into the darkness. A puff of wind blew out my flame, but Dorcas kept hers sheltered as we made our way to the stables. Just inside the stable door, she found a lantern in which to shelter her flame.

I suppose we made a comical sight, chasing down Atlas and Hercules in the goat pen, and I did laugh out loud once, to be frantically shushed by Dorcas. The goats' hooves thudded like low thunder as they darted and bolted from one side of the pen to the other, trying to elude us. Surprisingly, Dorcas showed shrewdness in the way she patiently cornered them and got them harnessed.

"Do you often rope goats?" I whispered. "You do it so skillfully."

She snorted.

"And the whole surreptitious, sneaky thing—definitely one of your talents."

"Hush."

As we trotted off down the drive, the huge night washed over us, like drowning in deepest blue. The temperature was cool, and we were glad for our wraps. We passed the lake, wreathed with a gauzy lavender mist and illuminated by starlight.

Once we reached the forest, Dorcas asked me about the ghosts I had known. Since I would not discuss Leo, I could tell her little, except how they looked. She seemed annoyed that I had seen nothing of the spirits of Wyndriven's murdered wives, and that, even with my experiences, I knew so little about the whys and wherefores of haunting.

"It seems to me," she said, "that there's got to be a reason why spooks would choose to linger on when they're not supposed to. In tales it's always unfinished business, such as the apparitions need to expose their killer, or they want to tell their family where the treasure is hidden. That sort of thing."

"Sometimes they don't realize they're dead."

"Stupid of them."

I shrugged. "It's not as simple as it sounds in stories. Since you're asking me about it, does that mean you've decided to believe me?"

"I...suppose I have. But only because it's *you* telling me. You ain't a liar. "

"Thank you."

"So, what will you say to the light if we see it?"

"Hopefully, it'll appear to me looking like Bridey. And then I'll ask her how she died exactly and what's keeping her tied to the earth." My heart pounded oddly in my chest, in little jumps and starts.

We rolled silently through sleeping Chicataw and out the other side. As we neared the wooded cemetery hill, Dorcas swallowed and pointed. Above us, ice-green stars quivered, but toward the hilltop, a pinprick of yellowish light winked through the trees. Dorcas's stomach growled loudly and she clutched her arm across it.

We wrapped the reins of the cart around a stump and made our way along the rough path winding up the hill. Dorcas carried the lantern in one hand and clutched my arm with the other. I had to move slowly because of her dragging. Twigs crackled beneath our feet, and a screech owl hooted a distance away, but some of the other sounds we heard could not be explained away so easily. The tree trunks up ahead loomed black against a glow that was more spreading and more golden than a spirit would cast. At least in my experience. We broke through the last barrier of trees and —

There, beside Bridey's grave, shone a lantern. And huddled within the radiance, lay a dark mound.

We moved closer, holding onto each other.

Conor's black hair spilled against the grass. He was asleep, wrapped in a blanket.

He scowled and stirred when I whispered his name. His eyelids flickered open. He bolted straight upright, blinked, and rubbed his eyes. "What are you doing here?"

"Coming to see what *you* are doing here," I answered.

He looked down at the grave's black, raw soil. For a moment he didn't speak, his mouth oddly twisting. "She couldn't bear the dark," he said slowly, with a catch in his voice. "I couldn't let her lie alone in the dark."

"Conor," I said, laying a hand on his shoulder. "Oh, poor, poor Conor. So you've spent every night here since Bridey was buried?"

He nodded.

"But *she* isn't down there in the earth. You need a good long talk with Father Paul. Bridey is shining in heaven with her own brightness, where she need never again fear the night."

"How can you know that? I mean really, *really* know that?"

"Because," Dorcas piped up. "If Bridey was still here, Fiona would see her because Fiona can see dead people."

It certainly hadn't taken Dorcas long to tell someone my secret. But I supposed I would have told Conor myself, if she hadn't.

He looked as a drowning man might if someone tossed him a lifeline. He wanted to hope. He wanted to believe.

We stayed like that, talking in our little circle of light, for hours. We watched the black night sky and then the grayed night sky. By the time we knew we must leave, I felt as if Conor was a friend. And he believed.

CHAPTER 15

THE BLASTED WOOD

"Why would anyone style a *walking* dress with a trailing train?" I asked crossly, yawning and tugging at the swathe of white cotton pique that snagged on every woodland shrub and briar it encountered. I had hoped a ramble in the woods after classes would wake me up, but I continued droopy, with eyes that felt as if they were being scratched by sand. One cannot stay up till the wee hours several nights in a row without paying the price, however interesting one's chatter with an attractive ghost.

"Perhaps because, when worn and walked in gracefully, the lady's silhouette is delightful." Monsieur's eyes raked over me, and I felt as if I were something being poked at in a cage. Obviously I did not dress or walk gracefully.

I had not felt the same toward Monsieur since he blazed up at me at the ruins. He had been extra gracious the first times we met after that, but his manner had struck me as false. Gradually he seemed to sense this, and his attitude toward me had changed. His conciliatory thoughtfulness had worn off and, perhaps it was my imagination, but I believed that I was finally starting to experience the real Monsieur. I wondered if it was a relief to him to not have to *try* with me anymore.

Warm blood heated my cheeks as he carelessly gestured at my skirt. "And the arabesque design at the hem almost lends a rhythmic visual effect. A sheikh I once knew had a similar pattern embroidered on each of his tents."

I wished he would begin one of his tales about his travels. They were my favorite part of our random meetings. "Back east, everyone is wild over Orientalism in everything," I said, to encourage him.

However, Monsieur did not seem to be in the mood to recount stories. Not even when I asked if he'd ever been in a land where they ate people, which I would have thought would have at least invited a few gruesome anecdotes. He simply looked down his nose at me and strode on ahead in brooding silence. His limp was more pronounced than usual.

I glared at his back. If he didn't want to chat, he should have left me alone. I had been perfectly happy basking by myself in a sun-sweet glade carpeted with newly sprung-up plants that resembled thousands of tiny umbrellas. It was a wild woodland place glowing with spring green light. I had been right in the middle of a splendid daydream. Leo was alive in it, and stretched out beside me, leaning on his elbows and chewing on the stem of one of the umbrellas.

Is it Leo's vitality of spirit that makes me conscious of him as I've never been conscious of a young man before? Or is it simply the fact that we share a bedroom?

Anyway, Monsieur had sauntered up out of nowhere, as was his habit, spoiling the daydream. It always made me uncomfortable that perhaps he had been there all the time, blended into the shadows, and I hadn't noticed. *He* had been the one to ask if he might join *me* in my explorations, yet somehow, in the last few minutes, he had taken the lead. Although we were following no path I could see, there was a determination in his stride that made me ask, "Is there some particular place we're going?"

"*Oui*. I want to show you a spot up ahead."

I twitched my skirt wide to avoid a prickly clump. "You know what? Tonight I'm going to hack away half this fabric so I can actually walk in this walking dress." I paused. "Except then I would have to re-hem it. I'm getting better at basic stitching, but I'm still not much of a seamstress."

Monsieur paused in mid-stride. "I had forgotten. You are without the services of a maid. Well, can you not hire some old lady to do your mending? And in the meantime, why not be sensible and toss the provoking train over your arm? I promise I will not peek at your exposed ankles."

I actually did as he suggested because I was certain he told the truth. The real Monsieur felt no temptation to leer at my limbs or any other part of me. He no longer dabbled at the habitual flattery and casual flirtatiousness he had shown the first few weeks I knew him. My awkwardness frustrated and annoyed him.

He ducked beneath a plumy pine bough. He did not hold it politely out of my way. His lack of manners more than ever confirmed my conviction that he did not find me attractive.

So *why* did he seek me out? I couldn't be all *that* entertaining. Loneliness, I could only suppose, although one would have thought someone as stimulating as Monsieur would have a great many connections, if not friends. Perhaps the answer to this question lay in his mysterious background, if only I could discover more about it. He evaded my queries with skill. I had asked Dorcas about him, but she had said she knew nothing of the business side of managing Wyndriven.

I picked up a satisfactorily-shaped stick and whacked at a low-hanging sweetgum branch.

"Stop that," Monsieur spat out, and I felt as if I were five years old. When I tripped over a root, Monsieur made no effort to help me up. He only gave an exasperated groan and plunged on ahead.

I gritted my teeth. Well, if he often found me irritating, I often found *him* even more so. I should stop following him now. I wished he'd go away. Or else I wished he were Leo. If only Leo could leave our suite to join me in the woods. He had been so restless when I left him that morning, pacing the floor like the lion I had once seen in a traveling menagerie.

"I ought to go back," I said, pausing and half-turning.

"Oh, no, no, no." Monsieur shook his head, and waited impatiently for me to catch up. "Just ahead is the glade where some natural phenomena occurred and did a great deal of destruction. I find ruin fascinating. Don't you?" His voice had taken on an edge.

"Not if people are hurt." Although I remembered uncomfortably my interest in sketches of the devastation of the Great Natchez Tornado of 1840. "And I particularly hate to see damage from the war."

"*Oui*, you told me so when I met you beside the shed riddled with bullet holes from the armies' target practice." His tone was distracted, as if he hardly noticed what we were saying. "Your family's artillery business, I believe, was part of your problem with such things. If it were me, I should enjoy seeing such evidence of my own power."

"I prefer power to heal and build rather than to hurt and destroy."

"Must you turn conventional?"

"Trix prides herself on being unconventional," I announced, picking accumulated burrs from my train and flicking them into the undergrowth.

A spark of interest kindled in his eyes. "Oh, ho. So you recognize that in the vixen."

"Well, I don't find her original. To me she acts and thinks exactly like every other mean-minded, bossy girl I've known. However I suppose she believes she's different because she curses sometimes and smokes gentlemen's cigars behind the tool shed and brags about her pet snake. Oh — and flaunts an infinite supply of ugly, supposedly artistic hats. All very studied."

He gave a dark, oily chuckle.

A sudden breeze I could not feel on my skin sent the leaves above us snapping together to make a sound like tiny, clapping hands. We skirted our way through a grove of blackened pine skeletons, and found ourselves standing at the top of a sharp drop. Below us was the vista he was seeking.

A terrible thing happened there.

I drew in a harsh breath. The forest had been...blasted. It was as if giants had wrestled, ripping out undergrowth, uprooting and knocking over great trees so that they were stacked and twisted about each other like enormous jackstraws. It had occurred long enough ago for the logs to be rotten and for vines to clamber over, binding and squeezing, but not long enough for saplings to mature. A tornado?

There was a troubled feeling about the place. I said out loud what I thought. "A terrible thing happened there."

"*Oui.*" Monsieur's voice held an odd note. "I met an accident there several years ago."

"Did you fall off this bluff?"

"No. I was down below. I was in a hurry, not watching where I was going, and I stepped into a trap."

"How dreadful. I've noticed you limp now and then. Thank goodness you've healed as well as you have, though. Does it still pain you?"

Monsieur didn't answer. He was staring downward with distorted features, as if he were seeing something other than a snarled mess of trees and undergrowth. Something horrible. I followed his regard. From within a tangled growth of creepers like moldy hair, the decaying bark on one log resembled a grotesque face, with a dark cavity for a mouth and sunken eyes glaring up at us. A demon from hell.

At that moment, I felt something emanating from Monsieur. My throat closed up from a knowledge shooting straight to my heart. I leaned against a jagged stump as my knees went weak. What I had suddenly sensed was a deep and dangerous darkness in Monsieur, that I was immediately terrified of stirring up. A dread of incurring his hostility against me.

Why had he brought me to this frightful place? "It's late. I must get back for supper."

He did not respond. I turned and left him to brood alone at the top of the pit.

As I made my way back through the woods, I tried to banish

the thoughts I had just had, telling myself that although Monsieur was not a very nice person, it was because he was unhappy in the normal way that some people are unhappy due to "the slings and arrows of outrageous fortune." And he liked me, at least in a way. As if I was an ungainly puppy. I couldn't begin to imagine what frightful thing Monsieur had just been reliving, but it had nothing to do with me.

The vague hints he had dropped made me aware that he'd had a sad sort of life, full of disappointments, betrayals, and losses. He was not the sort of person I normally felt sorry for — he was not a helpless innocent — yet pity for him did tickle at my heart. Pity now mixed with this new, lingering fear.

My name was called from behind, and, although I wished I could ignore it, I turned to wait for Monsieur to catch up. When he reached my side, he strode along in silence.

"Why do you stay on at Wyndriven?" I could withhold the question no longer. "If you dislike the Petherams so much and your memories here are so miserable, why don't you leave and start over somewhere else? You could find employment where you'd be more content."

"I shall never leave Wyndriven Abbey."

"But you don't find it a *comfortable* place. Neither do I, really. It has a troubled atmosphere. Did you know that several murders happened here?"

"I am aware of it."

"Dorcas told me about the former owner who killed his wives. I thought she might have been making it up."

"No. Women did indeed die in the house. Because they had betrayed their husband."

"You're excusing murder?"

"Terrible deeds bring about terrible retribution. It was not pleasant or pretty, but real life is rarely pleasant or pretty. I knew the gentleman. I must wonder sometimes if there was also too much influence by *la fée verte*."

"La-what?

"The green fairy. Absinthe — a kind of spirit which can make a beast of a man. The husband kept it a closely guarded secret, but he was a slave to it."

"How many people did he kill?"

"Seven. Four wives and three others."

"How horrible. And he chopped them into bits and buried them in the garden?"

He looked at me, black brows arched, incredulous. Then he gave a short laugh. "No, indeed. What you have heard is simply the stuff of legend. The disloyal ones were all interred in a church."

"What happened to the murderer?"

"He died before he could be hanged."

I was in a brooding mood of my own as I wandered back into the school, leaving Monsieur in the gardens. These days the entire world seemed darker and more shadowy when I had been with Monsieur.

Chattering girls' voices met me. I was careful to avoid them.

A little more than a month had passed since I had arrived at Wyndriven Academy and my only companions remained Monsieur, Dorcas, and Leo. I had thought that perhaps Trix's group might take Dorcas and me up after what we'd been through together, but that had not happened. Monsieur disturbed me, a little unrelieved Dorcas went a long way, and the problems with my relationship with Leo were obvious. I enjoyed the companionship of my unnatural roommate, but so many evenings spent with someone dead could not be healthy. Whenever I watched the other girls with their easy camaraderie, a chill of lonesomeness clutched at my insides. Would I always be like this—an outcast, looking on?

Up in my room, Leo was present, still—or again—pacing to relieve his pent-up vitality.

"Have you been doing that all day?" I asked, tossing my bonnet onto the bed.

"'Twas you suggested I practice calisthenics, and walking is exercise. Although I fear—" he whirled to face me, "that I shall burst if I don't find a way out of here soon."

"Sorry I'm such a boring companion," I said, perversely stung that my occasional company wasn't enough entertainment for him. Even though that was exactly what I had just been thinking about him.

"No, it's not that," he was quick to say. "It's only that when you're not around I begin to feel agitated. I over-think. Is there some purpose to my existence that I need to fulfill? Is there something I'm supposed to do? I need to *do* something."

I wearily dropped to the edge of the bed.

Leo ceased his pacing to look at me closely. "Poor Fiona," he said remorsefully. "I've got to stop keeping you up so late. I forget that you need sleep, even if I do not."

"How could I go to bed last night when I had you as a captive audience for my poetry?" I tried to say it lightly. "I'm shy about my writing. I have never before shared it with another soul, so having you listen was intoxicating."

"I was honored. Your way with words *is* intoxicating. I could have drunk in several more hours of it and that's saying a lot because I've never been a literary sort of fellow."

"You put my maiden cheek to the blush."

"Fiona, don't turn every compliment into a joke."

"And you haven't even heard me sing yet," I said, laughing feebly so he would know I was still jesting, even though he had told me not to. "My rousing rendition of 'Finnegan's Wake' was ever so popular in the servants' hall back home."

He dropped to the floor at my feet and ringed his arms around his knees. I noticed something about him I never had before. Silver light hovered about his skin, angel-like in a subdued sort of way. "We'll come back to your singing—don't think we won't—but I've been thinking and I've come up with a theory about the spirits you see and why sometimes they exhibit the effects of their death and sometimes they don't. Perhaps if the *manner* of the entities' death is very important to them—such as the suicide of that pair back at your grandmother's place—then they continue to display it. However, with me, even the headache I had at first is gone. So I think I really don't care whether or not Godfrey murdered me."

"Hmm."

"Is that all you can say about my clever insight?"

"Sorry. I'm too tired and hungry to think. I'd better go down to supper." Still I didn't move.

"I've thought about you all day. For one thing, you're part of another of my theories."

My chest tingled briefly at the pleasure of being thought about. "Oh?"

"Yes. I've got to wonder if your arrival here is what brought me out of my oblivion—the No Place in which I was existing for so long. That I was drawn to you because you could see me and because…well, because you're *you*. And haven't you noticed how lately I'm around more than I was right at the first?"

"I have. Do you think," I asked cautiously, "that my hoping to see you is what brings you?" Swiftly I added, "Because of course I do like you and enjoy your companionship." I sighed. "If only the girls here liked me as much as you do. Just my luck…" I didn't finish the sentence, but he knew what I meant.

Sometimes I was so tired of being me.

I turned away from him. When my fingers felt touched with ice, I looked down and saw that he had reached up to cover them with his own large brown hand.

The next day Varina arrived.

If I could buy a wit, whip-like
And bright,
If I could trade a toe for beauty
That bites,
If I could change into another —
I might.
— By Fiona O'Malley

CHAPTER 16

VARINA

That morning I passed the bedchamber that the new girl was to share with three twelve-year-olds. Miss Petheram had explained the necessary reasons for this, but still I felt sorry for the girl. I heard Varina before I saw her. She was singing a popular new ditty, "The Daring Young Man on the Flying Trapeze," slightly off key. Through the doorway I glimpsed her drowning in a sea of billowing trunks and clutter. I scurried on when she met my eyes. She was extremely pretty. It scared me.

At breakfast, she bobbed a curtsy and beamed at us as Miss Petheram introduced her. The entire student body smiled back.

Varina Carlaton was exquisite and small-boned, with enormous azure eyes, a slightly cleft chin, and hair like spun marigolds. She was in all my classes throughout the day, and whenever I was near her, I felt like a hulking troll beside a fairy.

During the social hour that evening, Dorcas and I were slinking past the crimson saloon, when we heard Varina's voice from within. Like moths to a light, we were drawn to the doorway, where we hovered awkwardly, watching and listening. Trix, Sylvie, and Mary Dell clustered around Varina who was holding court on a sofa, her grass green challis skirts spread wide.

"Oh, y'all can have no idea how gallant General Gregg was," she was saying. "Why, when I wept before him, for fear he might succumb in battle, he actually gave me one of his old swords. With some rusty-red specks on it that *might* be blood. I shall never wash it, just in case. I have it on my wall at Twisted Trees—that's the name of our plantation. Mama wouldn't let me bring it here, or I would have."

"Did the Federals ever occupy your place?" A shuttered look came over Mary Dell's face as she asked her question.

"Of course they clomped all over the house," Varina said. "Had to, or they couldn't carry off everything that wasn't nailed down."

I swallowed with difficulty at the thought of my former Northern schoolmates, who had bragged openly about the souvenirs their soldier brothers had plundered from the South. At that moment I hoped no one would point out to Varina that Fiona O'Malley was from New York.

"You should've seen what those mean old devils did at ours," Sylvie said brightly. "Claimed every hen and cow were Secesh hens and cows and slaughtered even the babies. Left us to near starve. There was a battle waged in our cornfield, so we were having to dart around with pails and wet cloths to put out fires from minie balls shot into our walls. Afterward there were dead and wounded lying everywhere. One old dead soldier was sprawled for days by the well. We had to walk past it to get water."

No one could respond to that. Who would have thought that pretty, flighty Sylvie and quiet Mary Dell had come through such horrors?

Varina reached over to squeeze her hand. "Bless your poor, poor hearts. Nothing so dire happened to us. The Yankee officers stayed in a big ol' mansion in town. I am so glad they weren't closer because you never can know what one of those commanders, with the power of life and death over people, will do. Can you believe what that old Beast Butler ordered when he occupied New Orleans?"

Even those who most likely already knew what she was about to relate leaned forward to hear. I would have expected Trix to resent Varina for becoming the new queen bee, but Trix seemed as mesmerized as everyone else. There was a sort of magic about Varina. I nearly expected sparkles and glitter to fly from her fingertips as she moved her hands expressively. Could this be what Leo had meant about his Marietta's "pretty ways?"

"Why," Varina said, "he announced that any lady who behaved toward his soldiers with less than friendliness and courtesy, should be treated 'as a woman of the town plying her avocation.'"

"What'd he mean?" asked Mary Dell.

Trix yawned to show how boring she considered Mary Dell's ignorance. If Varina were the good fairy, Trix more than ever resembled a bad pixie.

"A fallen woman," Varina said. "A strumpet. Scandalous. And all any of the ladies had done to provoke it was to empty a chamber pot over Officer Farragut's head. Why, I can't imagine how I should have gone on had I been in New Orleans at that time."

The others agreed that they couldn't imagine either. I think everyone, including Dorcas and me, huddled outside the circle, felt as if we had received a personal confidence from the new girl.

"I mean," Varina cried, her eyes flashing with righteous indignation, "not *all* is truly fair in love and war."

There followed several stories from Trix, Sylvie, and Mary Dell about other atrocities committed by the hateful Yankees.

I could hold myself back no longer. "We're not army ants."

They all stared. I particularly felt Varina's regard turned on me in the doorway.   *Oh dear.*

"What were you doing, hiding there and listening to our conversation?" Trix said. "And what on earth are you talking about? I never understand a word you say, Fiona O'Malley."

I tried to look her squarely in the eye. "You make it sound as if northerners come to the South like African army ants to devour everyone and everything to the bone."

Trix sniffed. "We're well aware that y'all are people. Cold-hearted people are far more to be blamed for their brutalities than creatures."

"It was vital for the Union to be preserved." A little heat crept into my voice and my jaw tightened. I truly believed in what I was saying, even though I was alone with these Southerners. "And the South had no valid moral argument for holding people in bondage. Thousands of Federal soldiers were killed as well. Besides, it was the South who fired the first shot."

Fire blazed in eyes, shoulders were drawn up, and (I guessed) thoughts were gathered to argue fiercely with me. However Varina wouldn't allow it.

"You're right—Fiona—that we shouldn't lump folks together as if they're not individuals. You know, I've never once heard a real live Northerner share their side of the issue. Interesting." Varina indicated Dorcas now. "And who are you?"

Dorcas told her name.

Varina held out her hand and beckoned. "Won't you two come and sit down?"

Due to past experiences with pretty, popular girls, Dorcas and I both hesitated. Was it some trick? Would there be an unpleasant joke at our expense? A noisemaker hidden beneath the cushions? Would she try to make us ridiculous?

When Varina continued waiting expectantly, with the others watching, we had to move. I drew a shrinking Dorcas along with me. Varina squeezed over to the corner of the sofa and patted the horsehair cushion beside her. "Right here. Both of you."

As we settled ourselves, skirts squashed together, stiff on the edge of the seat, Varina began again. "There's a ghost at Twisted Trees. Or rather a haunt—that's what the Negroes call it. Under the trees that grow as one, twining round each other to give our plantation its name, a spark of light sometimes shines like a candle flame in the night. It'll move back and forth, back and forth, steadily, as if pacing. The story is that it's the haunt of a beautiful quadroon maiden, murdered by a jealous lover."

Dorcas glanced my way and I knew what she was thinking. That it was possibly as authentic a supernatural manifestation as the one that had supposedly been Bridey. Dorcas and I had never actually sworn each other to secrecy, but still, I considered it understood that we would never speak of that business to anyone else.

What would these girls say if I told them the real things I've seen?

My fingers nervously sought the rosary in my pocket.

"Does no one ever see anything more than a light?" Trix's voice was high, and she tightly clutched the crimson silk cushion she held in her lap. "Or hear anything?"

Her tone was so odd that the rest of us stopped whatever we were doing: me fiddling with my beads, Dorcas biting her fingernails, Sylvie nibbling pralines from a paper twist, Mary Dell twining her dark locks around her finger. We all waited.

"No, as far as I know, just the light," Varina said, and gave Trix a sharp look. "Honey, have you experienced something spooky yourself?"

Trix's lips tightened to a blade sharp line, as if she were deciding whether or not to tell us something. Then she said slowly, "I sleep in a wing removed from everyone else. My parents paid for a private room as I need it to be very quiet or I'm too tense to sleep. I requested this one particularly because it overlooks the topiary garden. Anyway, for the past several weeks, I've been hearing things at all hours of the night. It seems to be from above my ceiling, although it's hard to tell from where exactly. Footsteps and thumping and clicking—not rustling and scrabbling sounds such as mice would make."

Mary Dell brushed her hair from her face and gave a wavery smile, as if she were hoping Trix was joking.

"You actually *do* hear things that go bump in the night?" Varina said with a grin, alluding to the old Scottish prayer. "Do you suppose a long legged beastie in hobnail boots is frolicking about in the room above?"

Trix's mouth twitched slightly, but I could tell she was not amused. Her face was pallid within its frame of maroon hair. "And sometimes—" she spoke so low we had to strain to hear— "my things will be moved around. All the many cushions from the bed will lie scattered on the floor. My hairbrush will be on the bed when I left it on the bureau. A letter from my mother was lying open when I had returned it to its envelope. Once I found Jasper—he's my pet snake—out of his box and down in my bed-covers. He...*wriggled* when I put my feet down there."

"Why didn't you ever tell us this before?" Sylvie squeaked, indignant.

"I couldn't," Trix said. "It's all too crazy."

"Is anything ever stolen?" Varina asked.

"No. Just moved around so I'll know someone has been in there. I believe it *wants* me to know—that's its whole purpose for what it does."

"No doubt it's one of the girls teasing you," Sylvie said comfortably. "You know, an awful lot of people think you're a spiteful minx."

"Thanks." Trix scowled.

"Sylvie!" Mary Dell remonstrated.

"What?" Sylvie shrugged. "We all know it's true. You aren't very nice a lot of the time, Trix. Plenty of the girls would adore a chance to get back at you."

"If I'm not mean sometimes, I'll start to cry in front of every-one," Trix said, very low, "and I'd rather be mean."

"Or," Dorcas whispered, when no one had a response to Trix's confession, "do you suppose it's the ghost of one of those wives who were murdered?"

Everyone stared at her. I was surprised Dorcas had dared to bring up the subject in this group. Maybe that was why the others stared as well.

"It might be," Dorcas said, defensive. "It has to be someone, so why not them? We should find out more about what happened in this house. One of them could have died in Trix's room."

"Oh, *please,*" Trix groaned. The room seemed to grow colder, and she quivered from head to toe in a manner that was alarming to witness. It was hard to equate the Trix I had known up to now with this girl. She still wore her flamboyant fashions—her dress was a gaudy purple print—along with her flamboyant hair, but there was nothing confident or confrontational about this young lady.

"Oh, poor Trix!" Mary Dell cried. "No wonder you don't hardly eat these days. I declare, your back and chest have gotten *bony.*"

"What's this murder business?" Varina asked.

Dorcas told what she knew of the killings committed at Wyndriven, which wasn't much, and was incorrect.

"There aren't any cut up body parts," I had to say, "and there were seven of them, and they weren't just wives." Now it was my turn for everyone to look at me. "Sorry, Dorcas. That French man I was asking you about told me that much. He also said the wives had betrayed the husband, and the husband died before he could be hanged. That's all he told me." I spoke matter-of-factly—I had to, in order to convince them that the story was unimportant to me.

"If you get a chance, ply him for more details," Dorcas said.

"I don't think I could. He acted so peculiar about it."

"Well, Trix," Mary Dell said. "You must ask Miss Petheram for a key and keep your door locked. A girl needs to watch out for herself."

"I did get a key," Trix said. "Although I didn't explain why I wanted it. So I always lock it now, day and night. And still someone gets in."

"Tell Miss Petheram what's going on so she'll let you move to a room closer to ours," Sylvie said. "Better yet, move in with us.

We'll squeeze in another bed."

"No," Trix said, and a touch of her bravado returned, as she lifted her sharp chin. Two spots of color showed in her chalk-pale face. "I like my room. I'm not going to let it chase me away."

Sylvie shook her head. "Well, I think you're a stubborn goose. We're like to find you murdered in your own bed."

Everyone gave her shocked and annoyed looks. Sometimes people other than me stopped conversations with their ill-chosen words.

"You know we might." Sylvie refused to back down. "Look what happened to Fiona's maid."

"She wasn't murdered," Trix said flatly.

I said nothing while Mary Del hastily told Varina about poor Bridey.

"That happened so recently?" Varina looked shocked. "How awful for all of you, and especially for Fiona. I'm so sorry."

I didn't know anything to say, so I looked down at my lap.

Sylvie popped another praline in her mouth. "Maybe we should hold a spirit rapping session. You know, as in the song. Maybe we didn't have any luck with that séance we tried, but another time…"

Mary Dell jabbed her sister with her elbow. "Hush, Syl." She put her arm around Trix, and Trix did not shrug it off. "Anytime you want to sleep in my room, sugar, just come down and hop on in."

"Or mine," Dorcas said, surprising me once again.

The rest of us nodded in agreement.

"Let's not talk about it anymore." Trix's voice was shaky. "Anyway, if I die tonight—"

We all leaned in to hear what important thing she was about to say.

"—someone please take care of Jasper. And get rid of my box of cigars. Mama would never survive the shock if she knew about those things."

"Oh," Sylvie said, wrinkling her nose. "I thought you were about to tell us how much you love us."

Trix actually laughed. "That too."

"I expect it's like Sylvie said—one of the girls trying to vex you," Varina said. Then she clapped her hands together. "I know what let's do! Let's lay a trap for her."

"What kind of trap?" Trix asked.

"I don't know…a bucket of water over the door. A string connected to a bell somewhere that will ring if someone walks into it. Tar on the doorknob so if we see someone black-handed we'll know who the guilty party is. Nothing deadly."

"Why nothing deadly?" Trix gave a roguish grin. "Why not rig an arrow aimed straight for the heart?"

"Because, darling," Varina said, patting Trix's head, "that would be horrid."

"If it really is one of the girls," Mary Dell said, "we could bait the trap with chocolate, then fix something to pounce on her while she's devouring it in bliss."

The heavy atmosphere lightened as we all made suggestions, some realistic, some not.

Finally it was decided that for the first trap, we would spread a light coating of flour on the floor just inside Trix's doorway. That way, if it was disturbed, we could see for sure that the door was the culprit's entry point, and not some secret passage. We also could follow the tracks.

"Mary Dell and I will snitch the flour tonight," Sylvie announced, "and bring it to you to spread around tomorrow morning before breakfast. Miz Jump is always going on about girls stealing food, so she can just figure one of us is up to a little sneaky late night baking if she notices any gone."

"Doesn't Miss Petheram check to see if you're in bed?" Varina asked.

"She patrols the halls once a night around 11:00," Sylvie said. "She usually doesn't even open the bedchamber doors. If she does, she barely pokes her nose inside. The only care you have to take is to stuff pillows under your bedding or else don't get up till she's made her rounds. I declare, there's constantly folks flitting about this place at dead of night and no one ever gets caught."

"And," Trix said, "The Petheram's too lazy to ever check my room because I'm away from the others."

"I've never noticed her coming to my suite," I said. I had been worrying about it, because of Leo.

"That's because you're privileged here," Trix explained.

Shortly after, Miss Petheram rapped smartly on the door. "Lights out in fifteen minutes. Morning comes early. Good night, girls."

"Good night, woman," Sylvie said, and Mary Dell giggled.

Everyone but Trix, Varina, and I trickled off to bed. I didn't know why Varina lingered, but I stayed because I was wondering if I should urge Trix more strongly to move in with the others. Traps were all very well if it were some girlish mischief-maker, but what if it really was a spirit? Whatever was coming into contact with Trix could not be Leo, since he was limited to my rooms.

Perhaps it was Bridey's smoke, and if so, and it had caused Bridey's accident, it wasn't harmless. And if it could actually move objects…I had heard of ghosts who wreaked havoc because they could do so. The idea worried me—if this alleged Trix-spook could make a physical mark on this world, it could do real harm to people. However, even though I'd lately revealed it to a few others, the habit of keeping my Sight a secret was so deeply ingrained that I didn't know if I could speak up even now. Especially to someone as insensitive as Trix and someone like Varina, whom I wished to impress.

Yet I must say *something*.

While I was deciding how to begin, Trix spoke. "I didn't even tell y'all the worst thing."

"There's more?" Varina asked, wide-eyed.

Trix licked her lips. "I have nightmares. Or maybe they're not dreams. Maybe I'm almost asleep, but not quite. In them, someone is whispering, so low I can't tell if it's male or female. Sometimes it's just the same sound murmured over and over again, until it's almost a vibration in the air. Other times it taunts and calls me cruel names. And then it tells me to—to do things to myself. Vile things."

Varina and I were silent, from horror.

"Trix," I finally begged. "Please move in with someone. You could sleep in my sitting room till other arrangements are made. Please. And don't play around with séances anymore. These things are really, really dangerous. This place *is* haunted. Bridey—I haven't told anyone of this, but just before she died, Bridey told me she saw a very nasty spirit here."

"Really?" Trix raised her eyebrows. "Huh. What did she see?"

I told them.

"Goodness," Varina said, "what sort of school have I wandered into? My mama would *not* approve."

Trix actually giggled weakly. "Oh, you have no idea!" She looked thoughtful as she rose and tossed the cushion she had been holding onto the sofa. The old, delicate silk was shredded where she had clawed it. "Well, we *have* agreed to stop the séance business because it was silly anyway. But—" her voice grew defiant—"as I said, I'm not abandoning my room. Not for scheming schoolgirls and not for nasty spirits. I like it there. If I give it up I'll never get another to myself, and I can't ever sleep with other people around. Anyway, it's only been the last month that things have been happening."

"You could sleep better with other people than with a noisy ghost." I had to say it.

Trix gave me a withering glance. "Whatever Bridey thought she saw, I'm sure my particular specter is a mere stupid mortal. Besides, these things are aimed at *me*, not my room. They would most likely continue wherever I was. And nothing has actually hurt me. I bet eventually whoever is doing it will get bored and stop."

"Honey, you are awfully brave," Varina said as she stood, "and maybe just a trifle addled in your brains. But hopefully we actually will find out something with the trap. In the meantime, we'll walk you to your room every night."

Trix did not object. We moved upstairs together, each carrying a lamp.

My nerves went taut as we entered Trix's bedchamber, anticipating whatever might be awaiting us there. However, I could sense nothing otherworldly—no cold, no quivering air, no eerie sights or sounds.

The room was not large. It was furnished with heavy, ornately carved furniture. The wallpaper was spotted with a faded brown medallion pattern that looked like many miniature faces ogling down. It was a chaotic place, with clothing and shawls and a myriad of ugly hats strewn about, so it was surprising Trix could even detect if anything had been moved.

"Yes, it's muddled," Trix said, defensive. "*I* don't have a maid to clean up after me."

"Neither do I, anymore," I said.

Trix mumbled something that I took to be an apology.

I scrutinized the details of the room. "Let's see if we can find a secret tunnel or a priest's hole or something else they used to build in these old places."

"I've checked," Trix said. "I'm not a dunce. I've gone over every inch of paneling and mantel. If someone wanted to enter any way but through the door, they'd have to scale the stone wall up three stories and come through a window. There are no trees or decent footholds. Only a monkey could do it."

We poked around, but found nothing. The windows fit loose and rattling. Rusty stains streaked down the frames where rain had leaked and one latch was broken, but Trix was right—no one could have climbed up so far. Maybe not even a monkey.

"Oh," Trix said, "there is something else." She drew an overflowing trinket box from the top of her bureau and rummaged through it. Finally she held out an ivory shard, an inch and a half long and very slender. "I found this beneath my carpet a couple days ago. It poked into my foot. I know it wasn't there earlier because I had actually lifted up the edges of the carpet and swept beneath them the week before. The Petheram stood there and watched me do it because she said my room was a disgrace. I would have seen this. What do you think it is?"

Varina took the thing in her hand. I squinted down at it.

"It seems to be made of bone," Varina said. "Sharp as a nail. And look at the marks — it's been carved into this shape with a knife."

"Perhaps it was there all the time," I said. "You just overlooked it in your sweeping."

Trix shrugged. "Maybe, but I don't think so. I suppose whoever put it there hoped it would stab right through my foot, but it barely poked it." She replaced the splinter in the box. "Y'all go on." She hesitated, looking embarrassed. "Before you leave, though, will you wait while I check under the bed and in the wardrobe? Of course no one's there, but…"

Varina and I nodded, and I held my breath as Trix looked in the two places. Of course no one would be there, but…

No one was there.

Varina and I bade our reluctant goodnights to Trix, and heard the lock click as she turned the key.

And so we left her behind.

CHAPTER 17

FRIENDSHIP

As we stood where the corridor branched, Varina shook her head. "If I was her, I'd have all six of us in bed with me, and ten lamps blazing through the night."

"Me too," I said, shuddering.

I thought of the expression on Trix's colorless face as she closed the door between us. "And I'm wondering how, in all conscience, we can abandon her alone in there after what she told us."

Varina frowned. "What could we do? She wouldn't leave with us and we couldn't stay forever." To my surprise she took my arm. "Let's not think about this anymore right now. Trix will be fine—her type always is. Do you know, Fiona, from the moment I saw you this morning, when you passed by my room, I've thought we were going to be bosom friends."

Was she serious? She gave an open smile. Strangely, amazingly, unless she was a flawless actress, she was sincere. How should a girl respond to such a declaration? "That's nice," I said at last, and immediately thought I had chosen the wrong words. I bit my lip. "Would you—would you like to see my rooms? Or maybe you're too tired?"

"I'd love to."

I took a deep breath. "The fact is, Varina, I've never actually had friends." I made my declaration of guilt in a stilted sort of voice.

"Why ever not?" Varina asked.

I was so grateful that she didn't act as if what I had just revealed was only to be expected, that I continued the confession. "So often I simply don't know what to say to people. I look at them and my mind is blank. I can't think to ask someone where she got her darling hatpin. But then other times, when I don't consider at all before I speak, I'll come out with some outrageous comment."

Varina squeezed my arm. "Maybe that will be my favorite thing about you. With most people, even if you don't realize it, you have a pretty good idea of what they'll say next. You, Fiona, will continually bring surprises."

As we walked on together, I couldn't believe this was happening. In the past I had witnessed such spontaneous friendships as I studied other girls—pairs who instantly attached themselves to each other as if they were stuck with glue. After being together every possible moment, eventually they usually got into a bitter squabble, called each other spiteful creatures, and parted ways. Already I was terrified that such a fate might befall Varina and me.

There was no sign of Leo when we entered my suite. I was glad—I couldn't talk naturally to someone else with him listening.

Varina wandered throughout. "Your rooms are too sweet for words. And your clothes," she said, sweeping a loving hand through my gowns dangling from hooks in the wardrobes, "are amazing. You must have employed a dozen fine dressmakers."

"I don't know, really. My grandmother ordered them. You can borrow anything you like," I said, embarrassed lest, even though I hadn't boasted out loud, my possessions were bragging for me.

"Thank you for offering," Varina said, "but I like to make my own dresses. I have strong opinions on style and I'm clever with my needle."

"I'm so sorry."

"Sorry for what?"

"Well...For being able to afford fine dressmakers. And not being clever with a needle. Or anything else."

She burst into laughter. "Goosey. You didn't make your fortune—sorry, honey, it's obvious from your things that there's a deal of money—so you needn't be proud of it, but don't feel guilty either. I, on the other hand, am excessively vain about my dressmaking and you just heard me unashamedly boasting. I honestly prefer making my own things. I feel as proud of myself when I put on one of my creations as if I had painted a masterpiece. And unlike canvases, I can carry them about on my body to flaunt them." She paused, and put her fingers to her lips. "Come to think of it, I wonder if I could paint with watercolors on a silk panel and stitch it into a bodice? What do you think?"

"I think it would be lovely. You should do it."

"Hmm. I believe I will." She twirled in a pirouette, making her skirts bell out wider, and I saw that there were tall, thin triangles of shiny green satin sewn into the pleats of the challis, only noticeable in flashes as she moved. Her bodice fit sleek and perfectly tailored. The cut was stylish, but somehow different, and exquisite.

When she swirled over to the mantel, she picked up a framed

silhouette and asked, "Who's this?"

"My mother."

"What a splendid profile."

"It's the only likeness I have of her, and my memories of her aren't much. I believe she was considered beautiful. She was a stage actress before her marriage. I try to fill in her face with things my father told me, before he died a few years ago, but the picture I dream up stays blurred."

"Bless your poor little orphaned heart! So all you have of her is her shadow. From the looks of it, you do favor her, if that's any comfort. I'm so sorry you couldn't know her." She slipped an arm around my shoulders and gave them a squeeze."

"I had a more than adequate home and a caring grandmother. I've managed all right," I said, hoping now to change the subject.

Varina studied me for another sympathetic moment, then gave one last squeeze before she dropped her arm. Her mouth tightened. "Well, it's a crying shame for you, of course, since I'm sure your mother was a splendid person, but be advised that sometimes mamas aren't the most pleasant people to have around. Mine for instance. If my mother was here she'd be trying to worm out where your fortune came from and how she could benefit from it, and she's just so awful. "

I waited for Varina to expound further about the awfulness of her mother, but she did not. Instead, she told me that her father had been killed early on in the war. "I didn't want to mention it around the other girls because I didn't want them to feel sorry for me."

I wasn't sure if I should say I was sorry, since she said she didn't want that, so I said nothing. I was gratified that she had trusted me enough already to tell me.

"By the way," Varina said carefully, glancing up at me right after glancing down at my sewing basket, "it was truly dreadful about your maid. If you're having trouble managing without her, I'm quite good at hair and I actually like to mend rips, should you ever need any rip-mending. I also love to dispense too much unsolicited advice about becoming styles—it's one of the obnoxious ways I have." She cocked her head to the side and narrowed her eyes. "Your hair is such a nice color. I envy you those raven tresses."

I touched my coarse black locks. "Truly?"

"Why, yes. Light hair like mine is so common. And I'll tell you something, since we're to be good friends—do you see this?" She patted the ringlets cascading from a bun on the back of her head.

I nodded.

"False," she whispered significantly.

"False?"

"False. I haven't enough hair to fix as I like, so, lamentably, I must add to it artificially. You have a wealth of hair and should show it off more. If I was you I'd arrange it differently."

"Differently how?"

"I declare, if you would wash it at night, and then plait it when it's still wet, in lots of skinny braids like a little Negro child, all the way up to the roots, by the time it dries it would be entirely rippling. Then, in the morning, knot it at the base of your neck, but only loosely, or pull part of it back and let the rest fall free. I'm dying to see you that way."

"But wouldn't it be considered outlandish? My hair falls past my waist when it's unbound."

"And mine evidently stops growing once it reaches halfway

down my back. I wonder why?"

"I've never seen anyone else my age with their long hair worn the way you said. Not in company, anyway."

"Wearing yours partly down may not be the current style, but who gives a button for that? Your face, all bones and eyes and long full lips, is perfect for it. You would look dramatic and so — so medieval, and actually medievalness — medieviality — whatever — *is* all the fashion. Among painters, anyway. My cousin Archer told me, and he knows ever so much about art. Your locks would be a beautiful black waterfall."

I blinked several times, flustered. "Maybe more like a tangled black jungle," I said finally. "But I'll wash it tonight and try it that way tomorrow, if you don't think I'd look too silly." I would be brave enough to follow Varina's advice, since she was so good as to bother with me.

"And," she continued, drawing back and looking at me once more with that measuring sparkle in her eye, "we simply must pierce your ears. Dangly earrings would add to your marvelous drama."

"You think so?" I asked doubtfully, never having thought that bored ears were the lot in life for a girl such as I. "I love *your* earrings." They were golden squirrels each standing upon a golden walnut. "The squirrels have the naughtiest expression."

"Oh, if you like them you must have them," she said firmly, "for I have ever so many pairs. We buried all our jewelry and silver before the Yankees came, you know, so they remained safe, though I worried we'd forget where in the woods we planted them. I needn't have feared. Mama can smell out gold." She reached up and lightly touched my earlobe. "Let's bore them now, so you'll have the night to recover. Have you a big needle and a swatch of silk?"

I dug a needle and a bit of silk from my workbox and dropped into a chair. Varina loomed over me.

"Now, hold back your hair," she commanded. "There'll be a prick."

There was much more than a prick. The boring seemed to go on forever, and my nose stung like it did when I was about to cry, but finally the scraps of silk were pulled through each earlobe.

"Now," Varina said, "you are the proud owner of fine, newly-bored ears. You must wriggle the silk often, and apply cold cream nightly. In a month your lobes will be ready for rings." She removed her golden squirrels and tossed them to me. "There, take them now to remind you why beauty is worth the trouble. Goodnight, honey. Sweet dreams. I'm so glad you exist." And she sailed out the door.

"Nice ears," Leo said dryly, from beside the window. I had quit closing the draperies at night so that he might not feel so closed-in. Moonglow poured around him, and he shone with the same intensity.

I started. "How long have you been standing there?"

"Only about the last twenty-or-so minutes. You were so busy giggling and doing normal, girly things that you never noticed me, even when I made faces at you. Because I told you I wouldn't do any spying when you were unaware of my presence."

"I didn't actually giggle," I protested as I gingerly touched the silk in my ears. Ouch.

"Oh, yes, you did. Most definitely. A nice sound, though. Not the annoying kind."

"Did you do your calisthenics today like a good ghost?" I sank down to my rocker. "You don't mind, do you, that I jest about you being dead? It makes the whole situation seem less...unusual."

"Indeed it does. And I did do my calisthenics. Thank you for asking. I feel a proper fool storming about, but I've got to believe that if I can push hard enough, eventually I'll find a way out. Or if I jump high enough I'll manage to fly."

I couldn't keep from smiling at the image of Leo leaping about the room, flapping his arms like a bird.

"Oh," he said, grinning sheepishly, "go ahead and laugh, but I promise that when I had a physical body, it obeyed me implicitly and I was quite the sportsman. I won foot races against gypsies, and everyone knows how fast they are. In contests on board ship I could clamber up the rigging like a monkey. I'd forgotten the pleasure I used to take in physical activity." He dropped prone to the floor, and commenced raising and lowering his entire body by straightening and bending his arms, like a lever. Muscles swelled beneath his shirt.

"Goodness," I said, "how long did it take you to be able to do that?"

"Oh, only about a hundred and forty years." He hopped back up to his feet.

"With all your hard work, you're bound to make it out of here eventually."

"I will. I must. Of course I want to move on to my just reward, but if I can't, I fully intend to at least haunt the entire abbey someday."

A frightening thought occurred to me. "You won't ever leave for a different location of—of any sort without saying good-bye, will you?"

"Of course not, Fiona."

"You must miss everyone and everything so much," I said, looking down and picking at a thread that was pulled loose in my lace cuff. "Has all this changed you a great deal? Other than your body, I mean. Do you have the same character you had in your old life?"

"I'm steadier. I did seek a good time before."

"I guess you never have a good time now."

Bite your tongue! There you are being pathetic again. And jealous as a cat.

Such a nasty, tight feeling in my chest. I did not want to be an anxious, insecure creature. Begging for reassurance. Until I met Leo I hadn't known I was a jealous sort of person. But here I was, envious of Marietta, envious of his long-dead friends. It had to stop.

His expression turned gentle. "I have splendid times with you, Fiona. You know I do. I can't imagine how I'd manage without you now. I'm ashamed of the hours I once spent in public houses and low company. Be assured that your sharp wit is far preferable to any drunken, silly, crude mischief I might have once been amused by. And I truly appreciate some of the advantages of this spirit body."

"Such as?"

"I don't have to worry about changing clothes. Evidently my riding gear is simply part of me now."

"Is it actually stuck to you?"

He tugged on his collar, but it remained tight against his neck. "It certainly appears that it is. As if some of my skin is now white linen and brown broadcloth." He flopped down onto the sofa, with his knees hung over the arm.

"I would hate wearing the same dress every day."

"Ah, my girl, that is one way in which we differ. I take pleasure in the convenience. Never have to decide what to wear and never have to bathe."

"And I love a hot bath. Can you *feel* with your shirt skin?"

"I don't feel heat or cold, but when I'm lounging here I can sense there are these soft cushions beneath me."

"Speaking of cushions, I heard something disquieting tonight."

"Ah, disquieting things are usually interesting. What did you hear?"

"Objects, including cushions, have been moved around inside Trix's room, even when she leaves her door locked."

"So someone else has a key."

"Oh. A key. For some reason none of us thought of that. Anyway, we're going to set a trap—flour on the floor by the door—so we'll know if that's how the person gets in."

"Ingenious! Besides cushions, what sort of things were disturbed?"

"A hairbrush. A letter. Small objects of no consequence."

"Hmm…Which part of the abbey is your friend in?"

I described the location of Trix's bedchamber.

He looked thoughtful. "There is—or was, anyway—a secret staircase beside the chimney going up from the kitchen and into the attics, but that is nowhere near that room. Could someone climb in the window?"

"It doesn't seem possible. Too high and no footholds to speak of. I worry that it might be a supernatural thing, and that's what's so scary."

"Why?"

"Well, if it can shift material items, what if it hurts her?"

"Why must it be an evil spook?"

"Because—oh, you know..."

"Because, like Bridey once said, if people are good at all they're supposed to be caught up immediately into heaven." His tone was flat.

I looked at him miserably. "Well, you're clearly good, and you can't shift things, so I guess we made that assumption." My words sounded fumbling.

"It's all right, Fiona. You haven't hurt my feelings. You know I ponder these things all the time. Now back to your friend—it's far more likely to be one of the girls playing tricks, but if it's a spirit doing these things, it truly could be someone ordinary and relatively decent like me who was somehow left behind."

"Except that it also says mean things to her. Although she admits she might be dreaming. Let's hope you're right and it is harmless. But Trix isn't my friend. At least not yet. Till tonight I hardly knew her."

He looked puzzled.

"The girl with the moving cushions. You called her my friend, but she isn't one yet, though maybe she will be eventually. Stranger things have happened."

"I thought just now that you two acted as if you were close."

"No, the girl you saw isn't Trix. She's Varina, and she is indeed my friend. She's beautiful, isn't she?" I tried to make my tone light as I asked this, but there was a cold little flutter in my stomach while I waited for his answer.

Leo rolled over till he was face down on the sofa. "I suppose she looks well enough," he said in a muffled voice, "if you admire that style."

"What style?"

He raised his head. "If you must know, I thought she had the figure of a twelve-year-old boy and her face was that of a very pretty doll."

"So you do think she's very pretty."

He looked at me as if he could see right through me, which was odd when I was the mortal one. "Of course. Anyone would think so in an objective way. But I prefer the statuesque in females. And features with character."

"What about Marietta?"

"What *about* Marietta?"

"She was dainty and doll-like and you were in love with her."

Jealous cat! Stop it!

"I was, wasn't I?" He rolled to a sitting position. "Although I can hardly remember it now. I suppose — it's hard to explain — but since I told you my story, my mortal life has receded. As if those hundred years have finally come between the now and the then. However, yes, Marietta was beautiful. I guess it just goes to show that a gentleman's tastes can vary. Or else it shows that it's the spirit shining through that attracts me."

I stood and removed myself to the dressing room because the conversation was making me fidgety, even though I had brought it on. Leo followed. "You'll have to leave these rooms completely if you want to get away from me, my girl."

"I don't want to get away from you."

He whipped around in front of me and stood close — so close that I could have felt his breath if he had had any. My head was tilted back to meet his eyes, my five foot nine to his six foot two — or so.

A little smile played about his lips. "What I have learned since meeting you with your majestic height, Fiona O'Malley, is that I don't believe any girl who was much shorter than my nose would suit me these days."

I swallowed, and turned away from him as I sank down to my dressing table stool. As if it was the most important thing in the world, I commenced brushing out my hair for the braids Varina had suggested.

Leo said something more, which set me brushing more furiously.

What he murmured was, "My raven-haired princess. I shall call you 'Princess' from now on. Do you mind?" And then, in the mirror, I saw him reach out a hand as if he would touch my hair, and his fingers melted into the dark strands.

After a moment I shook my head, still with my back to him.

CHAPTER 18

TRAPS

"What do you think of Fiona?" Trix's tone held again the snippy edge it always contained whenever I was concerned. Except for last night.

Her voice was carrying. It reached me before ever I neared the doorway to the banquet hall. I was late for breakfast because I had been gathering up my courage to wear my hair down as Varina had suggested. First I had put it up, and then down and then up again, and finally I left it down. Leo had laughed. "Does it matter so much?" "Yes!" I proclaimed as I left him.

I paused just outside the hall, holding my breath to hear what the response would be from whomever.

"She's interesting and clever and fun," Varina answered in her delightful drawl. "I just love her."

"Didn't you see how she flaunts her wealth? And however much her clothes cost, they look appalling on her gangly body."

"D'you think so? I didn't notice any flaunting and I find her attire ever so smart." Varina said it simply, pleasantly, without arguing. And she didn't even know I was listening. It was so much nicer than having the same thing said to my face. The sweetness, the warmth of her words washed into the empty, starved bits of me.

Trix's thin lips were still compressed when I entered the hall a second later.

Varina jumped up. "Oh, Fiona, your hair is perfect! I knew it would suit! You look like a Greek goddess, or—or Joan of Arc! Isn't she perfect, girls?"

There were a few unenthusiastic murmurs, but Varina's reaction was enough.

She touched the chair beside her. "I saved this for you, and the one across for Dorcas." Then she looked up at Trix, who was sitting catty-cornered from her. "Ooh, Trix, honey, did you embroider your collar yourself? Would you teach me that stitch? It's gorgeous."

"Isn't it, though?" Trix's expression softened. "I learned it from my grandmother, who is Danish. I always called her Mimmy." She flicked a quick glance my way. "I'm thinking we should call *you* Fifi, by the way. As a nickname."

"Please don't."

She grinned, and it was actually somewhat friendly. She lowered her voice now. "The flour trap is all set, so maybe I'll know tonight how the intruder gets in. And today, if y'all want to have some fun, I'll share my cigars. They're simply delicious smokes."

Varina and I exchanged glances, and together said, "No, thank you."

Trix scowled and looked down at her grits. After a moment, she raised her eyes and asked, with studied lightness, "Did y'all do anything else after you dropped me off last night?"

I pitied her. She was jealous—an emotion with which I certainly could commiserate.

Varina gave an exaggerated yawn. "Oh, nothing much. It was *boring*." She met my eye, let out a soft, unladylike snort of laughter, and flicked the silk dangling from my left earlobe. I winced because it hurt, but immediately found myself overcome with laughter—something I didn't remember ever having happened before. The young ladies around us looked either mystified or irritated. Then Varina grinned at everyone, up and down the table, and filled them in on how she had "bored" my ears with a needle. The frowns disappeared, and instantly came requests from other girls for Varina's hole-pricking services.

She had the gift of friendship. She had wit, but was never unkind. As the days passed after her arrival, again and again I witnessed that Varina had only to smile at someone to make them feel as if they were well-liked allies. Often, at my past schools, I had noticed that the most popular girls weren't actually the most well-liked—they were simply the most admired. Varina, however, was both liked and admired.

Although she was everyone's friend, it was me, Dorcas, Trix, Mary Dell, and Sylvie, who formed The Club with her.

Mary Dell, I learned as the days went by, was good-hearted and sweet nearly all the time, although she could get into a peevish mood now and again. I saw her now as quite pretty in her own right, rather than as the unfortunate twin.

Sylvie was never cross, but I could understand how she might drive Mr. Harry crazy, since her silliness often drove *me* crazy, if not for the same reason. However, I still liked her.

Even Trix appeared to have finally mellowed toward me, especially when she saw that I let people borrow anything of mine they liked. And that I wasn't picky about how soon my possessions were returned. Or in what condition. I learned to ignore her sharp tongue and to realize that she didn't mean half what she said—she simply couldn't resist a witty, waspish remark.

The flour trap had not caught the culprit in her room, and neither had any of the other snares we had set, mainly because, according to Trix, the incidents had ceased happening. She grew less tense and more fun to be around by the day.

"Y'all know what we should do?" Varina said, a few afternoons after the molasses-on-the-doorknob trap had yielded no results. Her eyes sparkled as she roused the girls of The Club from where we had been lounging in the crimson saloon. We had all been sluggish throughout the day, and only after supper did we confess and blush and learn the reason—that morning four out of six of us had started our female time. "Enough moping. Forget that you're cramp-ish. We shall go inspect the room over Trix's. Her villain is getting boring."

I for one was glad the villain had stopped livening things up for Trix.

"Oh, dear," Mary Dell said doubtfully, "we're supposed to be working on our needlework. What if Miss Petheram catches us?"

Trix's eyes took on a roguish sparkle to match Varina's. "As if we'd let The Petheram catch us! Let's go." Evidently the villain's recent calmness allowed Trix to act flippant about it now.

The rest of us dragged ourselves up and out. Only Varina and Trix could have got us to do it. We made our way to Trix's wing and on up to the floor above, where we peeked in a few doors before Trix finally announced, "From the window's view, this must be the chamber directly above mine. This is where someone moves around."

We began to haphazardly inspect the space until Varina declared, "Y'all, stop where you are. We're messing up the tracks. Thank goodness no one cleans up here. Look!"

She pointed to where footprints marred the dust-dimmed wooden floorboards. Prints of narrow, bare feet.

We were silent for a moment, taking it in. They were so real.

"So it's no ghost," Dorcas said.

"There must have been more of them," Varina said, "but we've mussed everything up with our clodhoppers." She set her shod foot beside one of the prints. "It's only as long as mine. Some girl was sneaking about up here. But which one? Anyone can wander around anywhere in this place without being found out. And why would she go barefoot?"

"For silence," Mary Dell suggested.

"The fact that they're around the window...but then they're everywhere." Varina moved now through the prints and shoved up the window sash, which rose easily, and stuck her head out, peering downward. After a moment she drew back in. "It's still hard to believe anyone could climb down to Trix's window from here. It's a straight drop and a long way, with barely any crevices between the stones. Whoever it was would have to be *really* determined to get into your room. Not to mention brave. And a lunatic. So, Trix, how long has it been since something was moved?"

Trix licked her lips. "A couple of weeks. Not since I told you about it when you first came."

"And the voice?"

"What voice?" Sylvie squeaked. "Y'all didn't say anything about a voice."

"Trix sometimes hears someone talking," Varina explained. "Have you heard it lately?"

Trix shook her head. "I think whoever it was got tired of the whole thing."

"What did the voice say?" Sylvie asked.

No one answered her. Varina commenced poking around in every corner. "I know you couldn't find a secret entrance in your walls, but I wonder if we can find something from here?"

Sylvie opened her mouth once more, but closed it again, and began poking as well. We all joined them, even though we weren't sure exactly what we were looking for.

I lifted the dustcover draped over the bed and squatted down to see beneath. A pale-colored object lay just under the edge. I drew it out. A string of beads. A few of them fell off and plinked to the floor when I lifted it. I held up both ends so no more would fall, and retrieved the scattered ones.

"What have you got there?" Dorcas asked.

"Some sort of broken necklace."

"Not very pretty."

It was true it wasn't pretty, but it was interesting, although evidently only to me, since the others immediately went back to their searching. The beads were made from a pale wood, roughly carved into small oval and cylindrical shapes, and there was a grimy crimson tassel in one spot. I knotted the string, and slipped the strand into my pocket.

After a bit, Trix gave a soft gasp and a loud profanity.

We thronged to her side. She had pulled back a needlepoint

stool from against one wall. At first I could see nothing, but then Trix's finger disappeared into a dark little hole in the floor right beside the baseboard.

She bent now and put her eye to it. "It's a tunnel bored all the way through to my room, almost like a pipe. I can't see into it, but there's a glimmer of light. Whoever was up here could whisper into it and the sound would carry down to me. I wonder how the opening is concealed in my room?"

We all dashed then, our feet clattering down the long corridor and a flight of stairs, then through another corridor, until we reached Trix's chamber. She unlocked the door and we filed in.

"All right," Varina said. "Let's get our bearings." She eyed the proportions of the walls, measuring with her hands. "The hole has got to be up there," she said finally, pointing up at the ornate plaster decoration nearly hidden by the tester on Trix's bed. "It must be concealed by the curly-cue leaves, but it's got to be there."

I felt shaken by the discovery, but Trix seemed pleasantly satisfied. "Well, well, well. Now that I know for sure that it was a living person with solid skinny feet and a real mouth and voice, I'm no longer distressed by the whole thing. If some wretched snip of a girl at this school wants to scare me, so what?"

"But Trix," Varina said, "don't you find it creepy that she would go so far as to bore a hole through the floor?"

Trix laughed. "I admire her dogged strength, whoever she is. Maybe she's not so pathetic after all. The clever girl never let herself get caught in our snares — she's a formidable opponent. But no more traps. Too messy."

We seemed to laugh a great deal. When I was on the outside, girls' shrill peals of amusement annoyed me, but on the inside, I found us delightful. Who wouldn't want to be us? I felt almost heady with this life. I wrote no poetry, read little, and viewed my lessons as irritating interruptions. This was what I had been missing all my life — this sense of belonging and camaraderie.

Dorcas, however, was slower to trust the happy state of affairs.

"It's wonderful to have friends these days, isn't it?" I commented to her once in handwriting class. "Varina, of course, is perfect, but Sylvie and Mary Dell and even Trix are surprisingly nice now too."

Dorcas shrugged. "They've chosen to decide that your quirks are charming."

"They're nice to you too, aren't they?"

"Only because you pulled me along with you."

"Oh, that's not true. They like you."

"Do you think they decided my smallpox scars are charming? No, it won't last. Can't you feel it? Something horrific is going to happen soon and mess up everything. There's a buzzing in my bones just as there was right before my family all got sick."

I rolled my eyes. "Well, I intend to enjoy this life."

"Just you wait and see," Dorcas said.

"Just you wait and we don't see."

CHAPTER 19

BEING US

April 20, 1867

Darling Grandmama,

 I am sorry I have been remiss in my correspondence. You see, I have been enjoying life so much here the last few weeks that I haven't written anything except school compositions (and I hardly can bear to do that!). Since you always disapproved of my scribbling, as you called it, I expect you will be relieved to hear that I haven't penned a single poem lately.

 When you used to disparage my verses, it did make me cross and dejected. No longer. I understand now that you simply feared I might come to harm if I were always wandering about in a poetical trance. I suppose I have done some growing up.

 Anyway, you may set your dear, old, wrinkled mind at rest. Your beloved granddaughter is no longer solitary — I have real flesh-and-blood friends! And they are very nice girls, except for one, and I like her anyway. My best friend is Varina Carlaton. She has helped me ever so much. She has made me believe that I am actually not an awkward oaf, who people hate to see coming. Which thing amazes me. Varina says that I simply have so many interesting thoughts bouncing about in my head that sometimes I don't notice what my body is doing. She also said that generally other girls like you better if you're not perfect, so long as you don't get all upset and dramatical when you make mistakes. They like it if your hat is cattywampus (how to spell?) now and again. "Cattywampus" is a splendid word Varina uses and I have taken it up as well. Anyway, partly people are relieved that they aren't the one who's askew, and partly they're glad you're as big a dolt as they sometimes are. Varina said that every single person in this world has their secret fears and foibles, even if it looks as if they don't. Now I know that one of your secret (or not so secret) fears was that I would become a sad eccentric living alone with only books for company. (And ghosts, I might add. Did you know that your house is haunted?) I'm curious about what Varina's fears are, since she seems so self-assured, but I will wait until we know each other longer to ask.

I believe that what she said is true, don't you? It makes me think of a line from a poem by Robert Burns. "O wad some Power the giftie gie us to see ourselves as ithers see us! It wad frae mony a blunder free us." (He wrote it with an annoying Scottish accent, in case you can't tell.)

As I thought about it later, something occurred to me that maybe you have realized all along. In the past, whenever I sought out connections with others, it was usually with those who seemed in a worse position than myself—servants, abused animals, etc. I always thought it was kindness on my part, because I wanted to help, but was it perhaps because they were the only individuals I felt superior to and therefore could be comfortable around?

I feel very wise and insightful to have realized this. It helps my confidence now to know that inside every pretty girl or swaggering male there is hidden vulnerability. I had never considered that pretty girls and swaggering males ever, well, felt. Now I look at people such as Monsieur (he's a French man who works here, and for a few days, was my only companion, but I don't need him now nearly as much as I once did) and I sense mysteries. I wonder what hurts inside them.

I am enjoying myself so much that it frightens me.

Now I will give you an example of how your granddaughter is learning confidence. Picture this (and, as you conjure up my image, imagine my hair falling long down my back, since that is how I wear my tresses these days. And I am wearing my olive plaid taffeta skirt that we bought at Arnold and Constables.):

In fancywork class, I am listlessly jabbing my needle into an especially ugly bit of knobby petit point. (You know how I hate needlework — although perhaps I am getting a leetle bit better at it these days.) Suddenly I realize that Varina is signaling me. I look at her questioningly.

She motions slightly toward my hem. My petticoat is not showing. I had not stepped on the hem to tear the band of velvet trim. I hold out my hands, mystified. What?

She lifts up the bottom of her own delaine gown to show her beaded slippers.

I lift my skirt, and absolutely freeze. I am mortified.

Peeking out is one scalloped leather boot and one bronzed kid slipper. How have I come out with mismatched shoes? As you know, with me there is no telling. So I had been walking around like this all day. Who has noticed? I jerk my feet back in and puff my skirt carefully over my shoes, but not before everyone in the circle has seen. They wait in silence for me to do…something. Apologize? Run humiliated out the door?

Varina's shoulders shake. She begins to titter softly, and then louder. Her infectious giggle sets everyone else, including myself, laughing. Then Maggie Simmons snorts loudly, and Mary Dell cries, "I think I popped my corset!" and soon it seems that we all will split our sides, we laugh so hard.

"*I hoped to start a new fashion," I say loudly. (This shows how confident I am becoming.)*

"*Oh, you have, honey child." (All the girls here are very Southern, and often call each other "honey" or "sugar.") Immediately Varina takes off one of her slippers. "Who wants to trade?" Soon everyone in the room has mismatched shoes.*

I stopped writing.

Even then, even as I was laughing, I had looked closely to judge whose feet might be the same size as the prints in the room above Trix's. It was hard to tell anything with feet inside stockings.

Varina was always coming up with brilliant ideas to keep us in scrapes and to entertain us. A light would spark in her eyes, she would tap her fingers together in a captivating manner, and say, "Y'all, you know what we should do?" And then she would tell us, and we would do it. It seemed as if I were receiving an intense course in what young ladies do for amusement.

During the social hour in the evenings, The Club usually gathered in my sitting room, since it was cozier than the public places. I was grateful that if Leo were present, he would slip into the other room, so as not to intrude and distract me.

Too bad he distracted me wherever he was. These days I could feel his essence even when I couldn't see him. (Especially when I was in the bathtub, and I knew he was somewhere close—at those times I felt particularly naked.)

The Club called these gatherings our "soirees," in honor of my grandmother's social events. After a collective loosening of corsets, we would do our school work or chat or play games or arrange each other's hair. I served macaroons, as well as grape juice, which we declared wine, and poured it from a crystal decanter into my own brought-from-home jewel-colored crystal goblets.

Often Mary Dell would play the piano and we would raucously spin out popular tunes such as "Annie Lisle" or "Camptown Races." Sometimes, though, all by myself, I would sing Irish ballads my nurse had taught me—"The Black Velvet Band" or "The Last Rose of Summer."

One evening, we were all trilling away on "Wildwood Flower," when Varina said, "Y'all hush now. Let's hear Fiona sing this by herself."

And so I sang, self-consciously at first, but soon with growing confidence:

"I'll twine 'mid the ringlets of my raven black hair,
The lilies so pale and the roses so fair,
The myrtle so bright with an emerald hue,
And the pale aronatus with eyes of bright blue.
I will dance, I will sing, and my laugh shall be gay,
I will charm every heart in this crowd I survey,
But I'll long to see him regret that hour
When he hurt and abused this pale wildwood flower."

There was silence for a moment, so I knew I had stirred them, and I noticed that Leo was watching from just inside my bedchamber doorway, his luminous blue gaze bright. A little thrill tickled through me as he turned and slipped from view.

Everyone but Varina was soon chattering again after the song, dragging my attention away from Leo. Because Trix began a rousing rendition of "That Daring Young Man on the Flying Trapeze," and I joined in, it took me a moment to feel Varina's fingers tightly clenched on my arm. I looked at her, bewildered, and stopped warbling.

"You sing of pain with such understanding," she whispered. "No one ever...*hurt* you, did they, Fiona?"

"What?" I drew in my brows. "What do you mean?"

She shook her head hastily. "Oh, nothing. It's just the way you sang that...Never mind. But if they did, you know you're not alone and you have a friend in me, no matter what." She was unusually quiet the rest of the evening.

Although I understood that many others had experienced worse, life had given me a healthy (or unhealthy) share of pain— my mother's desertion, humiliation at school, the abuse by The Two. Did something of the hurt of those encounters show in my countenance? My manner?

I wandered over to the open window, to gaze out into the night.

Below me, bathed in the watery starlight, stood a figure. I caught only a glimpse of an upturned, narrow face and shining eyes reflecting the moon, surrounded by a cloud of wild black hair, before she caught sight of me, and the girl was off, dashing lithe and barefoot into the shadows. I had seen her before—in the woods, when I sat on the ruins with Monsieur.

I turned slowly back to the others, slightly dazed by the girl's odd, rapt, intense expression. "There was someone out there. A Negro girl. Listening to the music."

"Sparrow, most likely," Trix said carelessly. "Was she creepy? Sparrow is particularly creepy. She lives over yonder in the woods with her grandmother. She flits around Wyndriven's grounds sometimes, and for the two minutes she went to school here last semester, the only time she seemed happy was during music class. You know — music soothing the savage breast and all that."

"She was actually a student here? Why ever did she stop coming?" I asked.

"Oh, bless her poor heart," Mary Dell said. "She hated it. I felt sorry for her because she was so different from everyone, being the only colored student and all, but then I saw that she didn't care a fig about that. She didn't hardly notice the rest of us. Including the teachers."

"When she was younger," Dorcas said, "Miss Sophie taught her to read and write, out at her grandmother's place."

"Her grandma is a witch, by the way," Sylvie chimed in.

"A witch? What kind of witch?"

"She uses herbs and potions and African magic," Trix said. "And there's always animals lingering around their cabin. Bears and wolves and skunks and snakes. Although, I think the animals are bewitched by Sparrow, not the grandmother. The witch's name, believe it or not, is *Anarchy*."

"We don't have witches up north," I said. "Except in Salem, of course."

"Anarchy supplies Wyndriven with honey and herbs," Dorcas continued the story. "Some girls are a little nervous about the food because of that. Anyway, Miss Sophie tried to get Sparrow to come here to school. She stood up to all the folks who threatened to withdraw their daughters when Sparrow started attending. Sparrow didn't stay long enough for any of them but Deborah Wirtz to actually leave, though. Sparrow was only here about a week, and I don't believe she did a lick of schoolwork the entire time — just stared out the windows. Don't y'all think that the main reason she quit coming — " Dorcas glanced at Mary Dell, Trix, and Sylvie — "was because she's a wild thing and couldn't stand to be shut inside all day?"

"She's an animal all right," Trix said.

"A shy woodland creature," Mary Dell said, brushing her stray hair back with her hand. "You don't expect her to talk English when she opens her mouth, but she did, just the one time I heard. It was when Mr. Moss recited that line by Edgar Allan Poe — "

"Who's no gentleman by the way," Trix broke in. "Mama says no school should teach Poe's trash. I like him, though. He's rather daring."

"Which line?" I asked. I was losing the trail of the conversation.

"'The silken, sad, uncertain rustling of each purple curtain,'" Dorcas, Sylvie, Trix, and Mary Dell said in unison.

"'Thrilled me, filled me with fantastic terrors never felt before,'" I joined in, licking my lips over the luscious words. "What did she say?"

"Why," Mary Dell said, "she let out this really long breath, and said out loud, 'Say it again.' Just like that. And Mr. Moss slapped her hand smartly with his yardstick and sent her out for interrupting while he was reciting. She ran off and never returned. That was the only time I ever heard her speak, but I suppose she talks to her grandma and Miss Sophie."

"Her clothes were the best part," Sylvie said. "Miss Sophie bought her all kinds of nice things, but she wouldn't wear anything right. Made me itch to fix her all the time."

"She was wearing a full skirt just now," I said. "It was too short. You could see her long limbs."

Sylvie grinned. "Do y'all remember when she showed up barefoot, with only a red satin petticoat for a skirt?"

"Was it a pretty red satin petticoat?" Varina asked.

"I guess so," Sylvie said doubtfully.

"Then I don't blame her," Varina said. "Who decides what's underclothing and what's overclothing? Is there a law? And why make the prettiest part of our apparel the part no one gets to see? Ridiculous. Admit it, you've always wanted to wear it showing outside yourself."

"There should be. A law, I mean," Trix said. "Seems to me that Fiona *wants* her underclothing to be seen. Don't you ever close your draperies at night, Fiona? They're always wide open. Even in the dressing room. Do you think you have such a sweet figure that all the world should see you dressing? Or do you just want to display your extra fine embroidery?"

"Balderdash!" I exclaimed, borrowing a word Leo sometimes used. "All the world can't see in. I tested it once with Bridey standing below. Unless you practically lean out the window, no one can peek in from outside. Besides, who'd be trying to look in?"

"The bad boys from Albion Academy for one," Trix said, "who have been known to haunt the woods watching for girls. And Sparrow for another."

"She wasn't looking, she was listening." I sighed and walked back over to the window. "I wish I hadn't chased her away."

"She'll be back," Dorcas said. "She loves the gardens. Especially around the summerhouse. I see her sitting there often."

"Y'all know what we should do?" Varina said. "We should leave Sparrow a present in the summerhouse. Think how surprised she'd be."

"Maybe a nice box of caramels," Trix said, giving me a sly nudge.

I wasn't sure how to respond, since that trick still rankled, so I took the mature, ladylike approach and stuck my tongue out at her.

Because Varina suggested it, everyone agreed, and that was how we started leaving little gifts for the shy, fey Sparrow — ribbons and sweets and a copy of "The Raven," by Edgar Allen Poe, all printed out in Mary Dell's best handwriting. We set the gifts on the stone table in the summerhouse, with Sparrow's name attached, and they were always gone within a day or two. Hopefully not taken by the bad boys from Albion Academy.

And one day, to our delight, we found a chunk of honeycomb, dripping with sweetness, wrapped in leaves. Sparrow was giving back to us.

During these weeks, the two men in my life — Leo and Monsieur — behaved true to character. At night, after my friends were gone, Leo was amusing when I needed to laugh, interesting when I needed to be stimulated, and serious when I had real concerns.

I enjoyed his viewpoint on every subject, and felt so protected because of his nearness as I drifted off to sleep, that I no longer needed a night light. Continually I reminded myself that Leo's companionship and humor were dead companionship and humor, the lips that smiled had been dust for a hundred years. His very existence at this time and place was unnatural and some sort

of cosmic mistake. We should have spent all our time trying to figure out a way to send him on, and yet it was as if we had forgotten
we were supposed to be doing that very thing.

Leo always called me "Princess," now—and I loved it—but
he had said nothing more that might be equated as "lovery." I
was anxiously waiting for more, however impossible our circumstances were.

It was ridiculous to be sweet on a ghost.

If only he didn't seem so very alive.

Unlike Leo, Monsieur's charms did not grow with acquain-
tance. I didn't see him often, but when I did, he no longer related
entertaining stories. Instead he glowered, criticized, and accused
me of neglecting him, always in a careless, amused tone, but his
real displeasure was palpable. His contempt of everyone.

Speaking with Leo warmed and restored me. Hearing Monsieur's malice again and again, was exhausting. I found myself
shrinking back or recoiling at everything he said. In spite of my
pity for him—for he was terribly unhappy—and my gratitude that
he had comforted me when I was lonely, eventually I could stand
his company no longer. Since he never approached me when others were near, I tried to stay close to a group. On the occasions
when he did find me alone, I would make excuses and scurry off.

I reveled in my new friendships. However, perhaps because
of Dorcas's comment about these good times not lasting, I could
not shake the uneasy sense that something was hanging over our
heads. That sooner or later something ghastly would occur to ruin
everything. And so I set myself to enjoy life frantically before that
happened.

CHAPTER 20

DANDELIONS

The woods were lit now with redbud and dogwood blossoms. Pink azaleas in the gardens ruffled in spring gusts, the peach orchard was a mist of white, and the first dandelions dotted the grass like spilled gold. The students of Wyndriven Academy often basked on the raggedy lawn, soaking up sunshine before it became too summer-hot and before carnivorous insects came out in famished fury. We made dandelion chains. We played with sweet new kids, keeping a watchful eye out for Atlas, the foul-tempered billy goat.

Sometimes I would see Mr. Willie, trudging about with his wheelbarrow or his pruning shears.

One day I showed him a bouquet of dandelions I planned on leaving for Sparrow. "Aren't they pretty?" I asked, beaming because I always beamed at Mr. Willie. "Dandelions are my favorite flower. I love their lion faces."

As usual, he did not look me in the eye. This time he seemed to gaze off to the left somewhere. "Most folks hates them things 'cause they reckon they is noxious weeds. I considers them lilies of the field, clothed glory-bright by the good Lord himself." He smiled shyly and the lines deepened in his leathery cheeks. "Back before the war busted everything wide open, I was a preacher man. Back before I done lost my congregation."

I knelt beside a black-spotted kid who had come trotting up on dainty hooves. I rubbed his hard little head and budding horns. "You must miss your preaching. What happened to your congregation?"

"Once the Bluecoats come round, in them first days, no one could stay put. Folks hankered to seek their kin or wanted to see if something might would be better yonder. Always yonder." He squinted up at the sky, where geese, flashing silver from sun on their wings, passed overhead. "I try not to grieve over them, 'cause the Lord'll care for my lost flock just as He cares for them birds, and all us lambs of His fold."

"What's that?" I leaned in to put my ear beside the kid's mouth, paused, and then looked up at Mr. Willie. "This little fellow says that at Wyndriven we should consider ourselves the kids of His fold instead."

It took a second for me to realize that the rusty, creaking sound I heard was Mr. Willie's laugh. "Ain't he a caution? We sure got fine goats hereabouts. All except old Atlas. That beast done got the devil in him."

I looked into the kid's freakish, slit-shaped pupils, and decided I needed to consult the preacher man. "Mr. Willie, do you believe that after death spirits sometimes remain behind in this world?"

He didn't seem surprised at the question. "I reckon angels and demons both does walk the earth, unseen."

"Why is it allowed by God?"

"Could be the angels been set a chore they got to complete."

"What about the demons?"

He rubbed his chin, considering. "Might be they're trying to flee from the good Lord so He won't cast them down to the fiery pits. But they can't hide out long, any more'n ol' Jonah could."

"What if someone—a regular person—can see them?" I said slowly. "Is it a mistake God made?"

"The good Lord don't make no mistakes. I'd say He got a purpose for that regular person seeing them things."

"If only the person knew what it was." I sighed and held up the dandelions. "Well, I'm taking these to the summerhouse to leave for Sparrow. Do you know her?"

Mr. Willy nodded. "I swannee, 'course I does. She's named Sparrow 'cause of that scripture about them birds—so she won't never fall to the ground without the Lord knowing it. And that child minds me of a bird too, flitting about the woods. They done tried to tame her and keep her at school, but she up and left. Couldn't never be caged nor tied."

I left one dandelion with Mr. Willy, and took my leave.

The summerhouse rose on a hill above the lake, its weathered stone carved into fretwork with circular windows. Gray, gnarled wisteria trunks snaked up the sides, while branches and leaves roofed the structure. It had been dazzling when the wisteria was a lavender cloud, but seemed drab now with the blossoms drooping all yellow-beige and withered.

She was there inside. Sparrow.

The girl was sitting on the table, with slender brown ankles crossed below a bright green calico dress. She started and jumped down when I entered, and cast about with those slightly slanted, bright brown eyes, poised to dash away. However, there was no way out, with me filling the doorway with my skirts.

"I'm glad to finally meet you, Sparrow," I said, trying to speak lightly, in a particularly friendly tone, so she wouldn't consider me the least threatening.

She acted as though she didn't hear me, still edging along the wall, possibly hoping to slip around and break free.

I thrust out the dandelions. "These are for you."

She looked at them for a moment, then took them carefully, with a little perplexed line between her eyes. "Y'all been leaving presents. Why?" Her voice was so soft I had to lean in to hear.

"Because we wanted to be friends. We loved the honeycomb. Delicious."

"From Memaw's own hives. Sweetest there be. But..." She paused. Sparrow evidently was not like most people, and certainly she was the opposite of me—she didn't speak without reflection simply because someone was waiting. Finally she continued. "Didn't no one spare me a thought when I stayed at that school. Thought I mattered less than a chigger bug. That's why I cleared out. No need to mess with them fools."

I smiled at her opinion of the young ladies of Wyndriven Academy. "I'm shy around them myself. I expect they didn't understand you, so you made them nervous."

Her thin shoulders twitched. "They sure jittered *me* up."

"Also they think your grandmother is a witch." As soon as I said this, I worried she'd be insulted, but Sparrow merely rolled her eyes.

"Memaw ain't no witch," she scoffed. "She don't eat no one's souls and she don't ride no one by night, nor turn herself into no animals." She eyed me thoughtfully. "*You* wasn't there at the school when I stayed there. You the one I seen that day out yonder on the rocks. And then up in the window when I was listening to the music."

"Yes. I saw you those times too. I wanted to talk to you. You looked so interesting. Dressed like a gypsy and running like a deer."

Her eyes narrowed as she pondered this. I couldn't decide whether she was beautiful or merely striking. "I done read about them gypsies. They favor music and dancing and freedom. Could be I *am* a gypsy."

Perhaps I had passed some test, because she now climbed back up to perch on the table, resting her hands loosely in her lap as though preparing for a nice long chat. Her limbs and feet were covered with scratches and scrapes. I hoisted myself up beside her.

"You like poetry," I said. "Do you also like to read?"

"'Course. After Miss Sophie learned me my letters, she said I took off and flew with the words. Since then, I read everything. Miss Sophie keeps me in books." Her glow dimmed. "Education ain't all good, though. I ain't so wild and easy as I was before I got it. I got responsibility. Right this minute, I feel responsible to tell you to beware that man."

"What man?"

"That man you was talking to on the rocks. He ain't no good."

"Monsieur? Well, I have to admit he isn't very nice. Stimulating, though. And I feel sorry for him."

She considered this. "Folks ain't like beasts of the forest, all simple and clean inside. Some folks is twisted in their guts and in their thoughts. That's why I stick mostly to critters. I'm just telling you, that man's the twisty kind."

I remembered the fear shooting into my mind that day in the blasted wood. It seemed a very long time ago. "I don't suppose he's actually dangerous. Some people aren't pleasant, but they would never actually hurt anyone." I didn't want to talk about Monsieur any more. "Since you enjoy music, won't you come into the school now, and we can play the piano and maybe sing a little?"

She seemed torn. "I got a dulcimer at home to play, and I liked a piano I heard when I was at school that time." Then her lips tightened and she shook her head violently, such an arresting combination of fey and fierce. "No. I ain't studying on seeing them fool girls again."

"We'll sneak you in. We'll go through back ways up to my rooms so you'll meet no one." I held out my open hand to her. She stared at it. Then she raised her own hand, and gingerly took mine. Her palm was small and rough and dry. She hung back a little, and I had to pull her a bit at first, but gradually she moved swiftly, gracefully, on her bare feet. We slipped from bush to bush, sneaking into the building at last by a side door.

She padded along beside me over soft carpets and cold marble, up twisty stone back stairs, and at last, undetected, we were in my sitting room.

Leo was sprawled on the carpet, his elbows thrust out and his hands behind his head, gazing up at the ceiling.

Sparrow's eyes started at sight of him, and she turned to run back out, but I still held her hand tight.

"You see him!" I cried, as I slammed the door shut behind us.

"You see Leo."

He bolted straight up, staring. "She does?"

Sparrow snorted. "Of course I does. I ain't blind."

Our eager story of Leo's haunting my rooms fascinated Sparrow so much that she *almost* quit gazing longingly at the piano. With Sparrow there was no artifice, no wasting time on things that did not matter to her. No wonder she hadn't lasted long at the school. "So," she finally said to Leo, "you're a haunt. I could've guessed, you shining bright as new silver."

She dropped the bouquet of dandelions she had still been clutching, ran to the instrument, and sank down to the stool. When it shifted as she first sat, she whirled around on it with her legs poked straight out. After coming to a stop, she touched first one key, then another, intent. She gave a satisfied sigh and began spreading her fingers to play chords. Within a few minutes she was picking out "Listen to the Mockingbird."

"Forget mockingbirds," I whispered to Leo. "Listen to the sparrow. She can just sit down and miraculously play a melody."

"A girl with such a name *should* be musical."

I gathered up the dandelions and bunched them in a glass with some water. "My favorite flower," I told Leo.

He chuckled. "It would be."

Leo and I settled down in the armchairs and listened as Sparrow played one tune after another, some I recognized and some I did not. Often she sang along, in a high, clear, somehow haunting soprano.

The clock chimed the hour. She dropped her hands and jumped up from the stool. "What?" she said, as if the clock had just spoken a word.

"That's just the clock," I said. "It's nearly five, so I must dress for dinner now."

"I got to go," she said. She turned and touched one piano key. "Bye, piano," she whispered.

Leo laughed. "You'll see it again, Sparrow."

"I'm so glad I finally met you," I told her. "And I'm so glad Leo is visible to you too. It's a relief that someone else sees him. It proves he's not a dream."

Leo looked at me curiously. "You've been thinking I'm a dream?"

"Not really," I said, with confusion. "But…It's hard to explain."

"I know what you mean, of course," he said. "With no one else to back you up, you have to sometimes wonder about me. Sometimes I wonder myself if I'm in my imagination. So good to know for sure that I am not. Thank you for that, Sparrow."

She laughed a pretty laugh. "How you know *I* ain't part of the dream?"

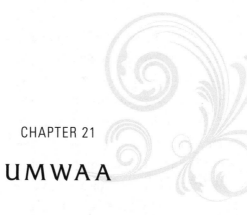

CHAPTER 21

UMWAA

One bright, apple-green late-April afternoon, the older students were told to gather together in the cavernous kitchen for a candy stew. The younger girls would have their stew later. Ours was to provide some sticky refreshment for our evening festivities — a supper and "practice" ball, with the gentlemen from Albion Academy joining us. It had been an annual tradition at the school in the last years before the war and it was to be taken up once again. I idly wondered if Mr. Thatoor, the young man I'd met on the stagecoach, would be there.

Varina and I reached the kitchen first and stood gazing about while we waited for Miz Jump, the cook, to notice us.

No one could have realized what a pretty day it was outside by this dusky, stifling interior, with its gigantic bake ovens and hanging silver covers that bulged out large enough to enclose a goat. Even my grandmother's enormous kitchen was a cozy place compared with this. Maybe it was my imagination, but I fancied that, lurking beneath the enticing scent of molasses boiling in two great copper kettles, I could detect the ghosts of centuries of food that had been prepared within these walls—the odors of blood, smoke, and spices soaked into the stones.

Miz Jump frowned when she finally saw us, as if she wasn't best pleased with this activity, and stalked over to thrust a voluminous apron at us, each in turn. She clucked as she watched Varina's small figure drown in the white folds. "Lawzee. Some of you gals at this school ain't no bigger'n a pot boggin," she said in her raucous, hoarse voice. From the set of her lips, she disapproved of smallness, possibly because it might be considered a criticism of her cooking.

Varina grinned and gave me a significant look. I knew we would laugh about Miz Jump later on. She was a tall, raw-boned woman who reminded me of chewed twine—I would be sure to tell Varina that. She had a drooping, gray-beige, sweat-beaded face outlined by colorless brittle hair pulled back in a tight bun, broken strands poking out frantically.

"What's that?" I asked Miz Jump, as I pointed to a massive block of wood in the center of the stone floor.

"The killing block," she said, nervously glancing about as more of us filed in and crowded around her to don aprons. "How many of y'all is there, anyways? Miss Petheram never said there'd be such a passel."

"This is all of us now," Varina answered. "The younger girls and boys are coming after supper tonight. What does the block kill?"

"It be where animals' heads is chopped off. When the beast is butchered right here in the kitchen, the flesh is freshest there is." Her mouth twitched and I guessed she was taking malicious pleasure in educating us on where our food came from.

Varina nudged me. "That must be where they got the boars' heads they were always wolfing down in the old days." She made a face as she whispered and I knew she felt as I did—that we wished we wouldn't have to eat another bite prepared in such a place. Even though we would, of course.

"By the way," I whispered back, "What exactly *is* a pot boggin?" We both giggled.

Some of us set to cracking nuts and picking out the meats to toss in pots. Others (Varina and I among them) hovered red-faced over bubbling cauldrons, stirring like schoolgirl witches. Sylvie and Mary Dell, who had the forethought to bring fans, wafted them vaguely about to stir the air.

Miz Jump wrung her hands and gnawed her lip. She made me nervous because we made *her* nervous. She looked as if, at the least provocation, she might do something barbarous—slap, scream, snatch away spoons, dash the hot mixture to the flagstones.

She was on me in an instant when I spilled a blob of boiling syrup as Varina and I turned it into the greased, shallow pans that were set out on chairs, stools, and even the floor. "And why," she shrieked, "I got to play mammy to a passel of clumsy, spoiled, useless gals, is more'n I can guess, when I got a whole fancy supper to fix for tonight." She snatched up a towel and threw it in the face of one of the jittery kitchen maids, who had been standing watching the process with guarded brown eyes. "And when y'all go about filching victuals like you do, I never know from one day to the next what'll be left to cook with."

"Who steals food?" Trix questioned. "Really. Have you any idea?"

"As if you didn't know," Miz Jump snapped. "Y'all sneaking around at all hours of the night, gobbling up anything that ain't nailed down."

We looked at each other guiltily, trying to remember if, other than the flour and molasses for our traps, we had ever done such a thing. It sounded so likely that we thought we probably had, although we had forgotten it.

As the candy cooled, we buttered our hands and began pulling the gooey stuff. Some of it we twisted into thick, golden-brown sticks, others we braided or yanked into long, rope-like pieces to be cut into drops. Dorcas and Mary Dell and a few other artistic types fashioned wreaths and baskets and animals. It made me snicker to see Mary Dell's hair hanging down in her eyes, since her hands were so sticky she couldn't shove it out of the way as she habitually did. We were applauding a particularly graceful swan she had just created when a knock sounded on the outside door.

Miz Jump jerked it open to reveal three skinny, ragged children. "Please ma'am," the oldest one said, "we got all of us kids ain't had nothing to eat all day, and our mam, she stay powerful sick, and our pappy, he passed. Please might you spare some cold victuals? Any old leftovers at all."

Miz Jump's lip curled. "Oh, I'm sorry, young-uns," she said in a nasty, falsely-sweet tone, "but the only victuals we got here are fresh and piping hot, so I regret I can't oblige you." And she slammed the door on them.

She turned to us and pulled a face. "Always the same story." Now she made her voice high and squeaky. "'There's all us hungry kids and our ma is sick and our pa is dead.'"

With the same thought at the same moment, Varina and I looked at each other. I scooped up several sticks of candy from the table while Varina snatched a basket of bread from a shelf. Before Miz Jump could stop us, we opened the door and ran after the astonished children, shoving the food into their arms.

"Nasty little thieves. Eat us out of house and home." Miz Jump muttered from the doorway, and shut and locked the door against us.

She would never tell Miss Petheram on us because Miss Petheram wanted to teach us to be charitable.

We were to use the opportunities of the supper and ball to polish our manners, our conversation, and our waltzes and reels. We girls also intended to use it to polish our sense of style. After the candy stew, the Club gathered in my bedchamber, wallowing in a sea of puffs and furbelows as we pulled dress after dress from my wardrobes. We held up one after another against us, crowding about the tall pier glass mirror, trying to decide what looked best.

Between her thumb and forefinger, Trix picked up the dress I had worn the day before from the pile of clothes that lay crumpled in a corner. "Honestly, Fiona, you don't deserve nice things."

I sighed. "I tell myself that all the time."

"Don't you try at all to take care of them?"

"I do try 'at all.' Just not a lot. When it's me who has to do it, it doesn't seem near as important as it used to seem to hang things up. I do get them to the laundry, though, if they're dirty."

Varina already appeared ravishing in a celestial blue organdy gown of her own making. She offered us suggestions, but there were simply too many possibilities. The rest of us could make no firm decisions, and eventually we tired of trying to choose.

Dorcas looked embarrassed as she held out her arms to me. "Fiona, will you remind me of the steps to the schottische? Not that anyone will ask me to dance, but if they do…"

"You'll get asked," I said. "And I could use the practice too."

We pushed the furniture to the edges of the room. Soon all six of us were making the short runs and hops of the schottische, puffing and laughing, rendering a mess of it without music. When Varina and Trix crashed into Dorcas and me, we finally ceased.

"Now," Varina said slowly, as she sprawled across the ottoman recovering her breath, "I suppose I should warn y'all that I don't intend to dance tonight. I'll come down to watch maybe, but I shan't dance."

"Why ever not?" We all could not believe what she had just said.

"I don't — I really don't like to be…touched by gentlemen."

Sylvie shook her head in incomprehension.

"I don't blame you," Dorcas said. "I went to a barn dance last summer and I only danced once. It was a polka and the fellow kept squishing the roll of flesh around my waist. Horrid."

Sylvie sniffed. "If you can't bear a little touching, then I don't know how either of you will ever have a real beau."

Varina looked away so we could no longer see her expression. "I don't ever wish for a beau." Her voice was soft. "Since the war, and even before, I've never thought I would marry. So many Southern boys are gone. From my home county especially. Their brigade got into a nasty spot in Sharpsburg and most of them were slaughtered. A great many Southern girls our age will never marry, so why shouldn't I be one of them?"

"Bless your heart, Varina," was all Mary Dell said, from the chair where she had dropped.

"How will you support yourself?" Trix asked. "I can understand a little, but how can a female survive without a husband to support her?"

"I don't need a man," Varina said, squaring her shoulders. "I'll manage somehow."

How curious. Everyone wanted to be married someday... didn't they? I thought of several remarks to make, but perhaps I was learning discretion—I held my tongue.

"To each his own." Sylvie reclined luxuriously against the pillows on my bed. "There'll be fewer boys here tonight than girls, so even when people do start dancing, plenty of y'all will be standing out. Not me, though, if I can help it."

"How do you suppose Miss Petheram will feel when she sees Mr. Crow again? So heartrending to be jilted." Mary Dell perhaps thought she was changing the subject from the distressing one, but in reality it was simply more of the same.

I quickly set about serving lemonade, hoping that refreshment would prove a pleasant distraction.

Trix took a glass, drank it down quickly and began pacing. She always had difficulty holding still.

"Excruciating," Sylvie drawled. "She's an old maid now, and how sad to be that old and to never once have had a gentleman love you enough to tie the knot."

Varina appeared to be completely engrossed in the careful drinking of her lemonade.

Dorcas refused a glass. She looked as if something was hurting her. I hoped it wasn't her stomach. "Would it be better to be painfully forsaken than to never be loved at all?" she asked abruptly.

"Well, I've been in love two—no, three—no, four times before, and it's always been most enjoyable. What's that Shakespeare quote?" Sylvie asked. "Something like, it's better to lose the fellow than to never have had him in the first place."

"Tennyson," I said. "'Tis better to have loved and lost than never to have loved at all.'"

"Will Mr. Harry attend tonight?" Trix asked, pausing in her pacing to give Sylvie a challenging look.

"Of course," Sylvie said, trying not to look pleased with herself. She lifted her glass to her lips to hide a lurking smile.

I wondered what her feelings were for Mr. Harry. Was he attractive to her because he was older or was it simply that he was an available male? Was she practicing? Or did she really care for him? He was nice-looking and amusing, but he had no ambition or prospects. For all we knew he might spend the rest of his life lingering about Wyndriven, half-heartedly hammering at woodwork, guzzling his secret spirits, and admired by schoolgirls (for the next few years, anyway).

One of the maids popped in just then with a card attached to a nosegay of azure bachelor buttons and hyacinths. "A gentleman asked me would I carry these to Miss Varina."

"Thank you, Charity," Varina said, taking the posies and tossing them onto the night table.

"You should at least read who they're from," Trix insisted.

"Don't have to," Varina said, through her teeth. "And I wish he'd leave me alone."

"They're from Jimmy, aren't they?" Sylvie said, picking them up.

"Who?" Mary Dell asked.

"Jimmy—or rather Mr. Casper—that boy from church." Trix said tartly. "Girls, remember that using given names encourages unpleasant familiarities in gentlemen."

Trix was so changeable—one never knew if she were going to be the arbiter of all etiquette or if she were going to suddenly swear. It always left me unsure of her.

"Fiddlesticks." Sylvie wrinkled her nose and poked at the flowers. "Look. In the language of flowers, they're bachelor buttons for anticipation and hyacinths for sincerity. How sweet and how perfect for the occasion. Blue to match your dress. And Jimmy's so handsome with his fine side-whiskers and all. I declare, Varina, if he was interested in me, I would follow him around like a puppy dog, with my tongue hanging out."

Varina frowned, but refused to meet anyone's eyes. "Then why don't *you* set your cap for him?"

"Because he only cares about you. Why don't you like him?"

"I like him just fine, when he doesn't act silly."

"Oh, yes. You don't care for beaus." Sylvie shook her head again, still mystified.

We had become acquainted with Jimmy and several of his Albion cohorts at church (which I had been attending with my protestant friends—a deep, dark secret from Grandmama). Every one of the boys had instantly become Varina's devoted vassal, but Jimmy was the most handsome and the leader of the group. He had also been a soldier in the war when he was very young and had lied about his age. I supposed it was this that made him seem older than the others. As well as the fact that he could grow luxuriant sidewhiskers, which his friends could not yet manage.

The rest of us had admitted to each other that we could not help being a bit envious of Varina's effect on males. We all studied her to learn how she did it, but could not discover the secret. We agreed that she never flirted or strung anyone along. Her manner with boys was exactly as it was with us girls. If any of the gentlemen tried to walk too closely, she would smilingly give him a little shove and tell him to scoot. If he flattered or flirted, she would say absently, as if she couldn't be bothered to listen, "Stop being absurd." If he persisted, she would sigh with exasperation, and say, "Would you please go away? I'm tired of your nonsense."

"You're simply too enticing," I said now, lightly. "That is your trial in life, you poor, abused thing."

I was expecting her to laugh, or to playfully throw something at me, but instead my words hung in the air so heavily that I wanted to bat them away. After a moment of awkward silence, Varina jumped up, set down her glass on the table a bit too hard, making it wobble before it righted itself, said, "Excuse me. I need a minute," and whirled out the door.

I stared, open-mouthed.

"What's wrong with her?" Mary Dell asked.

"She said she needs to go out for a minute," Sylvie said, adjusting her hair ribbon.

"Obviously Fiona said something wrong!" Trix snapped. "As she so often does."

I went out after my friend. "Varina," I said, touching her arm, "I didn't mean—"

She paused, as if composing herself, then turned to face me. I was taken aback, because her expression was not what I had expected it would be. She was smiling brightly. A false smile.

"Sorry, honey," she said. "How can I help acting silly when I ain't no bigger'n a pot boggin? Whatever that is. All this dance talk and beau talk. I can't handle it."

I looked at her, perplexed, but couldn't think what else to say. From a girl who had always seemed to handle any situation smoothly, her words struck as false a chord as her smile had. Varina had me worried.

We returned to the others and she offered the same excuse, but I was not convinced. While the rest of us brushed out our hair and applied creams and lotions, Varina commenced to act overly-merry, swathing a lengthy Norwich shawl about herself like an East Indian woman. She pulled a giant leaf from an aspidistra plant, and fastened the nosegay onto it. With a flourish, she pinned the whole cumbersome creation to her chest as a corsage, and capered about, looking ridiculous.

"Mister Casper would eat his heart out if he saw you like that, Varina," Trix said. She scanned the label of a silver-lidded jar on my dressing table. "Goodness, this lotion is called 'Oil of Aphrodite.' How hard do you think they had to squeeze her?" She slathered her arms and then grabbed Mary Dell's hand to wipe off the excess, before turning on Sylvie with narrowed eyes. "*Don't* tell me you just dropped the hairball you pulled out of that brush onto the floor."

Sylvie tossed her head. "Can't a person clean a brush without you acting like my mama? I did nothing shocking—there's always hair floating around places where girls live. If you look close, the upholstery in Wyndriven is covered with it—as if particularly shaggy dogs are shedding. It's a wonder we're not all bald by now."

"Don't be disgusting," Trix said.

"Why is talking about hair disgusting?" I asked. "There's strands of mine in the basin this minute, from when I washed it. They look like interesting cracks in the porcelain." (Actually, I also thought loose hairballs were disgusting, but I wanted to argue with Trix.)

Trix gave a snort, aimed at me rather than the others, but said nothing more. Sometimes lately she squelched me in a much nicer fashion than the way she used to squelch me.

We dusted our skin with fragrant powder and used so much perfume that the air became choking and we had to open all the windows.

Sylvie painted her mouth with the lip rouge she had brought with her, since I owned none. It looked so fetching that the rest of us couldn't go about pale-lipped, and thus had to redden our mouths as well.

"You know what we should do?" Sylvie said as she studied herself in the mirror and wiped away some stray color. "We should each blot our mouths on a sheet of paper so we can tell how good a kisser we are — or rather *will be* someday — by how pretty the lip marks are."

Trix laughed with scorn, and the rest of us giggled. However we wanted to do it no matter how silly it was. I dug out paper, and we each gave a sheet a smack, trying to make nice, even marks.

"Look at Mary Dell's!" Trix howled. "La, child, you would gobble a man whole!"

"So," Mary Dell said, stung out of her usual sweetness, "yours are lopsided. And fat."

Privately I thought my lip marks quite attractive — nice and even and gracefully shaped, if rather wide.

"We should change our name to the Umwaa Club," Sylvie said. "Because that's the sound you make when you kiss. Like this — umwaaaa." She smacked her paper again with a flourish.

"Maybe when *you* kiss Mr. Harry," Trix said. "You needn't bother to deny it, Sylvie. We all know you do."

"Trix," Sylvie said, "you really must wash off some of that powder. You favor a corpse."

Trix started to say something scathing, but Varina lifted her head and intervened. Only then did I realize that Varina had not joined in the fun, but had silently removed the shawl and her enormous corsage and sat a little away from the rest of us, turning the button on a chair cushion round and round. "Now dear ladies," she said, "remember that really you love each other. Enough of this squabbling and, er, smacking. We must attend to the matter at hand. We've made a giant mess of Fiona's room and still none of y'all have decided what you'll wear tonight."

We began seriously making fashion choices. Trix was in great demand for corset lace-tightening because she was strong and had no pity — important qualifications for a successful lace-tightener. She pulled our stays until we were nearly cut in half. I plunged determinedly into a cobalt silk with black ribbon-appliqued squares all over, and surveyed myself in the mirror. Cobalt was a nice color, but something was wrong. What? The dress was darling, so it must be me that was the problem. Whenever I looked in the glass, I never knew what I would see — it was as if different countenances, sometimes pleasing, sometimes plain, would come and go over me, sliding into place, then melting away. Did most girls really not know how good-looking they were until they heard the opinion of others — attractive or un?

"No, Fiona," Varina said. "No, no, no. Not that ugly thing."

"Where is it ugly?"

"All over."

I sighed. "It doesn't work, does it? This is from Paris, and the design is ever so admired, but it doesn't look right."

"Why is the design admired?" Varina asked. "So people can play tic-tac-toe on you if they get bored at the ball? And don't wear a necklace either. Remember, simple, graceful, and elegant."

"But I can't be necklace-less."

"Oh yes, you can. Repeat after me—simple and graceful. And you, Trix—can't you see that the spotted ribbon stitched over that skirt looks like a boa constrictor uncoiling? Why, I declare, it's swallowing you and regurgitating yellow taffeta."

We were all taken aback.

Trix started to set her jaw—after all it was a stylish dress—but then grinned sheepishly, admitting that Varina was right. Varina wasn't being mean and we all knew it. She simply had a talent for fashion, took it seriously, and was honest about it. She *wanted* us to look nice and helped in any way she could.

I plopped myself on the edge of the bed, my hands hanging between my knees. "What then? If I look dowdy and clumsy in something as fine as this, is there no hope for me?"

"Bless your heart." This from Mary Dell, naturally.

"Stop that right now," Varina said, pulling me up. "There's no need whatsoever to feel sorry for yourself. You've a lovely figure, but you shouldn't wear a gown simply because it's from Paris, is expensive, or because everyone else is wearing it." She began rummaging among the shining pile on my floor. "You're crying out for something more classic, like…this." She held up an evening gown of delicate, diaphanous, ivory silk. The soft kind of silk that doesn't rustle.

I eyed it doubtfully. "It's meant to have the lacy overskirt and tassels with it."

"Wear it without. The smooth lines will let you shine. You should be dressed simply, but at enormous expense. You don't want fringe and ribbons and rosettes and panniers and — and festoons flying about every which way. You want luxurious, beautifully draped fabric. A toga would suit you nicely."

"Well, I'm afraid I have nary a one," I said tersely.

"Poor deprived girl. Not a single toga? Well, then, honey child, put this on, do."

She helped me lift the silk over my head, and fastened it. I peered at my reflection — and drew in my breath.

"It's like magic, isn't it?" Varina said. "And now, let's start on y'all's hair." She and Sylvie proceeded to puff, crimp, and curl everybody with hot tongs.

With my black hair styled by Varina, I did indeed look romantically classical. I swayed in the Grecian bend, which our dance teacher had required us all to execute to perfection.

Varina crowned me with a circlet of wiry silver leaves. "And now Fiona, may Mary Dell borrow your ruby collar? You can see she requires it."

"Actually," I said, "it's a collar of purest red glass. Grandmama doesn't give me any truly valuable trinkets because I'm so bad about losing things."

I attached the collar for Mary Dell and more jewelry for the other girls. Only I was necklace-less.

Varina examined herself critically in the mirror, twitching this and adjusting that. Finally she asked if she might borrow a set of jeweled hairpins. She wore her bright hair in a simple, smooth chignon, with the hairpins—they were blue flowers on the ends of steel points—poking out.

Even though I looked well tonight, still I felt wistful as I watched her. The fuss and feathers of the current fashion—and the styles were only growing more elaborate— suited her. I did like overdone opulence, especially since it was in style.

But it doesn't like me. Drat it all. I should have been born two thousand years ago.

Sylvie ended up in pale blue chiffon, Trix in green and beige lace, Mary Dell in white tulle trimmed with currant-colored velvet, and Dorcas in her own rose-striped taffeta with scallops, since my gowns wouldn't fasten on her. (But she did borrow an amber necklet and bracelet set.)

As we admired each other, and tweaked a strayed strand or bunchy petticoat or crooked sash here and there, Trix said, "Y'all make exemplary lady's maids. I'm glad I have five of you in my employ."

We all laughed, but it was true—I actually looked better than I had all those years with someone paid to wait on me, and it felt good that I had helped myself and others. There was that pain in my heart that always throbbed when I thought of Bridey. Perhaps someday I would have another servant, but not for a long while.

Eventually everyone left in order to search out their own dancing slippers, as mine were too large for any of them.

Leo wandered in from the sitting room and gave a low whistle. "Breathtaking," he said. "If I had breath to take."

I fretted over straightening my jewelry chest so he wouldn't see the silly smile that played at my lips. Why couldn't I ever accept a compliment graciously? "There's a ball tonight," I said.

"So I gathered."

"With the boys from a school near here. In the banquet hall. It's to teach us nice company manners."

"Your manners already seem fine to me, Princess. So the gentlemen will be youngsters?"

"Fourteen to eighteen. The boys and girls under fourteen are to have a candy stew in the kitchen while we're dancing."

"Poor things."

"No. The little girls are all excited for it—they chattered like a flock of tweeting birds when they heard the plan."

"I wish I could whirl along beside you. Or would that prove too distracting?"

"Much too distracting."

"I suppose you wouldn't be able to flirt easily with the fourteen-year-olds if I were there."

I rolled my eyes. "Please. *Fourteen?* Of course it would be diverting to be the only one who could see you clomping clumsily along in your riding boots."

"Clumsily! I cut a graceful figure with the minuet in my day, I assure you, my girl. Although it helped that I wore dancing slippers rather than boots."

"Dancing slippers on a man!" I laughed.

"Yes. Rose satin with high heels and pointed toes. Why, what do they wear now?"

"It's easy for gentlemen to choose their ensemble these days. For dancing they wear only black shoes, with black trousers and tail coat and a white shirt and cravat. And white gloves."

"Oh. Boring. My favorite attire for balls was my mulberry brocade coat with white breeches and stockings. I was impressive, indeed. I was told I had a fine leg."

"I'm sure you looked very...pretty."

He tried to muss my hair, to no avail, of course.

A great boom sounded outside and at the same moment we turned to look out the window, and at the same moment said, "Oh, it's storming," and at the same moment laughed.

The earlier beautiful weather had ended. Clouds let loose now and rain came down with a low rumble. However, in spite of the conditions that raged outside, around us there was a warm softness in the air, a flowery sweetness. Perhaps it was the left-over perfume.

Leo lay down on my bed, lounging back on his elbows, one boot crossed over the other. He watched as I adjusted the silver leaves in my hair. His gaze traveled up and down my body in a way that made me self-conscious. "What are you looking at?" I demanded. "My sweet figure?"

"No!" he said, averting his head. "Of course not. I wouldn't—"

"Why not? What's wrong with it?"

He threw back his head and laughed. I joined him, perched on the edge of the bed. "I really am sorry you can't be there at the ball," I said.

He sighed. "Think how tragic and romantic I would look—a dancing phantom in the style of a hundred years ago."

I couldn't tell if he was jesting, but I was suddenly serious myself. "Any girl who could see you would fall in love with you," I said softly.

"Promise?"

I nodded mutely.

"May I look at your paper?"

"What paper?"

"The one you kissed."

I gasped and jumped up. "Oh, you *didn't* hear all that."

"I did. I'm surprised the sounds of my sniggering didn't reach you." He stood, and hesitated. "To be honest, Princess, I wished it was me instead of the paper you were practicing on." He had the humorous quirk to his mouth that always made me think he was teasing, so I drew back a little. But he followed, stepping closer, and leaned down till his eyes were gazing straight into mine.

This is happening.

My eyelids fluttered shut and heat surged through me…no—ice…Whatever it was, it was delightful and intoxicating as I felt the chill on my lips while I received my first kiss from a ghost—or anyone else for that matter.

My lips were still tingling when I slowly opened my eyes.

He was gone.

I thought I knew what love is,
When now and then I'd fall
For a boy who never noticed me —
But that's not love at all;
For now I'm filled with joy and pain
Over a phantom! This strange youth
Who isn't of my world at all —
Can this be love in truth?
—By Fiona O'Malley

CHAPTER 22

A HAIRPIN

"Ready?" Trix called, as she poked her head into my room. "Time for our glorious society debut."

"Ugh," came Sylvie's voice from behind. "Surely not. If fifteen or so schoolgirls and ten or so schoolboys make up my coming-out ball, I call that horrid."

Trix gave an evil laugh. "Sorry, dumpling, you're unlikely to get any other."

I was still standing rooted to the spot where Leo had left me. It took two tries before I could speak. "So Varina really isn't coming," I managed to say.

"She said she'd possibly be down after supper," Mary Dell said. "Just to watch."

I might have given Varina more thought, but at the moment I could only think of Leo.

We girls moved together like an upside-down bouquet of blossoming skirts down the staircase toward the banquet hall. Everyone chattered around me in excited anticipation. For them, who knew what momentous thing might happen at their first ball? However, my momentous thing had already happened to-night, and I could not speak because of the recently aroused emotions struggling in my chest—pleasure against pain.

I touched my lips.

I was in love with Leo and it was the sweetest and most ridiculous thing in the world. And the saddest.

Why couldn't I have been born in his time, or he in mine?

Don't wish for such a thing. If you had lived a hundred years ago, Leo would not have noticed you beside his lovely Marietta.

Ah, but she didn't want him. I could have stepped in and comforted him when she married his cousin Godfrey.

She married Godfrey only after Leo was dead. It's a simple fact— you're not the sort of girl gentlemen fall in love with. If Leo could leave your rooms, if he could speak to other girls, he would not be paying you comely attentions. You have no flirting banter or "pretty little ways" at your disposal.

I made my two provoking selves hush as we approached the banquet hall.

When we entered, I blinked, and one of my companions inhaled sharply, at sight of the flames glittering, as if all the light in Wyndriven had been gathered to this one place. Normally, oil lamps were lit for our meals, three on each long table. I had never before seen candles burning in the massive chandeliers hanging by chains from the two-story-high ceiling. Dozens of tapers shone in them now, as well as in many-branched floor candelabra and all down the centers of the tables. Reflected sparks winked and flickered in china and silver set on snowy damask. In niches and corners, banks of billowing brilliant red azaleas and trailing greenery had been arranged, seeming to glow with their own light.

The near-magic that turned schoolboys into gentlemen and our school into a dazzling ballroom dazed me.

The Albion gentlemen all stood behind their chairs, standing until every young lady was seated. When the last girl lowered herself into her chair, Mr. Crow gave a curt nod, and the boys dropped into their seats.

The Reverend Brother Gideon Stone sat at the head of one table, and his wife made her way now to the foot. My place was beside her, so I finally got to meet the owner of Wyndriven Academy. Miss Sophie was smaller than Varina, with bright molten bronze hair piled on her head, and a gown of black Chantilly lace over russet silk. She made me think of a butterfly. Not because she appeared at all featherheaded, but because she moved with a kind of winged grace and lightness. I spied a dancing-eyed look flash down the table between her and her husband. Brother Gideon was not handsome, but he had a likeable, humorous appearance. Their three red-headed children were there as well, huddled in the great chairs near Miss Sophie—two sturdy boys, introduced as Jack and Roo, and a tiny beauty of a girl, who looked just as her mother must have when she was small.

Miss Sophie gave a short speech, in which she proclaimed her happiness at Wyndriven Academy hosting a fete once again after the long war years. Her voice was breathy, and somehow enchanting to listen to.

Undercurrents pinged back and forth and bounced off the tapestried walls. On each side of the tables, bright-eyed, self-conscious Wyndriven girls, brittle and edgy because they were feeling pretty, were interspersed with the bright-eyed, self-conscious gentlemen from Albion, brittle and edgy because they were uncomfortable in their evening clothes and their company manners. Stilted conversation ran up and down the tables, except for Sylvie and Mr. Harry, who were seated near one another, and who flirted expertly.

Miss Petheram sat at the head of the other table, with her former fiancé, Mr. Crow, at the foot. The headmistress looked splendid for a woman her age, in pale violet silk. I studied the headmaster to see if he were studying her. He seemed to look everywhere except in Miss Petheram's direction. He had aquiline, sculpted features, and would have been handsome, except for a tightness about his mouth that give him a look of cruelty. He seemed edgy, and snapped several times at his charges. It amazed me that Miss Petheram had stayed engaged to him for so long. I wished Father Paul were present, although he would have appeared out of place in such an elegant setting. I wondered if he and the headmistress had seen each other since that first meeting.

We nibbled away at roast turkey, buttery Sally Lunn bread, sweet pickles, and waffles, with custard pies for the pastry. It was a splendid supper—Miz Jump had pulled through—but my nerves did not let me enjoy it as I would normally.

Miss Sophie tried to set me at my ease, as she asked about my home. I wished she would stop trying, since she herself seemed preoccupied. Gradually the conversation trickled off, to our mutual silent agreement, and she began gazing about the banquet hall, with a distant look in her eyes.

"You know," she said suddenly, "so many layers of the past cling to the abbey, don't they? These surroundings give rise to intense emotions in me. Part of me loves it because of some of what has taken place here—it was here that I first met my dear husband, and it was here that my eldest children were born—yet part of me loathes it because of vile things that happened in this setting. Does that make sense?"

"It does to me." Again I wondered if Miss Sophie had been connected with Wyndriven when the murders took place, but it was too terrible and personal a thing to inquire of her.

"Of course Wyndriven is merely mortar and stone—and the stone was ancient as the earth before ever it was dug up and shaped for the walls. Buildings are not of themselves good or evil. It is the people within who give them their character." She visibly shook herself. "But this is no time for dwelling on the past—we're in a ballroom, and who can think of anything serious while wearing dancing slippers?"

"You can if they pinch."

"Do yours pinch?"

"A little." I took meager helpings of the dessert, which consisted of jellies, almonds, and raisins.

I became aware of Miss Sophie's little girl, Daisy, staring my way from across the table. I touched my hair to feel if it was mussed, and dabbed at my face with a napkin in case I'd smeared jelly on my chin.

Daisy whispered something to her mother. Miss Sophie smiled. She turned to me. "Daisy thinks you are a beautiful princess. I agree. That dress suits you perfectly. I remember when I was your age, and I had a white ball gown as well. Fine linen lawn with trailing streamers down the back, and trimmed in purple…"

Once it started, our practice ball was not the fairy tale sort of affair one reads about in society columns.

We had no fashionable dance cards. If we had, things might have gone more smoothly. When the tables were cleared and pushed against the walls, and the musicians struck up for a reel, the young ladies and gentlemen about the edge of the dance floor shuffled their feet and cast sidelong glances. None of the fellows would conspicuously cross the floor to ask a lady to join him for the set. We stood about in groups separated by sex, talking with animation, absorbed in our brilliant conversations, lest anyone think we were concerned about asking, or being asked, to dance.

"I love your dress," I told Dorcas. "If only you would—"

She let out her breath in a hiss. "Don't say it."

"Don't say what?"

"Don't say that I would be pretty if only I slimmed down." She spoke so low that only I could hear.

"I wasn't about to say that," I said shortly. "What I was about to say is that, if you would only notice, you would be pleased to see how many covert looks you're getting from the gentlemen."

"Oh. Really?"

"Yes, really."

What would have been a modest neckline on anyone less well-endowed was shockingly revealing on Dorcas, showing much curvy, lily-white flesh that was normally hidden.

By now I was enough in the present to worry a little about how Varina was feeling, and to wonder if it would be me, among my friends, who would be a complete wallflower. My toes twitched inside my slippers in time to the music. My feet, at least, wanted to dance. Silently, sternly, I told them they must wait to be asked.

Jimmy Casper's group of youths was clustered by the massive hearth. There was Jimmy, with a perplexed expression on his handsome face, perhaps wondering where Varina was. He was flanked by Morgan Thompson, who was the sort of fellow who laughs at everything, and Frank Gentry, whom I considered droll, since he dryly commented on all that everyone else said and did, without offering up original observations himself.

Jimmy's suddenly lit-up face made me glance toward the entrance. There stood Varina, framed by the doorway, looking pale and ethereal as she stood poised for a moment, her lips half-parted as she took in the hall. She saw us and slipped around the edge to our group.

"I'm glad you came down," I said.

A waltz began playing.

"A clever trick," Sylvie whispered, "is to stare at the gentleman you want to ask you to dance. Then, when he meets your eyes, you blush very ladylike and look away. Watch this."

"You can blush on purpose?" Trix asked. "What a useful talent."

Sylvie paid her no heed—she was busy casting an arch smile toward Mr. Harry. When he looked up, she turned swiftly away, as though embarrassed. In a ladylike way.

Mr. Harry marched confidently across the dance floor to capture Sylvie. She grinned significantly at us, laid her hand on his arm, and sashayed off. Her chiffon skirts swirled around her like spray in the wind as she and Mr. Harry commenced their whirling.

Varina was acting peculiarly. She stood so rigid that she looked as if she would shatter if touched.

"Varina," I whispered, "I don't understand you. Has someone…who made you feel this way?"

"What way?"

"Don't pretend you don't know what I mean. Your attitude

toward men. Why do you hate them?"

Her expression was pensive. "I don't hate them. I simply don't care for them in a romantic way. If you must know, something horrid happened once. Something I will never reveal to another soul. Not even you, and you know I love you dearly. I suppose most everyone in this old world is walking around secretly wounded in one fashion or another, aren't they? How sad. Well, I'm going back upstairs. I shouldn't have come down when I knew I'd put a damper on things. Y'all, have a jolly time without me."

As she turned to depart, Jimmy Casper came striding up with determination to claim her.

Varina smiled faintly, and said, "No, thank you. I don't care to dance. I'm leaving now."

Jimmy groaned. "You can't go already, beautiful Varina. Don't torture a fellow so. Just this one waltz." He snatched her left hand and grasped her tightly about the waist, as if to whisk her off to the dance floor by playful force.

A faint shudder passed through Varina, like a ripple through a pond. Something bad was about to happen.

Should I step between them?

I had only a second to wonder what I should do, when Varina snatched one of the sharp steel pins from her hair and stabbed it hard into Jimmy's hand that held her.

He staggered backward, clutching his palm. "Are you crazy, girl?" he gasped.

Varina held the blue-jeweled pin, her chin trembling and her face dead white. "I—I said no, Jimmy." Then she whispered, "I'm so sorry." There was a drop of blood on the pin. She stared at it and wiped it off with her finger. It was horrible, then, when she slowly, carefully, replaced the pin in her hair.

Jimmy pulled out a handkerchief and wrapped it around his hand. He shook his head in disbelief, and, without another word, stalked back to his friends. They whispered and looked our way, while Trix and I hustled Varina to the door and out into the corridor. She moved like an automaton.

We were silent for a bit, still shocked.

"Well, I declare Mr. Casper deserved it," Trix said finally, as we led Varina up the staircase, "calling you by your first name and pawing at you so familiarly. I guess he won't try that again."

Varina was shaking. "I didn't even know what I was doing. What is wrong with me?"

"It's a good thing you didn't have a knife," I blurted out.

We all winced. Even me, and I was the one who had said the horrible thing.

In her bedchamber, we would have helped Varina out of her dress and into her nightgown, but she prevented us.

"Stop, please," she begged, as we tried to lift the gown over her head. "I've pulled myself together, so you needn't worry about leaving me. Let's not make too much of this. Please go back down and enjoy yourselves and apologize to Jimmy for me, if he'll even listen after what I just did to him. It was inexcusable . I suppose I'm having an attack of melancholia. It's happened a few times before."

"Uh-uh," Trix said. "We'll stay with you."

"No, indeed." Varina shook her head so hard that one of the horrid hairpins fell out and struck the floor with a tinkle. "No more fussing. I couldn't bear it if I thought I'd ruined y'all's evening. In the morning, you can tell me how grand it was." She settled into a chair, snatched up a book, and opened it determinedly, pretending we were already gone.

Still we couldn't leave just yet.

She gave an exasperated sigh. "All right, girls. I'll tell you the truth then. What I really want to do is cry my eyes out for a half hour or so, and I can't do that if y'all stay on and keep comforting me. Now, shoo."

Finally we shooed.

CHAPTER 23

AT THE EDGE

Back at the ball, everyone inquired after Varina, questioned what could have gotten into her, found no answer, and then went on as if the incident hadn't happened.

There was a moment of intense, thrilling drama (for Dorcas and me, anyway) when the doors were flung open and Father Paul entered. He appeared out of place and uncomfortable in ill-fitting evening clothes, just as I had thought he would. Immediately I looked for Miss Petheram, and there she was, floating across the floor to Father Paul's side, face flushed and eyes glowing. Evidently *she* did not find him intimidating. Or perhaps she did, and liked it.

Dorcas clutched my hand. "Oh, mercy, will you look at Mr. Crow's expression?"

I couldn't help feeling sorry for the man.

Trix looked down her nose at Father Paul. "I don't think a priest should dance."

"He's the kind of priest who may," I said.

"It still isn't right," Trix said.

"Well, you're not even Catholic, so you really aren't allowed an opinion, are you?" I was proud of this remark. Trix raised her eyebrows, but smiled slightly, as if she conceded a point for me.

However, Father Paul never did dance. Instead, he and Miss Petheram retired to a secluded corner and immersed themselves in conversation.

Mary Dell settled down on a chair with a heaping plate of refreshments, even though we had just had our meal—"I might as well enjoy *something*. A girl shouldn't feel as if she's Cinderella *before* the ball while the ball is going on," she told me between bites; Sylvie complained because Mr. Harry was dancing with another girl—"He claims he cannot spend all evening with me, or there will be talk. As if I care about silly gossip;" and squat Dorcas danced with a tall, gangling gentleman who seemed to be speaking constantly and earnestly into the air above her head.

It was Mr. Thatoor.

Trix watched. "Oh," she said with glee, "that's too delightful."

"Don't tease her about it," I said.

She narrowed her eyes in assessment. "Actually if you ignore the fellow's gawkiness, he's strikingly handsome, isn't he? Exotic-looking."

"He's from India," I told her.

She looked at me inquiringly.

"I met him on my trip here."

"Well, Miss Fiona, aren't we full of surprises?"

When he restored Dorcas to our group, Mr. Thatoor turned to me and gave an ungainly bow. "Would you care to dance?"

"Yes."

"With *me*?"

He made me laugh. "With you."

Trix gave me a little shove, and I bobbed an awkward curtsy. The others smirked as my partner led me to the dance floor and put his arm about my waist.

The music struck up a polka. I took a deep breath. Soon we were whirling about so speedily that all I could think about was how to keep my feet moving without them becoming twisted up in my partner's.

"Have you settled well into your school?" he asked, over the music.

"Yes," was all I could gasp out, as we narrowly missed a horrendous crash with another couple. I kicked him. Not on purpose, but hard. It must have hurt him dreadfully, because inside my slippers my toes felt as if I they were broken. "I'm so sorry. Please, let's sit the rest of this one out."

"Very well, Miss O'Malley," he said, wincing from the pain in his shin. "I too am feeling the disparagement of others on the floor. Shall we retire over there?" He indicated a small sofa near the refreshment table.

I let him lead me on, trying not to hobble with my hurt toes. At least we were on the outskirts now and no longer on display.

We sat in silence while Mr. Thatoor scrutinized the dancers as if they were an alien species. A species that was becoming increasingly rambunctious. Occasionally he would toss back his long, shaggy black hair. "The polka," he finally said, "is a recent import from Bohemia, did you know?"

"Yes."

"But I would wager you do not know that the dance and music originated with a young woman named Anna Slezakova, who danced to accompany a local folk song called '*Strycek Nimra Koupil Simla.*' That means 'Uncle Nimra Bought a White Horse,' in case you do not speak the language."

"I don't. Do you?"

"No. I must admit I do not. Except for those four words. I only speak English and Hindi."

He looked so crestfallen at this admission of ignorance that I gave him a friendly grin, and he returned it with a sort of spasm that might have been meant to be a grin in return.

"Actually," I said, "I'm hopeless with languages. Except for English, that is."

By now the polka had turned into such a wild romp that Mr. Crow abruptly ordered the musicians to cease. A few minutes later, they commenced a sedate quadrille.

Surprisingly, since Mr. Thatoor had been so silent during our coach trip together, he never stopped talking now. I had always prided myself on my vocabulary, but he often used long words of which I was not entirely sure I knew the meaning. Because he had been so kind as to keep me from being a wallflower, I tried to make myself pay attention to his droning on and on. To no avail.

Gradually my mind wandered first to what had happened with Varina, and then, when those thoughts were too disturbing, I drifted on to darling Leo.

What is he doing at this very moment? Does he regret kissing me? Or is he waiting to kiss me again…and again…and again?

When Mr. Thatoor became involved in what he was saying, he forgot to throw back his hair, so it hung over his eyes. Currently he was relating a drawn-out story, punctuated with foreign words, about his early childhood in India. He mentioned again that his father was a maharajah. His mother had been an American governess to the older children, before his father had married her and she had given birth to Sebastian Thatoor. It would have been fascinating and romantic if I hadn't been so distracted. As it was, I heard bits and pieces: "wrapped in old rags…my ayah disappeared…a fakir…hadn't even been ailing and then deceased within an hour…found it beneath the carpet…"

I was forced to pay more attention to Mr. Thatoor when we found ourselves rolled together because of the uneven sofa cushions. We looked at each other square on for the first time, and laughed self-consciously. Really, he was terribly good-looking. He would have made a splendid hero on stage, if only he could move properly. How odd, though, to have felt more delicious physical thrills from a young man without a body, than from a flesh and bone masculine thigh squashed against me. (Separated by lots of clothing, of course.)

We scooted awkwardly back to safe territory. Mr. Thatoor continued with his history and I continued with my daydreaming. I was vaguely aware that he had said something about being smuggled out of India in a cartful of gourds, when he asked me a question.

I had to hastily gather my wits and figure out what he had just said. I was trying to decide if I could respond with an "Oh, yes," without committing myself to anything, when something he had related earlier came into focus in my head. "Did you—did you say something about a snake bone beneath a carpet?"

"Yes," Mr. Thatoor said. "All that uncanny sort of occurrence was what made my mother so anxious to leave. Mostly the tricks of fakir's are innocuous—they recline on beds of nails or charm snakes, that sort of thing. But this particular fakir had a vendetta against one of my elder brothers. He murdered him by hiding the snake bone and reciting a *maran* mantra."

"What's a mantra?"

"It is a sound capable of generating transformation."

"I beg your pardon?"

"It is a chant repeated again and again and again in cycles, usually a hundred and eight of them, so that the vibrations and sounds awaken the *Kundalini*, or spiritual life force. People use *malas*, which are necklaces of beads, to help them count how many repetitions of the mantra they have completed."

"As I use my rosary beads — sort of. But what exactly is the mantra supposed to do?"

"That particular mantra — the *maran* mantra — combined with the bone, kills an enemy without leaving a mark on the body. For several years now, I have made a study of fakir magic. My mother dislikes my interest in it. I tell her it is part of my heritage."

I drew in my breath. This was going to take some consideration when I was alone. "Goodness. I've never heard of such a thing. I'm so sorry about your brother. That was an awful way to lose a loved one."

He lifted one shoulder. "He was not loved. Most who knew him detested him. I myself did not know him well, so it did not make me sad. My father was an elderly man when I was born, and my siblings are all at least forty years older than I."

I needed to get away to think. "How remarkable. Well, Mr. Thatoor, I hope I shall get to know you better another time, but I really must go now." I started to rise.

"Is it because I am too loquacious?"

"Pardon?" This time I *had* been paying attention and I still had no idea what he was talking about.

From what I could see below the shaggy hair hanging over his face, his expression was glum. "My mother has told me I speak too much at times. Or do you wish to leave because of my dark skin? Some Americans object to it. Mr. Crow, of course, welcomed me to Albion Academy because my father is nobility, but when I first arrived, some of the fellows were uncomfortable because they could not discern my race. To people in the south of the United States, everyone should be of either African or European descent. They jested with me, but I did not find it amusing."

Poor Mr. Thatoor. I could well imagine how unmerciful those young men might be toward an outsider.

I leaned back to view him dispassionately. "To tell you the truth, you make me think of a stage hero. I shan't name names, but you have been the object of, um, pleasant discussions."

"Stage hero? Well, Miss O'Malley, I thought *you* resembled a Greek goddess when I first saw you in the coach. That is why I did not dare speak for days. I suppose a polka is not the right sort of activity for a goddess. Too bouncy." He paused, then—"You are also enjoyable to talk to. A good listener. I read a great deal, and know many things, but often others are indifferent to my interests. Perhaps we might converse again."

"I would like that. But right now I need to go check on my friend."

"Very well, Miss O'Malley. Good evening."

He bowed and went off in search of another partner.

I slipped along the edge of the wall, but came to a spot where I would have to noticeably cross in front of the musicians in order to reach the doorway and leave. Instead, I retired into the niche of a deep bay window to wait until this set ended. I untied the golden rope that held back crimson velvet draperies. They fell into place with a swish, leaving me in a tiny room with a tall black casement window for one wall. It had been the sort of evening when you don't notice what the weather is like outside — only now I realized that the storm still raged. Wind moaned and rattled the panes and spattered dark raindrops against them in gusts. Drafts crept inside as well. I shivered.

Those things Mr. Thatoor had said about *malas* and mantras and bones...It was impossible, of course, that a fakir from India was here at Wyndriven trying to kill Trix by placing a snake bone beneath her carpet and chanting deadly mantras. Unless...Could it be Mr. Thatoor himself who was doing it?

I shook my head. The idea of that awkward, earnest boy sneaking from his school, creeping about Wyndriven at night, and hissing deadly spells down a hole into Trix's room was preposterous.

It was odd, though, how Mr. Thatoor's words explained some things — the strange string of beads I had found in the room above Trix's, the ivory sliver beneath her carpet, the voice droning as she drifted off to sleep...Was this something truly serious or was the bone a bit of unswept rubbish, the voice a fragment of nightmare, the necklace a trinket dropped by a servant?

If I told Trix about it all, would she be grateful, or taunt me unmercifully? Easy guess. Besides, there hadn't been any unusual incidents in weeks. As a matter of fact, we had recently stopped walking her to her room at night. I chuckled to myself — foreign magic indeed.

I parted the draperies a crack so I could peek out at the ball. By now, nearly everyone had lost their shyness, and was galloping about the floor. Dorcas and Mary Dell were swinging around the two little Stone boys, who hooted with laughter. Brother Gideon and his wife had stepped in to join the throng, carrying little Daisy between them so she wouldn't be left out. She laughed and squealed. Everyone seemed carefree. A few seemed graceful.

Trix was extremely, glowingly alive and healthy at this moment, sailing about on Mr. Harry's arm. His eyes kept wandering over Trix's head to find Sylvie. I smiled…until I saw Something very tall, very elegant, very masculine, with just a slight limp, weaving through the couples. Monsieur was making his way toward my hiding place. No one paid him any heed, too engrossed in what they were doing. He had not bothered to change into evening clothes. Doubtless he hadn't expected to be here — in the past he had seemed to avoid all company but mine.

He stood in front of the gap in the draperies and gave a deep, mocking bow. Reluctantly I parted the curtains farther to let him enter. "How do you do, sir?"

The draperies swung into place behind him, but not all the way. I held back one panel so I would not be too intimately enclosed with Monsieur.

He did not answer. Instead he stared out at the swirling mass of color on the dance floor, his jaw set in a sharp line. I followed his stare to Miss Sophie.

"Look at her," he said, and his expression was so nakedly intense and hungry that I was embarrassed for him. "Still beautiful. And that hair. How can it be that I remain drawn to something I so hate?"

I stood rigid, unsure how to respond. "If you mean Miss So-phie," I said finally, "she said something similar at suppertime."

"Is this true?" He turned on me sharply. "What did she say?"

"That part of her loves Wyndriven and part of her loathes it, because of things that happened here."

"Ah. *She* is haunted as well. Karma." He turned back to the dancers, his eyes smoldering.

I pictured a brief but passionate, long ago romance. Monsieur would have been persuasive and charming, of course, but Miss Sophie had wisely chosen Brother Gideon. "Do you think 'twas better to have loved and lost than never to have loved at all? You were in love with her once, weren't you?"

"You are overly inquisitive. Not an attractive trait. But I will tell you. Yes, I was. And she rejected and ill-used me. Destroyed me."

"Then you *don't* think 'twas better to have loved and lost, do you?"

He ignored me. "I have unfinished business with the lady, and have waited too long." Some desperate emotion twisted his features. "See how she taunts me. She shall pay, and pay dearly."

His menacing talk combined with his expression made me feel as if all the breath was knocked from my lungs, until a great clap of thunder shocked me into breathing again.

At that moment, Daisy wriggled and nearly fell from her father's arms. He caught her, and he and Miss Sophie laughed.

Monsieur's face contorted. "Sophia and her family. Such a pretty scene, and always together. But people do not stay together always, do they? The child looks very like the mother. Something bad might happen to the child. *That* would destroy Sophia. *Oui. Ça y est.*"

His words were like black, acrid smoke in my eyes. He spoke as if he were talking to himself, as if the things he said echoed into nothingness. Almost certainly he thought me too stupid to understand the threat he had just made. I willed a faint, frozen smile to remain on my lips. Let him continue to think me too stupid.

I swallowed, and found some bits and pieces of a voice. "It's been an interesting evening, Monsieur, but I'm tired. Please excuse me."

He simply continued to stare. He did not blink. "And there is her brother, as well." His tone was disdainful as he watched Mr. Harry execute a comic pirouette that set the surrounding dancers laughing. "Always playing the fool. He's prancing with the red-haired vixen. Your enemy."

"Trix is no longer my enemy." The curtain hissed shut behind me as I abruptly deserted Monsieur.

The evening ended soon after. As the last strains of music ceased, Mr. Crow stood on the musician's platform to give instructions. The Albion students were to spend the night at Wyndriven, due to the violent storm which had been steadily rising. Miss Petheram, Mr. Harry, and the servants who had stayed late because of the ball, all left to make up long-unused beds in long-unused bedchambers.

I could not warn the headmistress about Monsieur until morning. Surely, surely it had been an empty threat.

As they wandered off to their bedchambers, the Wyndriven girls, excepting my good friends, were flushed and tittering. Having so many gentlemen under the roof was a novelty. Beside us, little Sally Haney said, "Do you suppose one of the boys will have to share our room?"

For a moment I thought Trix was going to really box the girl's ears, but she only pretended to.

I would have expected Sylvie to lead the whispers and giggles, but she was conspicuously absent. Mary Dell appeared concerned, Trix tense, and Dorcas wilted and stomach-y.

"Where's Sylvie?" I asked.

"Something happened between her and Mr. Harry and she stormed off," Mary Dell said. "You think I should try to find her?"

"She'll find her way to bed eventually," I reassured her. "Once she's tired of being dramatic."

I left the others and slipped into Varina's bedchamber, as I had told her I would, to report on the ball. Her roommates hadn't gotten there yet. The light from the doorway shone on Varina's face as she rose up from her pillow. She was almost at her prettiest when she first awoke, with droopy kitten eyes and mussed, marigold hair.

She yawned. "Lose any glass slippers?"

"No," I said. "Although Mary Dell did say she felt like Cinderella before the ball, while the ball was still going on."

"Mary Dell danced some, though, didn't she?"

"Oh, yes."

"And you did too?"

"A very little. Are you feeling better?"

"Much. I still don't understand what happened to me. It was as if another person took over—someone who would absolutely die if poor Jimmy touched her. But let's not talk about it. So dreadful, and so embarrassing."

"All right. I know all about embarrassment. My lips are sealed on the subject from now on."

"I'd appreciate that." She laid her head back on her pillow. "In the morning I want to hear who everyone danced with. 'Night."

Varina's eyes were closed. I had been dismissed.

Her roommates poured in through the door.

"'Night." What else could I say?

There was no sign of Leo in my rooms, and for once I was glad. I wriggled out of my clothes and into a nightgown. I supposed I wouldn't be able to sleep for hours after all that had happened, so I took up my book and stacked pillows behind my head. The printed words were elusive.

Thoughts surfaced through a throbbing fog. Leo's kiss. My first ball. Varina had acted so strangely...Father Paul and Miss Petheram looked perfect together...Mr. Thatoor was an interesting fellow...Monsieur was terrifying...What would I tell Miss Petheram? Would she understand that it hadn't been so much the words, but the tone and the look in Monsieur's eyes that was frightening...?

I couldn't sort out any of it. Too tired to think.

Close your eyes for just one minute...

CHAPTER 24

LONG HIDDEN

"How did y'all sleep?" I asked The Club when I joined them at breakfast next morning.

"Ooo, listen to the girl. She said 'y'all.' Bless your heart—" Mary Dell squeezed my arm—"we'll make a Southerner of you yet."

I hadn't even noticed I'd said it. "Well, it *is* a convenient thing to say. I'm so tired. I tried to stay half-asleep while I dressed."

"We can tell," Trix said, raking her eyes over me, but only in a half-hearted sort of way. Her eyes had dark smudges beneath them, and there were pinched lines around her mouth. Was she simply tired or was she ill or was her tormenter tormenting her again?

"I didn't sleep well either," Sylvie said in a wavering voice. She dabbed at her face with a lacy handkerchief.

"Mr. Harry?" I asked.

Trix groaned. "Mr. Harry told Sylvie that it was over—all the annoying secret meetings and stolen kisses. Evidently she spent the night moaning and weeping and keeping everyone up. How can she continue at Wyndriven without Mr. Harry at her side? Oh, grim and woe-some woe! How can she help but wail over the deep and precious love that is lost to her after it had lasted for, what, two whole months?"

"Hush, Trix," Mary Dell said, and put an arm around her sister. "I shouldn't have told you. You're mean."

"He even called me *Miss* Blake!" Sylvie wailed.

"How *dare* he?" exclaimed Trix.

One of us was missing. "Where's Dorcas?" I asked.

"Stayed in bed with her stomach," Varina said.

I would bring her some peppermint tea later.

Varina raised a forkful of scrambled eggs, but then lowered it. "I do believe a round of naps is called for after the boys leave."

I refrained from asking her how she was feeling since I had promised to never again bring up what had happened the night before.

Down the table from us, Jimmy Casper was carefully *not* looking our way. There were a few watchful glances between boys and girls, but today nearly everyone who had been beautifully dressed and sparkling the night before, appeared either listless or cross. The fellows also were rumpled, since they must once again wear their evening clothes. All glamor had worn off. Princes and Cinderellas should never meet each other the morning after the ball. The boys were to leave shortly, and it would be a good thing.

"My bed was lumpy," one fellow said.

"Mine was hard as a rock," his companion answered.

"Mine was too short," came another complaint.

"Honestly, y'all sound like the three bears," Trix said loudly. She laid her head on the table and covered it with her arms.

"Then I'm the papa bear," the first boy said. "Lipscomb and Smith, you're the mama and baby. But seriously, besides the mattress lumps, there were things moving around in the walls all night."

"Oh, there was not," someone sneered.

"Was. Ask Lipscomb. He was in with me and he'll tell you. Elephants stomped around in there."

The reference to Things in the walls made me glance at Trix, but she didn't raise her head.

Mr. Crow announced that the boys would be leaving within the hour. Miss Petheram smiled sweetly. There was a new glow about her, and I guessed why. Too bad I would have to spoil her mood shortly, even though, in the pale morning light, the incident with Monsieur didn't seem as menacing as it had the night before.

Mr. Thatoor came up behind and tapped my shoulder. "Excuse me, Miss O'Malley, there is something I must show you. Come with me quickly."

"What is it?"

He shook his head. "I do not want to tell you. You must view it for yourself. Leave your friends and come."

"Can't they come too?"

Again he shook his head adamantly. "No. Only you. It will only take a few minutes and I must exhibit it to you before we depart."

Sylvie made a face, which looked pitiful due to her red-rimmed eyes. "Oh, the excuses gentlemen use to get a girl alone. I wouldn't go with him if I was you, Fiona."

"Yes, you would," Trix muttered from beneath her arms.

"I have to go," I said. "I'm curious. But come rescue me if I'm gone more than half an hour."

Sylvie gave a tremulous giggle. "Well, we shan't bother to chaperone you since a girl your size can easily defend herself against any fellow's amorous advances."

Mr. Thatoor winced, so I stood and kindly told him, "You may call me Fiona, if you wish."

He smiled. "And please call me Sebastian." He offered his arm and I took it, ignoring the curious looks we generated. We left the banquet hall and went first up the grand staircase, next down a few corridors, and then up a flight of narrow, twisting stone steps, with hollows worn in the granite where centuries of feet had trod. These were the stairs where one of the girls had tripped during the dreadful tour of Wyndriven.

"Be vigilant right there," Sebastian warned. "That is the trick step."

"What do you mean, trick step?"

"The one they made two inches higher than the rest, to throw a marauding enemy off balance as he leaped upward. I hurt my shin—not the one you kicked, the other— on it when I was led to my chamber last night. I had read about such devices in medieval edifices, but never thought I would come upon such a wonderful thing in Mississippi. This is an amazing place. You are fortunate to attend school here."

"Yes. And thank you for the warning."

"The room I was given is in the Renaissance part of the building," he told me, as we turned down a dusky hall, hung with rich tapestries glowing midnight blue, royal purple, red, and gold.

"I didn't know there *was* a Renaissance part of Wyndriven."

"Indeed there is. I should like to stay here and inspect every inch of this place. I have read many books on architecture and so many styles could be studied here."

The plaster ceiling overhead was molded into elaborate shells, swags, and fantastical designs. "Observe," Sebastian said, pointing upward. "Obviously Renaissance."

"Obviously."

I felt shy about entering Sebastian's chamber with him, but I told myself that it was not really a gentleman's room—he had only slept in it the once. Still, I hovered just inside the doorway.

The walls were draped from top to bottom with rectangular panels of leather, stamped in gold leaf with intricate, swirling patterns of butterflies and vines. "Spanish leather," Sebastian said. A vast, ancient, heavily carved bed jutted out into the middle of the room. Sebastian pulled aside the tapestried bed curtains. The covers were in a shambles, which made me even shyer. So very personal to see the naked sheets where he had slept.

There was a movement within the mound of coverlet. Strange. A dog lay curled there. A plump little red and white spaniel. It jumped up on its short legs and barked sharply.

"Here," Sebastian said, beckoning. "Draw closer. What I wish to show you is right up there. On the headboard."

I did as he said. The dog trotted over to the edge of the bed, growling. Hesitantly I reached out a hand. My fingers went through his nose. I stiffened. "Fenris?" I whispered.

The dog ceased threatening and eagerly wagged its tail.

Sebastian had slept with a ghost last night.

"I beg your pardon?" Sebastian said.

"N-nothing." This must be Marietta's dog. He looked exactly as he had in the painting. I looked determinedly up from Fenris and peered into the gloom beneath the canopy. "What did you find?"

Sebastian had clambered onto the mattress and stood where he could reach high onto the towering paneled headboard. He pressed and poked at the oaken floral design. "It is here somewhere."

"What is?"

Even as I asked the question, Sebastian pushed upon a certain rosette, and a little door shot open out of the headboard.

"There is a coiled spring," he explained.

It took only a moment to scramble onto the mattress myself and peek into the cavity Sebastian had revealed, my chest still fluttering from the moment when the secret compartment popped open. Fenris tried to jump up on me and fell through my skirt. He backed away and watched with bright, curious eyes. From the recess wafted a faint perfume, the ghostly fragrance of a rose garden in some long-ago June. The shadowy cubbyhole was not empty.

"Well," I said, "from now on I shall never rest until I have pressed every last bit of carving on every last bit of wood in Wyndriven, which will take forever, of course, but who knows what all might be hidden here?"

Sebastian agreed. "I wish I could help with the pressing. I have not yet inspected the contents. It did not seem right to do so last night, since I do not live here. I could hardly wait for you to come down this morning, as I thought you might find it as exciting as I do."

"That was kind of you. Such self-discipline."

Sebastian drew out a roll of yellowed paper. Hundred-year-dead brown petals showered down onto the sheets.

Gingerly, I reached in to remove some folded cloth. Clouds of fine dust rose from it as it stirred beneath my touch. The fabric was silk, of a beige color I guessed used to be pale pink, and so fragile, it tore in places no matter how carefully I handled it. Something small and hard fell from the center as it unfolded, and landed on a pillow. Fenris sniffed at the object, and Sebastian's hand went through the dog as he stooped to pick it up. A gentleman's signet ring. He shoved it on his finger.

The cloth was a long strip. Some sort of scarf. Irregular stains of dull maroon-brown blotted at intervals, large at one end, and then steadily smaller. The stiff brown cracked and flaked in places as the fabric shredded and frayed.

Meanwhile, Sebastian unrolled the paper coil to reveal writing in a round, childish hand, in faded brown ink. "It must be something remarkable if someone hid it away all these years. Oh. It is a love letter. Huh. This is unusual. And poignant. It is written to someone who had just died. Someone's 'darling Leo.' And it is signed 'Marietta.'"

I gasped. "Please let me have that," I said, reaching for the paper.

"Look, it is dated. It says 1745. Can you believe it, we are most likely the first to view this writing in more than a hundred and twenty years?"

"Please." I tried to pinch it from his fingers. "I know who Leo is. He's a man in one of the gallery paintings. I've wondered about him."

Sebastian handed me the sheaf of paper. "Take it, then, if it means so much."

My cheeks grew hot. "Thank you." I couldn't tell him why I was acting greedy.

"And take the ring too." He handed it to me. "That, at least, ought to be turned over to your headmistress."

I slipped it onto my thumb. "I suppose so." I changed the subject. "How ever did you discover the secret door? You were so clever."

He gave a short, awkward chuckle, and I had the impression that Sebastian did not laugh often. "A bat came swooping in just as I climbed into bed. I whacked at it with the pillow, and must have hit the concealed knob square on. Quite astonishing."

"What happened to the bat?"

"I wafted him out the window."

"Well, you were terribly brave."

A funny, giant smile spread across Sebastian's face, as he flushed a dark crimson. "May I—if I can find a way, may I come visit you here sometimes? We could investigate carved objects and—and converse."

"That would be nice. Actually there are some things going on that I would like your advice about. You seem to know so much. Is there a way you could come one evening next week?"

"I will find a way. Mr. Crow allows me great freedom."

"Because of your noble blood."

"Yes. Because of that."

A short while later, we girls stood about the drive, beneath a mist-shrouded silver sun, watching as the forest closed around wagons full of Albion boys. At my ankles, Fenris made a hulla-baloo for my ears only. He had waddled along behind me when I left what I must assume had been Marietta's bed. I had tried to shut him up in my suite when I deposited the items Sebastian and I had discovered, but he popped right out through the closed door to follow me. I had never been around dogs before. How did one

engage with them? How did one keep them from barking? Even if
no one else could hear him, I could, and it hurt my ears.

Marietta's letter beckoned. Perhaps it was not entirely hon-
orable, but I needed to read it while Leo was absent. I took
only a moment to drop a cup of tea off for Dorcas, and then
finally could seat myself in my rocker with the items in my lap.
With great effort, fat little Fenris braced himself and jumped up
among them. He curled into a round dog cushion, and oozed
over the letter, ring, and scarf. I felt no true warmth, no weight
from him, yet his presence caused a velvety warmth and comfort
to spread inside me.

"Good puppy," I whispered. "Good Fenris." I moved one
hand over his form, hoping he could receive some pleasure from
my un-touch. He twitched and his black lips stretched into a
contented smile. Really, in his own way, he was a fetching little
spaniel. How had it been for him all these lonely years haunting
Wyndriven?

My hands trembled as I unrolled the sheaf of papers. The two
yellowed sheets cracked as I forced them flat enough to read. A
few petals drifted down through Fenris and onto my lap.

*June 16, 1745. My love, did you have a premonition this would be
your last day on earth?*

I can barely write for weeping. (The ink was blotched. Marietta's
tears.)

*They destroyed the beast who cracked your poor skull against a limb.
You said you had tamed him gentle as a lamb. Tamed! Ha! I almost
laughed just now, and it was a dreadful sound.*

*It is a small comfort that you waited to die in your bed, and also that
I think you did not feel a great deal of pain. When you lay with your poor*

broken head in my lap, all wrapped about with my scarf, you actually smiled a little. The scarf lies beside me on the desk, your blood upon it.

You lived until twilight. Your spirit departed with the sun.

I do not understand. How can it be that you returned from those years of danger at sea, only to expire here at your home?

Darling Leo, when you came back I thought we had all the time in the world for love and joy, for declarations and caresses. I remember it now – on that Christmas Eve when you returned home, we all made merry, although Godfrey glared at you sometimes when he did not know I saw. Poor thing, he feared he was about to be replaced in my affections, which was not true – you have never for a moment ceased to hold my heart. We sang carols, and as we did so, the strains of the choir sounded from outside. We served them spicy hot pies and rum punch. You stood behind me, very close. It seemed at that moment as if the thing I wanted was near.

True, as the days passed, I knew you did not love me as I love you. Lately you cherished only the company at the tavern. You certainly did not seek MY company. While you lived, though, I had hope that somehow I could make you care for me.

Now you're gone with all those words unsaid. So much unrealized. But perhaps you saw me kiss your marble cold lips. And perhaps you can read this over my shoulder. Are you with me now, Leo? I shall say the words out loud as I write: I love you. I always have and I always will.

I must leave a trace of my love. I shall hide this away never to be found, and then, in some way it will live even if you and I do not. I shall put this letter in the safest, most secret place I know. I thought to put it in the passage behind the chimneys, but there is a chance that Godfrey is aware of the concealed entrances. Certainly, though, he knows nothing of the compartment in my bed.

Godfrey is anxious and eager to comfort me — as if anyone could! He is always patience itself to me, even when he is short-tempered with others. I am afraid that Godfrey has been jealous of you ever since we all grew old enough to understand how things were. I suppose it is natural. You owned everything. You had my heart and, once Uncle Robert and Cousin Edwin died, you also had an inheritance. Poor Godfrey must feel very guilty tonight about the resentment he has carried.

What does any of this matter now? What does this solid body matter? Godfrey may have it, as so many long, empty years stretch ahead, but the true part of me, the shining, winged part, will never be his, but only and forever yours, Leo.

Oh, my darling, I shall see you again. Not in this world, but in that bright place to come.

Adieu, from your Marietta

I sat holding the curling yellowed pages. A piece of me wanted to keep this back from Leo. I didn't want him to know that Marietta had loved him because I didn't want him to think of her. I had been envious of her the first time he said her name, back on that first night I spoke to him. He had cried out in anguish, asking where Marietta was. I remembered the pain in his face when I told him of the portrait of Marietta and Godfrey and their children.

I allowed the sheets to roll back up, and carefully, deliberately, stood, leaving Fenris in the rocker.

I am done with jealousy.

A most unattractive quality and one calculated to drive away the very person one is anxious over. No more silly begging for Leo's attention or reassurance or compliments.

I placed everything on the table. I used books to weigh down the edges of the two pages of the letter so they wouldn't roll back up. So Leo could read them.

Fenris lifted his head and growled. At Leo.

"Who is that you have there?"

I didn't answer. Leo's lips parted as he considered the dog more closely. "That looks just like—Fenris?"

The dog jumped from the rocker and scampered behind my skirts, still growling.

"It is him, isn't it?" I said. "A little ghostly spaniel. I came upon him this morning and he's followed me ever since."

Leo shook his head. "I can't believe it." He squatted down beside Fenris and held out his fingers. The dog drew away, trembling. Leo chuckled. "He always hated me." He continued patiently courting Fenris, speaking in a quiet voice. Gradually, the spaniel allowed himself to be stroked. "I used to dislike him, but not anymore. Oh, Fiona, this is *nice* to have Fenris here."

The dog rolled on his back and Leo rubbed his belly.

Tears pricked at my eyes as I watched the two of them together. After such long, empty years, with everyone they knew gone away, the two could have ghostly company from their past.

"There's something else," I said quietly.

It seemed hard for Leo to tear his attention from Fenris, but he glanced over, mildly enquiring.

My chin trembled as I indicated the paper lying on the table. "That's a letter from Marietta, written to you after your death. It's been hidden away all these years."

Leo's expression was a study. Incredulity, hope, fear. Pain gnawed at my heart as he began to read.

These yellowed sheets — this fold and crease —
This ink gone light as water stains —
This loving cry — all dead, all dried —
That echoes out the same, the same.
—By Fiona O'Malley

CHAPTER 25

THE MADMAN'S GHOST

"There's something you need to know." I twisted the handkerchief in my lap into a tight coil.

Miss Petheram sat behind her desk. Perhaps the velvet draperies over the window behind her had once been a brighter crimson hue, but now they had faded to the maroon of old blood. "What is it, my dear?"

"It's about Monsieur."

"Monsieur?"

"I don't know his name. I only know him as Monsieur."

"And who is the man? From where do you know him?"

"He's here. I met him when I first arrived at Wyndriven. He told me he's a manager for the estate or something like that."

"I don't know who you're talking about." Her voice was brittle. "What does he look like?"

"Tall, good-looking. A French man around forty or so. He has black hair and beard. Oh, and he wears silver earrings. You must know who I mean."

In the shocked silence I could hear a goat bleating out on the lawn.

Miss Petheram's mouth became a thin line. "You have seen a picture somewhere. That is what you're describing. Or is this a jest? I understand schoolgirls and their jokes, wanting to plague the headmistress. But Fiona, child, I'm surprised at you. This is far more unkind than you can imagine."

My eyes widened. "There is no jest. I'm aware there's trouble between Monsieur and your family, but he seemed nice and amusing, at first anyway. Now, though, some things he said…"

"Now — what?" She leaned in closer. "You say he has spoken to you? Tell me what he said. Tell me *exactly* what he said."

I drew back at her sudden vehemence, but I did my best to recount word-for-word what Monsieur had stated at the ball about Miss Sophie and Daisy.

Miss Petheram held an ivory letter-opener and began tapping against an inkwell, first slowly, then faster, faster.

"It's not just what he said," I explained at the end. "It was his tone and the way he looked at them. He hates all your family. You have got to beware of him. He's dangerous. I can sense it. I also brought this for you to see." From beside my feet I picked up the little chest that had been in the library. I opened the lid so the headmistress could see the savagely shredded scraps of tapestry. "I — I may be wrong, but somehow lately I feel as if he's connected with *this* as well."

Miss Petheram's face blanched and seemed to melt. She jumped up and ran to the doorway. "Harry!" she screamed. "Harry!"

Mr. Harry must have been close, because he was with us in only a moment. "What is it?"

Miss Petheram clung to him, shaking. She struggled to collect herself enough to say, "Harry, he's still here!"

"Who?" He pulled back and took his sister by the shoulders.

"Bernard de Cressac. Even now we aren't rid of him! We're none of us safe!"

"What on earth are you talking about?"

"Tell him, Fiona. Tell him what you just told me."

And so I did.

Mr. Harry's jaw hardened as he disentangled himself from his sister. "Nonsense. She's heard the story somewhere. From whom, Miss O'Malley? Who told you about de Cressac? The servants?"

His tone was so harsh that I shrank against the back of my chair. "No one. No one's told me anything. I've never heard that name before. I met Monsieur out by the chapel the first time. Since then I've talked with him several times, all over the place."

"She knows details about him," Miss Petheram said, "and besides, why would she lie, Harry? Fiona isn't that sort of girl. *De Cressac's spirit is haunting Wyndriven.* I knew he was too strong to die so easily. Oh, why did we ever think we could stay on here?"

At the word "spirit," my mouth fell open. I looked at the open window, the desk, the walls. "Are you saying—" my tongue seemed to swell so I could hardly push out the words—"are you saying that Monsieur is dead? That he's a ghost?"

Miss Petheram bit her lip, then nodded slowly, significantly.

"I'm not saying any such thing!" Mr. Harry exclaimed. "I don't for a second believe anything so preposterous. I will concede that Miss O'Malley is not making this up on purpose, but I'm afraid I must agree with the great Ebenezer Scrooge. It's all humbug. What you've seen may be caused by a disorder of the stomach. Your Monsieur is undoubtedly an undigested bit of okra."

I would have laughed if I wasn't so wretched. Miss Petheram

and I both shook our heads.

"Look!" Miss Petheram cried. "Look at the tapestry Sophie stitched for him. It's been ravaged. Who would do that? Only de Cressac, he hated her so."

Mr. Harry barely glanced at the chest. "Nonsense." Evidently he thought that if he proclaimed something nonsense, it automatically became so.

I bit the inside of my cheek, trying to think how to explain myself. "I see them often," I said softly. "Spirits. I guess it's my Irish peasant legacy. But Monsieur appeared so real, I never suspected. He isn't limited in where he goes, at least around much of the house and grounds. And he wears different clothing at different times. In the past, the ones I've seen always dressed the same. Other people—a few times other people seemed to view him as well. Mr. Moss once, and Sparrow—Oh, I'm so stupid. Sparrow also has the Sight, so she didn't know either." Now that I knew, it was all obvious. Why he never touched me. Why he never spoke to anyone else. Why he avoided me when others were around. He never blurred about the edges or faded in and out as Leo sometimes did. He wouldn't. He was too powerful and too clever for that. He had learned his way around many of the restrictions that limited Leo. "He wanted me to believe he was living," I said bitterly. "It must have amused him."

Miss Petheram reached over and lightly touched my hand. "Is it possible he hoped he could use your—your hands? To make you do things for him? To spread his hate through you?"

Mr. Harry had been listening with a face like stone. Now his expression changed to one of disgust. I understood. It was the only reaction he could come to terms with at this moment. "So was it you who tore up the tapestry?"

"No!" I cried, shocked. "No. I didn't. Why would I do that when it means nothing to me?"

"It was a gift from our sister Sophie to de Cressac." Carefully, rigidly gathering her composure, Miss Petheram now related the history of her family with Monsieur. "M. de Cressac was Sophie's guardian. She came to him at Wyndriven Abbey at the age of seventeen, an innocent in every way. And he was obsessed with her. He flattered her and showered her with luxuries. You — you have seen how he is. He had an overwhelming personality. He isolated her and tried to undermine her agency, distort her view of the world. She pitied him and was deceived for a long while about what he truly was. We all were. She made excuses for his ill humors, since she did not know that de Cressac's fits of fury, his possessiveness and selfishness, were actually madness. How could she fathom that? How could any normal person? For various reasons, all selfless, she allowed herself to become betrothed to him. The tapestry was her Christmas gift to him that year. She stitched it with her own hair. And strands from the tresses of his murdered wives." Seeing my look of horror, she added, "Yes, it was ill-advised, but she didn't understand what she was dealing with."

"How horrible. And yet, I can understand how easily she could be fooled, especially since she is a kind person. She would want to help a troubled man."

"Exactly." Miss Petheram took a deep breath. "When Sophie finally stumbled upon the knowledge that her *fiancé* was a murderer, she barely escaped with her own life. After she inherited the estate, she kept the tapestry in that box as a sort of honor to the dead women. Who on earth could have done that to it?"

No one could answer that question.

My legs were jittering, and I didn't even try to still them. "So Monsieur, the man I have known these weeks, is the murdering husband." I shook my head. "How he must have laughed when I questioned him about the killings at Wyndriven. He told me so many half-truths." The thought of Monsieur's laughter made my skin crawl as if worms were wriggling over it.

"Half-truths are also half-lies," Miss Petheram breathed. She looked appalling, even her lips bone-white.

"With Monsieur," I declared, "the lies were the bigger half. How could he hide his madness so well? How could he act normally when he had performed such gruesome deeds?"

Mr. Harry had been standing, elbows on the mantel, with his forehead pressed against the wall above. He turned now. A harsh color stained his cheeks. "He—he was not always mad. He truly had a painful life. His adored son died terribly, and then Victoire—the first wife—set him off by her adultery." He compressed his lips. "There was also the absinthe. He over-used it, and everyone knows *la fée verte* turns men into beasts."

"Don't make excuses for him!" Miss Petheram exclaimed. "And I had never heard about him drinking absinthe. Where did you learn such a thing?"

"Don't recall." Mr. Harry sank down onto the window seat, and put his head in his hands.

"How did he die?" I remembered my walk in the woods with Monsieur. "I know it was before he could be hung. Something happened in the forest, didn't it?"

"His leg was caught in the claws of a trap," Miss Petheram

said. "That was how Sophie escaped and he was apprehended by the law. Gangrene set in, and it killed him."

"He told me about the trap, but not, naturally, that he died from it. He limps still."

No one spoke for several minutes, as we all tried to come to terms with everything.

"What should we do, Harry?" Miss Petheram finally said. "Should we ask Gideon or Father Paul for assistance? Perhaps they — "

Mr. Harry started and looked up. "Why should we *do* anything? If — and I'm not saying I believe it — but *if* some shade of de Cressac lingers in this place, then he's been here for twelve years, and Miss O'Malley is the only one to notice. We were fine until she came. If she will only ignore any unnatural manifestations in the future, then how can he hurt anyone? He can do nothing himself, so I should think we're safe."

"That's just it!" I wailed. "I don't think anyone *is* safe. Now that I know what he is, I fear he may have caused Bridey's death. I believe she saw him, only he appeared to her as malignant black smoke trying to take on a man's shape. How did I not realize it? He asked me about her once. I thought it odd that he should have an interest in my maid."

"He couldn't have pushed her down the stairs," Mr. Harry said. "If there is such a thing as a spirit, it would have no substance."

"Perhaps he couldn't have pushed her," I said as I dabbed at my eyes, "but he could have purposely frightened her, hanging over her there at the top of the steps, so that she fell backward. He killed her just as much as he killed those others. I should have sent her away when she first told me about the smoke. It's my fault she died."

Miss Petheram put her arm around me. "No, dear, it was not. No one could have imagined such an outcome. It's been two months since your maid's death—don't rake it all up again. And you cannot know that is what happened anyway." At a sudden thought, she stood straight and gasped. "De Cressac couldn't be standing here listening to us, could he? Invisible?"

To me this was a perfectly logical question, but Mr. Harry rolled his eyes. "Anne! *Please!*"

"I believe I would see him if he were," I reassured her. "It's not as if he's always around. Although…I don't know what he does when he's not with me. Perhaps he wanders around spying on anyone he wants to. Certainly he's aware of some of the goings-on at the school."

"Miss O'Malley!" Mr. Harry glared. "Bite your tongue. Now my sister will be imagining a spook in every shadow."

Miss Petheram sank into her chair behind the desk. "No, Harry, I won't," she said carefully, licking her lips. "I refuse to become nervous and foolish. The girls would sense something is wrong, and I will not have that."

Mr. Harry stood and loomed over me. "Promise you won't mention any of this to the other young ladies, Miss O'Malley. We don't need hysterics and parents pulling their daughters out." His voice was cold. So unlike the light-hearted Mr. Harry I had known up until now.

I looked from side to side, trying to think. "I can't promise absolutely," I said finally, "but I'll say nothing unless I feel there's a great need. That's the best I can do." As I stood and started to leave the room, I whirled around. "But what about the tapestry? Who ripped it?" If Monsieur had done *that*, what else could he do?

They had no answers.

I met Sylvie on my way back to my rooms. She was heading to the banquet hall. I myself was going to miss supper — too ill-at-heart to eat.

It took a moment to realize that Sylvie was looking cheerful — even smug — which was puzzling since she'd been distinctly pitiful all morning.

"I see you've recovered," I said.

"Yes," she said, "because I know I'll get him back. He's told me countless times that he can't resist me. Sometimes his mind is haunted by all the terrible things he saw in the war. I'm betting that's his problem now. I shall use all my powers of attraction to make him forget. Watch — before a week is up he'll be at my feet."

"Hmm."

She floated blissfully on her way, entirely sure of her powers.

I doubted them. Mr. Harry hadn't seemed like himself at all when I had just seen him. Of course, how should I have expected him to behave? I had just told him something unbelievably shocking. And poor Miss Petheram. But I had been right to tell them. I could not handle the knowledge of Monsieur on my own, and, appalling though it had been, I had needed to learn what he really was. I was equally appalled at the fact that, even after so many clues, I had not been able to discern a spirit from a living person. How had I been so dense?

Marietta's things still lay on the table in my room. The pages of the letter were still spread out so Leo could re-read them again and again, as he had seemed to want to do last night.

Even though it was only late afternoon, still light, I changed from my day dress into my night clothes and crawled into bed. Fenris lay at the foot. I wished I could feel him, curled up warm and furry. I wished I could fall asleep now and sleep and sleep.

This same time last night my friends and I had been in here, laughing and cavorting, preparing for the ball. How long ago it seemed that Leo had kissed me.

Since then he had read Marietta's letter. Nothing would be the same since he knew now that Marietta had loved him. In his face I had read conflicting emotions. I tried to envision what he was experiencing. He had said it was hard to remember his old life, but those old feelings must be surging back. He was recovering his love for Marietta, even though at this time she was as distant and unattainable as the sun. He had no way of knowing if he could ever go to where she was. Meanwhile, I was here and he liked me. What should he do? How should he feel?

At this very moment, did Marietta kneel at the throne of God, pleading for Leo? How could the Lord long resist the prayers of someone as perfect as Marietta?

And Monsieur...Now that I knew he was the murderer, I pictured him squatting in the heart of Wyndriven like a toad in a hole—his handsome face changed to a dark, bloated thing. How should I react when I saw him next? Walk past him? Somehow will myself not to see him? I had tried such a thing before, with The Two, but never succeeded. Perhaps Miss Petheram could call on Father Paul to bless the house? But if he did, would Leo be driven out? Consigned to hell? Again and again I had to tell myself that Monsieur could do nothing without hands of flesh and bone to do it for him. But the tapestry? Perhaps I should leave Wyndriven immediately. Mr. Harry had been right—everyone had been fine here until I arrived.

Everyone except Leo and Monsieur.

Neither of them should be here, whether living people knew of their wrong, skewed existence or not. Somehow each needed to move on to their proper place. But oh! I did not want Leo to leave. And I did not want to leave either.

Fenris suddenly leaped up, gave one short bark, and wagged his tail so hard that his fat jiggled. I looked up, and there stood Leo at my bedside. The sunset glowing through the window behind him was bright, but he was brighter.

He watched me for a moment, then, without a word, lay down, facing me from the other pillow a few inches away.

"Oh. How are you?" My voice sounded sleepy even though I wasn't.

"How are *you*?"

"I've been better. I thought you didn't need to rest."

"I don't. I just wanted to lie here near you. To watch over you as you slept. I have felt extra protective of you since Bridey's passing." Fenris padded up and snuggled against Leo's chest, in between the two of us. "It's still daytime. Are you unwell?"

I sighed. "I've had a shock." I told him about Monsieur.

Leo sat straight up. "I'm...speechless."

I pushed up on my elbows. "It's all so dreadful."

He wriggled back to sit up against the headboard, his face drawn. "And so this madman's spirit, this Monsieur, not only might well have caused Bridey's accident, but has been — what? — *dallying* with you all these weeks? Entertaining himself at your expense?"

I wriggled back to join him. "I guess that's what he's been doing. I hope he didn't hope to use me for some sort of malicious mischief."

"You must avoid him at all costs. If only I could get out of here and find the man, I would slam him past the moon."

I had to laugh, but only for a second. And weakly. "If that ever happens, may I watch?" I pulled the bedclothes up higher around my neck without disturbing either Leo or Fenris. "It will take me some time to figure out all this Monsieur business. But really it's not something you need to worry about. I can take care of myself, and the Petherams know about it too. What I do need now is for you, Leo, to tell me something."

"And what is that?"

I paused, trying to put into words what I must know. "You've read that letter. Now that you're aware how much Marietta loved you, does it make you more anxious than ever to move on to where you can be with her? At first I had meant to exhaust all possible resources to figure out how to send you on over, but we've sort of ignored all that for a while."

Leo didn't answer for a moment. He examined his hands and fiddled with his emerald ring. So amazing that the tangible ring was in my possession. Finally he looked up. "Fiona."

"Yes. That's me. Right here."

"It was a queer experience reading that letter. As if two worlds were colliding. I'm not someone who is good with words, as you are — "

"Oh, I'm not good with *speaking* words, I'm only good with writing — "

"Please, let me finish. I was only trying to say that it's hard for me to explain how I feel. In the first world, Marietta was wonderful, and I adored her. Even in this world, her memory holds a piece of my heart. But she's far, far away and long, long ago. The letter was sorrowful for that long-ago Marietta and bittersweet for that long-ago Leo. Now this Leo—me—I am here and I am now and I am so happy to have you with me. And the rest of my heart, except for that little piece, is full of you, Princess."

"But Marietta was so charming and beautiful, how can you care for me when I'm completely unlike her?" I had promised myself that there would be no more insecurity or fishing for compliments, but once and for all I had to hear him say that I was what he wanted. At least here and now.

"Marietta was perfect for Marietta, and Fiona is perfect for Fiona. What can I say? Evidently a fellow can fall madly in love with two entirely different types of ladies."

"So you're madly in love with me? Here and now? Can you really love an awkward schoolgirl?" I spoke softly, shyly.

"I am. I can. I do." There was a breathless note to his voice. "And what about you? Can you love an outlandish spook?"

"I can. I do." My own voice was equally breathless.

He groaned and encircled me in his arms. My flesh could feel nothing, but my heart pounded as if it would burst my chest.

"All this is unreal, you know," I said.

"Of course."

"Every moment we're together is stolen."

"Heaven is barred to me, but when I'm with you, I don't miss it."

I didn't want to say it, but I said it: "We need to unbar it then. It isn't right for you not to miss it and strive for it."

"Fiona." His tone was firm. "Forget all that for these few, stolen moments."

CHAPTER 26

HIDE AND SEEK

A pile of musty calf-bound volumes lay on the table in my sitting room, with titles such as *A Book of False Ghosts Who are in Truth Devils in Disguise,* or *A Treatise of Apparitions; Verily Whether the Spirits of the Dead do Indeed Roam the Earth,* all penned by Learned Doctors and Ministers. None of them dated from later than 1700. Leo and I had tried to peruse them several times, but the reading was not easy and nothing we studied seemed pertinent to either him or Monsieur.

During the week since I had learned that Monsieur was dis-embodied, I had not spoken again to the Petherams. Sometimes I would catch Miss Petheram watching me with haunted worry in her eyes. As for Mr. Harry, until hearing my story, he had always seemed to like me, tossing out a bantering word or two whenever we met. Now he would see me coming and duck the other way.

Luckily, I had been distracted by my present world from feeling too anxious about any what-ifs. Every moment with Leo was delightful, I continued to enjoy soirees with The Club, and I had seen neither hide nor hair nor earring of Monsieur. Maybe

I would never see him again. Maybe. However, Leo and I had discussed what I should do if Monsieur sauntered up one day. I would either act perfectly natural, as if I knew nothing, or, if I could, I would simply ignore him. Walk right on past. Or through. Although the latter seemed rather terrible.

Late one afternoon, I was half-heartedly turning the thick, yellowed pages of a ponderous volume, with Leo looking over my shoulder, when my attention was drawn to Fenris wriggling on his back at my feet.

So sad that I couldn't give the little fellow the attention he craved. "Would you please rub Fenris's belly?" I asked Leo.

Trix burst in just as I said this, and paused in mid stride, her bonnet fallen back on its ribbons and her hair tussled. "Rub whose belly?"

Leo, who was sending Fenris into ecstasy by scratching the dog's stomach, laughed out loud.

I resisted the temptation to give him A Look. "Oh," I indicated the weighty tome at my fingertips, "just reading out loud."

"You are the oddest girl in the world," Trix said. "And you have the oddest taste in literature."

"I am and I do. What did you need?"

"You've a visitor."

"Really? Who?"

"This will thrill you." She gave a wicked grin. "Your conquest of last week—Mr. Thatoor—has come courting."

"Oh, my goodness. It's not like that at all. Sebastian said he would call—"

"And it's already 'Sebastian.' Sly boots."

"I am not a '*sly boots*'—whatever that's supposed to mean,

anyway. Pray stop acting like Sylvie. Sebastian said he would call, but I didn't think he really would." I glanced nervously up at Leo. He winked at me and strode into the other room.

"We're all gathered on the terrace since it's a lovely evening. If you'd like us to help you entertain Mr. Thatoor, he's out there right now."

I went with her to the terrace, where my friends had pulled wicker chairs into a circle at the top of steps leading to the garden. The reclining stone lions flanking them seemed to be standing guard.

Sebastian was already entertaining everyone with stories of India. Eventually I needed to get him alone to consult about the beads and bone, but I couldn't do it now. I seated myself, and this time I really listened to his tales. They were fascinating. As usual his speech was punctuated with words I had to translate in my head, since I wasn't *exactly* sure of their meaning.

"Did you swallow a dictionary?" Trix interrupted sharply at one point.

He flushed. "What do you mean?"

"Never mind her," Mary Dell said. "She's always teasing."

A quicksilver movement just beyond the rose garden caught my eye.

"Sparrow's out there." In a flash I was on my feet, dashing to catch the girl. "It's me, Sparrow!" I called. "Wait!"

The girl hesitated, her fingers resting lightly on a great urn that billowed with scarlet geraniums. She seemed to be wearing only a white lawn chemise, her hair all clouded around with purple wildflowers tucked in haphazardly. "I been wandering about here, hoping I'd see you," she said, looking shyly up through her lashes.

"For any particular reason?"

"Nope. Just hoping. Haven't seen you in a squirrel's age."

"My friends are all gathered outside," I said. "Won't you come and meet them? They really are nice. There's Varina—you'll love her, everyone does—and Dorcas, Mary Dell, Sylvie, and Trix. Trix acts mean, but it's all a show."

Sparrow peered with suspicion toward the terrace. "And a feller."

"That's Sebastian. I don't know him well yet, but he's awfully smart."

Her lips tightened as she nodded. "All right. But I ain't going inside."

I led her up to the group, silently beseeching everyone to be kind. To be friendly, but not too friendly. To ignore her apparel. Trix did narrow her eyes meaningfully at the sight of Sparrow, but other than that, somehow, they all did it exactly right. They smiled and spoke nicely, but did not swarm her. And Sparrow—well, she latched onto Sebastian immediately. She alighted on the back of the stone lion next to his seat, and openly gazed at Sebastian in fascination. He didn't seem to notice the attention, but began rattling off a long story about the time some of the Albion boys left a pair of opossums with their tails tied to a stick, hissing in his bedchamber.

Sparrow's lips parted in indignation. "Why, the poor little critters. Them bad boys hadn't no call to treat God's possums so!" Then she reached out a delicate hand to brush back the black hair that so often hung in Sebastian's face. He started at the touch. His eyes met Sparrow's for the first time. She began her slow-blossoming smile, and he kept looking at her face until it was in full bloom. And after.

One of the kids trotted up the steps from the lawn, his hooves making a trip-trap sound like one of the three Billy Goats Gruff. He poked his nose under Sparrow's elbow. She dropped her gaze from Sebastian to stroke the kid and whisper to him, and finally to lift him into her arms. If only I could paint her as she was, cradling a baby goat while perched on the rump of a lion.

"You charmed him, Sparrow," Varina said. "I've heard about the animals that come to your home. Won't you tell us about them?"

Sparrow looked from face to face, as if deciding something. Then she gave a little nod and told of the deer that poked its nose into the cottage every time the door was left unlatched, and of the wildcat who let her use its tawny body for a pillow. Every one of us fell under the Sparrow spell.

At last she blew out her breath and said, "I don't believe I've blabbed so much in all my born days. I ain't saying no more."

Trix jumped up. "I know what let's do. How about hide-and-seek? That lion is the home free. We can hide anywhere between this side of the building and the woods."

A chorus of "Not its" sounded, while Dorcas announced that she would not play. Too stomach-y.

"I will do the finding first," Sebastian said. "It is the gentle-manly thing to do."

"No fair," Sylvie pouted. "You can easily catch girls in corsets because we get winded when we run. And our fat petticoats and hoop are hard to squish in for hiding."

For a moment we were taken aback.

"Why, Sylvie Blake," Trix exclaimed. "For shame! The idea of mentioning undergarments in mixed company."

Sylvie flushed and giggled.

"We'll have to find extra good hiding places, then," Varina said quickly, hoping, I knew, to stave off a further Trix lecture.

Trix would have gone on for several minutes if she were in her arbiter-of-all-etiquette mode. However, since Sebastian took the undergarment-mentioning in stride, and since he had not appeared to notice in the least even Sparrow's revealing garb, Trix said nothing more.

"We can play the kind of hide and seek where he has to find everyone," Trix said. "So no running and chasing or home free."

We explained the rules to Sparrow, who had never played before, but who, I was sure, would take to the game like a duck to water. Sebastian dropped his head into his arms and began counting, while the girls, minus Dorcas, scattered like dandelion fluff in the wind.

I raced to the peach orchard, mainly because the idea of hiding among the flowery trees while wearing a pale rose gown seemed like something from a dream. Since the tree trunks were too thin for concealment, I sank down to the petal-strewn grass and waited to be found.

Dream-like indeed. I removed my hat and laid it beside me. Although shadows grew long, late sunshine embraced my cheeks. The air smelled tenderly sweet. I lifted my face, closed my eyes, breathed in the scent, and —

"Mademoiselle Fiona."

My entire body tensed and flinched, as if fingernails traced my spine. Monsieur. Slowly, reluctantly, I opened my eyes.

I swallowed, then flashed a bright smile. "What a splendid hide-and-seek player you are. I didn't hear a thing when you crept up."

His commanding presence towered above me. "One of my talents." He lowered himself to the ground. "So, we meet again at last. You have been avoiding me, Mademoiselle."

"No," I said, too quickly. "I've simply been busy. Schoolwork and friends and all. And you're elusive. I never know where to expect you."

"You are no longer the pitiful, solitary young lady I first met. I glimpse you at times with the others. The last time I could catch you alone was behind the curtain at the ball. Have you spoken to Sophia since then?" A breeze had picked up. I was careful not to notice that it did not so much as ruffle Monsieur's hair. The blue-black strands lay absolutely still, even though my own locks tickled my cheeks. Why had I never noticed such a thing before?

"I haven't. I—"

What happened next was so abrupt and so strange that I was too stunned to take it in immediately.

A swift, intense gust suddenly sent petals showering down, and lifted my hat from the ground where it lay. My hat blew right through Monsieur. Right through his golden brocade waistcoat.

I could only stare.

I should have looked away swiftly, pretended not to have seen. *But I saw it and he knows I saw it.*

My mouth went cotton-dry.

He turned his head slightly and appeared to watch my hat until it caught against the trunk of a tree. When he turned back, his face was frozen and his mouth was set, his eyes blank. Petals still drifted through him. "So," he said mildly, "now you know."

"Now I know." It came out as a whisper.

He gave a short laugh. "What a way for you to find out. So

absurd. So undignified. Being blown through. I do not recall that ever happening before."

My mind worked furiously. Somehow it seemed best that he believe this was the first time I had suspected. Always with him it was important to act unaware of things. That I give him as little information of any kind as possible. "Why didn't you tell me? I've always seen spirits."

"Have you indeed?"

"I would have accepted it as normal."

"How could I know that? I didn't want to lose you to hysterics. I had not spoken to another being in so long. And you were *très simpathique*. I could not risk frightening you away, *tu comprends*? Oh, Mademoiselle, it has been such a long, empty time, wandering alone. And now you are not afraid? You will continue to chat with me?"

"Ye—es," I said slowly.

He clapped his hands together. "This is splendid. I am pleased."

I smoothed out my skirts, not looking at him. "But may I ask a few questions? I haven't spoken much to spirits before. I'm curious."

"*Mais oui*. Naturally you are curious. The defining characteristic of females. I imagine you have a great deal to inquire of me." He ran his hands through his hair, his eyes sparkling. "Oh, this is good. Good. At last I can discuss this world of mine with someone else. I have told you in the past that I am happy you are unconventional. Now I grasp your difference in a new light. Another girl might have gone into the vapors. But you, Mademoiselle, simply ask, 'Why did you not tell me before?'" He gave a bark of laughter. "So, out with it—what do you wish to know?" He leaned forward, eager, watching me closely. His attitude seemed much more intimate than it had in the past.

"Can you move freely? Go anywhere you wish?"

"At first I was limited. Very limited. Bah! That I should be unable to roam at liberty about my own estate! I worked at it, straining my mind, my agency, my spirit body, until one day I found I could break through many barriers."

"You still have limitations, though, don't you? You can't enter my suite, for instance." If he could have, he would have.

He did not answer the question, but his honey brown eyes oozed over me, slow, suggestive, making me squirm. Even in the first days, before I began to irritate him, he had never looked at me like this. "If I do pay you a visit one evening, we might find it mutually enjoyable." He leaned in so that I felt the cold of his lips tickling my neck. "There are abilities I have discovered now that I am not caged in the prison of my former flesh. I can enter into places not built of wood and stone. Places of skin and bone. If I were to enter into you, you would find it an experience deeper, more personal, than any mortal sensual encounter."

I wiped ice cold sweat from my brow and forced myself not to leap away. "Could—could you do that? How?"

"Invite me in. Surrender your will to mine." His voice was a hiss.

My gaze was locked on his. His face moved so close that my eyes crossed. I tried to laugh and failed. Did he forget who he was? What he was? That he should play the seducer with me was nauseating. "Ha!" I exclaimed loudly. "No. I don't think so."

He pulled back. A little annoyed spark shone in his eyes. "You have always made it plain you do not find me attractive in that way. I wonder why?"

"And you have always made it plain that you don't find me attractive in that way either, so we're even."

He seemed nonplussed for a moment, and then roared with laughter. "Oho! So we are even!"

"You know," I said, "one of the reasons I never suspected you weren't alive is that you change clothing—do you have a spectral wardrobe floating about somewhere?"

He lifted his hands carelessly. "No. It is nothing of my doing. My attire changes with the setting. Inside the house my apparel is different from when I am outside. In the woods it is different from in the orangery. Perhaps it has to do with what I wore in those places when I was living, but I do not know."

"And have you learned to move objects, to make physical changes in the world with your spirit body?"

A shuttered look came over him. "No."

"What about Bridey?"

"Ah, your maid."

"It was you, wasn't it, who made her fall?"

"It was never my intention for that to happen. I had played with her a bit once before. Simply because it was distracting to have her see me. I am so unused to being noticed these days. It is a vast loneliness, a vast frustration—this existence. Surrounded by others, but invisible to them. The girl was standing at the top of the stairs and I simply came up behind her. She glimpsed me over her shoulder and lost her footing. It was regrettable."

"It was more than regrettable! It was tragic! She was so young and she must have been terrified. I have never gotten over the thought of her lying there, perhaps not dying immediately, in the dark." As always, my eyes welled at the image. "You killed her."

Monsieur shrugged. "Bah! Even if I did, what does it signify?" He sighed and ran a hand over his jaw. "How can I make
you understand? It makes no difference that one little person's
temporal life was extinguished. The girl simply moved to a new
existence. Please forgive me, Mademoiselle, if my thoughts on the
'tragedy' of discarding a mortal shell are not what yours are. *I* am
still here. Transformed."

I wiped my damp palms on the grass. Such a bizarre conversation. Sebastian's voice and Trix's sounded from a distance. I
yearned to flee from Monsieur, to join them, but I sat there, frozen
except for my tongue. "What about when the Stones lived here?"

"What about it?"

"How did you feel, seeing her always? With Brother Gideon.
With her children."

"How do you suppose I should feel?" For the first time he
spoke with passion, and his long fingers pressed into the earth,
sinking into it. Then the fire dowsed in his eyes and they became immeasurably bleak. "Sophiaaa..." The name came out in a
breath. "At first I had thought I had escaped retribution, but I discovered that, because of Sophia, hell was wherever I was. Always
it was where I was—living or dead."

I was trying to keep my voice level, but an edge crept into it
when I said, "And so you plot revenge. Did you think you could
use me for it?"

A small, cynical smile played about his lips. "Surely you
would not believe me so foolish as to think I could influence
Mademoiselle Fiona O'Malley to carry out my plans. Perhaps it
crossed my mind at first, but I quickly knew what you were. And
I was proved right, just now. You are stronger than you realize, in

your own innocent, dense, bumbling way. No, I shall not try to use *you*. Nevertheless, I shall soon have my vengeance against the Stones and Petherams."

Innocent. Dense. Bumbling. So be it. "And *you* are the murdering husband," I said steadily.

He flicked his pale fingers as if shaking away a subject with which he had little patience. "*Naturellement*. Can you not still see the blood on my hands? So drenched in it that I could never wash them clean. My intention was to snuff out the existence of those *sorcières* so they could do no more harm with their lies and treachery. Where they could hurt and betray me no longer. But, as I have said, my conception of the finality of death is now different from what it once was."

"Did you never feel remorse or guilt when you were alive? Did you never have nightmares about your victims?"

He did not speak for a moment. His eyes were hooded. Finally he looked up. "Only when I was awake."

I was shivering cold and yet perspiring as I grasped for command of myself. Confusion tangled in me. In a way, I pitied Monsieur, and this was dangerous if I were to fight him. From history books I knew that many tyrants and tormenters were also selfish whiners, shifting the blame to excuse dread deeds. This man was a beast — no sympathy should trickle into my heart.

He was considering me. Greenish flecks sparked in his amber irises. "Now," he said, "you are wishing you knew what I am plotting. You will be watching my strange and mysterious ways. It is tempting…"

I opened my mouth, but he raised his hand, halting me. "No, I shall not tell you my plans. You must wait and wonder and worry."

Enough was enough. I stood abruptly and brushed off my gown. "I am leaving now and I do not wish to speak to you again. Don't come near me. I am going to study and learn and do whatever I can to send you away from Wyndriven. And I will succeed."

He sucked in his cheeks and gave a bitter laugh. "So then, you choose to believe I am the monster of the story."

"You're a demon."

His furious glare burned.

I turned and started to walk away.

"It is a mistake to make an enemy of me, Mademoiselle," he called out. "A spirit I may be, but powerless I am not."

I flinched as if an arrow had shot between my shoulder blades. I had done it. The thing I had dreaded doing. I had brought Monsieur's hatred down on my own head. Without stopping, I said lightly, "How dramatic you are. Now you sound as if you're the villain in an amateur theatrical."

I walked on, slowly and stiffly, to keep my knees from buckling.

Tiger, tiger burning low
In the forests where they go
To hang the bandits from the trees--
There the fire, still un-seized

Is flickering. The tiger leaps
At nothing. As its rumble seeps
Into the dark, it licks the blood
Dried on its claws and tastes the mud

It hunted in. It bites the black
And bitter air. It arcs its back.
It twitches at a metal snap--
The distant closing of a trap.

I know (though I may be a lamb,
As young and flimsy as I am)
Though we may cower, by and by
Tigers, tigers also die.

— By Fiona O'Malley

CHAPTER 27

A GIFT FROM MONSIEUR

"There you are," Varina said, as I rejoined the group once again gathered on the terrace. "Where were you? We gave up on ever finding you."

"In the orchard."

"Well, that was off limits," Trix snapped. "I told everybody, y'all had to stay on this side of the building. Between you and Sparrow…Honestly, some folks can't ever follow rules."

"Sorry."

They were all watching me.

"Your face is as bloodless as a dead fish's underbelly," Trix observed charmingly.

"What's wrong, honey?" Varina asked. "You look as if you've seen a ghost."

I dropped to a seat, crushed beneath the weight of Monsieur's words, in spite of my parting bravado.

"Have you?" Dorcas inquired. "Have you seen a ghost?"

I put my hand to my forehead, squared my shoulders, and lifted my head, nodding slowly. "I just did." It was time. I had to confide in them. I needed help.

Trix snorted. "You lie."

"She's not—or rather, she doesn't!" Dorcas cried. "Fiona does see ghosts. She's told me all about them."

"Well," I said carefully, "not entirely all."

Varina reached over and took my hand, squeezing it. "What just happened?" she said quietly.

"I know how hard it is to believe, but it's true." I found myself giving a shaky, nervous smile, and could not imagine why I smiled, when what I wanted to do was cry. "I do see spirits. Often. And do you remember the murderer? The one who killed his wives in Wyndriven? Well, I was just chatting with him." My friends were silent, gaping, perplexed. "He was there in the orchard." And then I unburdened to them as much about Monsieur as I knew, including the fact that he vowed to hurt the Stones and Petherams, and that he had just now threatened me. "I need your help. We need to be rid of him. I don't know how, but we must," I finished. I had told the Petherams these things, but somehow had still felt as if the load remained on my shoulders. Now, as I revealed it all to my friends, the burden lightened. I looked up and waited for their reactions.

For a moment no one moved or spoke. Trix sat as still as I had ever seen her. Then she gave an incredulous laugh. Once this broke the silence, Sylvie trilled a line from "Spirit Rappings." "'Softly, softly hear the rustle of the Spirits' misty wings; they are coming down to mingle once again with earthly things.'"

"Hush, Syl," Mary Dell said. She had twisted her hair so tightly around her finger that her fingertip grew red and she had to quickly unwind the strands. She looked up at me apologetically.

"I'm so sorry, sugar, but I just can't believe in ghosts. Why would God allow such a thing?" She hastily added, "Bless your heart, though."

"I don't know why God allows it either, but for some reason He does." I sighed.

"So," Trix asked, "have you seen Bridey?"

"No."

"Why not? Why not her?"

I shrugged. "I don't know. I suppose because she was whisked straight off to heaven."

"And these other folks you see are all the bad ones?" Trix raised her pointed chin. "Is that what you think?"

"No. I don't know." I lifted my hands. "I've never had an understanding of any of it. Obviously I've only seen a few of those who've passed on, good or bad." All energy seemed to drain from my body. I was so tired. The load pressed down once more. "I don't blame you for not believing me, but it's a fact. They're there. The spirits I see aren't the chain-rattling, misty-sheet-wearing type. They're people caught in a between place. Sometimes they're horrible, but more often they don't really seem to know what's going on or what they are. Monsieur, of course, is horrid."

"What an extraordinary life you must have led," Varina said. "So you've been facing all this alone? Why on earth didn't you tell us before?"

"Of all people, you should understand why," I said to her sharply. "You keep secrets as well."

Varina looked away and crossed her arms.

Dorcas bit her fingernails thoughtfully. "I guess most folks have their own embarrassing or guilty skeletons in closets."

"In India, my ayah told stories of phantoms," Sebastian said. "She believed in them implicitly. They are called bhoots. Their feet face backward."

A pain shot through me. "I've heard of them."

"So the bad man is a haunt," Sparrow said. "Huh. I should've guessed.

Leo talk to him too?"

I shook my head.

"Leo?" Trix immediately latched onto the name. "Who's he?"

With one finger, I traced the vine pattern on my skirt, reluctant to have my Leo's name bandied about. Still...Was it possible they might help him as well? "He's the young man with the horse in the portrait gallery. He remains here too. It's time both spirits moved on—Monsieur because he's evil and Leo because he's good."

"Ooh." Sylvie waggled her eyebrows. "The eyes on that portrait follow you when you walk past them. Haven't y'all noticed? No wonder he's a spook."

Her casual dismissal of Leo made me wince. I related a smattering of his story. I did not mention that he shared my rooms, but I did include how Sebastian and I had found Marietta's letter.

"Aha," Sebastian said. "That is why you desired it."

"Yes. Leo had a right to read it."

"It was a love letter, as I recall." Sebastian nodded. "No wonder the fellow is eager to move on. Perhaps he hopes to be with the girl."

"Almost certainly." I couldn't help but grimace. No one noticed.

"How incredibly romantic," Sylvie said.

I gazed out into the sunset. Beyond the black lace treetops, pastel bands of color tinted the sky. Above us, bats swooped about the turrets.

"Anyway," I said after a moment, "if you'll only believe what I'm telling you, I need your help if we're to rid the place of Monsieur before he manages any more harm."

"And to assist Leo to move on," Mary Dell said. She gave a little smile. "I guess I do believe a little."

"I'm so glad you do. Yes. And to help Leo move on."

"To be with Marietta. How lovely." Sylvie sighed.

I was determined to be unselfish, but must they twist the knife?

"I'll ask Memaw about haunts," Sparrow said. "To her, they be common as pig tracks, and they never fool her, no ma'am, no matter how tricksy they get. There was one kept hiding Memaw's sassafras root till she stuck a broom at the door to keep it from coming in. That's what folks supposed to do."

"Please do ask her," I said. "We must find out all we can from every source if we're to fight Monsieur."

"So that's why all those books were in your room," Trix said, her eyes alight. "All those incredibly boring-looking tomes about spirits. Tomorrow let's each take one and study it till we're an expert on our book."

So Trix was coming around.

"We also ought to talk to Brother Gideon," Varina said. "And Father Paul."

"And Mr. Willie," I added. "Did you know he was a preacher?"

"Why haven't you told any of *them* about this before?" Trix asked.

"It's not something I tell people. I did talk to Miss Petheram and Mr. Harry. Perhaps they've spoken to the others."

"Oh, *Harry.*" Sylvie sniffed. "Maybe that's why he's acting so unlike himself. He's worrying about all this."

"It's *Mr.* Harry to you now," Trix said smartly. "Since he appears to be cutting off all contact with you."

"He *is*, isn't he?" Sylvie wailed. "But why? I've done nothing wrong. I've used every last little wile I possess, yet when he passes by me he acts as if I mean no more than—than Mary Dell."

When Sylvie first started speaking, Mary Dell opened her mouth as if she would offer a word of comfort, but at the finish she clamped her lips tightly shut.

"He's simply come to his senses, Sylvie," Trix said, in a patient voice that was meant to be kind. "He knows he's a fool to have traipsed after a schoolgirl."

"I declare, you should've seen the look he gave *you*, though, the other day," Sylvie said, glaring at Trix. "You just better stay away from him, Trix Pringle!"

Trix rolled her eyes. "Ha. Silly folks always say that sort of thing, and it's ridiculous. How can anyone ever tell what kind of 'look' anyone is giving anyone? I bet he didn't even see me and was dreaming of curling up to his cozy bottle that night, or some such thing."

"No." Sylvie said, shaking her head. "He was *ogling* you. I could tell."

I watched them wearily, one after another. Not a one of them was taking my news as seriously as they ought. They should be frightened. They shouldn't have room in their minds for anything but how to either avoid or combat Monsieur. They simply didn't understand the reality of the situation. "And so," I brought them back to the subject at hand, "our goals are to figure out how to send Leo happily off to heaven as soon—as soon as can be contrived, and to deal with Monsieur. Monsieur, who is very strong and very evil and very *driven*. I wish you could meet him so you could know what we're up against."

"I don't wish it," Sylvie said. "He doesn't sound at all nice."

Dorcas had been determinedly chewing one fingernail after another. "In life that man slaughtered seven people, and as a spirit he caused another death. That's the sort of being he is." Perhaps Dorcas did understand.

"No matter what," Varina said, "we must especially protect Fiona. He is far too interested in her." And perhaps Varina did as well.

"We must rid the place of this demon," Sebastian said, "before he manages to injure anyone else. He is cunning. He will find a way before long." And Sebastian.

I rubbed my arms. The goose bumps remained that had grown there since Monsieur first spoke. Silence hung heavy. It was all finally sinking in.

"Let's all go warm up some milk and molasses in the kitchen," Mary Dell said unexpectedly. "Miz Jump's gone for the evening, and a snack will make everything better."

Sylvie began to giggle, and the rest of us followed suit.

"So," Trix choked out, "is that a promise? Everything will be delightsome after milk and molasses? Well, then by all means let's go get some of that magical brew."

"Sebastian, can you stay?" I asked.

"I will," he said. "Mr. Crow knows where I am and will not thwart me."

"The convenient maharajah," I said.

"Yes. Indeed my father is convenient."

We all trouped toward the kitchen, including our guests. Sparrow sidled up beside me, just ahead of Sebastian. "In all my born days," she whispered, "I ain't never seen a finer-looking fellow. He makes me think of a deer — all brown eyes and narrow face."

"Of course you haven't seen a great many fellows. You do live in the middle of the woods in Mississippi and — how old are you, Sparrow?"

"Fourteen," she answered absently, gazing dreamily at Sebastian's back. "So tall. But too skinny. I'm fixing to feed him on honey and cream, and to take him often out into the sun."

She slowed until Sebastian caught up to her, and from then on she clung to his side. I heard him say, "What other information has your grandmother given you about spirits?"

Sparrow answered, "She says that on one plantation where she stayed there was the haunt of a wicked master who come back from the grave to keep on tormenting his slaves. They was as a-scared of him dead as they was of him alive. And on another there was a slave returned from the grave to seek revenge against his wicked master. Memaw says…"

After our magical warm drink, when everything actually did feel better, Sparrow announced that she was going to walk Sebastian home, in spite of his protests that he should accompany her to *her* place. They wandered off, arguing. It was nearly lights-out time by then, so the rest of us parted ways. I hurried to my suite, eager to inform Leo of the latest developments.

However, the moment I opened the door an echoing emptiness reached out to meet me. No Leo. No little dog. I moved from sitting room to bedchamber to dressing room, rigid with every one of my senses tensed to pick up the *feel* of Leo. Even when I could not see him, I could feel him. But not now.

He is gone.

I sank into my rocker, trying to take this in. It had happened. Leo had finally managed to move on. Which was good. Which was right. Which was what I wanted for him. And he'd taken Fenris along.

But perhaps they had only moved *out*. Perhaps even now they were roaming the expanses of their old home. If Leo had broken through the barriers he would certainly be eager to explore every corner. Afterward, certainly he would return to me. He had promised he would never leave for good without telling me goodbye.

Unless he had had no choice.

For several minutes I sat with my head in my hands, feeling hollow.

Well...unfortunately *I* was still here. And needed to go to bed. Tiredly, I stood and reached behind my neck to untie my cameo ribbon. I removed each earring as well, lifted the lid of my jewelry chest—and shrieked.

Inside writhed a wriggling knot of earthworms, pinky-gray, twining amongst my jewels.

I staggered backward, retching.

I made myself approach the chest and drop the lid, because—horror-of-horrors—what if the worms should get out and slither to other places? What if I should step on one barefoot? What if one got into my bed?

I snatched up a lamp and dashed for Varina.

Gradually I slowed. Although the house was silent, there

was something vigilant and listening about the quiet. Behind one of these closed doors, in the darkness, someone was awake and aware of my movements. I began to tread softly so as not to alert whoever it might be as to my whereabouts.

I slipped into Varina's room, and knelt by her bed. She was still awake. "What is it?"

In a whisper, I babbled out what was wrong.

Varina took it in immediately, and without judging my cowardice. My dear friend. I blessed her soundlessly as she threw on a wrapper and returned with me to my suite. With no hesitation, she picked up the chest.

"Take it far away," I said in a fierce whisper, because who knew if someone nearby might be listening, gleeful over my distress? "And after you get rid of those—those beasties, you and anyone else may have everything in the chest. I shan't touch any of that jewelry ever again."

"But Fiona, we can scrub all the slime off your pretty earrings and necklaces. They'll be fine. You can't give away all your jewelry."

"I can and I do. It's all paste anyway."

She reached out to touch my arm, but since she held the box to her bosom with one hand, I flinched away, shuddering. She gave a perplexed smile. "You've calmly faced all manner of ghosts, but you turn to jelly over a few earthworms."

I lifted my shoulders. I didn't understand it either, but the sight of the chest continued to make my stomach roil.

A line pinched across Varina's forehead. "Do you suppose…"

"*He* did it!" I cried passionately—and quietly. "I know it. He was aware of my repulsion for them. I can't imagine how he put them there, but somehow he did. And don't you see? It means he can enter my room?"

"Oh, I don't think so, honey. How could he? Trix wouldn't do it to you now, but some of the girls heard about her little joke before and thought it would be funny to do it to you again. You mustn't blame them. They couldn't know how badly it would affect you."

"No," I said, shaking. "It was him. And what will he do next, if he can do that?"

For a moment she watched me with compassion. "Very well. It was him. Now come and sleep in my room."

In spite of everything, I shook my head. If Leo were to return I needed to be here. With an effort, I steadied my voice. "No, but thank you. I'm sorry I'm so silly. I'll be all right once that box is gone. Please get it away from me."

"If you're sure..." Varina left, and I stumbled to the corner of the room, where I dropped to the floor and ringed my arms around my knees, watching. I would not sleep tonight. Edgar Allen Poe had called slumber "those little slices of death." I would huddle here, waiting for Leo and guarding against Monsieur.

CHAPTER 28

A DEPARTURE

The next morning, cottony mist rose to meet low clouds so there was no way to detect where one began and the other ended. A burning orange ball of sun peeked out for a moment before vapors drifted across it again.

I stood at my window feeling as if the fog had entered my brain. I had gotten a little sleep last night—at some point I had given up and finally crawled into bed, fully clothed—but still I could hardly think.

Varina stopped by on her way to breakfast. "Now," she said, "no talk of anything bad today. 'God's in his heaven—all's right with the world,' and those worms are snuggling their way deep into the lawn."

"Ugh," I groaned. "I hoped that was all a nightmare."

She took my arm.

I pulled away. "You did—you have *washed* since you handled that box, haven't you?"

"Goose of all gooses. Of course I have." She grasped me firmly. "Remember, no talk of anything bad. After lessons today, we'll each take one of those spirit books and do some studying."

"I can't find him, though, Varina." My voice shook.

"Can't find who?"

"Leo. Even when I can't see him, these days I can still sense his presence. But I don't feel it anymore. If he's found his way to heaven, why couldn't I at least have been allowed to say goodbye?"

"Honey, you wanted him to move on. Why are you so—" She broke off and looked at me closely. A sad little smile quirked her lips. She put her arms around me, and I slumped onto her shoulder, since she was so short and I was so tall. "He'll turn up. Or else he won't. But whatever it is, it will be all right."

I blew out my breath. "What would I do without you, Varina? And what will I do at Grandmama's house this summer? Y'all have made me unfit for that solitary life."

"Well," she said slowly, drawing away, "if you want, we could still be together. My mother has instructed—ordered me, really, since that's how Mother does things—to invite you for a visit to Twisted Trees. I've been telling her about you in my letters and she's eager for you to come. Perhaps it's for my sake. Because I would be lonely without you. Would you like that? Would you like to come?"

"Oh yes!" I cried. "I should like it of all things. I should love to meet your family."

"Don't expect too much. We're a rather uncomfortable group of misfits at the Trees. But if you'll write to your grandmother and ask permission, we can start making plans."

"Grandmama's health is poorly—the housekeeper wrote to tell me. I'm quite sure my grandmother would be relieved to not have me knocking about these months. She often says I fret her nerves."

The idea of a stay with Varina lifted my spirits, until, at breakfast, Trix was absent.

"Bless her heart, she's slept in," Mary Dell said. "Let's go bang on her door."

Cold trickles like spider legs slithered from my middle. Something about this was so familiar...

The Club trailed to Trix's door. The sharp sound of Varina's knocking splintered the air. "Trix, are you there?" No voice answered. She smote on the panels a second time. We waited, listening till it hurt. No sound stirred from within.

"I'm going to fetch Miss Petheram." Varina's voice was quiet and steady.

We waited, wide-eyed and silent until Miss Petheram arrived, a little breathless, holding out a key. We all clustered around as she turned it in the lock and the door swung open.

Someone began screaming and the screams echoed to fill our heads, the room, the corridor, the entire building.

Trix was hunched in a chair at her dressing table. Hunched in a way that showed she had been there a long time. Items from the table—a hairbrush, a spilled powder jar— scattered on the floor. There had been a struggle, but someone had restored Trix to the chair and placed her hands in her lap, her stiff fingers contorted into claws. She wore her white nightgown. In the mirror her reflection stared straight ahead with distended, empty eyes. Her skin was a gruesome purplish shade, with a darker stain around her mouth and nose.

My throat closed. Pins and needles numbed my fingers and crept up my arms. I could not move except to look lower.

Something yellow was knotted about her neck. Some sort of scarf.

"Girls," Miss Petheram said, her voice clipped, "I want you all to go downstairs. Quietly and without fussing. No hysterics. We must be brave for each other. One of you find Mr. Harry and tell him to send someone for the marshal and then to come here. Please wait for me in my office—don't speak of this to the other girls. Stay there until I come to talk with you."

It was good that someone told us what to do. After a moment we could force our limbs to move. We went in search of Mr. Harry all together. No one could bear to be parted from the others. Since he hadn't been at breakfast, we went first to his bedchamber and knocked on the door. A voice muttered for us to enter.

Mr. Harry slumped in an armchair, doing nothing, wearing a brilliant paisley dressing gown. He glanced up from half-closed lids.

"Something—something has happened to Trix," Varina said, without waiting for him to ask what was needed. "Miss Petheram desires you to send someone for the marshal and then to join her in Trix's room."

I expected him to question us briskly, to leap into action. He did not. Mr. Harry rose slowly, lethargically.

Sylvie broke from us and ran to him. "Oh, Harry, it's so dreadful!" Possibly her plan was to fall into his arms, but since his hands remained at his sides, instead she fell at his chest as if it were a brick wall. After a moment, he placed her away from him, said, "Excuse me," and ambled from the room.

"Harry! Please!" Sylvie cried after his back, but he did not turn around.

We stared at one another.

"He must be ill," Sylvie said. "Terribly ill. He's not himself."

"Let's do as Miss Petheram said," Varina said, through teeth that had begun to chatter. "We'll go to her office."

I put my arm about her waist, Mary Dell took the other side, Sylvie and Dorcas latched on, and we moved together, arms clinging in a chain of girls, even down the stairs, to the office, only letting go when we had to enter the doorway.

I fell into a chair as if I could no longer hold myself up. The others dropped as well, wherever they found a seat. Varina huddled in Miss Petheram's place behind the desk. She appeared ill. Sylvie looked bewildered. Dorcas slumped boneless and listless, her face without expression, but covered by a sheen of perspiration. Every once in a while her hands twitched. For a while the clicking of Mary Dell's coral beads as she fidgeted with them was the only sound in the room.

How could this be? Who would do this to Trix? To us? We were just girls. Young, innocent girls. And something horrible, something unspeakable, had happened to us.

Finally I said it. "We should not have let her sleep alone in that room. How could we have allowed it after what she told us?"

"I can't believe it," Varina said. "I can't believe she's really gone."

"I told y'all we were like to find her murdered in her bed!" Sylvie said, wiping her eyes with the back of her hand. "Of course it wasn't actually in her *bed*, but still I was right. Who will it be next? It could be any of us!"

"We must watch out for each other," Mary Dell said. "We must—"

"You know what?" Dorcas cried, clenching her fists. "I wouldn't care! You hear that? Y'all are fretting about who'll be next. Well, I don't care if it's me. If someone wants to give me a glass of poison, I'll guzzle it right down." She had been talking loudly and stridently. Now she visibly withered, and said, with a whimper, "I don't want to be in this awful world anymore."

We all looked at her with widened eyes. Once, during my lonely times, I might have echoed her. But not now. Now the thought of dying, leaving so much unlived, was dreadful. Varina cried, "Oh, my Dorcas!" and jumped up to throw her arms around our friend. The rest of us followed suit. We told her how we couldn't bear it if anything happened to her. We told her how wonderful she was and how we loved her, even if her father and stepmother did not. We told her that her stomach problems simply could not continue making her miserable and that everything had to get better—we would make sure of it.

After a bit we let go of one another and pulled our chairs close. Sniffles began, and then tears, sobs. It seemed forever, and still Miss Petheram did not come. At one point male voices sounded from the great hall and we assumed the marshal had arrived. We wiped our eyes and waited.

"Do you suppose they'll notice?" Dorcas whispered.

"Notice what?" Mary Dell asked.

"The prints in the powder."

"What prints?" I asked.

"Didn't y'all see?" Dorcas said. "In the powder spilled around Trix there were bare footprints. Like the ones we found in the dust in that room above. And they went toward the window."

The implications of this hit me hard. It was not Monsieur who had somehow done this thing to Trix. It was someone living. Who had entered through the window.

"We'll have to tell the marshal everything," Varina said. "All that Trix told us and all that we've noticed. How could we have been so silly as to think it was simply some girl's mischief?"

"We couldn't know," Mary Dell said. "No one normal would have believed anything different. No one really believes anything unspeakable as this could possibly happen."

Marshall Gibbons, a round and ruddy-faced individual, listened to our information without comment. He was holding the yellow silk scarf, stretching it back and forth between his hands. Our eyes riveted on it, even as we each spoke our piece. He had shown us how a coin was knotted in one end so that the scarf could be swung around Trix's neck and then tightened, strangling. He seemed to be enjoying our dismayed attention.

When we finished speaking, he turned to Miss Petheram. "You'll keep on thinking which no 'count servant might've got ahold of a key to that room?"

The headmistress nodded. Her face was the color of chalk, making her blue eyes shine unnaturally.

"And be watching if any of them don't show up to work or acts out of kilter. Sure as shooting, it's one of them. The gal probably caught them thieving."

"But—but you just heard us," I sputtered. "Whoever murdered Trix came in the window."

"Ain't no one could have slithered up or down that wall," Marshall Gibbons said. "I done investigated."

"But didn't you see the prints in the powder?"

"What powder?"

"The powder scattered on the floor."

"O' course I investigated that. Everything was all tromped through. Couldn't no one see nothing in it."

"But—"

"I'm fixing to continue my investigation," he told Miss Petheram. "Try to keep these fool girls from spreading nonsense all over the countryside, setting citizens ascared of their shadows. Don't you worry none, ma'am. The law's got everything under control."

A telegram was sent to Trix's family. Her parents came two days later to carry her body home to Louisiana for the funeral and burial.

While they were upstairs boxing up her possessions, we sat around on the lawn. There were no thoughts in my head and no words for my tongue. Only a cold void. No one else spoke either, so perhaps they felt the same.

At one point, Trix's father set a small wooden box down beside the front steps.

"Oh, my stars," Varina whispered, "that's Trix's snake."

Eventually the wagon was loaded. There were Trix's possessions, as well as the long wooden crate containing her body. I choked on a sob when I saw her hat boxes full of the ugly hats. We watched them drive away. The crate jiggled from the bumpy drive.

After several silent moments, without saying a word, Dorcas stood and retrieved the snake. She returned to us, clutching his box. "Poor little Jasper," she said. "Remember how Trix said if she died—" She lifted the lid and we all peered down at the little green snake.

"She asked us to find him and her cigars before her parents

did, and we forgot." Varina stroked him with one finger. "We'll have a memorial to Trix when we turn him loose."

We took turns, then, telling a memory of our friend. Soon we stopped the turn-taking and our words spilled over each other. Sometimes we wept, but sometimes, to our amazement, we found ourselves laughing a little as we remembered one outrageous comment after another that Trix had made.

"I wonder what her mother thought when she found the cigars and snake," Sylvie said, and clapped her hand over her mouth to stifle a giggle. Trix's mother had appeared excruciatingly ladylike and proper. That must have been where Trix got her arbiter-of-etiquette tendencies. And her contrary desire to rebel.

"How can we laugh?" Mary Dell asked, with a tremor in her voice.

"We all know we care about Trix," Varina said. "We're all grieving. But Trix of all people would like us to still laugh."

Dorcas lowered the snake's box to the grass and lifted the lid. For a moment he did not move.

"Run, Jasper, run!" I cried. "You're free, little fellow!"

The snake blinked, flicked out his tongue, and slithered off, slowly at first, but then whipping along so swiftly he was soon lost in the green grass sea. I pictured Trix's spirit doing almost the same when it was released, hesitating at first, then wriggling with delight at the sudden freedom and shooting straight off toward the light.

Trix's was the first departure.

I could tell from Miss Petheram's sad, resigned eyes that she was certain this was the end of the school.

"Young ladies," she announced at suppertime that evening, "I understand the desire many of you have to flee to the bosom of your families, and no one could blame you. Letters have been dispatched to your parents and guardians, informing them of what has happened here. For those of you who remain, the staff of Wyndriven Academy pledges to continue lessons as usual until the end of the term, which is only a little more than a month away. Hopefully the perpetrator will be caught soon. Until then, we ask that you stick together, and travel in pairs. We hope that you support each other and the academy. Please don't indulge in hurtful gossip. Brother Gideon will be here for the next few days to speak with any of you who desire God's comfort and guidance."

I sent my own letter to my grandmother, telling her I was not frightened or anxious, and that I wished to stay at Wyndriven till the term ended, and then proceed with my plan to visit Varina's home, if I might have her permission.

A good many girls trickled off in the next few days. It was obvious who had mindful, concerned parents and who did not. Several were quickly scooped up.

"The parents are having a jolly time," Varina said, "having something they can disapprove of so thoroughly as the murder of a girl at school."

I heard nothing from Grandmama. I supposed that the mail delivery to New York and then back to me would take so long there was no way I would have to leave before the term ended.

Every member of The Club remained. Sylvie and Mary Dell's mother wrote and asked if they wished to come home, but they sent her a reassuring note that begged to be allowed to stay. "We're not about to abandon y'all," Sylvie cried passionately. I had to wonder, though, if her main reason for staying was that she still hoped for a reconciliation with Mr. Harry. Unlikely, since he was more aloof than ever.

I could not blame her. I refused to move in with any of the other girls, even though there were vacancies in their rooms now. Neither would I allow anyone to move in with me. I needed to remain alone in case Leo returned. I wanted to believe he was in heaven, but that seemed too pat. Too anticlimactic.

No one mentioned the missing ones, but we always seemed to be clustering pathetically at mealtimes and in class. At bedtime, I cowered excruciatingly alone in my room.

I ached inside with mourning Trix and missing Leo. The first numbing shock of Trix's death was past and now I felt everything keenly. In the middle of the night I would awaken and find myself picturing her last moments: hearing some slight sound, but before she could turn, a sudden tightness about her neck, terror, flailing, fighting to breathe, bursting lungs, and then...death. It was odd, when I thought of it, that I experienced the grief and horror as much as everyone else. After all, I absolutely had a knowledge that Trix's spirit continued. Still, the sense of loss, the sense of waste from a life cut short, was deep.

Then, one night, I heard a scratching sound, and Fenris popped through the door. He waddled as fast as he could across the space to make the leap onto my bed.

I ran my hands over the fur I could not feel. "Dear, darling Fenris, where is your friend Leo? Was he with you?" Fenris wagged his tail madly, but, naturally, did not answer, since even a ghost dog cannot speak people words.

So now Fenris was back. Leo, however, did not return. I didn't see Monsieur either. Again I pictured him as a bloated toad in a hole, lying low in the heart of Wyndriven, making those vengeful plans he alluded to when last we met.

I would hear the creak of a settling board or catch sight of something with the corner of my eye, and would turn eagerly, expecting Leo. If only I could tell him everything. Sometimes I would imagine conversations with him, what advice he would give. We had gotten to know each other so well I thought I knew what he would say. Fenris also missed him. His forlorn tail hung between his legs. I was a poor substitute for his friend, especially in my current mood.

For a few hours after supper we always gathered in my sitting room — Varina, Mary Dell, Sylvie, Dorcas, and I. All wore black, but without any notion of showing off our mourning. Each day we threw on our apparel, hair in snoods or pinned back simply to keep it out of the way. Shadows smirched beneath our eyes. It was odd how our numbers seemed drastically reduced, even though there was only one of us missing. It made us cling even tighter to each other. We felt as soldiers must, who are going through a battle together.

Life had been so much simpler when I was a (somewhat) happy-go-lucky, solitary rich orphan girl skulking about the back halls of Grandmama's mansion, only being tortured by a few malicious ghosts. Now I wanted to care for these people, comfort them, fight for them. My enormous quantity of caring sometimes sucked all energy from my body and made my insides go hollow. If I spoke, I would cry.

Early in May, a few weeks after Trix's death, we gathered together, attempting to keep busy with needlework or schoolwork. None

of us seemed able to concentrate. My mind hopped from one disturbing thought to another and my legs jittered. Dorcas drank
peppermint tea constantly, to keep from chewing the skin at the
tips of her fingers, since her nails were bitten past the quick. Mary
Dell's hands couldn't keep still. They constantly played with
her hair or plucked at the cloth of her skirt. They twitched, they
jerked, they fiddled with her buttons and her beads, until Sylvie
grabbed her twin's fingers between her own and cried, "Stop it,
will you? No more." Sudden tears coursed down Sylvie's cheeks,
and she turned her face from us, all the while still clutching Mary
Dell, so the tears streamed unchecked.

There was a weighty pause until Dorcas shattered it by saying,
"Y'all can feel it, can't you? It's not over. There's more to come."

She was aware of it too, then—an electricity in the air. Whatever was happening at Wyndriven, it was far from finished with us.

Varina lifted her chin. "I don't know about y'all, but the only
thing that will keep me sane is if we take some sort of action. I pro-
pose we do what we were about to do before—before what happened to Trix. I can't help but feel that all this is connected with
Fiona's Monsieur. We need to figure out how to get rid of him."

"Don't call him 'my Monsieur.' And Varina, Fenris has jumped
up into your lap—will you please pet him?"

"Like this? Right about here?" She stroked the air just above
Fenris's back. He looked smugly satisfied. "You do believe all this
has got to be connected with Monsieur, don't you, Fiona?"

My hands clutched each other tightly. "It's like the worms. I
don't know how he did it, but he did. He hated Trix. He hated her
hair."

"Her hair?" Sylvie questioned.

"Her hair. He despises all red heads such as Miss Sophie. He couldn't use me, but perhaps he found some other hands to do his ill deed. Someone else here at Wyndriven."

Our eyes slid from one to another with something chill and frightened and suspicious in our gazes.

"No!" I cried. "It is *not* one of us."

Varina shivered. "Don't y'all find yourself wanting to say 'Is it I?' just like Jesus's apostles did when they knew one of them would betray him? But Fiona's right—it ain't—it's *not* one of us. We must think. Who at Wyndriven has been acting strange lately?"

Sylvie drew back in her chair. "I know what y'all are thinking. I know he hasn't been himself—but don't say it's Harry. He would never harm anyone. Unless... Although..." She bit her lip and turned away.

"Unless he was under someone else's control," I said. My voice sounded cold and flat.

"We'll watch him," Varina said. "We have to at least consider the possibility. He would have to be able to see, or at least hear, spirits, in order to carry out Monsieur's wishes. He never mentioned spiritualism, did he, Sylvie?"

"No. He laughed at me the only time I brought it up to him. He doesn't believe in ghosts. Or God either, for that matter. Maybe I'll sneak into his room sometime. I think I would know if anything's unusual or out of place there."

"So, you've been in his room?" Mary Dell hissed at her, low, but we could all hear.

Varina sighed. "For now, what we need to do is study those books."

Slowly, one after another, we each picked a volume off the

pile on the table. I lit an extra lamp. We opened the covers, and soon the only sound was pages turning and Sylvie muttering her reading out loud until Mary Dell shushed her.

After a long while, Varina tapped on her page. "Listen to this: 'Some holy scholars, renowned for their wisdom, assert that there is a singular form of spirit who may linger in this world as a guardian angel. In times of dire need, they do give what help and comfort they may to those in their watchful care.' Do you suppose that's what Leo is? A sort of guardian angel?"

"What Leo *was*," I said forlornly. "He's gone. So we don't need to research how to send anyone to heaven. All we need to look for now is how to send a spirit to the other place."

"If Trix was here, she would have mocked you for not saying the word 'hell,'" Sylvie said, with a painful little smile.

"You know what the servants are saying?" Dorcas said.

"No," I said. "You're the only one who knows that sort of thing. See how much we need you? So, what are they saying?"

"That the thing that killed Trix was something less than human. A creature of the dark. How else could it have entered her locked room so high above the ground? Perhaps we should be investigating the possibility of monsters as well."

Mary Dell moaned.

"Tomorrow —" Varina said, "tomorrow we'll look up monsters in the library."

I tapped a paragraph in my book. "Listen to what Edgar Allen Poe thought about the spirit world: 'Invisible things are the only reality. The boundaries which divide Life from Death are at best shadowy and vague. Who shall say where the one ends and where the other begins?'"

"He's so creepy." Sylvie wrinkled her nose.

"You think so? He's sort of my hero," I said.

A knock sounded. We all jumped, but it was only a maid come to inform us that we had visitors.

Wondering who it would be, we left the room. I ordered Fenris to "Stay!" I had learned that, amazingly, he would obey this command, even though he reached his neck amazingly far out the doorway after me, while keeping his body inside.

Sebastian and Sparrow awaited us in the yellow salon. Sparrow clung to Sebastian's arm. She wore a long, full, bright yellow calico skirt, snagged and stained at the bottom, and a simple white blouse. As usual, she had flowers in her hair and appeared so charming it was hard to look away from her. Sebastian's hat was in his hands and his head hung low on his shoulders. He and Sparrow leaned in to each other ever so slightly. I felt a rush of affection for them both. They were included in the bond between us all.

"Have you both heard about Trix?" I asked.

"Sparrow had not, so I went to her place to inform her. We have come to offer our condolences."

"Thank you. It's been awful. Please, won't you sit down?"

For a few minutes, we all tried to make casual conversation, but it was full of starts, stops, and gaps. Even Varina, who was usually so good at that sort of thing, didn't seem to be able to bring up a topic anyone could comment on. The subject always returned to Trix. Finally we gave in and discussed her murder.

"It's hard to believe someone could hate her enough to kill her," Mary Dell whispered. When we spoke of Trix, we always started out whispering, but gradually our voices would rise.

"There are many motives for slaying," Sebastian said. "Personal hatred is not always an element."

Sparrow wrinkled her brow. "Folks'd have to be plumb crazy to snuff out any life unless they're threatened. I don't even eat no victuals that's been killed."

For a fraction of a second I thought of pointing out that even plants are killed when they're picked, but I refrained. "You're right," I said. "There would have to be something wrong with anyone's brain if they would kill someone other than in self-defense or in a war. Or if they were threatening a loved one."

"Perhaps that is so," Sebastian said, "but many motivations might ignite the insanity, enflaming it into murder. There is greed and fear and ambition, for instance. It was the ambition of one of my father's advisors that caused the fakir to murder my brother."

"Jealousy," Sylvie announced. "That's a big reason for murder. Girls are always jealous of other girls. Or gentlemen are green-eyed over rivals for their sweethearts' affections."

"There's revenge too," Varina said. "If someone really, really hurt you in the past. Or what if someone threatened to expose something shameful?"

Again, for a flicker of a moment, I had to wonder what once might have been done to Varina.

Dorcas had been gazing thoughtfully down at her lap all this time. She looked up now. "Fiona, you said Monsieur's insane, murderous rage came about because of pride and jealousy and feelings of betrayal. And too much alcohol, maybe."

"Yes."

"How exactly did Miss Pringle die?" Sebastian asked abruptly. "I heard she was garroted—but with what?"

"She was strangled," Sylvie said. "If that's what 'garroted' means."

"By a yellow scarf," I said. "With a coin tied in the end so it could be swung hard."

Sebastian drew in his breath sharply.

"What?" we all cried.

He shook his head. "Never mind. It cannot be."

"You can't say that and then not tell us. What were you thinking?" I demanded.

He twisted the gold ring he wore around his thin finger before answering carefully. "There is a gang in India. A cult of professional assassins. Thuggee groups travel across the land and join other travelers, gaining their confidence. Thugs strangle their victims using a yellow scarf around their necks. They do it to honor Kali. She of the blue skin and many arms — the Hindu goddess of violence."

Silence hung heavy.

"But what could that have to do with whoever killed Trix?" Varina said finally. "That's India."

Sebastian raised his hands. "I only related it because you asked."

The lace around my neckline suddenly itched unbearably. I dug my fingernails into my flesh as thoughts ran feverishly through my head. Memories, images, words...A blue-skinned, many-armed statue with her tongue sticking out. Trix had laughed at her in the statue gallery. Gradually my mind slowed as an idea clicked into place. "Oh, no. Oh, my goodness. I've just remembered something. No. No, it's impossible. Never mind."

CHAPTER 29

BEHIND THE WALLS

All eyes were on me.

"Now *you* can't say such a thing and not tell us," Varina said.

I tapped my fingers against my forehead as if I could joggle out a memory. "I wish I could remember exactly what Miss Petheram said about him."

"About who?" Sylvie squeaked.

"When the Petherams first came here—it must have been when Monsieur was alive and master of Wyndriven Abbey—there was a servant from India." I struggled to gather my thoughts. "I think Miss Petheram said he was the valet, so he would have been close to Monsieur. His name was Achal. I don't know why I remember that, but I do. Miss Petheram had no idea what became of him. She said he had no identity outside of his master. Is it too crazy…could it possibly be that he's never gone away? That he's still here inside these walls? No. No, that's impossible. It's been years."

Sparrow glanced around. "This is such a heap of a place that anyone could hide out."

Something squeezed my lungs as my realization grew. "And it's not just the yellow scarf that's a clue—there was that bone under the carpet. At the ball, Sebastian, do you remember telling me about someone chanting something and then placing a snake bone beneath a carpet in order to kill someone?"

At the same moment, Varina cried, "That bit of carved bone Trix showed us!" and Sebastian said, "A *maran* mantra."

"Would you please tell everyone about it, Sebastian," I said, "while I run fetch something.

I raced up to my room and snatched from my desk drawer the beads I had found in the room above Trix's. Fenris howled miserably behind me as I left him once more.

When I returned to the salon, Sebastian was still describing in detail how the chanting of a *maran* mantra, along with a nail carved from the bone of a snake during a certain time was supposed to bring about the death of a victim. "Only," he said, "if such a thing was used on Miss Pringle, it did not work, so the murderer took more sure measures."

I dropped the beads into Sebastian's hand. He gave a low whistle. "It is a *mala*. People use them in meditation to help them count how many repetitions of the mantra they have completed."

"I knew it," I said. "Something in me knew it must be the beads you had mentioned. I wish I'd shown it to you before. If I had, maybe Trix…" I couldn't finish the thought.

"Don't tear yourself up about that," Mary Dell said. "None of us did all we could have to keep Trix safe. We didn't know."

"Trix heard a murmuring voice, and there's that hole bored down to her room," Varina said. "Any of those things—the voice, the scarf, the beads, the Indian valet, or the bone—"

"The worms in my room. And the torn-up tapestry," I inter-rupted. "I'll tell you about it later. So many things took a pair of human hands to accomplish."

Varina nodded. "All of these incidents would mean nothing singly, but when we have all of them together along with Trix's death and Monsieur's dislike of her...Oh, my stars. But how did he manage it?"

As she spoke, I stood and moved with agitation first here, then there. I couldn't hold still.

"Remember how Miz Jump is always going on about food missing?" Mary Dell spoke hesitantly. Her face was ashen.

I returned now to the sofa. "Someone—actually, it was Leo once, and then Marietta in her letter—said there's a secret passage behind a chimney. Leo said it went up from the kitchen."

"So. There's been a man hiding out at Wyndriven." When Dorcas's pretty voice said this, ridiculous as it was, somehow any lingering doubts ceased. Especially with what she related next. "I've never told anyone this, since at the time I decided I must not have really seen it, but I once saw someone—a very unusu-al person—rounding the corner of the orangery. It was his sly, sneaky quickness that caught my eye. As if some inhuman thing had slinked out of the forest. He was bearded and *little*—almost child-sized—with a cloth coiled on his head."

The prospect was so horrid. This stranger slipping about just on the other side of the walls, watching, spying...invading every-thing we had done while living here.

Mary Dell kept opening and shutting her mouth like a fish. Finally she spoke. "Why do you suppose Trix is the only person Achal's hurt?"

"The only person he's hurt until *now*," Sylvie said significantly.

They all looked to me as if they expected me to have the answers. "I don't know. I can only guess that he acts on Monsieur's will. Maybe Monsieur has never before been so active and *present* as he is now. Monsieur hates everyone, but the ones he hates the most are Miss Sophie and her children. They aren't here often, and when they are, they're surrounded by people. Achal couldn't get to them, but he could tease and torture and finally attack Trix. Monsieur always acted as if he detested her, mainly because of her hair. All of the wives Monsieur killed had red hair, and so does — did — Trix."

"Shall we go tell the Petherams right now?" Varina asked, her eyes intense with a mixture of alarm and excitement.

Sebastian shook his head vehemently. "Not without proof. All this is mere speculation. We must find validation of this person's existence."

"Aww." Sylvie grinned. "I know you fellows. You just want some adventure before we bring anyone else in on it."

Sebastian flushed, but smiled guiltily.

"It does make sense to seek proof before we go to anyone with such a wild story," I said. "If the passage does rise up from the kitchen, and if it pops out in the attics somewhere near where the person sleeps, that would narrow down our search."

"But does it make sense that they would have kept the secret passage when they brought the whole caboodle over from England?" Dorcas asked.

"The person who rebuilt the abbey over here—" Sebastian said.

"Monsieur," I prompted.

"—obviously strove to put everything back authentically. If it were me, I would have been especially careful to restore secret passages." He stood. "To the kitchen, then."

"Miz Jump won't let us poke around there," Mary Dell said.

"She is your cook?" Sebastian asked. "If she attempts to stop us, we shall overpower her. Tie her up."

"Dear me," Mary Dell said, "we can't possibly tie up poor Miz Jump."

"Ha," Varina said unexpectedly. "We could so. Remember, this is the same Miz Jump who sent little beggar children off to starve. I'd be happy to do the overpowering." She snatched up a lamp and we all trooped behind her downstairs.

Luckily for Miz Jump, she was elsewhere. The supper dishes were already cleaned and put away and the fire was out. We all stood, studying the wall on each side of the massive chimney. A few feet to the right of the chimney breast was a door to a cupboard. It wasn't large—about eighteen inches by two feet. When opened, the dark cavity was empty save for a dusting of crumbs on the bottom. Sebastian immediately began rapping at the inner surfaces. To me, all the sounds were the same, but he seemed to find differences.

"Aha!" he cried. He pressed an indentation on the side wall. It swung open. "Give me the lamp."

He held the light close to the revealed opening. Dust motes danced and iron rungs ascended into blackness inside a stone shaft. "I'm going up," he announced.

"I ain't staying behind," Sparrow quickly proclaimed.

"Is there a lantern—yes, there is." Sebastian lit a lantern he removed from a nearby hook, and hoisted himself to begin wriggling into the gaping hole.

The rest of us shuffled our feet.

"Sorry," Varina said. "I don't figure I'm scrambling into that. Let's allow Sebastian and Sparrow this privilege."

I didn't relish climbing through the dark, doubtless cobwebby, spaces either, but as I watched Sebastian's boots already disappearing up the ladder, with Sparrow behind, I lifted up my skirt and began divesting myself of my hoop.

"Mercy, Fiona!" Sylvie cried. "What are you doing?"

"Following. If the murderer's waiting at the other end, there's safety in numbers. And I can't fit in with the hoop."

"You're right," Varina said. "Also, neither Sebastian nor Sparrow belong at Wyndriven. If they should be discovered by anyone, perhaps some students with them would lend some justification for their presence. Should we all come?"

"No," I said, stepping from my skirt. "We'd make too much noise and most likely smash each other's fingers on the ladder."

"Well, then, we'll wait here and take care of your clothes. If you and Sebastian aren't back within—how long?—we'll go tell the Petherams."

"Give us at least an hour." I took a deep breath and hoisted myself up into the cupboard, and from thence into the shaft. Behind me, there was a brief giggle from Sylvie, evidently at sight of my long skinny legs dangling in stockings and pantalets.

As I climbed, wavering light from the lantern above shone down eerily. Echoes of Sparrow's and Sebastian's movements and breathing filled the space. The air felt thick and smelled of dank stone and fungus. The ladder rungs were slippery with damp, and the stone walls shone greasily in the dim light. A shivering started in me. I hadn't thought I was afraid of heights, but at this moment something that must be fear was making my feet and hands hesitate to release the rungs. "Move, feet. Move hands," I whispered, and was surprised that they obeyed.

Luckily, somewhere around the second floor, the shaft widened and the rungs ended at a platform. Sebastian and Sparrow waited for me. Sebastian reached out a hand to help me heave myself up.

"I would expect a skeleton to be sprawled right about here," I said.

Sebastian smiled. "I doubt they'd transport *that* across the ocean. Although I would have."

From here a narrow, steep, winding stone staircase rose. Now we moved more quickly, although it still seemed as if we climbed for hours. Round and round we took the curves, until my head spun. Once, Sebastian stumbled and from then on, Sparrow clutched his arm, presumably to support him.

Abruptly, the staircase ended in a rough wooden wall. Sebastian started to knock against it, but I whispered, "We mustn't warn anyone we're here if someone is on the other side."

We inspected every inch of the surface we could reach—it seemed thoroughly solid.

"Is there no exit?" I whispered. "Maybe there was a doorway somewhere along the way and we missed it because we were expecting it to be at the top."

"That would be unreasonable," Sebastian said. "Why build steps to lead nowhere?"

"To fool people?" I suggested. "To trap them at the end?"

Sparrow was kneeling on the floor. "A ladder was here once."

She held up a partial rung of rotten wood.

"There must be a door up high," Sebastian said. "Sparrow, climb on my shoulders."

Already they worked like a team. Sebastian knelt and cupped his hands. Sparrow placed one dainty foot into his palms and pulled herself onto his shoulders. I stood beside them, hands upraised to steady them if need be.

"Hold up the light," Sparrow said. "A door's got to be nearabout."

I held the lantern high.

"There is a crack, and...oh, yes. A latch that can be sprung." She sprang it. A waft of fresher air reached me, as the door swung open an inch.

"Now," Sparrow said, squatting, "I'm fixing to climb down, and Sebastian might could scramble on me and you, Fiona."

"No." Sebastian said. "I am too heavy for you ladies."

"That ain't so," she said. "Not if both of us holds you. The thing is that if you go up first, you're hefty enough you can pull me and Fiona up after."

"But how did Achal get up and down here all by himself?" I asked. I knew the answer even as I asked. He had climbed. Just as he had climbed down to Trix's window from the window higher above. The man must be half spider.

Sparrow and I squatted on the floor, holding out our hands. Sebastian removed his boots and thrust his stocking feet into our palms. "Forgive me," he said. My legs shook as I rose. I felt as if all the blood vessels would burst in my head, but glancing at Sparrow, she seemed unfazed. She must be very strong.

Sebastian peeked through the crack first and then pushed the door wider open. He succeeded in getting his elbows up onto the floor, and pulled himself up. He then reached down to hoist us, his face dark with effort.

At last we all stood panting together on the attic floor. The place was like a sloping-ceilinged maze, with steps going up, steps going down, and room after room leading haphazardly off each other. Cobweb-draped beams crisscrossed them, and dusty dormer windows were opaque from the nighttime outside, showing only the tiny reflected spark of light from our now-shuttered lantern.

"Perhaps," I whispered uncomfortably, "we're being foolhardy. The *mala* and the secret stair shaft should be proof enough. Oughtn't we to go back down and let the Petherams and the marshal handle the search?" I wiped sweat from my brow with the back of my hand. The attics were hot.

"Never!" Sebastian said, low and intense. Excitement danced in his brown eyes. "That would spoil everything. Dorcas said he was small—I can handle him." Sparrow watched as he flexed his arms. "Look at them muscles," she said softly.

We tread lightly and slowly, jumping when a floorboard squeaked, threading from room to room through crates, trunks, and shrouded shapes. Sebastian swung the lantern so the beam would reveal more.

"Here!" he cried triumphantly, forgetting to whisper. What he indicated was a pile of shabby mats and a coverlet, all stirred up like a rat's nest behind a massive dust-covered form. "His pallet."

This was all real. Someone—some man—actually had been living around us, above us, behind us, beside us, all this time.

I don't know what caused me to look, because there was no

sound. But something, some awareness sharper than noise, made me turn my head.

He was there, in the deep shadows beneath the eaves. My heart stopped beating for a moment, and then lurched, pounding madly. I couldn't speak, but I pointed, and the others' gaze followed the line of my finger.

Sebastian opened the shutter on the lantern. Light trapped the man, who did not blink. The three of us scrambled to stand between him and the door. Still he made no motion. He crouched there, watching us with bright brown eyes, his curiously long, thin hands dangling between his knees. He had frail, spidery arms and legs, leathery skin, a sparse, scraggly gray beard, and dark, ragged clothing. He reminded me of someone…something…

A weasel. He had the same wary, alert, malicious look as his gaze now slid past us, obviously seeking a way out.

Sebastian spoke. "*Tum kaun ho?*"

The man remained silent for a long while. Finally, in a low, hoarse voice, he said, "*Koi bhi. Kuch bhi nahi. Ek bhoot.*"

"*Tum Achal. Tum yaha in sabhi varsom raha rahe hai de Cressac se aadesha lene. Aur tum larki ko maar dala.*"

Achal responded shortly, ending with a peculiar, rattling laugh.

I caught Monsieur's name, and Achal's. I could guess what Sebastian, at least, was saying. He was telling the man we knew who he was, that he was Monsieur's henchman who had murdered Trix.

So quickly that we were left reeling, Achal bounded up like a coiled spring and was past us, darting to the open dormer window. By the time we moved to follow, he was already out and scuttling impossibly fast, fringed with silver moonlight, along the edge of the steep-pitched roof. Sebastian started to climb out after him.

"Don't!" I cried.

Sparrow grabbed him.

"He'll get away." Sebastian tore his arm from Sparrow's grasp, swung his leg over the sill, and was out on the roof.

"He has to come down sometime," I said. "Let's run get the Petherams, or Mr. Willie, or whoever, and we'll watch for them from down below."

Without looking back, Sebastian said, "All he has to do is go in another window and he'll get away. We'll never find him again."

"I'm coming too," Sparrow said, and was out the window as well before I could stop her.

I poked my head outside, sick with apprehension. Sebastian did not close the distance between himself and Achal, but Sparrow was soon at Sebastian's heels.

I actually found myself helplessly wringing my hands, something I thought people only did in books. Well, I certainly wasn't following the three of them.

The height made me dizzy and I could no longer watch. Instead I turned and raced down flight after flight of stairs. I skipped steps, leaped over expanses—thank goodness I was skirt-free. Still, it was a miracle I was never sent sprawling before I reached the first floor.

Much later, I would be teased about the way I pounded through the hall in my pantalets, wild-eyed and wild-haired, ignoring the girls who stared or asked what was wrong. "Where's Miss Petheram?" was all I said, breathless and urgent. No one knew.

Music drifted from down the corridor. Cello music, although

not spectral. This was a recognizable tune, but awkward, stilted, and scratchy. A couple of girls stood in the doorway, listening and grinning. Harriet Campbell said loudly, "Goodness, Mr. Harry! I didn't know you played the cello."

I pushed past her into the room.

"Mr. Harry!" I cried.

He paused, holding out the bow, and looked up sluggishly from lowered lids. He blinked. "You're only wearing your undergarments."

"It's Achal."

"Achal?"

"Achal. Monsieur's servant. He's still here. He's with Sebastian and Sparrow. All up on the roof."

I didn't blame him that it seemed to take forever for him to understand. The whole thing was unbelievable. Eventually, though, he roused himself to take action. Miss Petheram was found, a stable boy was sent for the marshal, I had gathered up the Club, and Varina had forced me to slip into my skirt.

Everyone, including all the servants, gathered now outside on the drive with our necks craned back, peering up at the silhouettes on the roof. They crawled along the highest ridgepole, outlined by a swollen yellow moon. The scene resembled some sort of weird pantomime. A sharp wind tore at our clothing, tossed surrounding tree tops, and mourned, very low.

Whispers slithered back and forth. "...an Indian man..." "...been living here..." "*Here* here?" "...think I'll faint..." "...killed Trix..."

"Is this a dream?" Varina asked, swiping back the strands of hair that blew across her face.

I didn't answer because I wasn't sure.

Achal hesitated at the end of the roof-line. His long shirt whipped in the gusts. He turned his head to observe Sebastian nearing. The only escape was a great leap to battlements several feet away. Achal was wiry and slick, but such a leap was impossible. His knees bent. He leapt. Collectively all of us down below held our breath.

He nearly reached it. But he dropped too soon, smashed into the stone wall, and plummeted.

That falling thing can't be a person.

There was a sickening thud and crash when it hit a roof below, then another gruesome final thunk.

In that moment the revolting memory of the smashed faces of The Two thrust into my mind. I stumbled behind a bush to vomit.

I straightened, gulped, wiped my mouth, and raised my head.

And there stood Achal. Achal who had plunged to his death seconds earlier. His appearance showed no marks of his fall...except that his feet were on backward. He screwed up his features in a sneer and the malice in his eyes as they met mine grew brighter.

His face stretched and distorted. His edges darkened and blurred. The wind snatched at him until the trailing, ragged vapor that was Monsieur's servant blew off into the night.

CHAPTER 30

WAITING

"Where is Harry?" Miss Sophie asked.

Miss Petheram shrugged. "How would I know? He's never where he's expected to be, and he's gotten worse lately." Her voice and her demeanor were drained. "Frankly, I can't worry about him with everything else that's happened." She had been up much of the night, first talking to the marshal, and afterward visiting each girl in their beds, administering comfort and reassurance. And almost certainly she hadn't slept after that.

Father Paul reached out and laid his hand over hers. It shocked me that in such circumstances I still noticed this, and even felt the tiniest, faintest of thrills. How could I have any attention left for such a thing, when I knew Monsieur was still up to something? Achal, Monsieur's hands, might be dead, but Monsieur was not done with us.

Brother Gideon, Miss Sophie, Miss Petheram, Father Paul, and I were gathered in Miss Petheram's office the morning after Achal's death to discuss what had happened. It felt uncomfortable to be the only young person included. I had been called in since I supposedly understood what had been going on at Wyndriven. Except that I didn't. Understand, that is.

"You know," Miss Sophie said, a pucker between her arched brows, "I hardly remember Achal from before. He flitted about in the background behind Monsieur Bernard while his master lived, and, evidently, continued to do so after his master was dead. For twelve long years. Who would do that? And why?"

I lifted my hands and let them drop. It was impossible to comprehend.

Miss Sophie had been sitting. She stood now and strode to the window, jerking back the velvet panel to stare outside. "Unbearable to think of him—them—oh, it's overwhelming!—spying on us for so long. Slipping around behind the walls." She turned to face us, all color absent from her face. "And we lived here! The children were here. The soldiers. The students have all been exposed to him." Her fist flew to her lips and she pressed against them so hard it must have cut inside. "Still, in a way I must pity Achal. What a wretched existence."

I twisted my handkerchief tightly. "Sebastian—Mr. Thatoor—you know, the young man from Albion Academy who was on the roof—spoke Hindi to Achal last night when we first discovered him. He told me that when he asked him who he was, Achal said he was nobody. Nothing. He called himself a *bhoot*—a ghost."

Miss Petheram shook her head. "How amazing that we just 'happened' to have a young man who could speak Hindi. How was that even possible?"

"Because," Father Paul said, with one of his transforming smiles, "coincidences are small miracles sent straight from God."

"Now that I think of it, I always used to feel sorry for Achal,"

Miss Sophie said. "Him and all the foreign servants. Because they were so far from everyone who truly cared about them. And the be-all and end-all of everyone's existences was to cater to M. Bernard. What a waste. So, do you suppose Achal could see and speak to Bernard even as you do, Fiona? And that was how he got his orders?"

"Sebastian said—he said the last thing Achal told him was that his master was in his head. Always talking in his head. Achal considered himself nobody save for Monsieur in his head. Some dreadful bond between them."

Brother Gideon put his arm around his wife and squeezed her shoulders. "Such an existence must have driven Achal mad long ago. I suppose he cannot be entirely to blame for his actions."

She looked at me, and the strange pain in her eyes was hard to bear. "What does he look like now?"

Some might have thought she meant Achal, but I knew of whom she spoke. "I know that he's handsome," I said slowly, "although I don't *like* the way he looks. He looks…cruel. But still attractive."

Miss Sophie gave a shrill, short laugh. "That's what I thought once I knew him. I never grew used to how desperately attractive he was. In the end it was one of the things that was most terrifying." Her voice shook. "I thought we had won, though. All these years I thought he was gone and we could be happy. Now we learn he's still here." She bowed her head and brought her handkerchief up to her eyes. "We can't go through this again."

Haggard lines were carved in Brother Gideon's face. "We'll close up the abbey. Tear it down to the ground. Let de Cressac be the Lord of Rubble. The King of Desolation."

"No!" Miss Sophie cried sharply. "What does that solve? This ancient building has been the home of far more good people than bad. It's not the abbey that's evil, it's Bernard. Perhaps it will never be a school again, but it can still be beautiful and interesting and useful. Bernard must be made to leave."

I thought of Leo and knew I did not want his home to be demolished, even if he never came back. I had told them all I knew about Achal and Monsieur. Now it was time to let other people—older, wiser people—make decisions. Take action.

"Gideon," Miss Petheram said, "Your church does not perform exorcisms, but the Catholics..."

Father Paul had been sitting silent, brooding beneath craggy brows until this moment. "I can bless the house."

"Would it send him to hell, though?" Miss Sophie asked.

Father Paul rubbed his chin. "In a manner of speaking, yes. If it works as it is supposed to, which is by no means a sure outcome. However, hell is not a physical place. It is the state of being banished forever from communion with God and the blessed."

"I don't know if I can be responsible for such a thing," Miss Sophie said.

At the same moment, Brother Gideon and Father Paul exclaimed, "*I* can!" They looked at each other, and Father Paul continued, "It is the creature himself who has freely chosen to close himself to God's love."

Miss Sophie shook her head. "I don't know. What if...We'll end the term early and the girls will go home. Wyndriven's reputation is in shambles as it is. I don't want them carrying home stories of spirits and exorcisms as well. We can make decisions after everyone is gone. My skin crawls to think that he's here, even if no one but Fiona can see him, but he can do nothing more now that his henchman is gone. And Achal *is* gone forever. You haven't seen *him* again, have you, Fiona?"

"Not since right after he fell. No. And I haven't seen Monsieur either, since before Trix…went. But…" I didn't think I could make them understand how I felt. Still, I had to try. "I know he's still lurking here somewhere, preparing something. He won't give up simply because he's lost Achal." They had never beheld his apparition. They couldn't understand how real he was, in spite of being disembodied.

"We'll wait," Miss Sophie said firmly.

That could be the hardest thing of all to do.

Days like splintered, broken glass followed—three, four, five of them, and there was nothing. I had told my friends they ought to leave. Now. They refused. School would be dismissed for good two weeks early, and, to them, that was soon enough. We attended class, gathered together in the evenings. Waited. Time weighed like lead on my back. Something was coming. My nerves were stretched taut and ready to jump out of my skin as I waited for The Thing to happen. The unnatural quiet wasn't a lull or soothing. Beneath, I sensed a soundless muttering that must precede something horrible. Sometimes it took on the vibration of cello music, just below the range of hearing. What would he, could he, do next? Where? When? To whom?

I stood now alone at my sitting room window, watching fog creep in. It ghosted the trees as tendrils of mist drifted up from the forest. Like a tide edging ever nearer, it lapped at the house, surrounded it, swallowed it in a murky shroud.

I feared, and yet longed for a battle with Monsieur. A final reckoning after which all would be over. I glanced toward the simpering shepherdess statue on the mantel and clenched my fists to keep control. Then I strode across the room, snatched up the figurine, and hurled it against the wall. Shattered to smithereens! That felt good.

"Missed me."

If all that existed of him were his voice, I would have loved him for that. I whirled around and there stood Leo. His tawny lion's-mane hair, his shoulders swelling beneath his white shirt, his quirky smile. Fenris leaped at him. He picked up the little dog and rubbed him between the ears.

I was speechless. I shook my head and closed my eyes. "Yes, I missed you," I whispered. "I've missed you so much." Fenris echoed me, whimpering.

"Have I been gone all that long?"

I moved closer, so that the luminous light surrounding him washed over me. "A little over a week. But it seems longer. Much, much longer."

"I hadn't realized. Oh. Time doesn't affect me as it does you."

"You're more—more glow-y than ever. Far more than the last time I saw you."

"Does it suit me?"

I drew back to look him over critically. "It's certainly impressive. And—are you wearing a sword?"

He glanced down. "Oh, I am. I wonder when that appeared? I like it."

His increased shimmer made him seem more alien. It made me uncomfortable, so I had to scold. "Where have you been?"

My voice squeaked. "You said you wouldn't go without saying good-bye."

"Sorry about that. I didn't mean to leave these rooms without letting you know. It was just that one day I was flexing my bulging spiritual muscles and I broke through the barrier that's held me in here. Fenris was with me at first, but he couldn't go past the edge of the woods. Looks as if he came back to you."

"So you went off willy-nilly, to explore the countryside?"

"I had to. You cannot imagine how good it felt to be able to go places. I like Mississippi. So wild and ragged and natural compared to my part of England. Like a wolf beside Fenris."

"I'm glad—" My voice broke.

"What's wrong?" he asked quickly, sharply. "Did something happen while I was absent?"

"Some *things*." He didn't know any of it. Not about Trix, not about Achal.

I told him everything, including my fears of the thunder building just beyond the horizon. It was a relief to pour it all out to Leo.

He listened with a glower dimming his glow. "This can't go on," he announced at the end of my recitation. "It's my house as much as it's his. And it was mine first." He gave a mirthless smile. "I'm going to go find him. Perhaps this is why I'm still here. Maybe this is my destiny. To trounce your Monsieur into hell."

"Not—No, Leo!" I buried my face in my hands. "Don't you dare try anything so that I'll have to worry about you as well as everyone else. You don't know him. He's strong and he's evil. I've somehow got to make him leave, so everyone will be safe, but I can't bear it. It's too much."

He sighed. "Stop it, Fiona."

"Stop what?" I looked up, glaring. "Wanting you to be safe? Sorry. I won't."

"Stop always trying to take care of everything for everyone. It can't be done and it's not your job. Comfort, yes. Reassure, yes. Commiserate, yes. Just as right now you're in desperate need of comfort and reassurance and commiseration yourself, and I want to give it to you. But the fact is, I'm already dead — what could this Monsieur do to me?"

I passed my tongue over my lips, saying nothing. I looked at him standing there so close, yet immeasurably far. The frustration of yearning to touch him, to wrap my arms around his body — or at least the place where his body had once been — was so overpowering, so painful, that I swayed on my feet.

He came toward me. Tentatively he reached a hand to my cheek. There was that flush of ice on my skin. Into my cheek. The cold ceased, and a warmth poured into my flesh. Slowly he edged closer, closer, until his face was inches from mine. My eyes fluttered shut. I gasped as the heat spread through me, along with a rush of... something...memories, thoughts — alien impressions crowded my own. Only not so alien because it was Leo. He had as tight a hold on my mind as strong arms might have had on my body. There was an exultation. So many sensations. I could feel — he — *we* could feel — air upon our skin. The scent of the honeysuckle in the vase on the table. The throbbing of our blood and pounding of our heart.

I don't know how long it lasted. At last he drained out, and stood before me. I was left panting and weak.

"I — I'm sorry," he said. "I didn't know I was going to do that. Or that I *could* do that. I just wanted so badly to hold you close."

"That was amazing," I whispered, shaky.

"It was. And—I don't know the words to say what all it was."

"There aren't any. That we know of. So you really do think I'm beautiful. I could feel it."

"So beautiful." His eyes were intent.

For once I didn't blush or turn away. I faced him and smiled. I *felt* beautiful. And safe. And loved.

"Will you write a poem about it?"

"I can't write poetry anymore. I've tried for weeks and it seems to be gone."

"No. It's still there. I heard it in you."

"I want you to have my signet ring."

"I thought maybe I should give it to Miss Petheram, since it was found in the house."

"Good heavens, no. It's mine to give, and I give it to you."

"Thank you. It will always be my treasure. But we're still going to find a way to send you off, you know. We should read those verses about heaven in Revelation once more. To remind you why you want to go there."

"I suppose so."

"Because you need to be with Marietta. Don't worry. It doesn't bother me anymore. When I was half you I could feel how happy you'll be with her. And I want you to have that."

"And I could feel how you need a flesh-and-blood man. A good man who will be the right one with whom to share your flesh-and-blood life."

"But we really are in love with each other."

"We really are. Deeply."

Oh Dearling, I have seen your shining
Through shuttered eyes, and opened them,
And blinked against the first true dawning
In all this world of shadow men.
Oh Wonderful, I've heard the pounding
Of your lion-heart, the beat
That drives the world from start to ending
(And then the voice will say "Repeat").
You were meant for truer things and other-kind,
Oh Morning-Light, oh Joy-of-Mine.
— By Fiona O'Malley

CHAPTER 31

AT A PICNIC

School would be dismissed in two days, and we were having an end-of-term outing today, together with the Albion Academy boys and faculty. I guessed that partly it was planned to give us something nice to think about, to fill the void until it was time to leave. I had dressed accordingly in a light-as-air pink voile summer gown.

We could not remain constantly in a state of dread and trepidation. It had been weeks since anything had happened. We were young and high-spirited. We were going on a picnic. And there would be pie.

Once the gentlemen had arrived, we were carried in wagons driven by Mr. Willie and Brother Gideon, Mr. Crow and Father Paul to the base of a hill. We poured out and surged up the slope like a swarm of insects, dabbing at perspiration with our handkerchiefs. It was a steamy day of low sullen clouds and mosquitoes.

We spread out various coverlets and tablecloths on the ground so that a giant, colorful patchwork quilt lay about us. Varina, Sylvie, Mary Dell, Dorcas, Sebastian, and I shared our green gingham cloth. Sparrow had been invited, but it was not the sort of occasion she cared for.

"Our tablecloth is the best," Sylvie announced.

She sounded so smug that I had to grin. "Three cheers and a tiger for *our* cloth!" I shouted.

For a moment everyone looked our way. Then they laughed and all began shouting huzzahs and hoorays for their own cloths.

The tone was lighthearted, in spite of heavy air that tingled on the skin. Everyone slapped and scratched and sweated good-naturedly. Fried chicken, corn, baked beans and sweet potato pie were unpacked from baskets and the feast spread out.

Dorcas and I noted how Mr. Crow glanced furtively, with lowered lids, toward Miss Petheram, who sat happily beside Father Paul. Mr. Crow winced each time his former fiancée laughed. And Miss Petheram laughed and smiled a great deal.

The three Stone children had come with their parents. They tumbled down the hill and raced back up, like puppies. When their mother tried to make them pause and eat, they would snatch up a bite or two, then dash off again. Finally Miss Sophie gave up. "Let them run outdoors while they can," she said. "It's going to storm later."

We devoured our meal with gusto. Everyone speaking over everyone else was a rumble in the ears. Afterward there was to be a tug of war between the gentlemen teachers and the Albion students. There were to be sack races and other games.

Brother Gideon headed down to the stables and boathouse to procure the rope and sacks just as Mr. Harry shambled up. Mr. Harry grunted in response to his sisters' greetings. It seemed as if I hadn't seen him in ages. Dark shadows splotched beneath his eyes, and his mouth hung open a little. When he stumbled and bumped me as he moved past, he mumbled something. He dropped to the ground and appeared to be preoccupied with studying his hands, as he flexed and extended his fingers.

"Drunk," Sylvie whispered. "Oh, I'm ashamed for him. Stop staring, Fiona. It's bad enough without you drawing attention to his state."

From that moment, the day changed. Everyone seemed languid and lazy if left alone, but when spoken to, they stiffened and retorted harshly. The hot air sagged. Insects shrilled out warnings. Frogs boomed and cicadas screeched.

Some of the boys stood and half-heartedly tossed a ball back and forth. The distraction of the flying ball made my head hurt.

Mademoiselle. What Mr. Harry had mumbled when he bumped into me, was, "Pardon, Mademoiselle Fiona." Alarm bells clanged through my body, accompanying the frogs and cicadas. "Where are the children?" I asked sharply.

Dorcas lifted her shoulders. "If their Mama don't care, why should we?"

Something was wrong. Terribly wrong. "And Mr. Harry — where's he gone to?"

"No doubt passed out somewhere," Sylvie said. "I declare."

"What's the matter, honey?" Mary Dell was staring at me.

Suddenly everything was falling into place. I was sweating, shaking, gasping for air, my heart racing. I jumped up and put my hand over my eyes to peer down the hill. Purplish-black, bruised-looking clouds blotted the sky to the west. Shadowed by them, the dark water of the lake spread out, studded with minute, bright-white swans. The tiny figures of Mr. Harry, carrying Daisy, with the little boys trotting alongside, approached the lake.

Even from this distance I could tell that the thing inside Mr. Harry's body made it move jerkily. It must take a while for Monsieur to become used to a different vehicle, like blindly driving a vastly unfamiliar horse and buggy.

"No!" I wailed under my breath. "Oh, no!" I ran up to Miss Sophie. "The children!"

Her eyes widened, mildly wondering at my unexpected behavior. "They're fine. They're with my brother." I could hardly hear her over the clamor surrounding us.

"He's not your brother now," I cried. "He's Monsieur. Monsieur is *inside* Mr. Harry!"

Without waiting for her reaction, I took off down the hill, stumbling once, sickeningly, over a clump of underbrush. Miss Sophie followed.

Our skirts flapped, our boots pounded, but we seemed to get nowhere. Time ceased to flow. Instead, it stretched like hot taffy. Slowwwww.

Spreading fields and gardens lay between us and the children. Too far ahead, Monsieur waded past the reeds. Dark green water lapped about him. A swan flapped away across the surface. Something must stop this. This ghastly thing could not happen before our very eyes.

The water was up to his knees. He bent and lowered the little girl below the surface. Nothing interfered. We were going to watch him drown Daisy.

I was vaguely aware that Miss Sophie was shrieking, but I hardly heard for the blood pounding in my ears. Bad Atlas-the-goat got in my way. I pushed furiously past him, and he was so surprised he didn't even try to butt me from behind. I scooped up a short, thick fallen branch, in case I could use it on Mr. Harry/ Monsieur.

Up ahead, Daisy sputtered and thrashed, a small, terrified wild animal, as Monsieur tried to hold her under. The brave little boys attacked him now, defending their sister. They clung to his arms, shouting, "Stop it, Uncle Harry!" "Let her go, Uncle Harry!" Jack swung from Monsieur's elbow. Monsieur flung his arm wide to toss the boy away. In so doing, he lost his hold on slippery Daisy, who was up in a trice, stumbling from the water. Monsieur grasped Roo now, and they thrashed wildly as he held him under, while Jack leapt onto Monsieur's back, tearing at his hair, clawing at his cheeks. Monsieur lurched backward, and Roo was up again. Monsieur thrust him down.

That was the position they were in, when Brother Gideon emerged from the boathouse, splashing through the lake and sending more frantic swans flapping. In a moment he had grabbed Mr. Harry — Monsieur — from behind, spun him awkwardly around, and slammed his fist into Mr. Harry's face. Blood poured from Mr. Harry's nose. He reeled, righted himself. Now he clenched his fists, lowered his head and charged like a bull, as well as he could with water dragging at his feet. He slammed into Brother Gideon, and Brother Gideon fell backward into the lake. Later I learned he struck his head against a boulder, hidden just below the surface.

Finally, we reached the reeds. Miss Sophie waded through to clasp her three dripping, sobbing children tightly in her arms and lug them to shore.

For a moment I watched in horrified fascination as Brother Gideon righted himself, reeling, shaking his head as if to clear his vision. Blood streamed from his hair and down his neck. The men's eyes locked, burning with jealousy and hatred on Monsieur's part and the force of defending loved ones on Brother Gideon's. They circled each other. Such primitive, terrible motion. Brother Gideon was tall, but Mr. Harry's body was bulky. Vaguely I could make out smoky smudges about the edges of Mr. Harry's shoulders and head, swelling to the outline of a taller man. They lunged. Brother Gideon got a fist square on his nose. He flailed out, fighting tooth and nail. Back and forth they slammed at each other, water splattering, gulping, spraying.

Grasping my branch, I plunged through the reeds. A craving to do violence burst through me like flames.

"Monsieur!" For a fraction of a second he glanced my way. As hard as I could, I swung my weapon into his face. The branch broke. He crumpled and splashed into the water.

Brother Gideon gasped for breath and stepped back. I looked at the two of them with confusion. "Mr. Harry?" I said. I lifted Mr. Harry's arm and pulled. After watching a moment, Brother Gideon took the other arm to drag Mr. Harry toward the lake edge. When Father Paul, Miss Petheram, and Mr. Willie arrived, Mr. Willie and Father Paul came out to take over for us. They hauled Mr. Harry up onto the grass.

Once we were reassured that he was lying quietly, Miss Sophie begged her sister, "Will you please take the children to the house? We'll explain everything later."

Miss Petheram gathered up the little ones and left.

Still panting, Miss Sophie and I babbled out explanations to the men, who, amazingly, took it all in. At this moment, anything was instantly believable.

"So," Father Paul said, "Harry Petheram was possessed by the spirit of Bernard de Cressac. I did not truly believe such things could happen, but….I feared it. Heaven help us. Who is he now?"

At his moan, we all looked over as Mr. Harry's eyes jiggled beneath closed lids. They popped open.

"Harry?" Miss Sophie said softly, tentatively, kneeling beside him. Her husband stood just behind her.

"Not…Harry." The creature looked up, and my senses swam because that was the most frightening sight of all. For the first time I could see it clearly—Monsieur looking out of Mr. Harry's green eyes. His gaze was as bleak and deep as if he were seeing an eternity of desolation and torture. He swallowed, and took a deep breath. "Do you not know me, Sophia?" The vocal chords were Mr. Harry's, but the slight accent was French, and the tone was all wrong. "*I* could never mistake *you*. Never, though we were separated for a thousand years. A thousand lives." In that instant the agony I read in his expression sent straight to my heart a stab of misplaced pity that left me confused for weeks afterward.

"And I could never mistake you, Bernard," Miss Sophie said, standing and drawing back. "You are as you always were—pitiless. You tried to hurt my children, and my husband. I shall never forgive you for that. Not for a thousand years."

Father Paul approached as Monsieur struggled to rise. Father Paul towered above him, terrible in his Old Testament prophet persona. Brother Gideon joined the priest, followed by Mr. Willie. Standing straight and strong, three men of God ringed Monsieur.

Mr. Willie spoke first. He pointed at the man lying there, and proclaimed, "I say unto you, in the name of King Jesus, leave this body!" In that moment, his voice held all authority.

Brother Gideon spoke next. "Begone, Bernard de Cressac, and never dare to trouble my family again!"

Next came Father Paul. "*Vade retro satana.*" Go back, Satan.

Nothing seemed to happen.

Father Paul repeated the order. "*Vade retro satana.*" His tone was so deep and resonating that I fancied I heard a gong sound along with each word.

The others later told me they saw nothing, save Mr. Harry falling back against the ground.

A contrary, writhing wind had picked up. Now it furiously whipped our clothing. My bonnet's ribbons strangled my throat as gusts sent my bonnet flying every which way. Sticks and leaves pelted us. Dark clouds rolled above, lightning streaked. From a distance, came shouts and squeals from students as they stumbled and streamed in confusion down the hill. Brother Gideon put his arm around his wife to help her stagger to shelter. Undulating waves of ink black roiled above, edged by a skinny streak of red, lurid sunset on the horizon. A great crash of thunder shook the ground. Vaguely I felt an enormous drop land on my nose. The deluge began.

Through eyelashes blurry with rain, my eyes riveted on tendrils of oily black smoke snaking from Mr. Harry's solid flesh. It coagulated into a shadow that twisted and coiled as it fought to take form. Two stumps were shaping where legs would be and two more where arms grew. In the nub of a head were three darker spots, shadow within the shadow, and from the lower one came a gibbering sound, as if the thing were trying to speak.

Before me stood Monsieur. He oozed malignance.

My teeth chattered. I backed up, prepared to run with the rest from this apparition, until I realized that it was only I who was afraid, only I who could see him. I must confront him alone — although Brother Paul and Mr. Willie were only a few feet away, although students swept right past us, wind-buffeted, yelping and bewildered.

In my mind's eye I saw Trix...Bridey...the vague forms of the seven victims I had never met. Suddenly I was quivering with fury. I was so sick of the pain and grief this man had caused. Sick of the dread, of the waiting on edge, fearing what he would do. Horrified by what he had tried to do today. Anger burst behind my ribs and blazed from my very soul. I held my trembling in check, looked him steadily in the eye and said calmly, sternly, "How much is enough, Monsieur? How many frightened school girls? How much death and destruction? Go. Go anywhere, but leave us alone." Rain filled my mouth and I clamped it shut.

His eyes narrowed. "I told you once, Mademoiselle, that I shall never leave Wyndriven," he said flatly. He took a step toward me, his bulk menacing.

And then some movement from above, through the driving rain, made me look up. I fell back on my rear end, staring. Because the churning clouds had turned into legions of gigantic, coal black rams, surging forward. Clutching their horns were demon riders, red of eye, distorted of feature. Some raised swords rippling with flame.

Maybe I was sobbing. Maybe I was praying. I shut my eyes.

A flash of brilliant light that pierced my eyelids made me open them. From the eastern sky, charging toward the creatures, were pale, glorious beings, mounted on silver-eyed, silver-skinned steeds. Their swords and spears glowed blue. Beautiful but painful, so that I must guard my vision.

At that moment, I felt hands trying to lift me. Someone—someones—flanked me. "Get up!" Dorcas shouted.

I shook my head frantically. "Not yet!"

So my friends all collapsed beside me, wallowing in mud, shielding me and each other with their arms.

Deafening clashes, that might have been weapons, might have been thunder, might have been trees falling, sounded.

Within the cacophony was the sharp sound of barking. Fenris—but not the Fenris I knew, because white light radiated from him—yapped at Monsieur's ankles, his teeth snapped onto Monsieur's trouser leg. Monsieur tried to shake him loose as Leo followed close behind. Leo strode in front of me and my friends. "Get back, all of you."

I made us scuttle backwards. The others' gaze followed mine.

"What is it?" Sylvie cried.

I could not answer.

"Hush," Mary Dell said.

Varina's arm tightened around me. "Fiona is seeing something monumental."

Leo flung back his head, standing straight and strong, one hand at his hip. It rested on the golden hilt of a glowing sword—an angel's sword. He did not rage. He simply allowed his regard to rest on Monsieur as if he were seeing him from somewhere a long way off and found him most distasteful. "I command you to leave my house and this sphere. Go, sir, in the name of God, to that state you have earned by your wretched life." In a flash the sword was drawn. He lunged at Monsieur, blue fire flaring.

Monsieur turned tail and ran. It made a ludicrous picture—

Monsieur, dignity shattered, with the exalted little dog snapping at his heels, tripping him up. Leo charged directly behind, sword outstretched.

Monsieur headed straight for Atlas, who cowered nearby. Monsieur's spirit dissolved into a funnel of inky smoke that dove into the black goat's flesh. Leo raised the sword — and plunged it deep into Atlas's side.

The goat sprang straight up into the air, back arched, as if stung. Smoke belched out. Atlas hit the ground, turned in circles, and bolted off through the dark haze, galloping madly into the woods.

Mr. Willie took off after Atlas.

A whirlwind of demons circled Monsieur's smoky form as it struggled. Black arms snatched at him, sucked at him, until all of them were absorbed into the — what? The only way I can describe it, is that there was a gaping hole in the sky. All the rams, all the demons, all the darkness, all the shadows, whooshed into the hole like water down a drain.

And they were gone.

So were the angels. All except Leo.

The rain turned gentle now, and warm.

Mr. Harry had been lying motionless nearby. He sat up, holding his head. "Ouch."

Father Paul rushed to his side. "Don't try to think just now." He assisted him to rise, and with a supporting arm about him, they made their slow way to the house.

Oh. All these people had been huddling close the entire time.

It was as though, thankfully, a veil had been lowered over

my Sight once again. And those I saw now seemed all the more precious.

Varina, Dorcas, Sylvie, Mary Dell, Leo, and I remained by the lake. Leo stood before us, watching me with bright, concerned, loving eyes.

"What happened?" Dorcas asked. "Start from the minute you left the picnic. Mr. Crow wouldn't let us leave to check on you."

Varina squeezed in closer. Her solid, human touch felt wonderful. "Can you tell us what you were seeing? Why did Atlas turn crazy beast?"

I opened my mouth and then closed it. Again. Finally, on the third try I said, "It's over. It's finished."

CHAPTER 32

SEEING AN ANGEL

"Fiona."

My friends waited by my side, saying nothing. I appreciated their quiet support as I tried to collect myself. I shoved aside the drenched strands that were plastered against my face so I could look upon Leo, who towered above me. I blinked through the raindrops that clung to my lashes.

"You've become an angel," I said softly.

"What?" Dorcas said.

Varina looked up and around as I spoke, then backed away.

White light streamed from Leo's entire body, so dazzling as to make me turn away a little. It glittered in the streams of rain surrounding him.

"Maybe. I don't know." He sank to his knees across from me.

I shielded my eyes with one hand. "You're clothed with the sun."

"Leo?" Varina whispered.

I nodded faintly.

"Then we'll leave you two alone."

I hardly noticed as they left because I was so enthralled by Leo.

He laughed. "Perhaps the brightness is the feeling of triumph. I am exultant. I have faced evil and conquered it with the sword of truth and he is gone forever."

"You did something amazing. You defeated a demon."

It was all too big. Too enormous for either of us.

At last I spoke again, struggling to understand. "Is that why you remained here? You were left behind—or else you came back—in order to overcome Monsieur and keep us safe from him."

"If I was meant to be here at this time, for that reason, so were you, Princess. I don't know everything, but this house is my stewardship and we both had a part to play. You were able to see in order to warn and prevent, I to protect."

"But we failed with Bridey and Trix."

"It must have been their time to leave. From my viewpoint, death isn't nearly as final as I used to think it."

Monsieur had said much the same thing. And I had long known it. "It was awful before you got here. Monsieur attempted to kill the children. Father Paul and the others tried to send him away, but only drove him from Harry's body, and no one but me could see him." I meant to take a deep breath, but it came out as a sob. "He was still here. And I couldn't think what to do next. How to keep him from always, always still being here."

"You were courageous. You looked an angel yourself, standing so straight and strong and lovely, so confident and sure of yourself. I shall never forget it."

My tears poured down unchecked, blending with the dripping rain.

"Look," Leo said. "There's a tunnel of light gleaming over there. It's pulling me."

I followed Leo's gaze to a deep, white, pulsating glow beckoning through the dusk and rain as if a star had fallen to earth. It bedazzled my eyes and got inside my head and exploded there as a desire for wings, so that I could soar. "I can see it!" I cried. "Oh, take me with you!"

He shook his head and smiled, a little sadly. "I can't. A long, abundant life lies ahead of you, full of people you'll love and be loved by. Much more fitting companions than a spook. And at the end of it, one way or another, you'll see me again. That's a promise."

There was a heavy silence. It weighed on the air, it weighed on our hearts. He was going. There was nothing more to be said, because that said everything. I made myself look at him straight on. Strong.

For the last time he stooped to kiss me, a cold, sweet kiss. Then he said, "Come, Fenris." The little dog trotted up to me. I bent toward him so he could touch my cheek with a cold, sweet tongue. As the two of them walked away, the light closed behind them.

All was still.

Of course there were questions, questions, and more questions from the Stones and Petherams. We had retired to the office, while nearly everyone else gathered in the banquet hall for hot cocoa. Miss Petheram was anointing Mr. Harry's wounds with ointment, while Miss Sophie did the same for her husband.

When the storm — almost a whirlwind — came up after the exorcism, all that the others had seen was me speaking to the air, as people rushed for safety. I told them about Monsieur, how he'd left Mr. Harry's body, and then materialized only to be confronted by Leo in all his glory. I told them of angels, of rams and chargers, of the violent clash between good and evil, and that demons had claimed the soul of Monsieur.

It was a lot to take in. No one questioned me further.

The first to speak was Mr. Harry. He turned to his brother-in-law and said, "You're a right mess, Gideon."

"You look worse, Harry," said Brother Gideon. "You can thank my right hook for that."

Mr. Harry grinned—his nice, normal grin—and rubbed his jaw. Then his smile fled. "I'm so sorry, Sophie. It's my fault de Cressac gained control. I drank to keep the war memories at bay and nearly lost myself and cost you your family. I've been—the only way I can explain it, is that I've been in and out of myself for quite a while. The more I drank the more I would be absent." He rubbed his forehead. "It's all awful."

"You've been shadowed by Monsieur, I think, since right after the ball." I had been going over everything, trying to decipher it. "That's when you began acting strangely, in lots of different ways. When I first informed you and Miss Petheram about Monsieur, you mentioned that he might have committed the murders under the influence of absinthe. Monsieur had told me that very thing once, but no one else seems to have known about it. I didn't tie anything together, though."

"It's easy to see in the aftermath," Miss Petheram said, "but none of us had the knowledge to interpret what was happening."

Mr. Harry closed his eyes and his lips tightened. "I'm so ashamed."

"Not your fault," Brother Gideon said. "But go on—what else do you remember."

Mr. Harry sighed. "Well, for the past several days I kept feeling myself coming and going. Huh!" He gave a short laugh. "I should've suspected something when I found myself trying to play the cello. And succeeding."

"Not really," I said.

"Not really what?"

"Succeeding."

"Oh." He laughed for real now, and the atmosphere of the room lightened. We hadn't heard Mr. Harry's infectious laugh in a long time. "But then this morning—is it still Friday?"

"That was yesterday."

"Astonishing. Anyway, Friday morning something poured into me. Like water into a glass. And I was still there, but I was squished down inside somewhere. Squashed too tight. That's all I remember. Nothing else until I awoke out in the rain."

A knock sounded on the door. Miss Petheram opened it to a waterlogged Mr. Willie. There was a movement in the shadows behind him, and Sparrow's pointed face peeked around his shoulder.

Miss Petheram invited them both to enter.

Mr. Willie twisted his hat in his hands. Water dribbled onto the carpet. "Reckoned y'all might would want to know about old Atlas. That billy always did have a devil in him, and it took over at the end. He ran off lickety-split through the woods. I had a right hard chore keeping him in sight. Pretty soon I lost him, but this child showed up to follow after him then. Tell the folks what you saw, Sparrow."

She stepped forward, her expression a combination of hesitation and fierceness. "I don't see how y'all could let your very own goat skedaddle off like that." She glared at Miss Petheram.

The headmistress's forehead wrinkled. "We really couldn't help it. We didn't mean it to happen."

Sparrow rolled her eyes as if that were no excuse. "He come to that cliff, the one above the ruined grove. Didn't even slow down. Just pitched right off." She swiped a hand across her eyes. "I looked down and he was poked clean through with a sharp branch. Poor old goat. I can't hardly stand to think of him stuck there all night in the rain." She tightened her lips and turned away.

Mr. Willie squeezed her arm. "I'm fixing to bury him soon as dawn breaks."

The blasted wood. The terrible place Monsieur had taken me, where he had once been wounded.

Miss Petheram patted Sparrow's back. "Poor Atlas. It was a horrible ending. I'm so sorry it happened and that you had to see it. I appreciate you both coming to tell us." Her shoulders sagged as she stifled a yawn. "It's late, Sparrow. Unless you'll stay the night, you really ought to go home to your grandmother."

I touched Sparrow's arm. "Would you please come with me to my room for just a minute before you go? I need to talk to you."

As we were turning to leave, Mr. Harry caught my hand. "Miss O'Malley." He lowered his voice, so I leaned in to hear him. "I believe I might've hurt someone very—very dear to me. Would you please...?"

I smiled and whispered in his ear. "I'll explain everything to Sylvie. Or at least I'll try."

Once we were up in my suite, Sparrow waited for me to speak, although I could see how her eyes were drawn to the piano. I perched on the edge of my rocker. It took me a moment to feel something lumpy beneath me and to smell a pungent, green scent. Beneath me lay a crushed bouquet. Of dandelions.

"Did you—" I looked at Sparrow—"bring me this?"

"Nope."

"No?" I blinked. "Could it—Perhaps it was Leo then. He figured out how to do so many things in the last couple of days."

She cocked her head to one side, like a curious bird.

I told her everything. She was bitter, but not surprised, that Monsieur was the cause of Atlas's demise. I told of mine and Leo's parting, finishing with, "I can't believe he remembered that dandelions are my favorite flower."

Sparrow knelt on the floor beside my chair and shyly reached to squeeze my hand.

I smiled then. "Would you please play us something happy on the piano? That would help so much."

She played a beautiful, heavenly tune I did not recognize. It comforted us both.

I think of you when in the night
I hear the softly falling rain;
And when the moon comes full again
With splendid radiance of light;
I think of you at sunset's glow,
And at the tender touch of dawn —
I think of you, knowing you are gone.
I whisper then, to God,
O, let him happy be!
Lord, let him happy be!
— By Fiona O'Malley

CHAPTER 33

LEAVETAKING

"And the city lieth foursquare…" I turned Leo's ring round and round on my finger, as I tried to picture where he was right now. I had wrapped yarn around the back of the band, but it was still too big. The trouble was, I simply could not *know* where Leo was, or if he were happy. I could guess, I could hope, I could imagine. And I could miss him with an ache that did not seem to lessen. This morning, probably the last I would ever spend at Wyndriven, it hurt as much as ever.

In a few minutes, The Club was to gather in my sitting room to say our good-byes. Already we wore our traveling clothes. Already conveyances were gathered out front to carry us to our various destinations. Varina and I would ride in a wagon to town, and then take a coach to Twisted Trees Plantation, where I would spend the summer.

My grandmother had sent a telegram, once she received the letters informing her of the occurrences at the school. There was a pitiful note to the message. It stated that, as Grandmama was indisposed, and as it was my wish, I had her permission to stay on at Wyndriven till the end of the term and to accompany Varina to her home for the summer. I felt a twinge of guilt that Grandmama was unwell and that I didn't want to be with her. The twinge was eclipsed by the excitement of remaining with Varina.

For the last two days of school, The Club had flailed about, trying to regain some sense of normality. Yet every moment we were aware that we would never be the same. Of course each of us had been affected by death in the past, since no one who lived in our world, and especially through the war that had ended so recently, could be innocent of it. Still, the passing of Trix and Bridey drove home to us how transitory life could be even for the privileged. For us. The young and healthy and generally blessed in life. The Club. One minute we could be present. The next we could be gone. It was as if the ground beneath our feet had become shaky and a great abyss dropped away close by.

Not to mention everyone else's new knowledge, and my deeper knowledge, of the transitory nature of *death* as well. The very plane of our existence had become wobbly.

If I could have discussed Leo with my friends, perhaps I would have felt better. If only I could talk about him so often, that, at the mention of his name, their eyes would glaze over and they'd give each other glances. But I couldn't do it. I could never let the others know all that Leo meant to me. My feelings went far, far too deep.

I loved him. I wanted to remember this. Someday, if I grew out of the Sight, I might tell myself that a lonely girl had conjured up an imaginary lover. If I didn't grow out of the Sight, and still believed in him, I might be so grown up and stolid that I might tell myself I had been *fond* of Leo, but that was all. I might say I was too young and too inexperienced to recognize a schoolgirl in-fatuation for what it was. "Fond." Such a shallow, silly word com-pared to my feelings for Leo. For my shining angel. If I did such an annoying thing as to consign my emotion to fondness, I would remind myself of this moment. This moment when I knew — ab-solutely — that at this time he was my sun and my moon and my stars. I did not ever want to cheapen what I had.

Was Alfred Lord Tennyson's conviction that "'Tis better to have loved and lost than never to have loved at all" true? I still didn't know. All I knew was that I was glad to have known Leo and to have the memory of those moments when I *was* him. It was hard to believe that I could possibly ever care for another young man, but I expected I would someday. People did move on. Or so they claimed.

Sylvie wandered in. "It's so final," she said, with a dramatic sigh.

The others came shortly.

"Miss Petheram was mourning the end of the school," Dor-cas said. "And then I heard Father Paul say — very meaningfully, I might add — that perhaps she might become something better than a headmistress in the fall."

"No one can know what may happen this summer. Even if the school started up again, we might not all be here in the fall anyway." Sylvie gave a secretive smile.

"You're not hinting more of us will be dead, are you?" Dor-cas's pale eyes bulged with horror as she gnawed her thumbnail. Dorcas, who had said, not too long ago, that she didn't care if she were next to go.

"No," Mary Dell said. "She means she may have eloped with

Mr. Harry. She's longing for him to say the word."

"You wouldn't, would you, Sylvie?" Varina said.

Sylvie's smile deepened. "I might."

"But think of the scandal."

"She would love the scandal," Mary Dell said.

"Not the scandal, precisely," Sylvie said. "More the romance."

Mary Dell reached into her pocket and pulled out a slender, pink kid volume. "Anyway, we need to get these books signed."

The day before, we had bought matching autograph books at Maloney's Mercantile. We had also stopped by the photography studio and had our portrait taken all together.

If only we had done it before some of us went missing.

As my friends bent their heads over the books, I watched them, with my own pen poised over Dorcas's album. I had a clever, sentimental little verse all prepared.

We had gone through pain and grief and fear together. We were fast friends, but we all had our mysteries. What had Varina once said? That most people carry about secret wounds and secret quirks. I saw ghosts and for a while was living with a male in my private chambers. Dorcas's unhappiness was deep-seated and none of us could truly understand what she had suffered in her unloving home. Mary Dell and Sylvie had endured experiences during the war that had to have changed them permanently in some ways. Something was wrong with Varina. Something had caused her to stab at Jimmy and to have a skewed attitude toward gentlemen. Perhaps in her home I would learn what haunted my best friend.

After a flurry of good-byes to the servants, the Stones, and the Petherams, we all trooped outside.

Varina had already climbed into the wagon, and I was about to, when Sebastian, clutching Sparrow by the hand, appeared out of nowhere.

"I am glad I caught you before you departed," Sebastian said. "I wanted to give you this." He thrust a small packet into my hands. "It is Indian jewelry. To help you forget the evil *mala*. Jewelry is important to Indian women. The Ramayana abounds in descriptions of ornaments. It is similar to what Sparrow wears, but yours has blue stones."

Sparrow proudly held up her wrist, and three golden bangles, flashing with red, gave a satisfactory jangle. She smiled up at Sebastian and he smiled down at her, and they had matching glows in their eyes.

"They're beautiful, Sparrow. And thank you so much, Sebastian."

I climbed into the wagon. Varina and I both waved to everyone expansively as we rolled away down the drive. After a moment, we looked at each other.

"Well, that's that," Varina said.

"Good old Wyndriven Academy. Isn't it interesting that they actually taught me not to slouch? I wouldn't have thought it possible since I've slouched ever since I shot up tall so early on."

"Carrying a book on your head really does help. And I'm proud of the fact that I can now regulate my breathing so that I shan't show it if I burn my mouth while drinking tea. Such a useful skill." Varina adjusted her bonnet. "I'm curious what you'll think of Twisted Trees."

"So am I."

The sky above us was brilliant, with a sun as golden as the gates of heaven.

It made me want to sing, so I sang.

ACKNOWLEDGMENTS

Without the encouragement of a good many people, this book would never have been, and I am grateful to all of them. Readers wrote to me, asking "What happened next?" Others stated on social media that they were looking forward to *A Place of Stone and Shadow*. My husband continually reminded me of my goals and was supportive in every way. My family and my friend Ellen enjoyed the story, and wanted to see it in print. If they hadn't, I don't know that I would have pressed forward with this, and *possibly* with one more future companion novel—if it continues to demand to be written.

All the poems in this book were penned by my two favorite poets: Carol Trost (my mother) and Stella Nickerson (my daughter). I can't get enough of their poetry—it's more delicious to me than ice cream, and that's saying a lot. I asked them to write them for the book and they graciously complied, with lovely results. I am so thankful for them and their talents.